VEIL of PEARLS

Print ISBN 978-1-61626-577-9

eBook Editions:
Adobe Digital Edition (.epub) 978-1-62029-014-9
Kindle and MobiPocket Edition (.prc) 978-1-62029-015-6

Unless otherwise indicated, all Scripture quotations are taken from the King James Version of the Bible.

Scripture quotations marked NKJV are taken from the New King James Version®. Copyright © 1982 by Thomas Nelson, Inc. Used by permission. All rights reserved.

This book is a work of fiction. Names, characters, places, and incidents are either products of the author's imagination or used fictitiously. Any similarity to actual people, organizations, and/or events is purely coincidental.

For more information about MaryLu Tyndall, please access the author's web site at the following Internet address: www.mltyndall.com

Published in association with the literary agency of WordServe Literary Group, Ltd., 10152 S. Knoll Circle, Highlands Ranch, CO 80130

Cover Photograph: Margie Hirwich/Arcangel Images

Published by Barbour Publishing, Inc., P.O. Box 719, Uhrichsville, OH 44683, www.barbourbooks.com

Our mission is to publish and distribute inspirational products offering exceptional value and biblical encouragement to the masses.

ecpa Member of the
Evangelical Christian
Publishers Association

Printed in the United States of America.

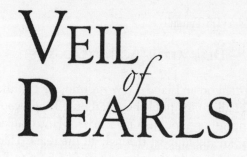

VEIL *of* PEARLS

MaryLu Tyndall

BARBOUR
PUBLISHING

Dedication/Acknowledgment

No book is written on an island. I owe my undying gratitude to so many people. First of all, to my publisher, Barbour. Thank you for believing in me and continuing to publish my stories. Many thanks to my agent, Greg Johnson, for his support through all the years. Thank you, Traci DePree, the best editor on the planet! Sending hugs to Rel Mollet and Michelle Griep, who read over this manuscript when it was raw and unpolished. And they still liked it! I thank my family, who has always been there for me. And I especially thank my Motley Crew for hanging with me during the storms. You're the best crew any captain could ever have!

Dedicated to everyone who has longed to be one of the "in" crowd.

The fear of man brings a snare,
but whoever trusts in the LORD shall be safe.
PROVERBS 29:25 NKJV

Chapter One

Barbados, the Caribbean, December 10, 1811

If Althea got caught, Sir Walter would whip her to death. It was why her heart hammered in her chest and her breath seized in her throat. It was why she stood at the top of the stairway unable to move. Darkness coated the main corridors of the house like molasses, so thick it nearly forced her backward down the long hall to her chamber. Where she belonged. Where she was usually locked behind a bolted door. But not tonight.

Not ever again.

Taking a deep breath, she pressed her valise against her chest with one hand, gripped the banister with the other, and began her descent. She slid her boots over marble, feeling for the edge of each tread, careful not to jangle the chains around her ankles. Careful not to even breathe too loudly lest she awaken anyone and her only chance to escape—the chance she'd planned for years—would dissipate like her childhood had the day she'd arrived on this plantation.

Her shackles rattled. She cringed. *Slowly now. Take your time.* Her breath huddled in her throat. She slid down another step. The tread creaked. The sound echoed through the house like an alarm. She halted, listening. Only her ragged breathing filled the air. No, wait, voices—whispers. But at well past two in the morning, all the servants and slaves should be asleep. She inhaled silently. No, it was just the wind whisking past the windowpanes. Warning her to go back to her prison or cheering her onward, she couldn't tell which.

Starting down again, she rounded the curved stairway. Firelight coming from the parlor licked the foyer tile, evidence that the ravenous monster slept within. Sir Walter Miles. Althea had amused him with rum and sweet smiles until he toppled like a felled tree onto the sofa.

She eased down the rest of the stairs, then halted before the open parlor door, bracing herself to hear his voice—his insolent, mad voice, beckoning her. Or worse, doling out some cruel punishment for being out of her room at night.

But instead, all she heard were his snores, deep and blubbering as they always were when he was besotted. The smell of rum and smoke bit her nose. Perspiration spilled down her back. Slipping past the parlor, she clipped the ring of keys from her belt—the ones she'd used to open her chamber door—and set them on the side table. She only wished they'd held the key to unlock her shackles as well. A tall shadow on her left gave her a start. Pressing a palm over her heart, she brushed past the grandfather clock, its *tick-tock tick-tock* hurrying her along, reminding her she hadn't much time to escape. Thunder rumbled in the distance. She stopped at the front door. Normally, there would be a guard on the other side as there was at each exit of the house. But tonight, Althea had overheard Sir Walter order the man to accompany the overseer into Bridgetown for an early morning slave auction. He'd already been well into his cups by then and had failed to post another servant there.

Or at least she hoped he had.

Gripping the handle, she took a deep breath and swung it open. The hinges squealed. A burst of rain-laden wind blasted over her and swept a whirlwind of leaves into the foyer. No one barred the exit—no man armed with a pistol to keep her inside. Emboldened, Althea stepped onto the wide veranda porch, shut the door, and hobbled down the stairs. Shadows dripped over the vast expanse of Sir Walter's plantation. A line of tall palms swayed in the breeze like henchmen waiting to capture her.

But not this time.

Clutching her valise, she gripped her skirts and shuffled down the dirt path, nearly stumbling over her chains. Iron bit her skin. *Clink-clank, clink-clank,* the vexatious sound reminded her of Sir Walter's voice: "You won't get far with those shackles on, my dear, so I would abandon all thoughts of escape. No. No." He laid a finger on his chin, a malicious glint in his tiny eyes. "You are mine. Forever. I will never let you go."

Althea trembled. She would not be *his* anymore. She'd rather die. She wished she had died with her sister, Delphia. Then she'd be at peace and would be with Mother and Father. But perhaps God would shine His favor on her this night. Hurrying across the open drive, she slid next to the vine-drenched shrubbery lining the pathway. Better to remain out of sight should anyone be out at this hour. Wind tore at her hair, loosening strands from their pins. Above her, fluttering palm and eucalyptus leaves laughed at her attempt to escape. Thunder growled. Branches and leaves slapped her face, scratching and stinging. She swatted them away. Nothing would stop her now.

Each step she took toward freedom loosened the fetters enslaving her soul until they began to slip away, one by one. All but the ones around her ankles. They grated her skin and jangled so loud she was sure Sir Walter's men would catch her at any moment. But then the wind picked up, drowning out the sound. Perhaps God was looking out for her, after all. Ignoring the pain, she pressed onward. She passed through the front gate and shut it behind her with a resounding *clank,* then stood frozen in place. Unsure, unsteady on her feet, for it was the first time she'd been outside the Miles Sugar Plantation in seven years.

Lightning scored the sky, flashing an eerie gray over the jungle. A jungle she had to traverse in order to get to Bridgetown by dawn. Where she hoped to find passage on a ship. No, she *must* find passage on a ship leaving early in the morning. Or all would be lost.

Thunder rattled the iron bars behind her. Althea jumped and swerved around. Just a gate. Not Sir Walter. Not his men intent on dragging her back to hell. Rain pelted the ground—her head. Catching her breath, she plunged into the lush forest.

Two hours later, as dawn's glow began to chase away the night, Althea emerged from the sopping jungle to the outskirts of Bridgetown. Water dripped off leaves, plopping and splattering into puddles. Her wet gown clung to her. Mud lined the hem of her skirts. Her sleeves were tattered from batting branches away.

And she could no longer feel her feet.

Which was a good thing by the looks of the rings of blood soaking her stockings at her ankles—blood that now trickled into her sodden shoes. Slipping into the shadows, she opened her valise and withdrew a bonnet, gloves, and a handkerchief. After wiping the leaves and dirt from her gown and ensuring her skirts covered her ankles, she pinned up her wet hair and placed the bonnet atop her head, lowering the veil over her face. She'd often been told that the quarter of her that was Negro was not evident in her features. But how could she be sure?

She hoped no one would recognize her. She hoped she could pass for a lady.

Instead of a slave.

Snapping the valise shut, she clutched it beside her. It contained everything she owned and yet more than she had owned in years: the money for her passage—money she'd hidden away bit by bit over the past three years—dried beef, bananas, and bread Cook had given her; pouches of dried herbs; her Bible, the only book Sir Walter had allowed her to keep; another chemise and gown; and her mother's pearls—the pearls Althea had retrieved from Sir Walter's room just before she left.

Her stomach growled. Her legs ached. Pain screamed from her ankles.

But she was free.

With chin held high, she made her way into the heart of the city, past the shops just opening for the day, the vendors setting up their carts, the sleeping taverns. A dog bounded toward a cluster of chickens, sending them squawking into the air. A pig snorted through a pile of garbage. A man and a woman argued in front of the drapers. The scents of tropical flowers and cou-cou, a cornmeal porridge native to Barbados, drifted past Althea's nose. A man tipped his hat in her direction, and she nearly fell backward. She'd never had a gentleman acknowledge her so politely.

Turning a corner, she headed for the docks, thankful the noise of the city covered her rattling chains. Soon, tall masts of ships poked above warehouse roofs. Ducking toward the other side of the street, she passed the now-vacant slave auction where Sir Walter's overseer would no doubt soon be found. She hoped to be long gone by the time it opened.

Further ahead, fishmongers slapped fresh marlin and tuna onto wooden racks. She drew a hand to her nose at the smell. The sharp clank of bells competed with the soothing rustle of water against pilings. Glittering sheets of sunlight swept across the bay in between roving clouds above. Even with the veil protecting her eyes, Althea squinted. Bare-chested slaves, hoisting barrels and crates onto their backs, tromped down the wharves, unloading goods from a recent arrival. Adjusting her skirts, she hobbled along as elegantly and swiftly as her shackles would allow and slipped inside a small clapboard shack that belonged to the port master.

A man sat on a stool behind a counter, shoving porridge into his mouth. Graying hair spilled from his queue onto a stained waistcoat.

"I would like to book passage to America."

The man continued eating, not looking up. "There's a ship leavin' for New York later today that's still takin' passengers."

Her stomach tightened. "That will not do, sir. I need to leave this morning."

He lifted his gaze. A drop of porridge slid over a jagged scar on his chin. He swiped it away, his eyes flickering delight at the sight of her. "Where are you heading, miss?"

"It matters not. Just away from here." Althea realized her mistake when the man gazed at her suspiciously. He glanced out the door.

"Are ye travelin' alone?"

She swallowed. "What difference does that make?"

Standing, he set down his bowl and scanned her. "I meant no offense. Just curious. The only women who travel alone, miss, are. . . Well, miss, they are a bit more scantily dressed, if ye know what I mean."

Heat flooded her face, even as anger stifled her fear. Footsteps sounded behind her.

"Ah, there's yer man, miss." The port master gestured over her shoulder. "Captain Faraday be headin' to Charleston this morning. Aren't ye, Captain? Ye've got a passenger here if ye've a mind to take her."

The captain brushed past her, handed the port master a paper, and said, "I don't take women on board. Bad luck," before he exited the building again.

Althea followed him outside. Scrambling, she stepped in front of him. "Captain, please. I beg you. I must leave this morning." Only then did she glance into a face that reminded her of crinkled vellum— aged and crumpled—and wearing a scowl that nearly sent her reeling backward. Instead her gaze was drawn over his thick shoulders to Sir Walter's overseer, Mr. Milson, who was headed their way.

Acid welled in her empty belly. Ducking behind the door to the port master's shack, she waved a hand of dismissal toward the captain. "Never mind. I'm sorry to have troubled you."

The man's eyes narrowed as they swept from her to the oncoming overseer. Understanding flickered across his face. He pulled from her hiding place, flung an arm over her shoulder, and eased her down the wharf, trumpeting in a loud voice, "I'm so sorry to hear that, Mrs. Pragin. A tragic death. And so sudden. Let me escort you to your husband."

Stunned, Althea played along, expecting Mr. Milson to come upon her at any moment. But thankfully, no sound of boots stomping on the wooden dock met her ears. Instead, one glance over her shoulder told her he had entered the port master's shack.

Her breath returned. "I must thank you, Captain Faraday."

"I ne'er could resist a damsel in distress." He chuckled. "Besides, I know that cur, Mr. Milson, an' I'm sure he's up to no good." Stopping before a group of sailors loading supplies onto a small boat, he faced her, squinting into the rising sun. "Now what sort of trouble could a young miss like you be in to cause that brute of a man to be lookin' for you?"

Althea lowered her head and swallowed. "It is. . .it is a private matter, sir. But rest assured, if you do not take me aboard your ship, I shall be dead before noon."

He scratched his gray whiskers then snorted. "Well, I don't want that on me conscience, do I?" He held out his palm. "That'll be three pounds, miss. An extra pound for the bad luck ye'll no doubt bring. An' I won't be feedin' ye neither."

Three pounds. Over half her money. But it couldn't be helped. She glanced at his crew ogling her from the boat. Neither could she help but place her trust in these men to bring her safely to Charleston.

But the alternative was unthinkable.

"Very well, but I will pay you half now and half when we get to Charleston." Opening her valise, she counted out the coins and dropped them in his hand.

He grinned. "Smart lady," he said before helping her onto the boat.

An hour later, Althea stood at the starboard railing, her heart in her throat, as the brig weighed anchor, raised sails, and drifted out of the harbor. She fully expected to see Sir Walter storming down the docks after her, his fist in the air, or perhaps ordering the fort to fire a cannon at them. Or worse, rowing out to the brig to drag her back home himself.

Instead, all she saw were the people and buildings of the town growing smaller and smaller until they blended into the green hills of the island before being swallowed up by the turquoise sea. Barbados had disappeared. Her home. The only home she'd ever known.

The home that had turned into a prison.

Two hours later, she found herself stuffed into a cabin the size of a trunk, being thrashed about in a massive storm like a whip in the hands of an angry master. The only thing worse than her aching muscles and bruised skin was the constant heaving of her stomach. Ravenous waves fisted the hull. Thunder growled, shaking the timbers. And Althea began to wonder if she hadn't indeed brought bad luck to this voyage.

The door slammed open, and Captain Faraday entered, ax in hand as if he was of the same opinion.

Althea shrank into the corner. Had she gone from one madman to another? *No, Lord, not like this.* The ship tilted. Faraday gripped the deckhead and made his way toward her. She couldn't tell from his expression whether he was angry, frightened, or— Althea touched her face. She had forgotten that she had removed her veil! Could the captain tell who she was? *What* she was?

Water dripped from his loose hair and clothes onto the floor. He smiled. Not a malicious smile, but an amused one. "I'm here to take care o' those." He nodded toward her ankles. "Ye'll balance better if you don't have them on."

Althea blinked. "You knew?"

"Hard not to." Balancing over the teetering deck, he gestured for her to sit on the bed and place her feet on either side of a stool.

Gripping the mattress, she lifted her skirts as modestly as possible and complied, stunned at the man's kindness.

The chain flattened across the wood.

Captain Faraday lifted the ax over his head. The brig canted to larboard. He stumbled and Althea squeezed her eyes shut. If he should miss. . .

Thunder split the sky.

The sharp *clank!* of metal rang, and her feet flew apart. Kneeling, the captain slipped the chains through the iron locks and tossed them into the corner. Althea stared at them as they tumbled over the canting deck, impotent without a victim. She'd worn them every night for the past seven years. Only her. None of the other slaves were locked up at night. Because she was his favorite.

"You are a kind man, Captain," she shouted above the screaming wind.

He tossed her some rope. "Tie yerself to the bed. It's goin' to get rough tonight." He headed for the door.

How could it get rougher than this? Her hands trembled as she grabbed the cord. "Will we sink?"

"Naw. It's just a squall, miss. If God be on our side, we'll make Charleston in a week." He winked and closed the door behind him.

Althea rubbed her ankles, wincing at the pain. She would have to put some comfrey on the wounds later.

Charleston. What awaited her in Charleston? A new city. A new world. But still a world where slavery existed—where women had few rights. How long could she survive with only three pounds? More importantly, would the light color of her skin veil her true heritage, or would she find herself once again a slave, only in a much worse situation? Though she couldn't fathom anything worse than what she'd endured.

She tied the rope to the bed as more questions assailed her. Would Sir Walter search for her? Was she really safe anywhere? So many unknowns. And with her survival teetering on the answer to each one, she felt no more secure than she did on this tiny brig being tossed about in the tempest. *Oh Lord. Help me. Please.* Yet after the Almighty had allowed so many tragedies to strike her, she wondered if He would.

Thunder blasted. The ship trembled, rattling Althea's bones. The deck canted, and she held on to the bed to keep from tumbling to the floor. For now, she must survive this voyage. But even if she didn't, even if she sank into the cold deep never to be seen again, at least she would die a free woman.

CHAPTER TWO

Charleston, South Carolina—one month later

Drawing the stool up beside the cot, Althea laid the back of her hand over the young boy's cheek. Burning hot. As she suspected. She already had a pot of yarrow and nutmeg leaves simmering over the fire. As soon as he awoke, she'd make sure he drank some of the tea. The boy shivered.

Releasing a sigh, she drew his ragged coverlet beneath his chin and glanced over the crowded room. Rows of cots filled the makeshift hospital that sat behind the Negro orphanage. Both run by the generous charity of Father Mulligan from St. Mary's Church. Without his help, these poor children would have nowhere to go. At least not until they were old enough to be sold as slaves. She took in all the young faces, some sleeping peacefully, others with droopy eyes and sallow skin, tossing in agitated slumber. They'd had ten new cases of this strange fever in the last week. And now the only doctor who would treat them was ill. Ill, indeed. If one could call inebriated ill.

A chilled breeze swirled about her. Drawing her shawl over her shoulders, she made her way to the window and eased it shut. Had the wintery air swept the sour stench of disease from the room, or was its absence only an indication she'd grown accustomed to the smell of sweat and vomit? An ache clawed at her stomach. She'd not eaten since yesterday when the last of her money had run out. Of course she still had her mother's pearls, but she'd rather die than sell the last remnant of her family—a symbol of the love she'd known before slavery.

After spending days being tossed about like a rag doll on the brig, she'd finally arrived in Charleston a month ago—happy to be on land once again. Thrilled to find the charming city full of life and opportunities.

But it didn't take long for her to realize those opportunities were not for her. At first, she had knocked on every doctor's door, seeking a position as an assistant. After each one turned her down, she'd sought work as a house maid, chambermaid, cook, laundress, even stable hand.

Nothing.

If Father Mulligan had not allowed her to sleep on a cot in the storage room in exchange for her help with the sick orphans, she would have nowhere to lay her head at night. But, aside from a few scraps, the orphanage could not afford to feed her as well. Today was the first day in which she had no idea from whence her next meal would hail. *God, I need a miracle.* Tears filled her eyes, but she forced them back. She had no right to complain when some of these children would not survive this new outbreak.

"Adalia."

Althea heard the name, but it floated through her mind like a visitor, unfamiliar, detached from anyone she knew.

"Adalia!" The voice was louder, startling Althea from her thoughts. She looked up to see Mrs. Charlotte standing across the room. The elderly woman who assisted with the orphans gave her a perplexed look.

"Oh my, forgive me. I don't know where mind is." Althea's pulse raced. She must be more careful. She must remember her new name— even when deep in her thoughts. For she was no longer Althea Claymore. She could never be Althea Claymore. Not as long as Sir Walter was alive. She was now Adalia Winston. She must get used to it—the sound of it. She must think it. Speak the name until it sounded natural on her lips. Besides, it suited her perfectly, she thought, as she wove in between the cots to stand before Mrs. Charlotte.

"Febee's stomach pains her something fierce, Miss Adalia." The rotund woman stared down at the girl who hugged her own tummy, a look of agony on her face. "Ain't there somethin' you can do?"

"I'll try." Adalia smiled. "Would you go check on the tea?"

As the woman scurried away, Adalia knelt before the girl and reached into her pouch for some peppermint leaves. "Here, chew on these, sweetheart." She placed them on the girl's tongue. "They taste good, and they'll ease your bellyache."

The little girl nodded.

A man's snort startled Adalia, and the little girl's eyes widened.

Springing to her feet, Adalia spun around to find an elderly gentleman, perhaps in his sixties, staring at the sick child with disdain. His thumbs were stuffed within the pockets of a satin-embroidered waistcoat from which dangled the gold chain of a pocket watch. When his gaze shifted to Adalia, his disdain turned to delight.

"May I help you, sir?"

"I am Doctor Langston Willaby."

Adalia released a sigh of relief. Finally. They'd sent posts to nearly every doctor in town requesting assistance. "We are so happy to see you, Doctor. Thank you for coming."

"I normally don't attend to Negroes, but since your doctor is ill, I've made an exception."

A sour taste filled Adalia's mouth. "How kind of you, sir." Regardless of the man's attitude, she would accept any help that was offered. She motioned toward the children. "Twelve cases of this fever and stomachache in the past week. I fear it is cholera or scarlet fever."

He studied her, not once glancing at the patients. "I will make my diagnosis shortly. However, I come on another matter as well. You are Miss Adalia Winston?"

Fear sliced Adalia's heart. Had she been found out already? She took a step back, glancing at the door. "I am."

"May I speak with you for a moment?" He lifted his brows, but there was no malice within his eyes. "Outside?"

Without waiting for her answer, he sauntered down the aisle and stepped out the door.

Despite his superior attitude and the fear etching down her spine, curiosity drove her to follow him. No one knew her full name in town save Father Mulligan and the staff at the orphanage. Besides, surely Sir Walter would have no idea where to start looking for her or under what name to make his inquiries.

She stepped into the courtyard between the orphanage and the sick house. The cold air stung her face, and she tightened her shawl around her neck. The *clip-clop* of horses' hooves floated on a salty breeze from the bay.

"Miss Winston, I see you have, shall we say"—he hesitated, wrinkling his nose—"no objections in treating the Negro."

"No, of course not." She narrowed her eyes. "How do you know me, sir?"

"I have a business proposition." He plucked out his watch, flipped it open, and gazed at the time. "I am in need of an assistant. I understand from Father Mulligan that you are looking for a position?"

Adalia nodded, barely able to contain her rising excitement.

Snapping the watch closed, he dropped it into his pocket. "He has informed me of your skill with healing herbs. Are you interested?"

Adalia swallowed. "Yes, I am." *Real employment! And just in time, Lord.*

"Fifty cents a day. Room and board are included." His brown eyes softened above a smile. "Are the terms agreeable?"

"Yes, quite agreeable." She tried to curb the elation in her voice. A moan sounded from within the hospital. "Would I still be able to help at the orphanage?"

He looked perplexed. "Of course. Of course. On your own time, that is." He gave her a quick nod. "Very well then. It's settled. You are hired."

Dare she believe such good fortune?

"I thank you, sir. I promise I shall work very hard."

"Yes you shall, Miss Winston." His gray brows raised. "In fact, you'll begin now. I need you to travel to the Rutledge plantation. One of the slaves is ill, and apparently Mrs. Rutledge is unable to attend to the matter."

The way he described a sick child as a *matter* settled like a brick in her stomach. "But what of these children?" Adalia glanced at the hospital behind her. "I cannot leave them in this condition."

"I will tend to them, Miss Winston."

She nodded, not about to question his orders. "How will I get to the plantation, Doctor?" Surely he knew she had no means of conveyance.

"My man, Mr. Gant, will drive you." He gestured toward a phaeton and horse waiting by the street. "My home and office are on the corner of Calhoun and Anson Streets. After you're done at the plantation, he will bring you there."

Adalia dared to gaze directly into the doctor's eyes. Whenever she'd been so bold with Sir Walter, she'd been slapped. But she had to know if she could entrust these precious children to his care.

The kind look in his eyes set her fears at ease. "I will tend to the wee ones," he huffed, as if reading her thoughts. "Never fear."

"Please allow me gather my things." Adalia entered the hospital, her feet and heart dragging. She should be happy to have found employment. She should be thanking God. Yet, she hated to leave the children. But what choice did she have?

After gathering her medical satchel and valise, and explaining the situation to Mrs. Charlotte, she climbed into the buggy and waved good-bye to Dr. Willaby, saying a prayer for the children as she moved out of sight of the hospital.

What she should also have prayed for was courage to enter the grounds of a plantation. Though she was nowhere near Barbados or Sir Walter Miles, and though no one knew her true identity, her heart clenched as the phaeton passed through the massive iron gates of Rutledge Hall. With each turn of the carriage wheels, her ankles burned as if phantom shackles clamped around them once again. Even the Spanish moss swaying in the breeze from the massive oaks lining the drive did nothing to becalm her rising angst. By the time the phaeton stopped before the big house and she had leapt from her seat—much to the dismay of Mr. Gant, who had jumped down to assist her—her legs nearly collapsed. Gripping the railing, she ascended the steps and knocked on the ornate door, gulping for air and half expecting to see Sir Walter standing on the other side. What she saw instead was a plump Negro woman with eyes as big as saucers, wearing a tattered scarf over her head.

The slave's gaze immediately dropped to the ground, causing Adalia's fear to turn to anger. She longed to tell her that she had every right to look Adalia in the eye—that she was no less a human being than Adalia was—but instead, she introduced herself in her kindest tone and inquired as to the whereabouts of the sick slave. The woman gave her the information and quickly closed the door.

Adalia found the slave quarters easily enough. They were the only ramshackle buildings on the plantation—nothing but flimsy shacks clustered together on the far end of the property, shoved out of the way like dust swept into a corner. On the way there, she passed manicured flower gardens that were no doubt beautiful in the summer, marble fountains, horse stables, massive storehouses, barns, a kitchen house, and a dairy. The scent of bread baking reminded her that she was famished. And everywhere slaves hurried to and fro, loaded down with baskets, bricks, wood, or tools, attending to their master's duties. In the distance, empty cotton fields lay fallow until early spring when the planting would begin.

A whip cracked the air. Adalia froze. It was a sound that haunted her nightmares and stalked her waking hours. A sound that tightened every nerve while at the same time urging her to flee. To flee anywhere outside the path of that leathery blade, as sharp as any knife's. Whether she was the object of its anger or not, she hated it and its predatory howl. *Snap! Snap!* Like the crack of lightning across a black sky. She unfurled her fists and dared a glance at the overseer standing over a poor slave at the edge of the fields. He raised the whip to strike the cowering man again. The slave winced and curled into a ball, offering the least amount of skin to his master, a subconscious posture the body took when threatened. One she knew all too well.

Tears misted Adalia's eyes. *Why, Lord, did You allow me to come here? To see this?* When there was nothing she could do. Nothing to save these people—her people—from their torturous existence. The overseer shouted obscenities then booted the slave and dismissed him. Feeling as though her own body had been whipped, Adalia watched as the man stumbled away. She wiped a tear from her cheek then started again toward the slaves' quarters. At least she could help one of them.

Her boots shuffled over the dirt floor of the tiny home as the smell of mold and sickness enveloped her. A rickety table guarded the glassless window on her right. A set of shelves perched beside the other one. A fireplace stood against the back wall surrounded by bundles of hay covered with tattered blankets. The sick lad lay on the one closest to the fire. Kneeling beside him, Adalia felt his skin, asked his mother a few questions, and finally determined the boy had eaten something that disagreed with him.

"The missus usually checks on us." His mother wrung her hands together. "But she sick today, I hears. Poor thing."

Adalia gazed up at the woman. "So, the missus is kind to you?"

The woman looked down and backed away. "Yes'm."

Rising to her feet, Adalia touched her arm. "You have nothing to fear from me."

"Yes'm." She dared a glance at Adalia. "Missus Rutledge is kind. Not the master, though. Or his oldes' son." She flattened her lips and gazed at her own son. "Thank you for tendin' my boy, miss. I's got to get back to the creek now to he'p wit' the washin'."

"You're welcome." Adalia handed the woman a pouch of nettle. "Make tea with these leaves, and have him drink it for two days. He'll be feeling better soon."

She nodded, her eyes riveted to the floor.

Adalia wanted to tell her she didn't have to live like this. She wanted to tell her that she could run away like Adalia had. Find a new life. But could she? Adalia could pass for white, but not this woman. Or her family. The only way they could be free would be to buy passage back to Africa, back to a place they had no memory of, a place where they would feel just as estranged as they did here.

"God be with you." Adalia closed her satchel.

"Oh, the good Lord's always wit' us, miss. Always."

Adalia smiled, pleased to hear such faith in the woman's tone. Her own faith had been the only thing that had kept her alive the past seven years. Perhaps God would set these people free someday, as He had Adalia. She would pray for that.

Hoping to avoid the sight of slaves, Adalia took a different route back to the main house through a small wooded area littered with pine needles and leaves and scented with moist earth and conifer trees. She drew a deep breath, trying to rid herself of the dour mood that had come upon her since she'd ventured onto the plantation. She was employed. She would have a meal tonight and a place to sleep. She had much to be thankful for.

Emerging onto a field overgrown with grass rippling beneath a cool breeze, she adjusted her threadbare shawl over her shoulders and vowed to purchase a proper coat as soon as she could afford one. Of course by then it would be summer, and she'd heard the temperatures in Charleston would become more tropical—much like those to which she was accustomed.

Soon the warmth of the sun soaked away her chill, and she gazed across the wide expanse of land. A gushing creek cut across the field. Horses grazed in the distance. The leaves of cedar and hickory trees, festooned in moss, laughed in the wind. So breathtaking. So much land. Did the owners appreciate how much God had blessed them? Or was all this beauty simply a veil that masked the agony of slavery?

The chime of steel on steel drew her gaze to two men fencing by a small unfinished bridge spanning the creek. No doubt the spoiled Rutledge sons the woman spoke of. Laughter followed the clank of swords, increasing her anger. They were playing, enjoying themselves while hundreds of slaves worked on their land and in their home. *Pampered urchins.* She knew their type, and she wanted nothing to do with them. Yet, unless she wished to circle back around, she could see no other way to cross the creek save to pass right by them. Fine. She would hold her head high and do just that. Besides, she was done allowing their kind to intimidate her, to dictate her life.

Clutching her skirts she stormed forward, her gaze on the ground and her heart encased in steel.

❧

Morgan Rutledge leveled his sword out before him. "Prove me wrong, brother." He grinned.

Hadley, ever the epitome of pompous composure, threw back his shoulders and lifted his blade. "Prove that I will always excel you at swordplay? My pleasure, dear brother." He sneered. "That I excel you at all things we shall prove one by one."

Morgan snorted. "I believe you have exceeded both Father and me in one thing—your overexaggerated belief in yourself." He thrust out his blade. "Not an easy feat."

Hadley smirked and met his parry. "Ha! Then you admit I am already ahead."

Morgan slashed at Hadley's right side.

Shuffling his boots over the grass in a ludicrous display, Hadley met his blade with a mighty clank then swung in on Morgan's lower right. Morgan repelled each parry with one of his own, defending himself with an ease borne to his station and skill.

"So, little brother has been practicing." Hadley backed off, his breathing ragged.

Morgan grinned. "Ready to forfeit lest we scar that handsome face and your paramours abandon you?" A light breeze flapped his shirt, sending cool air over his moist chest and neck even as the sun's rays lashed his back.

"I'd sooner utter a vow of celibacy than forfeit a fight with you." Hadley ran a hand through his black hair—so different from Morgan's light wavy hair. Tall, handsome Hadley was rarely seen without his retinue of lady admirers. He gave Morgan a look of boredom then kicked out his front leg and lunged forward.

Morgan leapt out of the way just in time, wondering how much of this duel was indeed sport and how much vengeance. He spun around and dipped low, striking Hadley across the leg but not allowing the blade to sink any deeper than to tear his nankeen trousers.

Hadley gaped at the hole. "I just had these tailored, you oaf."

"Then you shouldn't have challenged me." Morgan laughed, glancing across the vast plantation at the coachman working with a new horse in front of the stables. He ran a sleeve over his forehead.

"I was bored." Hadley huffed. "What else to do on such a dull day? I have no parties to attend until next week, and Ellen is furious with me." Leveling his sword once more at Morgan, he charged forward.

Morgan met his thrust with a resounding *clank*, forcing his brother back. "Then perhaps you shouldn't have arranged a tryst with Catherine. You know the two ladies talk."

"I didn't think they would discuss me." Hadley dove in low, sending Morgan springing backward.

Spinning around, Morgan brought his blade forward and twirled it tauntingly before his brother's nose. "You know nothing about women."

"And you do?" Hadley swept down from on high. "Miss Emerald has been dropping hints of a courtship with you for months now. And you do nothing."

"Perhaps I'm not interested."

"Then you are a fool. Emerald is the comeliest woman I've ever seen. And she's worth a fortune."

Morgan pitched his sword back and forth, engaging each of Hadley's thrusts and forcing him back. All true. With her golden curls, skin of ivory, and figure of Aphrodite, Emerald was a fine catch. And being the only daughter of Anthony Middleton III made her dowry substantial.

"Ellen will come around." Hadley shrugged and stopped to catch his breath. "And if she doesn't, there are dozens of others waiting behind her. Maybe I'll set my sights upon Emerald."

"By all means." Morgan chuckled. "But you'll have to choose one of them soon."

"Why is that?"

"Because you will inherit all this from Father." Morgan swept his sword over the landscape. He gazed at his brother. At seven and twenty, Hadley should have been settled down by now, helping Father run the plantation, learning the business.

"Bah!" Hadley spat. "I'll inherit it anyway. And you, dear brother, will serve at my pleasure."

"Never." Morgan lifted his chin along with his sword, determined to prove himself the better man, when a flash of lavender snapped his gaze to the left. A woman he'd never seen before marched across the field like a soldier into battle.

Intrigued, he watched her, wondering what her face looked like beneath those luxurious black curls.

"Ah, what beauty doth the fair winds bring our way?" Hadley said loud enough for her to hear.

Still, she did not look up. The closer she came, the more pleasant her curves formed in Morgan's vision. Who was this fair maiden? From the ragged state of her gown, a servant girl no doubt. Yet, why had he not seen her before? Surely he—and most definitely Hadley—would have noticed such a lovely creature on the plantation.

More importantly, how dare she ignore them?

He moved to block her way. "Milady." He hailed her with a bow. "Perhaps you can aid us."

She halted and slowly lifted her gaze to his. Eyes as dark and rich as the fertile soil speared him with a look of contempt. Her disdain shocked him more than vexed him. Lips the color of brandywine made him lick his own, his mouth suddenly parched. And her fiery cheeks only accentuated her beauty—and her anger.

She averted her eyes as if displeased with what she saw. "What aid could you possibly need from me?" Her tone, contemptuous and fiery, only intrigued him more.

"Can you judge who is the master at swordplay, milady? Me or my brother?"

๑๑

Adalia fumed. She should ignore the pompous scamp and head back to the carriage. But the man stood between her and the bridge. A rather handsome man if she were forced to admit. Hair the color of wheat and as wavy as the sea under a high wind. Eyes, as green as the moss hanging from the trees, glinted mischievously in the sunlight. His taut chest peeked at her beneath his loose shirt that flapped in the breeze. Tight black pantaloons led down to bare feet. Her body heated at his lack of attire. Did he have no shame?

He gave her an audacious grin, which only infuriated her further. She had been silent too long in front of men like these, and now she had a chance to tell them what she thought without repercussions. For they held no power over her. She must remember that. No one owned her anymore.

He waved at the other impudent devil. "We shall perform for you, miss, and you may judge the champion."

"I need no performance to make my judgment, sir."

"Indeed? Then, no doubt, you have been admiring our skill from afar?" The light-haired brat waved his arm with a flourish. "I implore you, do dispense with formalities and deem me the victor." He chuckled.

"I will deem you, sir. As nothing but a swaggering, vainglorious despot."

A gasp escaped the dark-haired whelp's lips, followed by a chuckle. At first a choppy sort of I-can't-believe-she-said-that chuckle but finally ending with a full-fledged belly laugh. The light-haired man gaped at her as if she'd grown a mustache. He planted his sword in the dirt and leaned on the hilt.

"I do believe the lady is acquainted with you," the dark-haired man stopped laughing long enough to say.

But she wanted no more to do with either of them. "Good day to you, sirs." Gathering her skirts, she headed toward the narrow bridge.

"I daresay, miss," the light-haired man called after her. "How can you say such a thing? You hardly know me."

"I know your type," she shot over her shoulder and took a cautious step onto the bridge, which didn't seem to be very sturdy now that she was up close. The wood creaked beneath her shoe.

"And what type is that?" His voice grew closer.

Adalia faced him. "The type who plays idly while men and women are enslaved to do your work."

His eyes sharpened. "You do not know to whom you speak, miss. I fear you will be horrified when you discover my identity."

"I know who you are, sir." She continued across the bridge, noting that the railing on the right side had not been fully completed.

His footsteps followed her, sending the bridge wobbling. "Well then, I demand to know who you are."

Demand, indeed. "No one of consequence."

"I could have you dismissed and thrown off my land."

"I will spare you the trouble. I am leaving."

"I insist you tell me your name." His voice bore more humor than fury.

Adalia clenched her jaw. She spun around. "You do not own me, sir, as you do the poor souls who work your land. Therefore, you cannot insist I do anything." She couldn't believe how wonderful the defiant words felt on her lips. How glorious! How empowering!

His handsome face scrunched. "You take issue with my slaves? They are only doing what they were bred for!"

Adalia slammed the heel of her shoe on his bare foot.

He let out a thunderous growl. Grabbing his foot, he hobbled backward over the wooden planks as the dark-haired man burst into another fit of laughter. But the light-haired brat was not amused. In fact, his face twisted in rage as he continued to rub his foot. Finally, he leaned against the half-finished railing in an effort to balance himself.

A *crack-snap* split the air. Before Adalia could react, the railing splintered, and the man toppled over the side into the creek with a resounding splash.

CHAPTER THREE

Y ou should have seen Morgan, Father. I dare say, shoved into a creek by a mere slip of a girl." Hadley sipped his brandy and chuckled as he leaned one arm across the mantle. "And she gave him quite a tongue-lashing as well." The crackle of the fire joined Hadley's laughter.

Cringing, Morgan poured himself a glass of Madeira then glanced over the drawing room, avoiding his brother's gaze. Their father needed no further evidence to fuel his poor opinion of him—an opinion he never hesitated to spout with great enthusiasm. Bracing for the oncoming lecture, or at the very least, a groan of utter disappointment, Morgan sipped his wine and stared at his father.

Franklin Octavian Rutledge sat in his stuffed leather chair, newspaper stretched out before him and cigar clenched between two fingers. "Humph," was his only response.

Their mother, however, looked up from the divan and set her sewing in her lap. "What girl was this, Morgan?" Her blue eyes sparkled with returning health, though her face still lacked its usual glow.

Morgan shoved a strand of his damp hair behind his ear. "No one." Though he would love to know who the mysterious woman was—the insolent servant woman with the sharp tongue. And even sharper heel! He shifted his weight off his right foot, where an ache gave evidence of the latter. Despite the way she'd utterly embarrassed him, he found himself longing to see her again. But by the time he'd pulled himself from the creek, she was gone.

"A true beauty," Hadley added in his make-sport-of-Morgan voice. "Perhaps she is a fairy, or a forest sprite? For she vanished as quickly as she appeared." He waved his hand about tauntingly.

Their mother laughed. "Oh dear, you read far too much Shakespeare."

Their father glared at Hadley over the top of his newspaper. "And not enough of what is important, such as *The Southern Cultivator*, or pray tell, an actual ledger."

His harsh tone dragged the levity from the room. Would that Morgan could leave with it before his father turned his scorn on him.

Too late. The man's dark eyes shifted his way.

Hadley shrugged and sipped his drink. "But that is your job, Father. And you do it so well."

Still gripping the paper, Franklin drew his cigar to his lips and took a puff before returning to his reading, his expression one of disgust as if he couldn't stand the sight of either of his sons. In fact, until the age of five, Morgan believed his father to be naught but a booming voice emanating from the *Charleston Courier*. Unless one roused the beast and the dragon emerged from his printed lair—scaly faced, anger steaming from his bull-like nose and embers sparking in his eyes.

Franklin puffed on his cigar once again only affirming Morgan's analogy, the sting of tobacco filling the room with his reproach. "Who is this woman, boy?" he barked, using the degrading word for Morgan. "I'll not have you philandering with common servants. It's bad enough neither of you can cease sampling every filly in town long enough to marry one of them."

Morgan's mother gasped, and she lowered her gaze at the lewd discussion.

Hadley chuckled. "With so many delectable treats, you can hardly expect me to choose."

The clock on the mantle struck seven, the chimes piercing the sudden silence like gongs of doom. Morgan sipped his drink, hoping the sweet wine would smother the bitter taste in his mouth as he watched the final rays of the sun retreat out the window. Much like his own feelings of hope and worthiness did whenever he entered this house. A servant dashed in to light the lamps then scurried away like a frightened mouse.

Morgan circled one of the Victorian stuffed chairs in front of the hearth, making his way toward his mother, who looked ready to cry. "I was hardly philandering, Father." Though he most certainly would not have objected if the lady had offered.

"Oh." His mother dropped her knitting again. "I'm sure she must have been sent by Dr. Willaby. He said he would send someone to look in on poor Jamon. His mother sent word the lad wasn't feeling well today."

"See, mystery solved, dear brother." Hadley tossed the remainder of his brandy to the back of his throat. "Though how embarrassing that a common working woman set you on your back." His chuckle grated over Morgan as it always had since they were young boys. Morgan scoured him with an angry gaze.

Hadley lifted his glass toward him and grinned.

"A disgrace, if you ask me," Franklin mumbled.

His mother's eyes lit up. "If she is the woman from the Negro orphanage at St. Mary's, she sounds rather interesting. I would love to speak with her about her knowledge of healing herbs."

Morgan slid beside his mother. Interesting indeed. Not only beautiful and spirited, but intelligent as well.

Hadley snickered and strode to the window.

"Regardless," Franklin said. "I insist you both cease these banal trysts and make your choice. There are plenty of ladies with good pedigree and excellent dowries."

Hadley choked on his brandy, exchanging a humorous glance with Morgan. "Are we choosing wives or horses?"

Franklin cleared his throat, but before he could growl his debased response, Morgan inquired as to his mother's health.

She patted his hand. "I am much better, thank you."

"I've warned you to stop attending those slaves, Mrs. Rutledge," Franklin said. "You probably caught one of their nasty little diseases. Leave them to this woman from now on." He lifted his paper back up to resume reading.

His mother's disappointment hung in the air around her. Taking care of the slaves was one of the few household tasks she enjoyed. Yet still she did not argue with her husband. She never did.

So Morgan would. "It is expected of plantation wives to tend to the slaves, Father. Surely you don't wish anyone to believe Mother is not fulfilling her duties as mistress of Rutledge Hall?"

Franklin peered at Morgan over his paper. "If you are so concerned with our reputation, boy, perhaps next time you will not allow a baseborn woman to demean you on your own land. Preposterous." He snapped his paper shut—not a good omen for Morgan. "At least the incident wasn't witnessed by any of the servants." He puffed on his cigar before grinding it out on a plate beside him, then faced Hadley, who stood with his back to the window, a rather pleased look on his face.

"Where were you this morning?" Franklin snapped. "I asked you to receive the inventory report from Jenkins."

"I was otherwise occupied, Father." Hadley stared at the painting above the mantle—a picture of two ships engaged in battle during a storm at sea.

Morgan had spent his youth getting lost in that painting, dreaming of commanding one of those ships, wondering how it would feel to order a broadside, to march across the heaving deck and breathe in the salty air. As he gazed at the scene, he felt the tug of the sea on him even now, luring him to another world where he had meaning, purpose, and freedom.

"I told you—" His father's strident tone yanked him back to reality.

"I know how to keep the ledger, Father," Hadley interrupted.

Franklin rose to his full six-foot stature, his lined face reddening. "You are seven and twenty, Hadley. Old enough to handle the responsibilities of this plantation." He folded the paper and tossed it on his vacated chair.

Six-year-old Lizzie bounced through the doors in a flurry of lace and giggles, scattering the dour mood that hung in the room like a demonic presence before an angel. Halting before her mother, she twirled around, sending her pink skirts spinning. "See my new dress, Mama, Papa." She faced Franklin, blond curls springing around a face that held a look of expectant adoration.

"Hmm. Yes, indeed. Very nice, Lizzie." The man placated her with a grin that seemed to crack his aged face.

Unaffected by her father's quick dismissal—oh, how Morgan hoped that would be the case her entire life—Lizzie dashed into Morgan's arms. He gathered the little girl into a bear-like embrace and set her on his lap. She smelled of sunshine and cinnamon, and he wished she would remain this young and innocent forever.

Hadley made his way to the buffet and poured himself another brandy.

Franklin's jaw bunched as he glanced between his sons. "All the two of you do is fritter away your time on gaming and women. You are both a disgrace to the Rutledge name."

"Oh dear." Mary glanced between her daughter and husband. "Must we always fight?"

"Until my eldest son owns up to his responsibility. . ." Franklin glared at Hadley. "What am I to do when I die? Hand over the running of the plantation to Morgan here?" His tone spoke of the complete absurdity of the notion.

The Madeira soured in Morgan's belly. He distracted himself by tickling Lizzie and allowing her giggles to sweep life into his empty soul. He'd accepted that Hadley was the favored son long ago, preferred it that way, in fact. Then why did the reminder never fail to twist the knife a little further in his gut? Not that Morgan wanted anything to do with the plantation. He enjoyed the privileges and wealth that came with belonging to the landed gentry, but in truth it all seemed oddly unimportant to him.

"I'll die before I'll watch my indolent sons squander everything I've worked for."

Hadley tossed his brandy to the back of his throat. "Father, you're too cantankerous to die. Why, you will no doubt live another hundred years." He gave a caustic smile. "Besides, we have more than enough to squander."

"I don't want Papa to die." Lizzie's blond eyebrows drew together. Morgan hugged her as his mother clasped her hand. "He's not going to die, Lizzie."

The maid entered, curtseyed, and lowered her gaze. "Supper is ready, mum."

Hadley set down his glass and straightened his waistcoat. "I fear I must miss our evening meal, Mother. I have an appointment in town."

"An appointment at the gaming halls no doubt." Franklin sneered.

"Hadley, please stay." Pain laced his mother's tone. "You so seldom dine with us."

"Some other time, Mother." He gave her an apologetic look then turned and left.

"I've lost my appetite." Franklin stormed from the room, his steps echoing up the stairs.

Morgan hated seeing grief shadow his mother's face. An all-too-common occurrence these past few years. Had she ever been happy? Though quite comely in her day, a permanent wrinkle folded the skin between her brows, and harsh lines framed her delicate mouth. Even her golden curls seemed to hang limp with despondency.

Scooting Lizzie from his lap, Morgan stood, took his mother's hand, and bowed gracefully. "May I escort you to dinner, madam?"

She smiled and stood, placing her hand in his.

Shoving aside the strife that always permeated the walls of the Rutledge home, Morgan escorted his mother and sister to the dining hall—the only two reasons he spent any time at all at home. But his thoughts drifted to another lady. A dark-haired woman with the prickly tongue. An educated, prickly tongue from her manner of speech. Yet, a mere servant? Regardless, instead of swooning at his feet as most women did, she had shunned him—insulted him! *Utterly and completely fascinating.* He grinned. *What a challenge.* And Lord knew Morgan needed something, anything, to add a spark to his humdrum existence. No, he must find a way to cross paths with this bold servant girl soon. Very soon.

๛

Nerves strung tight, Adalia stepped into the doctor's drawing room. Rich wainscoting framed the walls beneath paper painted with bright flowers. A woven rug covered the center of the wooden floor. A Hepplewhite settee and chairs sat upon it before a bay window that overlooked the gardens below. Flickering light from a fireplace and two painted glass lamps created a warm glow through the room. Her stomach rumbled. Yet this time, it was in appreciation of the food she'd just consumed: boiled mutton, okra soup, corn, and rice pudding. More food than she'd eaten in weeks.

Dr. Willaby looked up from his reading, took off his spectacles, and stood. "Do come in, Miss Winston, do come in. Is your chamber to your liking?"

Adalia smiled. Much to her surprise, she'd been given a beautiful chamber on the second floor, not one below stairs with the servants. But more importantly, it was a chamber that locked from the inside, not the outside. "Yes, it is perfect. Thank you. And supper was quite good as well."

"Ah, that would be Mrs. Golding, my cook's doing. I'm sure you were introduced."

"Yes." Adalia clasped her hands together, unsure of this man's intentions for her, beyond assisting him with his medical duties.

"Come. Sit and tell me how you learned to heal with herbs." He closed the book and set it on the table beside him. Only then did Adalia notice he'd been reading the Bible. Relief loosened the tight coils in her chest. A man who read his Bible was surely a good man.

The young Negress Adalia had met in the kitchen entered with a tray of tea. Though Adalia had tried to engage the girl in conversation, she had barely gotten a word out of her. The cook had informed Adalia that Joy was a new slave in the household.

"Joy, this is Miss Winston." The doctor's voice was curt.

The young girl set the tray down and nodded, keeping her gaze on the ground.

"She'll be staying with us and helping me with my patients. You are to assist her with anything she needs."

Adalia flinched. "I have no need of a maid, sir." Especially a slave. She'd rather die than have a slave serve her.

"Of course you do. Every lady needs a maid." The doctor frowned at Joy. "Don't just stand there, girl, go get another cup for Miss Winston."

His harsh tone grated over Adalia as Joy bobbed a nervous curtsey and left.

"Now, tell me how things went at Rutledge Hall." Doc Willaby said the name as if the mere sound of it poisoned his lips.

Adalia slid onto one of the chairs, feeling out of sorts conversing with her master—employer—as an equal. "The young boy had a simple bellyache. I gave him nettle tea." Her thoughts drifted to the Rutledge sons, but she wouldn't mention the incident. Her insolent behavior was inexcusable and could possibly tarnish the doctor's good name, something she hadn't considered in the heat of the moment.

Joy entered with an extra cup and poured tea for them both. Her hand trembled and Adalia took the cup from her before she spilled any and incurred the wrath of her master, as Adalia had done on more than one occasion with Sir Walter. She offered Joy a comforting smile, hoping to reassure her that she had nothing to fear from Adalia, but the girl wouldn't meet Adalia's eyes. The sip of tea turned to ash in her mouth. How could she work for a man who enslaved people—her people? But what else was she to do? Starve on the street?

Joy set the pot on the tray with a nervous *clank* and hurried from the room. At the very least, Adalia would do her best to make the young slave's life tolerable, if not pleasurable at moments. Perhaps that was why God had placed her in this home.

Dr. Willaby sipped his tea and leaned back in his chair. Though mostly gray, strands of dark brown revealed the original color of his hair. A brown that matched the warmth of his eyes, which now shifted to her with approval. She quickly lowered her gaze, afraid she'd be chastised for looking at him directly.

"Where did such a charming girl learn about plants that heal?" he asked again.

"From my mother. She studied healing from the local natives."

"Natives?" Disdain marred his voice. "Which island?"

Adalia hesitated. "Jamaica." Her insides cringed at the lie, but it couldn't be helped. She must give no indication of her true past or where she'd come from.

"And where are your parents now?"

"They are deceased."

"I am sorry, miss." His sympathetic tone touched her. "And leaving you alone so young."

She dared to meet his gaze. "I am nineteen, sir."

"Ah, a grown woman." He chuckled. "I daresay, when Father Mulligan informed me of your skill with the Negro orphans, I knew I'd found the right assistant."

"I am very grateful for the employment, Doctor." She sipped her tea, allowing the warm liquid to unwind her nerves. Peppermint tingled in her mouth.

Doctor Willaby proceeded to tell her the rules of the house, relaying in great detail the tight schedule he kept. "I expect you to attend church with me every Sunday."

"Of course. That would please me greatly." Adalia set her cup down on the table, trying to hide her enthusiasm. Sir Walter had never allowed her to attend church.

"You'll find me a quiet man who enjoys a quiet home."

"I assure you, Doctor, you will have no trouble from me."

He set down his tea and retrieved his Bible. "Very good. You may take your tea and go to your chamber. I'm sure you are tired."

Adalia thought nothing of the quick dismissal. In fact, being beyond exhaustion, she was glad for it. Bidding him good night, she headed upstairs, closed the door to her chamber, and lit the candle on her dresser. Golden light blanketed the room and warmed her heart. She dropped to her knees beside the bed and thanked God for all her many blessings: for a home, a bed, food, and employment. "Thank You, Lord. You do, indeed, supply all my needs."

Rising to sit on the bed, she withdrew a velvet pouch from her valise and poured a string of black pearls into her hand. Her mother's pearls. Pearls her father had purchased with money he'd saved for years. The beads shimmered like silvery onyx in the candlelight, dark and lustrous like her mother. She pressed them to her cheek. Cool and smooth. They were all Adalia had left of her. These and her sweet memories.

Closing her eyes, she pictured her father clasping the pearls around her mother's neck then leaning down to nibble on her ear. Her mother giggled then swung around and embraced him, gazing up at him with such love.

"What about us?" little four-year-old Delphia whined.

Their father, tall and as handsome as any regal prince, faced his daughters. "You both will always be my precious pearls." He knelt, and Adalia and her sister flew into his arms, where he showered them with kisses until they all collapsed in a heap of laughter.

That was six months before the hurricane swept them out to sea, leaving Adalia and Delphia orphans. Two days later, Sir Walter visited their farm on the pretense of checking on his neighbors. With soft words and promises of care, he stole them, frightened and hungry, from their beds. They never saw home again.

A breeze whistled through the cracks in the windowpanes and chilled the tear spilling down her cheek. Batting it away, she slid the pearls back into the pouch and began unpacking her things—what few things there were. She placed her extra petticoats and chemise in a drawer and hung her skirt on a hook in the wardrobe. After holding the Bible to her chest, she set it on a table by the bed, thankful her father had taught her to read and write. Not only that, but her father had insisted that she and Delphia receive a proper education, consisting of lessons in mathematics, literature, history, science, Latin, and religion. She'd never asked him where a simple farmer and fisherman had learned all these things, but she guessed he used to be a man of means, perhaps even of property and status, whose family disapproved of his marriage to Adalia's mother. Now, she would never know the truth.

Reaching back into the valise, her hand struck something hard and cold. The iron band that used to clamp around her ankle—at least one of them. She pulled it out. A chill scraped down her back that had nothing to do with the cool metal in her hands. Why had she kept it? She'd tossed the rest of her shackles into the sea. But not this. The candle fluttered, highlighting the engraved words, *Miles Plantation Barbados.* She snorted. How Sir Walter loved to brand everything and everyone with his name. She held the band up to the flame, exposing it to the light—if only to prove it had no power over her anymore. No, she would never wear it again. She had kept it as a reminder of just that, a reminder that she had once been a prisoner—a slave. But now, she was free.

Much the same as what the Lord had done for her and all mankind on the cross.

And she must never take that freedom for granted.

Tossing it back into the valise, she stuffed the case into the mahogany wardrobe, changed into her nightdress, blew out her candle, and crawled into bed. Drawing the quilt to her chin, she smiled. Warm, protected, and fed, she hadn't felt so content in years. So content *and* exhausted that within minutes, she felt herself drifting to sleep.

Sometime in the middle of the night, Adalia dreamt of shackles and leather whips and Sir Walter floating down the long hall like an evil specter, calling her name in slurred words. "Althea, sweet Althea." She cowered beneath her quilt, begging God to make him go away. But instead his voice grew louder. "Foolish girl! You can never leave me. You are mine forever."

Chapter Four

Morgan took a spot on the quarterdeck beside Captain Bristo and thrust his face into the wind. Sunshine spread a warm blanket over him as the scent of tar and the briny smell of the sea filled his nostrils. The merchant ship rose on a swell then plunged down the other side. Salty spray showered him. Bracing his boots over the wooden planks, he shook the droplets from his face and ran a hand through his hair.

"You are looking more like a true seaman every day." Captain Bristo smiled.

The compliment lifted Morgan's shoulders. "Remember my first week at sea when I clung to anything nailed to the deck?"

"You did provide entertainment for the crew." The captain chuckled as he folded his arms over the blue coat he always wore at sea. Though taller than Morgan's six feet, Captain Bristo was slighter of figure. And with his long brown hair pulled back in a queue, he looked much younger than his forty-three years. Many a sailor made the mistake of attempting to take advantage of the captain's presumed inexperience only to find that behind the gentle demeanor lurked a wise, valiant man who had no trouble maintaining order aboard his ship.

Morgan gazed over the blue expanse of glittering whitecaps. This was his world. The only place he felt at peace. In control. Happy. "I thank you, Captain, for taking a risk on this landlubber and teaching me to sail."

"Not just sail, Morgan. Command a ship of your own someday."

Morgan's heart both leapt and shriveled at the thought. "That is but a dream."

Sails thundered above. The captain lifted his gaze to the bosun on the main deck. "Reef topsails, if you please, Mr. Granger."

The aged sailor nodded and began braying commands to the crew, sending them leaping into the ratlines and scrambling aloft.

The captain eyed Morgan, his blue eyes brimming with wisdom. "Dreams can be made realities with determination, hard work, and God's help."

"My father would not see it so." Morgan snorted. "And God has not taken note of me in years." *If ever.*

Captain Bristo gripped the railing as the ship canted to starboard. "As to the first, you are not your father's son. As to the second, you *are* your Father's son."

Morgan rubbed the stubble on his chin and pushed aside yet another of the captain's many references to the Almighty. "You make no sense as usual, Captain."

In fact, if Franklin knew Morgan was learning to sail from a common merchant, he'd disown him on the spot. Yet ever since Morgan had turned ten years old and had been permitted to walk about Charleston on his own, he'd spent hours standing at the South Battery gazing at the sea, watching the ships sail into port, longing to hop on them and sail away to faraway lands. When he'd mentioned this desire to his father, the man had laughed. His laughter had turned to insults, then threats when he'd realized Morgan was serious.

"What's wrong with you, boy? The Rutledges are not common merchants. We are not pitiful sailors. We are landowners. We sit on the city council, respected and honored members of society. And by all that is sacred, you will not ruin that standing or our good name, or you will no longer be a Rutledge. Do you understand me?"

At age twelve, Morgan had simply nodded and skulked away.

But like a desperate lover, the call of the sea was relentless. It beckoned to him during the day as he strode past the docks and admired the masts of the ships waving at him from the harbor. It lured him at night in the sea breezes flowing through his window. Until he could stand it no longer. So, years later, when he befriended Captain Kane Bristo in the White Street Tavern and the captain offered to teach him to sail, Morgan could not turn him down.

Now at age twenty-two, he had accompanied Captain Bristo on several trips to the Caribbean, two to Baltimore, and five to Boston. All during the social season in Charleston when Morgan and his brother Hadley spent several months at the family townhome in the city, away from the plantation.

Captain Bristo slapped him on the back. "Yes, I'd say you are nearly ready to command your own ship, Morgan. The men respect you. You have a natural talent for sailing, an ability to lead."

Morgan tipped his hat against the bright sun and squinted at the captain. Waiting for him to laugh at his joke. But instead, when he only nodded in affirmation, mist covered Morgan's eyes, and he turned away, thankful when the breeze quickly dried it. He'd never received a single compliment from his father. In fact, quite the opposite. He'd been told his entire life that he was nothing but a disappointment and a wastrel. "I can hardly believe you think so highly of me."

Captain Bristo winked. "I never lie."

No, the man didn't. He was far too godly to lie to anyone. The most honorable, decent man Morgan had ever met.

"Sail Ho!"

"Where away?" Plucking the scope from his belt, Captain Bristo raised it to his eye.

A speck popped over the horizon like an ant crawling from its hole. The crew halted their work, staring at the intruder. Tension stiffened their postures. Many a story had filtered through Charleston's taverns of British war ships boarding American merchantmen and impressing their crews into the Royal navy. Not to mention that a few of Charleston's ships had gone missing recently and had never been heard from again. And of course they must always be on the lookout for pirates. The sea was not the safest place to be.

Yet Morgan could think of nowhere he'd rather be.

"She flies the Union Jack." Captain Bristo lowered his scope and slapped it against his palm. He faced Morgan, a twinkle in his eye. "Your command, Morgan."

"Me?" A twinge of fear poked him.

"Aye, you know what to do. Evasive action. Bring us out of danger." The captain nodded toward the crew awaiting command on the main deck, all eyes on Morgan.

He drew in a deep breath, feeding off the confidence he saw in Bristo's eyes while bringing to memory all the sailing knowledge he had learned the past few years. He glanced at the British ship. The ant had sprouted wings. White wings glutted with wind. And she was heading their way. He swallowed and faced the crew.

"Lay aloft and loose topsails! Up staysails. Clear away the jib." He glanced behind him at the quartermaster at the wheel. "Two points to larboard, Mr. Hanson."

❧

Medical satchel in one hand, skirts clutched in the other, Adalia crossed the cobblestone street, weaving in between a horse and rider and a four-wheeled landau. The clip of Joy's shoes sounded behind her as they made their way down Church Street. A cool January breeze swept in from the bay, stealing the warmth of the sun from her shoulders and bringing the smell of horseflesh and fish and sweet yellow jessamine, which combined into an oddly pleasant aroma. She smiled. The smells of Charleston. She'd been in the city for a month and a half—two weeks of which she'd spent in Dr. Willaby's employ. And she'd never been happier. Well, not since she was a little girl. She had already learned a great deal about medicine from the doctor, and he seemed equally interested in her knowledge of herbal remedies. Besides which, she enjoyed bringing comfort to the sick. Just as her mother had done. Not only did Adalia carry on a family tradition, but she was also able to independently support herself. How many women could lay claim to that?

Especially Negro women.

She glanced over her shoulder. "Joy, please walk beside me." She gestured for the girl to move forward.

"It ain't proper, miss," the young slave responded.

"You may be Doctor Willaby's slave, but you aren't mine. You are my friend." In fact, the more time Adalia spent with Joy, the more she liked the girl who lived up to her name so well. No matter the work, no matter the long hours, or menial tasks, no matter that Dr. Willaby oft scolded her, Joy always had a smile on her face.

Tugging the girl up beside her, Adalia turned down Chambers Street on her way to the apothecary, where she needed to purchase some additional herbs. Dr. Willaby informed her that the weather would soon be warm enough for her to grow her own herbs in the garden beside the house, but until then, she would have to purchase what she could.

She turned another corner and nearly bumped into a man. Leaping back, she threw a hand to her chest.

"Pardon me, miss." He tipped his top hat, his eyes appraising her as a slow grin replaced the frown on his mouth.

"Quite all right." Clutching Joy's arm, Adalia forged ahead, only to see a group of young dandies across the street looking her way.

Now that the social season had begun, Charleston's streets over-flowed with men and women dressed in silks and satins, feathers and top hats, lace and gloves—displaying all the fineries and fripperies representing their class.

Fingering the top buttons of her modest gown, Adalia avoided the men's gazes. The last thing she wanted was to attract the wrong kind of attention.

Joy stumbled, caught her balance, then leaned toward Adalia. "Lots of handsome men stare at you, miss."

"I assure you, they grant the same courtesy to anyone wearing a skirt."

"Not to me."

Adalia looked at her. Skin as smooth and glistening as café-au-lait, dark curls that would be the envy of any lady, and chocolate eyes framed in thick lashes. "You are lovely, Joy."

Joy gave her a disbelieving smile before they started on their way again. Regardless of the young girl's beauty, it was obvious she didn't receive the same attention as Adalia. Or any white woman, for that matter. And only because she was a Negro. Yet, Negro blood flowed through Adalia as well.

Pondering the injustice, she turned down Queen Street. A bell rang from the harbor. Chickens squawked as a young boy chased them across the avenue. Up ahead the masts of ships spired toward the sun.

A merchant ship must have just arrived, for boats carrying all manner of goods lined up at the public landing off Gibbs Wharf. A tall commanding man leapt from one onto the long quay. He adjusted his cocked hat, and bade another man farewell.

Something familiar about him kept Adalia's gaze locked in his direction. Only when he looked her way did she remember. The spoiled impish Rutledge son. The one she'd pushed into the creek. Tugging her straw bonnet lower on her face, she turned, spun Joy with her, and hurried in the other direction. The last thing she needed was trouble with the wealthiest family in town.

❧

Morgan blinked. It was her. The audacious healer woman. The one who had stomped on his foot. The lady he hadn't been able to force from his thoughts these past weeks. The one he'd been unable to find, though he'd gone to Dr. Willaby's house more than once. And now, she was snubbing him again! He had just evaded a British frigate, so surely he could command such a lowly woman. Morgan charged forward, threading in between slaves carrying loads from the ships, a group of sailors, and a horse and carriage. He gazed across the sea of bobbing feathers, top hats, and flowered bonnets, finally spotting her plain straw hat and wool shawl. Shoving his way through the mob, he nodded at passing ladies and answered a friend's greeting, and then finally, he leapt into her path.

Instead of looking at him and acknowledging his presence, she skirted around him, muttering a "Pardon me, sir."

Incredible! He stepped before her again. "Miss Winston, I believe."

She stopped and raised her gaze to his, a look of annoyance on her lovely features. "Is there something I can do for you, Mr. Rutledge?"

The slave girl took a step back, where she belonged.

Morgan gave Miss Winston one of his most beguiling grins. "So, you *do* know who I am."

She huffed and gazed across the street as if he were bothering her. *Him? Morgan Rutledge. Bothering her?* She should be thrilled he even spoke to her.

He cleared his throat. "I don't believe we've been formally introduced." Dragging the cocked hat from his head, he suddenly remembered he must look a fright in his seaman's clothes. He raked his hair, pressing down the wind-frayed strands. Regardless, he still had his good looks and Rutledge charm. Not to mention great wealth. Surely one of those would suffice to garner a smile out of her. Although why he needed one, he couldn't say.

She tilted her head. "Since you know my name and I know yours, I don't see the necessity."

She spat the words with an assurance and confidence usually found lacking among those of her station. But all he could focus on was the sensuous way her moist lips moved. She was as lovely as he remembered. With hair glistening like liquid obsidian, her tawny skin smooth and glowing, her deep, fathomless eyes, now sparking with. . .

Disdain?

He shook off what surely was a misunderstanding. "Since we did not meet under the best of circumstances, I thought we should make a better attempt."

She gaped at him as if he'd grown horns on his head. "Very well. Pleased to meet you, Mr. Rutledge." She dipped a curtsey then reached behind her to grab her slave's arm and proceeded past him.

Of all the— His name floated on the brisk wind, and he turned to see a group of ladies eyeing him from across the street. Yet this woman, this common servant girl, dismissed him as if *he* were a mere slave. Egad, she treated her servant better than him.

He followed her. Surely the woman was confusing him with someone else. "Miss Winston, if I may have a moment of your time."

"Unless you are ill, Mr. Rutledge, I fear not," she shot over her shoulder. "I have duties to attend. A concept that I'm sure escapes you."

Stunned, Morgan stared after her. He caught up to her again and touched her arm. She tore it from him as if he'd branded her.

Ignoring the fire in her eyes, he lifted his brows. "I wondered if you'd join me at the Bay Coffee Shop for a spot of tea. Or perhaps lemonade?"

Frowning, she looked at him as if he'd asked her to drink horse urine.

❧

Adalia brushed away a fly, wishing she could rid herself of this pompous rogue as easily. A spot of tea? What was he after? Men like him were always after something. And the only thing she could think of caused her stomach to curdle. By the way the ladies lining the marketplace gaped at him, Adalia assumed Mr. Rutledge was quite the *Don Juan*. Perhaps he wished to add another feather to his cap with the new lady in town. No doubt most servant girls would swoon over any attention paid them by this handsome, wealthy rake. For he was handsome, indeed. Even more handsome than she remembered. His face no longer held that look of abject boredom so often found on the spawn of the tediously affluent. In fact, he seemed much more alive. Maybe his common attire—a simple linen shirt, waistcoat, and trousers tucked within high boots—brought his usual arrogance down to a manageable level. In any case, it couldn't hurt to enjoy the way his wheat-colored hair flung about him in wild abandon, the sprinkle of dark whiskers on his chin, and even the spark of mischief in his stark green eyes. Though she'd spurned him, he held himself with authority as he awaited her reply. The scent of the sea clung to him, reminding her of her father.

But he was nothing like her father.

And she wanted nothing to do with him—or his kind. Like Sir Walter, men like him thought they ruled the world and all the women in it.

She intended to tell him just that when a gentleman called his name, and he and two ladies darted across the street toward them.

"Morgan, we've been looking for you. Hadley said you came to town weeks ago." A comely woman with brown hair addressed him.

Never moving his eyes from Adalia, Mr. Rutledge seemed annoyed at the intrusion. Not until the woman tugged on his arm. "And now you have found me," he responded curtly.

The other lady, a stunning woman with hair the color of alabaster, sidled up to Mr. Rutledge and brazenly looped her arm through his. "Morgan, do say you'll join us at Dillon's tonight." Her icy gaze locked upon Adalia then swept away. "And who, pray tell, is this?"

The gentleman with dark hair and an even darker scowl on his face tugged upon his lacy cravat and glanced at Adalia with curiosity.

Mr. Rutledge freed himself from the woman's clutches. "Miss Winston, may I present Miss Emerald Middleton, Mr. Joseph Drayton, and Miss Caroline Johnson."

Adalia dipped her head. "A pleasure."

But the feeling—as false as it was—did not seem to be mutual, especially not from Miss Emerald. She studied Adalia as if she were studying a disease through a microscope. "Miss Winston, how are you acquainted with my Morgan?"

Adalia did not miss the possessive form. "I am not acquainted with him in any way, miss."

"Then how did you come to speak to him?"

"He was speaking to me." Adalia flashed him a curt smile and found him gazing at her with delight. Straightening her shoulders, she collected Joy. "Good day." She dipped her head and headed down the street.

"Will you join us for tea later?" Mr. Rutledge called after her.

"No, I will not, Mr. Rutledge."

Joy raised a hand to her mouth, restraining a giggle. She glanced over her shoulder. "You've gone an' offended the richest bachelor in town, Miss Winston."

"Call me Adalia, please."

"He fancies you."

"Don't be absurd. He doesn't even know me." Yet how could she explain the interest on his face when he gazed at her. As though she were valuable, precious. No one had ever looked at her like that before. Especially not someone in such a high position. She had searched his eyes—those moss-green eyes—and found no salacious or nefarious intent. His pompous friends were another story. She knew how to handle the contempt she saw in their gazes. It was all too familiar.

One last time, she glanced over her shoulder and found his gaze still locked upon her even as Miss Emerald attempted to drag him away.

Facing forward, she forced down the confusion caused by his attention. She would never be a part of his world. Never.

CHAPTER FIVE

Eight-year-old Adalia pressed her knees against the pony's tummy. "See, this is how you make him go," she instructed her younger sister, Delphia, who sat in front of her atop the soft, warm gift their father had given them for Christmastide. "You squeeze his belly and tap the reins on the side where you want him to go."

The pony obeyed, heading down a pathway to their right.

"Let me try! Let me try!" Four-year-old Delphia tugged on the reins. Adalia relinquished them but kept a hold beneath her sister's tiny grasp.

Delphia pulled the reins to the left and squealed with delight when the pony turned around and loped back the way they'd come. "I did it. I did it!"

Adalia hugged her little sister, inhaling the sweet scent of her lilac soap. The same scent that always clung to their mother. They emerged from the jungle path into the clearing before their modest home. To the right, Adalia spotted her father in the fields tugging their stubborn mule, Fred, through furrows of fresh dirt. Beyond him, palm trees swayed in the tropical breeze. And beyond that, she could hear the waves of the Caribbean tumbling ashore. If her father wasn't attending the crops, he could be found in his boat fishing upon the sea.

Their mother waved from the front porch of their single-story brick home. "Be careful, dears," she shouted.

"Faster, faster." Delphia bobbed up and down. Adalia tapped the horse's belly and clicked her tongue as she'd seen Papa do, and the pony broke into a trot. Delphia giggled as they bounced down a small trail, leaves caressing their faces and the distant bubbling of a creek joining their childish laughter.

Then the memory faded and another took its place. Delphia's pale, sweat-laden face sinking into her ratty mattress. Her hollow cheeks and cracked white lips. Her dark hair matted to her forehead. The life ebbing from her eyes. Adalia crumpled into a ball by her side, begging her to live, begging God for her life. Offering up her own in the place of her sister's. But she was gone at only nine years old. Before her life had begun. Before Adalia had found a way to escape their enslavement.

Sir Walter tore Adalia from her sister's body and ordered two men to take Delphia away and bury her. Adalia screamed, fisting him with her hands. His slap stung her face.

She bolted upward, gasping for breath. Perspiration glued her nightdress to her body. Shadows formed in the darkness. Unfamiliar, yet safe. She was in her chamber at Doc Willaby's. Swinging her feet over the bed, she dropped her head into her hands. "Oh, Delphia. I miss you so." She drew in a staggering breath. "I'm so sorry, Mother, Father. I tried to take care of her. I tried."

But she had failed.

She never knew what disease had forever robbed her of her sister. She never had a chance to treat her. Sir Walter had forbidden her to use any of her herbs. "Black magic. The devil's elixir," he had called them.

Her door creaked. Wiping her eyes, she leapt to her feet. Joy crept inside, her gown slightly askew as if she'd donned it in a hurry. "Miss, are you all right?"

"Yes."

"You was screaming."

Shame stung Adalia. She glanced out the window, where dawn's glow tiptoed across the tree tops. "Was I?" She sank back onto her mattress.

Closing the door, Joy stumbled over something before stopping beside the bed. She moved her hand as if to clutch Adalia's but then halted, biting her lip. "Who is Delphia?"

The name spoken aloud caused Adalia's throat to clog. She drew in a shredded breath, trying to clear it. "My sister. At least she was."

"I's sorry, miss."

"It was a long time ago." Adalia wiped her moist cheek and stood. "She would have turned fifteen this year."

"Same age as me." Joy eased Adalia's hair back over her shoulder.

The caring gesture warmed Adalia. Especially since she knew the risk in touching a master without permission. But perhaps Joy sensed she had nothing to fear from her.

But then the girl took a step back and lowered her gaze. "Forgive me, miss."

"For what? You were being kind to me."

Joy dared a glance at Adalia as if to gauge her sincerity. She must have been satisfied, for her gaze remained steadfast. After offering her a reassuring smile, Adalia wandered to the window. The arc of the sun peeked above the massive live oak in the center of Doc Willaby's garden. She squinted at the bright light splintering through leaves as they frolicked in the morning breeze. "Have you ever lost anyone, Joy?"

"Never had no one to lose, miss."

The girl's nonchalant tone spun Adalia around. "No family?"

Joy shook her head and then glanced out the open door. "I'll go fetch water for your basin, miss."

"I can fetch my own water, Joy." Adalia longed to know more of Joy's story, but the girl seemed uneasy with the question.

"I don't mind doin' it, miss." She started to turn then halted. "That Mr. Rutledge came by agin yesterday when you was out wit' the doctor."

Adalia shook her head, her glance landing on the card atop her dressing bureau with the name *Mr. Morgan Rutledge* scrawled across it in fancy letters. What did the infernal man want? And, more importantly, why would he not leave her alone? Thankfully, she'd not been home on either occasion when he'd come to call.

"The doctor was none too happy when he saw his card sittin' on the receivin' table." Joy gave her a sideways glance.

Adalia wondered why but simply shrugged. "Well, I suppose Mr. Rutledge will stop coming when he sees his interest is not reciprocated."

Joy smiled. "I best be goin', miss. Cook will need help with breakfast."

Two hours later, Adalia slipped into the massive sanctuary of St. Michael's Church. Though she attended every Sunday with Dr. Willaby, the sight never failed to amaze her. Behind the altar, exquisite stained-glass windows depicting magnificent angels arched to a massive half-dome in blue and gold designs. The largest organ she'd ever seen, now regaling them with "Rock of Ages," sat behind a mahogany pulpit perched high above the pews. Separating from the doctor, she headed up the stairs to sit in the balcony with the other servants and those who could not purchase a pew box.

It wasn't until she took a seat on the hard oak bench that she saw him. Morgan Rutledge sitting in a box about midway toward the altar beside an elderly man and woman, a small girl no more than six or seven, and the man he'd been sword fighting with that day on the plantation. His brother. As she stared at Morgan, much to her horror, he turned around and scanned the balcony as if he were looking for someone. Before she could turn away, his gaze latched upon hers, and a grin lifted one corner of his lips. Heat rose up her neck.

Infernal, pompous man.

Thankfully the service began as the choir filed in from the side in their black cassocks and white surplices. During the recitation of the creed and the singing of the hymns, Adalia kept her eyes closed and her mind focused on God. She knew most of the words anyway. They were implanted in her memory and heart by a father who put God above everything else. She could still hear his melodious baritone belting out hymns as he worked the fields. Now, with the beautiful organ music and the harmonious voices of the choir, Adalia could almost imagine what it would be like to sing praises to God before the throne in heaven. She felt her spirit rising upward, wishing that day would come soon. For she had nothing left here on earth to capture her heart. No family. No friends. In fact, she could see no reason why God had taken everyone she loved.

And left her all alone.

Still she would not blame Him. Neither for that, nor for the cruelty of Sir Walter. *The Lord gave, and the Lord hath taken away; blessed be the name of the Lord.* She could still see her papa look up from his reading of the book of Job and smile. "There's a reason for everything that happens, good or bad," he had said. "Just trust and obey."

Adalia bowed her head. *I've done my best, Lord.*

I know, precious one.

Emotion burned in her throat as warmth swirled about her. She was not alone, after all. God was there.

Soon the music ended and the reverend mounted the pulpit. Though she tried to focus on the sermon, Adalia could not help but notice that Mr. Rutledge's gaze repeatedly swung in her direction. In fact, he didn't seem to be listening to the message at all. Rather he fidgeted in his seat, stretching his broad shoulders against the back of the pew and tapping his fingers atop the box frame. As well as repeatedly glancing over his shoulder at her! Adalia feared someone would notice. How could she focus on God when the incorrigible man kept staring at her? Finally she plucked out her fan and, though a chill permeated the church, she waved it beside her face, blocking him from view. At the end of the service, she couldn't exit the building quickly enough. Unfortunately, Dr. Willaby was detained within the foyer conversing with a couple of older gentlemen.

Slipping through the crowd amassing before the huge pillars of the church porch, Adalia found a spot out of view to wait for the doctor.

Unaccustomed to having such nice attire, she adjusted the lace at the cuffs of her Sunday gown. Well, not so nice if she compared it to the silk skirts, velvet sashes, and wool shawls adorning the genteel women exiting the church. But Adalia had purchased her cream-colored muslin gown with her own money. And she was proud of it.

She didn't see him coming until the tips of his boots slid up to the toes of her shoes. She knew it was him before she lifted her gaze. Her stomach tightened in a knot. In frustration, no doubt. But yet, something else lingered in her emotions.

When she did meet his eyes, he gave her that boyish grin that only further cinched her midsection, making it hard to breathe. Dressed in tight pantaloons of broadcloth, a fine cashmere waistcoat trimmed in gold, high boots, and a black overcoat, he presented quite the gallant.

"Why were you staring at me, sir?"

He leaned toward her, his warm breath wafting over her cheek. "Because you are beautiful, miss."

Her stomach unwound and fluttered. He smelled of exotic spices. She stepped back, trying to regain her senses. "There are plenty of comely ladies present." She pointed toward one particularly stunning blond who glared at them from afar—Miss Emerald Middleton, if she remembered her name. "Please do me the favor of casting your vain flatteries elsewhere."

"I meant no offense." The humor left his voice, and the odd longing she'd seen before filled his eyes. Over his shoulder she saw the elderly couple who'd sat with him in church climbing into a fancy carriage. The little girl, however, upon spotting Morgan, started toward him, a grin on her lips. She seemed to be making every effort to keep society's strictures and walk, not run, though a rebellious skip broke through her careful stride once or twice.

Upon reaching him, her face beamed even brighter, as if he were the most precious person in the world.

The sight stunned Adalia. Morgan hoisted the girl into his arms and spun her around in a twirl of petticoats and giggles. Adalia's thoughts drifted to her sister at the same age, and she swallowed at the tender display, so at odds with her first impression of the planter's son.

"Morgan, come with us in the carriage," the little girl said, clinging to his neck and giving him a pout. Golden curls sashayed in the wind around a face like a cherub's. But it was the adoring way Morgan looked at her that kept Adalia frozen in place.

"Not this time, Lizzie, but I'll come home soon."

"And then you'll take me on a pony ride like you said?"

"Of course." He tapped her on the nose.

"And you'll read Mother Goose to me?"

"Until you beg me to stop." He chuckled.

Morgan's gaze slid to Adalia as if only then remembering she was there. He set the little girl down and took her hand. "Lizzie, this is Miss Winston. Miss Winston, this is my sister, Lizzie."

The little girl dipped a curtsey, graceful and dainty.

"Pleased to meet you, Lizzie." Adalia smiled.

"Elizabeth!" A male voice boomed from within the carriage as the elderly woman leaned out the window and stared their way.

Adalia thought she saw a spark of fear cross the girl's beautiful green eyes.

Morgan knelt and kissed her on the cheek. "I'll come see you soon. Be good for Mother."

Her frown was miserable enough to melt a warrior's resolve. But then she nodded and squeezed her brother one last time before she dashed to her parents. Morgan's affectionate gaze followed her until she was snug in the carriage and safe on her way.

As if the girl had clipped a piece of his heart and taken it with her, Morgan gazed at the vehicle until it rounded a corner and disappeared from sight. The scene caused a piece of Adalia's own heart to soften.

"She's a charming girl," was all she could think to say.

"I adore her. She's the only bright spot in my otherwise dismal life." He faced her, and she saw emotion misting his eyes.

But his statement had already shattered any possible effect. "Ah, yes, poor rich boy. All that wealth, all those parties." She turned to leave.

He slipped beside her, keeping her pace. "I know you must think me some foppish primcock, but you know nothing of my life."

She wanted to respond curtly that of course she didn't, how could she? but the sorrow in his tone stopped her. She turned to face him. The usual devilish twinkle in his eyes dissolved beneath a hollow melancholy. She shrugged off the sympathy it caused. No doubt it was but another one of his tricks to enslave an innocent woman's heart.

It wouldn't work with her. She thrust out her chin, glancing over the massive columns of St. Michael's, desperately wanting to change the topic to something. . .anything that would bring the priggishness back to his eyes and the shield back around her heart. "I haven't seen you at church before."

"I don't normally attend St. Michael's, though now that I know where to find you, I'm sensing a call to deeper spirituality." He grinned and acknowledged the greeting of a passing gentleman.

She narrowed her eyes. "The only thing you are sensing is your own carnal nature."

"Ouch. Milady wounds me deeply." He pressed a hand over his heart.

"Is everything a joke to you?"

"No." He sobered. "I find no humor in receiving no response to my many calls to your home."

"No doubt you expect me to dash to your side every time you drop off your calling card?"

His green eyes flashed. A breeze loosened a strand of hair from his queue, leaving it dangling over his impervious jaw. She noted the way the sunlight glinted specks of gold in the dark whiskers on his chin. "Yes, now that you mention it, I do," he said with a grin.

She'd wager that most women did precisely that. Frowning, she eyed the parishioners exiting the church. Still no sign of Dr. Willaby. Surely it would be safe enough to walk home alone in the daylight. Anything to rid herself of this rogue and the odd feelings he invoked.

The *clip-clop* of horses' hooves and the grate of wheels grew louder as a landau passed. "If you'll excuse me, Mr. Rutledge." Turning, she started to leave.

He leapt beside her and offered her his arm. "May I escort you home?"

"You may not." She forged ahead.

"Why do you hate me so?" A pinch of sorrow spiced the shock in his voice.

She must remind herself that it was only the sound of his injured pride, not any true feelings he held for her. "I don't hate you, sir. I merely know your kind."

"And what kind is that?"

She stopped and eyed him. The social season had begun in

Charleston, and much like the season in London, it was a time when the affluent and powerful forsook their plantations to converge on the city for balls, plays, concerts, and general frivolous amusements. That was all she was to him—an amusement.

"The kind who have more wealth than they can ever spend, who fritter away their time in idle and often immoral amusements, and who think they are better than everyone else simply by nature of their birth and fortune."

❧

Morgan rubbed his chin, an unavoidable grin raising one corner of his mouth.

"I insult you, and you smile at me." She bit her bottom lip and blew out a sigh. Her dark eyes flitted about, looking for someone, or perhaps just avoiding him. How he longed for another glance into their fathomless depths. In the meantime, he satisfied himself by admiring the rest of her. Even in a plain white gown with a cambric frill, she stood out from among the dozens of more richly attired women. The garnet-red velvet bow tied about her straw bonnet matched the color of her luscious lips. A breeze brought her scent of rosemary to his nose and sent one of her ebony curls dancing across her neck.

He swallowed down the urge to caress it. "I find your honesty refreshing."

"Indeed. No doubt due to its rarity among your friends." Giving him a look of annoyance, she started walking again.

Egad, her shrewish tongue! He followed her. He couldn't help it. She reminded him of the sea: wild, tempestuous, unpredictable, and beautiful. "Would you honor me by allowing me to escort you to a soiree at Craven Hall Friday night?"

"No," she said without stopping.

The woman confounded him. Dozens of ladies awaited his invitation, and she spurned him without a second's thought. "Are you otherwise engaged?" It was rude to ask, but he could think of no other reason for her refusal.

"No."

He touched her arm, if only to slow her down. She leapt away from him as if he'd burned her. Her chest rose and fell beneath the ruffle at her neckline.

"My apologies, Miss Winston. I didn't mean to frighten you. I

51

simply wish to know why you refuse me."

"For the very reason that you are astounded that I would do so."

Morgan knew his vanity had been gravely insulted, but he couldn't help but smile.

The clamor of the gossiping crowd rang over them. Miss Winston tipped up the brim of her hat and finally graced him with a peek into those dark eyes. "Are you still confused, sir?"

"No, I believe you have been quite clear." He frowned, battling a frustration he certainly wasn't accustomed to with the softer gender.

She tilted her chin and fingered a black curl fluttering about her neck. The very curl he yearned to run his fingers through. "I suggest you continue attending church, Mr. Rutledge, and do spend more time listening to the sermon next time."

Dr. Willaby approached, stepping between Morgan and Miss Winston. "Mr. Rutledge." His tone was curt as usual.

"Doctor." Morgan nodded at the impudent man.

"If you'll excuse us." Taking Miss Winston's arm, Dr. Willaby stole her away before Morgan had a chance to utter a proper adieu.

❧

"What business have you with Mr. Rutledge?" The doctor addressed Adalia when they were outside the reach of prying ears.

"None, I assure you," Adalia said.

"I would stay away from the Rutledges, miss. Especially the men in the family. They are a danger to women everywhere." He patted her hand as a father would a daughter.

Adalia eyed him, wondering at the cause of his scorn. Surely anyone would consider a match with one of the Rutledge sons a great advantage. Regardless, she had every intention of following his advice. She glanced back over her shoulder only to find Mr. Rutledge standing amongst his friends, the alabaster beauty clinging to his arm. Sunlight shimmered off her silk gown and the jewels strung about her neck.

But Morgan's eyes remained fastened on Adalia.

She faced forward, her mind spinning from their encounter. During the torturous years enslaved by Sir Walter, she'd often dreamed of a charming prince who would come to her rescue. An honorable man who would cherish and protect and love her and take her away to a fairy-tale land filled with beauty and wonder.

But no such man came. In truth, heroes didn't exist.

Especially among slave-owning nobility. Yes, she admired the beautiful women and handsome men she'd seen strolling about town in their elegant attire. She'd heard their laughter and the music from their parties. But Adalia knew she was not destined for such a life. She would always be a pauper. Some days her belly might ache from hunger and her back from too much work. But God would take care of her. She knew that. Yet, as she stole one more glance at Mr. Rutledge mingling among the privileged crowd of aristocrats, she wondered just for a second what it would feel like to be a part of his world.

CHAPTER SIX

After one last glance in her dressing mirror, Adalia gathered her gloves, pelisse, and medical satchel and headed downstairs. She now owned three gowns. Three! Could she ever have imagined? Even though one of them was reserved for her Sunday best, she felt devilishly rich. And a bit ashamed. Having a salary for the first time in her life had made her far too frivolous. As she descended the stairs, she vowed not to purchase any more fabric for at least a year. She passed the housekeeper, who was carrying an armful of dirty laundry and a tin of coals. "Good morning, Mrs. Faye."

The elderly woman grinned and wished her a good day.

Adalia smiled as she made her way to the foyer. Every day, she thanked God for Dr. Willaby's generosity. She had a home, food, clothing, and worthwhile work. Work she was excited to begin on this crisp February day. Though she had assisted Dr. Willaby on several of his medical calls, many days he sent her to help at the Negro orphanage. Which of course she didn't mind at all. It was only that she'd hoped to learn more about true medicine from the doctor. Today, however, he had promised to bring her along on all his calls.

Happy at the thought, she bounced into the drawing room, and upon seeing the doctor sitting in his usual chair, cup of tea in hand and open Bible in his lap, she said, "I am ready to leave whenever you are, sir."

He looked up at her and smiled above the rim of his glasses. A gentle smile with a hint of sorrow. "I'm afraid there's been a change of plans, Miss Winston." He released a heavy sigh. "It's the Rutledges."

Adalia's heart grew heavy as she waited for him to continue.

"It seems they have more ill slaves. You'll need to attend to them.

Plus, I'd like you to drop by the orphanage on your way back. Apparently Doctor Patterson is...well, indisposed again." He huffed his displeasure. Everyone in town knew of the man's affair with the bottle.

Adalia tried to hide her disappointment. Rutledge Hall was the last place she wished to go. "Surely there is another doctor who could better attend the Rutledge slaves." She clamped her lips together, but the words had already squeezed through them. She shouldn't question her employer. It was just that she was so looking forward to absorbing his knowledge today. Besides, Adalia was beginning to wonder whether the doctor had employed her simply to attend to Negroes. For he always passed any calls to minister to them on to her.

He frowned. His jaw clenched. Adalia swallowed, chastising herself for ungrateful words.

"No respectable physician panders to the idle complaints of slaves." His lips curled in disgust. "Besides, that task normally falls to the matron of the plantation. Why Mrs. Rutledge refuses to do her duty is beyond me." His dark brows—so at odds with his graying hair—lifted in a stern line. "You will go, Miss Winston. Is that clear?"

She nodded, acid welling in her belly.

"Joy can accompany you." Setting aside his Bible, he stood, the harsh lines of his face softening. "I can see that you are disappointed."

Should she dare press her hand? "Forgive me, sir. But I thought you wished me to stay away from the Rutledges."

"I do. The men, not the slaves. Besides, I believe those unbridled sons are staying in town for the season." He glared at her. "Is there a problem?"

"No, I am happy to help them." Adalia lowered her eyes.

"You are a sweet girl, Miss Winston." Kindness shoved the last trace of anger from his tone. Raising a fist to his mouth, he cleared his throat as if overcome with emotion. "I thank God He brought you to me."

The gracious, sincere words, so foreign to her ears, trickled through her mind, awakening fond memories of her childhood, of a father's love, and washing away all traces of the doctor's vile attitudes in the process. "It is I who am thankful, Doctor, to have such a generous and good man as my employer."

A short while later, Adalia snapped the reins, sending the phaeton lurched forward. Joy clung to the edge of the carriage as they trundled down the street into the path of a cool ocean breeze that fluttered the fringe on the hood above them and brought the scent of fish and rotting wood to their noses. As they passed through Charleston, weaving among other carriages and horses, several gentlemen tipped their hats in her direction. Adalia ignored them, happy when the cobblestones turned to sand and the buildings faded into angel oaks and palmettos. At least the trees wouldn't ogle her.

Yet, Joy seemed anything but happy beside her. The farther they went out of town, the stiffer her posture became, and the tighter she gripped the edge of the seat.

"Are you all right, Joy?" Adalia raised her voice over the *clip-clop* of the horses' hooves and the rattle of the carriage wheels.

Yet the girl's wide eyes remained riveted forward. "I don't much care for visitin' plantations."

Adalia nodded. It was an emotion she could well understand. Her reaction had been the same the first time she'd entered Rutledge land. Though at the time, her fear had quickly turned to anger. And now at her friend's reaction, it threatened to do so again.

"I's afraid they'll steal me as their slave."

Adalia shifted the reins to one hand and touched Joy's arm. "They can't steal another man's slave, Joy. It's against the law. So, you have nothing to fear. Besides, I won't let them harm you."

I won't let him take you, Delphia. I won't let him make us slaves.

Adalia's promises to her sister echoed in her mind like hollow chimes. Empty, like her words were now.

The scent of pine and moss and a hint of rain swirled around them on a crisp breeze. Joy gave her a tremulous smile. But a smile, nonetheless. And that gave her courage to ask, "How did you come to be Doctor Willaby's slave?"

Joy folded her hands in her lap. "I was at the orphanage. The one where you hep out." The wind blew a whip of hair into her face, and she brushed it away. "When I turned ten, I was put up for sale."

Adalia's chest tightened. Humans beings sold like goods. It sickened her.

"I was a laundress for Mrs. Hentley for four years. But she up and died of the ague last year. Doc Willaby bought me a couple months ago," Joy continued as she gazed at the passing foliage. "I's very lucky. A friend o' mine went to the rice fields. She died from the malaria."

Malaria. How horrible. Adalia had heard that over half the slaves assigned to the rice fields succumbed to the disease within their first few years there. "Where are your parents?"

She shrugged. "My ma died givin' birth to me. I don't know where my pa is."

The phaeton emerged from the wooded trail onto a wide clearing of tall grass and shrubs. In the distance, the massive iron gate marking the entrance to the Rutledge plantation stood like an open prison door, luring unsuspecting victims. Adalia squinted and urged the horse onward, her heart as heavy and dark as the storm clouds rising on the horizon. She clasped Joy's hand again. At first the girl tugged it away, but Adalia tightened her grip. "I'm so sorry, Joy, for all you've suffered. But surely God has taken care of you. He is your Father now."

"My Father?" She huffed. "Naw, miss. He don't care much for me." Though her tone was somber, a smile soon washed away her frown. "But the doc treats me well. I's lucky. Very lucky."

Lucky, hmm. Though Dr. Willaby was nothing like Sir Walter, Adalia had not missed the harsh tone he often used with Joy. A completely different tone than he took with Adalia. Still, Adalia wished the girl gave more credit to God for all her blessings. Giving God thanks and being grateful for what He has done opened more pathways to getting to know Him better, to understanding His love, which, in turn, gave one the strength to endure struggles. Something Adalia knew all too well.

Joy tensed as they passed through the main gate and made their way down the long oak-lined pathway. By the time they stopped before the main house, the poor girl seemed to be having trouble breathing.

A footman scurried out to tend to their horse, but Adalia told him not to bother. They wouldn't be staying long. Tying the horse's reins around a post, she grabbed her satchel and Joy's arm. "We will check on the sick and then leave as soon as we can. There's nothing to fear."

Together they crossed the field to the slave quarters. But upon arriving, they found the shacks empty save for one elderly woman weaving a basket. "No one sick 'round here, far as I knows," she said.

Blowing out a sigh of frustration, Adalia headed back to the carriage, Joy at her side. The wind flapped their skirts. Thunder rumbled in the distance. Yet Joy kept her eyes on the ground as if seeing a plantation slave would doom her to the same fate. Thankfully, aside from a few women hauling baskets atop their heads and a group of men chopping logs by the stables, there weren't too many around.

Halfway across the field, an odd *Meroow* brought Adalia to a halt. She looked down to see a fluffy, beige-colored cat following on their heels.

"Where did you come from, little one?" She knelt, and much to her surprise, the cat brushed against her leg and chinned her hand in a brazen request for pets. Which Adalia happily provided. Joy backed away. "It's only a cat, Joy," Adalia said. "I had one as a pet when I was little." One of her many fond memories of childhood. Adalia swept the feline into her arms, noting her rather large belly. "A rather well-fed cat, I'd say." She chuckled. The cat draped its head and front paws over her shoulder as if it hadn't a care in the world. Several gentle caresses brought the expected response—deep purrs that tumbled into Adalia's ears like a waterfall.

Joy did not seem so convinced.

"You can pet her, Joy. She won't bite."

The young slave inched her hand toward the animal and hesitantly stroked its soft fur. A smile broke through her lips in a row of sparkling ivory.

"You shouldn't be holdin' it, miss. Don't it belong t' the Rutledges?"

"I don't intend to keep it."

"Greetings, Miss Winston." Adalia recognized the voice before she turned—that deep timbre with a hint of pompous playfulness. *Drat.* Why hadn't she heard him approach?

Snatching her hand from the cat, Joy stepped back and lowered her gaze.

"Good day, Mr. Rutledge." Adalia turned to face him and instantly regretted it. Sunlight streaked his hair in gilt and transformed his eyes into flashing jade. A white shirt, tucked within far-too-tight pantaloons, flapped in the breeze. A flush rose up her neck.

Looking away, she started walking. "Come along, Joy."

"I was pleased when I heard you were visiting us." His voice followed her.

"I am not visiting you, sir. I am here attending to your sick slaves." Of which there were none. A thought jarred her. Halting, she swung around. He nearly bumped into her. He smelled of tobacco and spices.

"You." Still holding the cat over her shoulder, she pointed a finger at him.

He gave her a slanted grin. "Me?"

"You called me here. There are no ill slaves."

"Indeed?" He shrugged. "How would I know?" He eyed the cat curiously.

Joy backed away from the altercation.

"Go back to the carriage, and wait for me there, Joy," Adalia said.

"Yes, miss." The words barely escaped her lips before she dashed away.

Mr. Rutledge fingered a blade of tall grass. "Since you won't respond to my invitations, you left me no choice." He crossed his arms over his chest and gave her an imperious look.

Adalia ground her teeth together until her jaw ached. "You have kept me from important work, sir. And all to feed your over-satiated ego."

His brows leveled. "Ego? My ego is quite satiated, thank you, Miss Winston." He reached out for her, but she leapt back. "I must know why you find me so repulsive. It's uncanny. Preposterous, really. I cannot shake you from my thoughts."

Adalia could only stand and stare at the man. Had he not heard a word she'd said? "You overbearing, self-gratifying"—she growled, attempting to control her tongue. Her attempt failed—"presumptuous, vain, pampered milksop."

He jerked his head back as if she'd punched him. Though humor flickered in his eyes, his features tightened like a taut rope. "Do you know who my father is?"

"No. Nor do I care." She swung about and stomped through the grass.

"He is Franklin Octavian Rutledge, one of the most powerful men in Charleston—no, in all of South Carolina. His father, my grandfather, was a senator."

"What difference does that make to me?" She waved a hand over her shoulder.

"Because you just called his son a number of unflattering names." He leapt into her path, halting her. "And you are stealing my cat."

"I am not. . ." Adalia pried the animal from her chest and set it down, regretting that she couldn't take it with her and spare the poor creature such an odious owner. "I was only petting it. You shouldn't feed it so much. It's fat."

The cat rubbed against Mr. Rutledge's leg. *Traitor.* There was no accounting for taste among felines, she supposed.

"It's a she, I believe," Morgan said. "And her name is Snowdust." He leaned and scratched the cat's head, causing a chink to form in Adalia's armor. Anyone who loved children and animals couldn't be all that bad. Unless it was only a ruse.

She growled and continued walking. "I realize you have nothing of import to do with your time, sir, other than flirt, drink, and gamble, but

I am a healer. There are sick people with real problems. I have no time for coddled brats who toy with people only to ease their own boredom."

ༀ

Morgan felt as though he'd been shot with a thousand arrows. The woman never failed to astound him. He thought she'd be flattered, amazed even, that he had gone to such lengths to see her again. Any woman would. Instead, she insulted him more than anyone had ever dared—or daresay, more than he had ever allowed. And now she turned her back to him and marched away. A common servant girl! Yet he could not deny that her words dug deep into his soul. He *was* bored. Terribly bored. And, if he admitted it, perhaps even a bit spoiled. And he had not considered that she had important work to do. In fact, the revelation pricked his jealousy, for he had no real purpose in life other than to be his father's son and make his father proud.

The latter of which he was naught but an abject failure.

He marched after her, grabbing her arm. She stiffened at his touch and sprang away from him, eyes blazing.

Was that repulsion on her face? Impossible. No, it seemed more like fear. But of what? He'd seen the way she looked at him, the way she blushed. He knew when a lady was attracted to him. But how to win this particular lady's heart? *I must do something drastic.* "Please forgive me, Miss Winston. I have behaved the incorrigible cad." He shifted his boots in the dirt and shook his head. "I didn't consider the inconvenience to your time."

Her obsidian eyes softened. She studied him as if deciding whether he told the truth. "Very well. Good day, Mr. Rutledge."

Feeling ever so much like a little boy who'd been scolded by a parent, Morgan watched her leave. Despondency weighed down his heart as he realized the hopelessness of his pursuit. He had found the only woman in the world beyond the reach of his expert seduction. And yet he wanted her more than any woman he'd ever met. His shoulders rose with prideful indignation. How dare she shun him after he had humbled himself by apologizing? Did she realize how difficult that had been for him? Yet as he watched her storm away, her cream-colored skirts swaying with each movement of her curves, all he found within him was admiration. Amazing, honest, wonderful girl. She challenged him. She had life within her. Something vibrant, spirited, dynamic.

And he knew above all else he must have her for himself.

⁊⁌

Adalia pressed a hand on her aching back. Grabbing a cloth, she took the kettle from the fire and poured the chamomile, thyme, and honey tea into several cups. There had been an outbreak of coughing at the orphanage, and with Dr. Patterson. . .well, indisposed. . .it had been left to her to help the five children afflicted by the incessant hacking. Setting the cups on a wooden tray, she glanced out the tiny kitchen window, where a magnificent sunset spread wings of violet and saffron across the sky. Where had the day gone? She'd sent Joy back to Dr. Willaby's to aid Cook with supper hours ago. She knew she should leave as well. Before she had to walk home alone in the dark. But the poor children. . . They suffered so much and were unable to catch a moment's rest without their frail bodies breaking into spasms. Carrying the tray into the hospital, she set it down on a table and lowered herself onto a stool before the first cot.

"Drink this, Charity." She held the cup out to the little girl.

The girl nodded and tried to smile. Her heart aching, Adalia eased a lock of moist hair from her forehead. So much pain in the world. "This will help you sleep too, precious one. Drink up now."

After the little girl drained the cup and sank back onto her pillow, Adalia stopped at the next cot. A young boy no older than three. As she urged him to drink, her thoughts drifted to her encounter with Mr. Rutledge earlier in the day. She'd long since relinquished her anger for his impertinent behavior. But what she could not shake was her astonishment at the measures he took to see her. Surely, if he sought only a frivolous assignation, he would have given up by now. Perhaps her serenade of insults today would force him to do just that. Oddly, a pinch of sorrow tweaked her heart at the thought, making her laugh at her own girlish foolishness. Indeed, any woman would be flattered by the persistent intentions of so handsome and wealthy a catch, but to dwell on it, to enjoy it, would be vanity. Besides, Adalia was grateful for the life God had given her. She had freedom and purpose and all the comforts she needed.

Yet. . .she had to admit it was nice not to be looked upon as a slave, as sub-human, an animal to be used for one's own needs. But instead to be gazed at as a princess, a cherished and valuable prize. As Morgan looked at her.

An hour later, most of the children had drifted into a peaceful sleep.

All save a young girl. Adalia sat with her and sang a song her own mother used to sing at night to comfort her.

"Sleep my child and peace attend thee,
All through the night
Guardian angels God will send thee,
All through the night
Soft the drowsy hours are creeping
Hill and vale in slumber sleeping,
I my loving vigil keeping
All through the night."

By the time she finished, the little girl had ceased her fidgeting and closed her eyes. Adalia took the opportunity to do the same. She leaned her head back on the chair, allowing the tension of the day to slip from her, and before long, exhaustion stole her conscious thoughts and dragged them to a past she'd sooner forget.

"Serve me my tea, Althea," Sir Walter commanded from his seat on the high-backed sofa. Adalia complied, keeping as much distance between them as possible. But it was not enough. When she handed him the steaming cup, he slid a finger over her bare arm. Nausea bubbled in her throat.

Then his face was floating in the air above her bed—hovering like an unholy specter. A ravenous grin breached his bloated cheeks. Darkness swirled about his head. He let out a maniacal, demonic laugh.

She ran down a thorny path. Lightning stabbed the dark sky. Iron shackles tripped her. She toppled to the ground. He reached for her.

Waking with a start, Adalia rubbed her eyes. She gripped her throat to slow her breathing. Her hand trembled. She gazed at the precious orphan now sound asleep. Only a dream. Like all the others.

After ensuring that the caregiver of the orphanage was in the next room, Adalia slipped out onto the street. Darkness had claimed the city, sending its minions about to stir up the elite into a festive frenzy. Music, laughter, and myriad voices tumbled through the roads and avenues, accompanied by distant thunder. A breeze, ripe with the sting of rain, swirled about her. She drew her pelisse tighter as the memory of Sir Walter sprang fresh in her mind, fanning her fear. A carriage filled with loud and obviously besotted men passed by. One of them leaned out the window and gaped at her. "Hello, miss." He lifted his hat.

Did these coddled urchins have nothing better to do? She knew all too well what they wanted. It was what Sir Walter had stolen from her on more than one occasion. She had been his toy, his "pet" as he had called her. He had stripped her of her childhood and her innocence and left nothing but an empty girl who clung to her God and her dreams of someday being a princess. But princesses were not soiled like her. Blinking back tears, she drew her shawl further over her shoulders and ducked into the shadows, where she wouldn't be seen. She wished she could do the same with her memories.

Up ahead, light spilled from a stately house onto the street. Ladies in brilliant gowns with jewels to match stood alongside men in top hats and tailcoats on the long piazza, chattering and sipping drinks. These parties were the sort of thing Mr. Rutledge had invited her to attend. Stopping for a moment, she gazed at them dreamily. Ladies decked in colored velvet spencers, scarves of cashmere, and fur tippets. Reticules of silk dangled from their wrists as they waved painted fans about their faces. The gentlemen sauntered through the garden, ladies on their arms as they bowed and addressed each other with the dignity of their class. High collars guarded lacy cravats that tumbled from their throats like icy waterfalls. Music from a live orchestra swirled about them. So romantic. Like a fairy tale from a storybook, or a dream that drifted through one's mind in the wee night hours. But one that could never be entered. Never be lived. Always out of reach.

Adalia shook off the spell. Silly girl. What was she thinking? Turning, she hurried forward. Just another block and she'd be home safe.

Footfalls pounded behind her. Her heart seized. Just one of the partygoers. Nothing to fear.

She hastened her steps. The thumping increased in tempo and volume.

A glance revealed a dark shadow. Someone followed her. She quickened her pace, saying a silent prayer.

A firm hand grabbed her arm and spun her around. Out of the darkness emerged an unusually large man, wearing a satin waistcoat and breeches. . .and a grin on his face as if he had just won a chest of gold.

CHAPTER SEVEN

Release me at once!" Adalia struggled to free her arm from the hefty man's grasp.

"At once, you say?" His words slurred. He wobbled, yet his grip on her arm remained firm. "Nobody tells Aniston Mulberry the Third what to do, especially not a"—he scanned her with glassy eyes—"common tart like you."

A metallic taste filled her mouth. She peered about wildly. No one was in sight. No one to save her. No one to hear her scream.

Just like at the Miles Plantation.

"Please, sir, I beg you, let me be!" She screeched, then slammed her medical satchel against him. It didn't faze him. He tore the bag from her hand and tossed it to the dirt then grabbed her other arm and forced her against him.

"How about a little kiss?" He leaned toward her, lips puckered. His stench of sandalwood cologne and rum suffocated her.

Cringing, she jerked her face away and fought to free herself. But the man's foppish attire belied his strength. Tears streamed down her cheeks. She gulped for air. She would not be a victim again! His wet lips landed on her neck.

"Off of her, Aniston!" A man's hand reached over her assailant's shoulder and jerked him around. The villain released Adalia. She stumbled backward. Catching her breath, she peered into the darkness. Mr. Rutledge, his body wound tight like a panther's, glared up at Aniston.

"Find your own entertainment, Morgan." The man gave him a look of disgust before he turned back toward Adalia.

Again Morgan pulled him back. "You're besotted, Aniston. Go back to the soiree."

Aniston Mulberry the Third staggered then tugged on his lapels and threw back his wide shoulders. "I will not. I saw her first." He shoved Morgan, sending him sprawling backward, then turned toward Adalia.

Clutching her skirts, she started to run, chastising herself for not leaving while she had the chance. But he caught her arm and yanked her to a stop. Pain spiked into her shoulder. Morgan barreled into him, sending both of them tumbling to the dirt. Grunts, groans, and curses saturated the air. "Run, Adalia! Run!" Morgan shouted.

Hugging herself, Adalia glanced down the street. She could make it home, but how could she leave Morgan in the hands of this massive brute?

That brute now leapt to his feet. With a groan akin to a rabid bear's, he grabbed Morgan's coat and lifted him off the ground. Then swinging an arm back, he slammed his fist across Morgan's jaw. Morgan's face snapped to the side. Blood spurted through the air.

It began to rain.

Adalia gasped and looked around for a rock. Anything to stop this mammoth. Surely by size alone, he would pummel Morgan into the ground. No rocks. No bricks. All she saw was her satchel, its contents spilled onto the sand.

Morgan wiped the blood from his lip, his face thundering in rage. "I warned you, Aniston."

Aniston chuckled and raised his fist to strike again, but this time, Morgan blocked his blow with one arm while slamming his other hand into Aniston's stomach. He bent over with a groan but still managed to swing at Morgan. Dodging the incoming strike, Morgan slugged Aniston's jaw. Still the man came at him. Would he never stop? But Morgan blocked each punch with lightning skill, forcing the man backward. Finally he fisted the villain again in the belly. This time, Aniston crumpled to the ground.

Thunder rumbled.

"Go home, Aniston," Morgan ordered in a tone that begged no defiance.

Struggling to rise, Aniston Mulberry the Third pressed a hand to his stomach and shifted his scowl from Adalia to Morgan before staggering away.

Raindrops tapped a nervous cadence on the cobblestones.

Adalia stood frozen in place, her breath heavy. Her eyes met Morgan's as he moved into the light from a streetlamp. "Are you all right, Miss

Winston?" His tone brimmed with concern. Rain pooled on his lashes.

"Yes," she finally managed to say. But her wobbling legs betrayed her.

Morgan steadied her with a touch. She moved back and glanced at the man staggering away. "Friend of yours?"

"More of an acquaintance."

"You keep rather debauched company." She wiped rain from her face.

"Indeed. I've been trying to rectify that as of late." He raised a brow and grinned.

Rainwater dripped from loose strands of his hair onto his coat. He raked a hand through them, slicking them back. Lightning flashed silver light across the sky, accentuating the yearning in his eyes.

Adalia looked away. "If you refer to me, sir. I'm hardly the sort of company that would foster your reputation." Water soaked through her shawl into her gown. She shivered and hugged herself, trying to control the tempest of emotions spinning within her: the terror of the attack and the horrid memories it resurrected; the appreciation she felt for this wealthy, arrogant slave owner; but worst of all, the look in his eyes that was doing funny things to her insides.

"I beg to differ with you, miss." Shrugging out of his coat, he flung it over her shoulders. She intended to step away from the intimate gesture, but the fine wool blanketed her in warmth, and she found she could not resist it.

Kneeling, he picked up her herbs and ointments, placed them back into the satchel, and handed it to her.

Thunder made her jump and brought the concern back into his eyes. "Did he harm you?"

She shook her head as a tear joined the rain sliding down her cheek. He reached up to wipe it, but she backed away, bumping into a lamp pole.

He approached. Blood spilled from his lip. But the look on his face threatened to crush her resolve to have nothing to do with this conceited knave.

"I won't hurt you, Miss Winston. I would never hurt you." He proffered his elbow. "Allow me to escort you home out of this rain."

෨ඬ

Her gaze flitted between his as if searching for his intent. Rain transformed her hair into waves of dripping ebony. Water beaded on her lashes, framing them in silver. He swallowed, not wanting to move for fear she'd dash away and vanish. She reached for him. Stopped. Hesitated. Bit her lip. But finally she placed her hand on his arm. He hated that she seemed frightened of him. Even now, as they started on their way, he could feel her trembling.

The rain lessened to a sprinkle. A breeze whipped around them, stirring the leaves of trees and loosening the raindrops from their tips. Droplets fell to the ground in a *tap tap* that accompanied the rhythm of their footsteps over the shiny cobblestones.

"I cannot thank you enough, Mr. Rutledge." Her voice was jittery.

"My pleasure, Miss Winston. I'm only sorry you had to endure Aniston's assault. It's not the first time he's forced himself on a lady." The anger that had raged when he'd first seen the man's hands on Miss Winston still simmered in his belly. *The prurient oaf!*

She frowned. "How did you know where I was?"

"I saw you pass the Crenshaw estate."

Her silence and the tension in her hand brooked further explanation. "I should have joined you sooner, would have joined you sooner, but. . .in truth, well, you made it quite plain that you wanted nothing to do with me. And I intended to honor your wishes. That was until I noticed Mr. Mulberry's absence."

"Yes, I suppose I did, didn't I." The spark of playfulness in her tone delighted him—encouraged him to find out more about this captivating woman.

"May I ask how you came to be a healer?"

She was silent for a moment. Almost sad. "My mother taught me. When we lived on Ba—Jamaica. She was quite knowledgeable of healing plants. For instance, did you know that nutmeg can cure a fever? And mango leaves can help you sleep?" Excitement edged her voice. "It is simply miraculous how God provided all we need for our health within the natural world. We just have to know where to look for the cures." She glanced at him. "Oh my. I'm talking too much. Forgive me, Mr. Rutledge."

"On the contrary, Miss Winston. I'm fascinated." And he was. With her intelligence, her enthusiasm, her kindness. "And where is your mother now?"

Wind howled against the brick wall of a building as they turned a corner onto Calhoun Street. "She is with the Lord. A hurricane took her life." Her voice broke slightly. "And my father's."

Morgan scowled, clamping his jaw. Of course. Why else would she have come to Charleston alone? Morgan couldn't imagine being an orphan, much less having to earn a living. What a brave girl. "Now, it is I who must ask your forgiveness, miss. I pry too much. It is a fault of mine."

Moments passed as they walked in silence, save for the clap of their shoes on the cobblestones and the distant rumble of thunder.

"I hear you volunteer at the orphanage at St. Mary's," he asked, hoping to recover her jovial mood.

She smiled. "I do. They are wonderful children. But I am at a disadvantage, sir, for you seem to know much about me while I know nothing of you."

"There is not much to know, Miss Winston. For one thing, I'm not nearly as charitable as you. Your devotion to those in need puts me to shame."

"Charity begins in the heart, Mr. Rutledge. And hearts can change."

He pondered her words as they walked on in silence. Wise as well as gracious.

"Do you enjoy working with Doctor Willaby?" he asked.

"Yes, he's a kind man."

"How wonderful it would be to have such purpose. To use your skills to help others. You are most fortunate, Miss Winston."

"And you, Mr. Rutledge"—she gave him a coy grin—"what do you do besides attend soirees and rescue ladies in distress?"

Morgan frowned, embarrassed that he had no answer. Embarrassed for the first time in his life that he had no answer. "You have found me out, miss. I fear those are my only talents." He forced a chuckle.

But she did not join him. "Surely you assist in running your plantation, managing the slaves?" Her voice turned suddenly spiteful, though he couldn't imagine why.

"My father handles things well enough, and it is my brother who will succeed him. I have naught to do with the slaves. My mother treats them quite well, I understand."

"And your father?" The spite remained.

"He can be a difficult man."

She stared down the dark street as if in deep thought. Streetlamps cast cones of golden light on the slick cobblestones. Her fingers shifted, and Morgan placed his hand on them to keep her from releasing his arm. He was enjoying her touch far too much.

They continued walking.

"If you will not manage the plantation in your father's stead, what will you do? Do you have no ambitions, no dreams?" she asked.

Morgan glanced toward the bay. Though he could not see them, he could hear the crash of waves beckoning him to the sea. To a place where he felt alive and had purpose. But that would never be.

"None that are possible, miss. For now, I will continue to rescue fair maidens." He grinned.

Sorrow passed across her eyes. No, not sorrow, it was something akin to pity. No one had ever looked at him that way before, and he found the feeling it invoked unsettling.

He opened the iron gate to the doctor's home and ushered her up the porch stairs.

Releasing his arm, she faced him.

He stepped closer. If only to get a better look into those tempestuous eyes. She smelled of rosemary and sweet rain. And he longed to take her in his arms and comfort her. Tell her he'd protect her forever.

If she'd only give him the chance.

She sniffed, and her face tightened in a frown. "You've been drinking."

He shifted his stance and looked away. "I had a drink or two."

"Or three?"

He shrugged. "Am I forgiven for earlier today?" One of her dark curls matted against her cheek. It took all his control to not brush it away.

She graced him with a tiny smile, all spite abandoned. And that smile was like sunshine breaking through a storm. "Yes, Mr. Rutledge, I forgive you. If you'll forgive me for all the names I called you."

Morgan chuckled and rubbed the rain from the back of his neck as he recalled the colorful titles. "I would rank your degrading litany among the finest I've heard from Charleston's learned." He grinned and she smiled in return. Certainly his odds with this lady improved by the minute. "But there is one name I'd prefer you call me."

She cocked her pretty head, awaiting his next word.

"Morgan."

Suspicion clouded her eyes. "That would not be proper." Easing the coat off her shoulders, she handed it to him then turned to the door.

Morgan sighed. He had been doing so well. He halted her with a touch. She jolted and faced him. How could he make her understand that he wished her no harm? Quite the opposite, in fact.

"Will you do me the honor of accompanying me to the Ashley

estate for a soiree this Friday?"

Her forehead crumpled. "I've already said no to your invitations, Mr. Rutledge."

Flinging his coat over his arm, he planted a boot on the step above where he stood. "I've proven to you I am no monster, Miss Winston. And I assure you, I can be quite chivalrous."

❧

Quite chivalrous indeed. And handsome and courageous and witty and charming and capable.

And so much more—sensitive, caring, and warm.

Adalia could stand it no more. Risking his touch, she plucked a handkerchief from her sleeve and dabbed the blood spilling from his lip. Blood spilled on her account. Perhaps there was more to this man than she first assumed. He gave her that grin again—that half-devilish, half-charming grin. Placing his hand over hers as she tended to him, he brought her fingers to his lips and placed a kiss upon them. Her bare fingers!

Instead of fear, warmth flooded her belly. She should pull her hand back. She should. . .

"What do you say, Miss Winston?" His green eyes absorbed her.

She retrieved her hand. "You should put some comfrey on your wound."

"I meant about this Friday."

"I say yes, Mr. Rutledge." The words floated in the air between them before she had a chance to check her sanity.

But his resulting smile was so wide and bright, she didn't have the heart to take them back. "Very good. I and my friends shall come for you at eight."

Adalia sighed. What harm could it do to attend one silly party? "Until then, Mr. Rutledge."

He leapt down the stairs, nearly slipping on the wet flagstone. "You have made me a happy man, Miss Winston," he shouted over his shoulder.

She resisted the urge to giggle. "It is only one party, Mr. Rutledge."

He stopped at the gate and bowed. "Ah, but it will be a grand affair with you in attendance."

Shaking her head, she entered the house. The man was a charmer, a Casanova.

Even worse, a slave owner.

What was she thinking?

As quietly as possible, she ascended the stairs, but the aged treads squeaked as loudly as a pack of frightened mice. She barely made it into her chamber when Joy scampered in behind her.

"Are you all right, miss? I was worried 'bout you."

"Yes, I'm well." Though her hand trembled as she lit a candle. Turning, she saw the concern on Joy's sweet face and felt horrible that she had been the cause of it. "I'm sorry you were distraught. I stayed late at the orphanage."

"But you tremble, miss." Joy scanned her. "And you're all wet. Somethin' happened."

Adalia swallowed, unsure how much to disclose. "A man assaulted me."

Joy threw her hands to her mouth, her eyes as wide as full moons.

"But Mr. Rutledge came to my rescue," Adalia blurted out before the girl became overwrought.

"Mr. Rutledge, miss?"

"Surprising, isn't it?"

"No." She shook her head. "I sees the way he looks at you. Oh, you're soaked through. Can I get you some tea, miss?"

Adalia smiled. She imagined her sister, Delphia, would have been much like Joy had she lived. "No. Please go back to bed." Without warning, she drew the girl close and hugged her. Though stiff, Joy gulped with emotion.

"Thank you, Joy." Adalia withdrew and saw Joy brush a tear from her face before she scrambled away.

An hour later, Adalia, dressed in nightdress with sleeves rolled up, stood over a basin, scrubbing her arms where Aniston Mulberry the Third had gripped her. A ritual she had performed every time and on every spot Sir Walter had marked her with his touch. The rough sponge grated over her skin, turning it red and raw, but it couldn't be helped. It was the only way to remove the filthy stain that branded her as debased and ignoble.

The only measure of control she'd ever had.

As she scrubbed, she thought of the ease and skill with which Morgan had dispatched the knave. He might be pampered and rich, but he was certainly no blubbery ninny whose muscles had grown soft from fine food and lazy living. The thought sent a thrill through her, sparking memories of fairy tales where a dashing prince swooped in to rescue the fair maiden. Trouble was, she was not fair. Nor a maiden.

Finally, she tossed the sponge down.

Oddly, the hand that had perched in the crook of Morgan's arm and been kissed by his lips did not bother her at all.

CHAPTER EIGHT

Y ou look beautiful, miss." Joy stepped back to admire the pink sash she'd tied around Adalia's waist.

"Truly? Do you think so?" Adalia laid a hand on her throat. Her pulse beat a nervous cadence against her fingers. "What is wrong with me? I'm acting like a silly schoolgirl."

Joy adjusted the tiny flowers pinned in Adalia's hair. "I would be nervous too, miss. I's never been to such a fancy party."

"Neither have I." Adalia turned to gaze at her own reflection in the dressing mirror. When she'd accepted Morgan's invitation, she had forgotten that she had nothing appropriate to wear. Neither did she have the funds or time to have a proper gown made. The best gown she had—her Sunday best—was nothing but plain, white muslin. But with Joy's help they had added a festoon of paste beads about the hem, a gold pin that belonged to the housekeeper, and a lace ruche around her collar. Adalia had considered wearing her mother's pearls, but she didn't want to draw attention to them. In addition, the housekeeper had aided Joy in pinning up Adalia's hair with sprigs of fresh flowers. A dab of beet juice on her lips and cheeks completed the transformation.

Transformation, indeed. For Adalia nearly gasped at the lady looking back at her from the mirror. In all her life, she had never hoped to look so elegant.

"Now, go and have fun, miss." Joy smiled warmly.

"Thank you, Joy. Pray for me, will you?"

"God don't listen to me, miss." Then at Adalia's look of censure, she added, "But I'll try for you."

Grabbing her gloves and shawl, she kissed Joy on the cheek and

73

headed downstairs. Morgan would be here any moment. She only hoped her heart would settle once she arrived at the party, or she feared she'd faint in the middle of the festivities and embarrass herself to no end. Flickering light poured from the drawing room into the foyer. She halted before it, not wanting to disturb Dr. Willaby. Or see the disapproval in his eyes once again. He'd made his feelings regarding her plans with Morgan quite plain, and his censure now would only add to her unease.

"Is that you, Miss Winston?"

Drat. He'd heard her. Sheepishly, she rounded the corner.

His brows raised at the sight of her then lowered into a glowering line. He tapped the open Bible in his lap. "The good Word says 'Be not deceived: evil communications corrupt good manners.' Do you know what that means, Miss Winston?"

Regardless of whether she did or not, she knew he would soon inform her.

"To associate with those who do evil may very well pull you down with them. I trust you will keep that in mind tonight?" His spectacles slid down his nose.

"You have my word, sir. It is only a party."

"Humph. A party of nincompoops, if you ask me." He released a sigh, but then a smile wiped away his frown. "However, you do look lovely, Miss Winston."

"Kind of you to say, sir." She knew he only meant well. In truth, it felt good to have someone care for her welfare.

A rap on the door jolted her heart. She turned as Mr. Gant opened it and Morgan Rutledge filled the entryway. If Adalia were the swooning type, she surely would have collapsed on the tiled floor, for she'd never seen a more handsome man. His silk-embroidered waistcoat peeked from beneath a long black tailcoat of fine broadcloth. Tight gray pantaloons disappeared within knee-high boots. A white silk stock graced his neck. He removed his cocked hat and smiled, but it was the way he looked at her—as if she were a precious jewel—that set her heart tumbling in her chest.

"Sir." Mr. Gant blocked his way. "Doctor Willaby requests that you enter no farther." The footman gave Adalia an apologetic look.

Morgan's perplexed expression transformed into a chuckle. "Very well." He held out his arm for her.

"I shall pray for your safety," the doctor shouted from the sitting room. Adalia turned to smile at him before she stepped out onto the porch and slipped her arm through Morgan's.

Beyond the gate, a coach pulled by four horses awaited, complete with lanterns perched on either side of the driver's box and serviced by three footmen dressed in fine liveries, one of whom held the door open for them.

Adalia drew in a breath, feeling very much like Cinderella attending the prince's ball.

That breath clogged in her throat when she saw a woman and a man gaping at her from within the coach. Only then did she remember Morgan mentioning friends accompanying them. Her heightened nerves knotted. How could she pull off this charade? She had barely left the doctor's home, and already she felt like a lump of coal among jewels.

Or worse, a slave among masters.

But it was too late to turn back now. Morgan held out a hand for her, and she climbed into the carriage, taking a vacant spot on the right. After he eased beside her, the coach rumbled on its way as all eyes scrutinized her.

"Allow me to introduce my friends, Miss Winston. This is Miss Emerald Middleton." He gestured toward the stunning blond sitting across from her—the one who stared at her as if she were a pesky gnat. And the one she'd seen twice before with Morgan. "A pleasure," the lady said, her tone stiff.

"Beside her, Mr. Joseph Drayton," Morgan continued.

Adalia nodded at the dark-haired man. He smiled her way, but it seemed to strain the permanent anguish that lined his face.

"Miss Caroline Johnson." Morgan waved a hand toward the woman on the end, a regal-looking brunette. "And you've met my brother, Hadley."

Adalia leaned forward to nod at the other Rutledge son, equally as handsome as Morgan, but darker, lankier, and clouded in pomposity. "I am pleased to meet all of you," she said.

"Indeed." Miss Emerald gave a bored huff. "Hadley, you were telling us about your recent winnings at the races," she said, brushing aside Adalia's greeting.

Forcing down the rejection, Adalia glanced out the window, focusing on the passing shops and inns, the Charleston Theater, the library, and the people strolling about. A distant bell tolled, and a hint of sea breeze reached her nose, wiping away the sting of expensive perfume and cologne that filled the coach. With each jostle of the carriage, Morgan's leg brushed against hers. He didn't appear to notice the contact as he continued to talk with his friends, but every touch sent a jolt of heat through her. Not fear, as she expected.

As they rounded a corner and came in view of the Ashley home and Adalia saw the lavishly attired people clustering around the doorway and heard the orchestra playing, she considered bolting from the carriage and running home. What was she doing with these people? Two months ago she had been a slave on a plantation! None of them would have given her even so much as a glance. She nearly laughed. Morgan's friends barely gave her a glance now. Perhaps there was something about her that marked her as unbefitting, beneath them—an inherent quality hidden beneath her skin that would always brand her as a slave, no matter her physical freedom.

The coach rattled to a halt before the large home, and the group disembarked. Morgan's eyes met hers as he assisted her down the step, and she found an odd reassurance within them. Enough to encourage her to continue on with the evening and make the best of it. As he led her to the side of the house, where stairs rose to a long piazza mobbed with people, greetings hailed the young Rutledge heirs from all around.

Miss Emerald and Miss Caroline ascended the steps before them, leaning their heads together.

"Can you believe what she is wearing?" she heard Miss Emerald snicker.

Miss Caroline giggled and glanced at Adalia over her shoulder.

Their belittling quips might as well have been spears for all the pain they caused Adalia's heart. She glanced down at her gown. What had been so beautiful in her dressing mirror now appeared like rags beside the luxurious attire surrounding her. Her eyes burned with tears. She'd been a fool to come.

But it was too late now.

Morgan led her through the crush of men crowding the piazza, drinks and cigars clutched in their fingers. Feeling their gazes assail her as she passed, she held her breath against the sting of tobacco and alcohol, until, finally, they entered the house.

Light from dozens of glittering sconces and chandeliers blinded her. She blinked as they greeted the host and hostess, both of whom barely acknowledged her. A servant announced Mr. Morgan Rutledge and guest. *Guest.* She supposed that was as fitting a name as any, for with each step she took, she felt more and more like a temporary visitor—a peasant passing through a pageantry of opulence that would always be outside her reach. Perhaps announcing her as *stranger* or *foreigner* would have been more apropos.

The foyer was ten times the size of the doctor's and abuzz with chattering people who all glanced her way to see what strange oddity Morgan had brought to the party. From a room to their left, orchestra music drifted atop the beaded and jeweled coiffures. Before she could protest, a butler took her shawl and Morgan's cape and hat. She didn't plan on staying that long.

Morgan patted her hand as he led her into the massive ballroom. No doubt he knew how nervous she was. The first thing Adalia noticed was how large the room was, the second, the intricately carved crown molding lining the ceiling above Dutch floral paintings and crystalline chandeliers—such beauty and lavishness she'd never seen. The third thing she noticed was that once again everyone turned to stare at her. In fact, the chattering faded as ladies leaned together behind fans in clandestine whispers. This time, however, Adalia lifted her chin, took in a deep breath, and met their gazes with equal alacrity. If she was to endure their reproach, she would endure it with courage and pride. What made them think they were any better than her? Yet that was precisely what she saw in their eyes as they tore their gazes away, all save a few of the men who ogled her as if she were one of the sweet treats being passed about on silver trays.

In the center of the oblong room, couples twirled over the floor in some sort of country dance. Adalia gulped. Dancing? She'd been so excited to come, she hadn't realized there would be dancing. But of course there would be. Her blood made a hasty retreat from her head, her heart, to her feet until they began to ache.

Morgan's friends gathered in a group to the left of the doors. She wondered if they were paired together, yet the men seemed more interested in a line of radiant young girls looking their way from across the dance floor than in their guests. Hadley excused himself to cross over to them.

Adalia's eyes were drawn to a man in a dark blue suit of fine-ribbed corduroy. Such a bounty of netted silk bubbled from his sleeves and neck, even the most ostentatious lady at the party would be put to shame. She would hardly have given him a second glance save for the intense glare he'd fixed upon Morgan, a glare that if armed would surely have inflicted a mortal wound.

Before she could inquire about him, Miss Emerald spoke up, "Oh look, Morgan, your nemesis is here to taunt you."

Morgan's eyes shifted to the man. He sighed. "And here I'd hoped to escape him this season."

"Who is he?" Adalia asked, wondering when the man would release his blatant stare.

"Fabian Saville. As you can see, he harbors little affection for me."

"Well, you did cause him undue embarrassment, Morgan," Emerald said. "In front of all of society."

"Five years ago." Morgan sighed. "You'd think the man would let bygones be bygones."

Drayton snickered. "But he hasn't lived it down. Once society dubbed him a limp-wrist, he has carried the stigma ever since."

"I can hardly be blamed for his continued reputation. It would help if he wouldn't dress like a fop."

"And his gestures weren't so…so…dainty," Caroline added.

Morgan stared back at the man. "Still, I do wish he would quit challenging me to duels in order to prove his mettle."

"Why not oblige him?" Drayton said with a yawn.

"I have no quarrel with him. And I certainly do not wish him harm."

Miss Emerald looped her arm through Morgan's. "I so adore your confidence, Morgan."

Mr. Saville finally snapped his gaze away and disappeared into the crowd, leaving Adalia to wonder what prank Morgan had played on the man.

But further thought of the matter seemed to vacate Morgan as soon as Mr. Saville was gone. "Would you care for a drink, ladies?"

"I'd love some punch wine." Miss Emerald smiled, her voice like honey.

"That sounds lovely, thank you, Morgan," Miss Caroline added, glancing over the crowd as if she were looking for someone.

"And what would Miss Winston like?" One brow arched playfully above eyes so forest-green she could get lost in them—wanted to get lost in them at the moment.

She swallowed. She had no idea what sort of refreshment they served, and she most certainly didn't want spirits.

"Lemonade, perhaps?" he saved her, easing a wayward lock of his wheat-colored hair behind his ear.

Why did this man always seem to sense her discomfort? "Yes, thank you."

He released her hand, grabbed Mr. Drayton, and disappeared into the crowd, leaving her with the two women. Two vixens was more like it.

"So, Miss Winston. Word is you are new to our fair city. From whence do you hail?" Emerald fingered the lace bordering her low neckline.

A gentleman passed by, tipping his head at them with an appreciative gaze.

"Jamaica."

Miss Emerald shivered. "I hear it is nothing but a cesspool of disease and squalor."

"Actually it's quite lovely. Beaches with sand as white and fine as powder. And birds and flowers of every imaginable color and shade." Though Adalia had never been to Jamaica, she assumed it was much like Barbados. Besides, the woman's impudent tone annoyed her.

Miss Emerald's eyes turned to ice. "And you came here for what purpose?"

"To make a living."

"A living?" She giggled and leaned toward her friend. "What on earth is that?"

Miss Caroline joined her mirth.

Adalia tried to keep the anger from her tone. "A living is putting one's talents to good use in order to provide for oneself."

"Of all the. . ." Emerald huffed. "I know what a living is."

"Oh, leave her alone, Em." Miss Caroline smiled at Adalia. "I admire any woman who doesn't have to rely on a man to survive, even if she must work at a trade to do so."

Speaking of men, two gentlemen emerged from the crowd, primped in silk, lace, and devouring grins.

The tallest man, who seemed to be the leader, kissed Miss Emerald's hand. "You look stunning as usual, Miss Emerald." The man to his left seemed to have forgotten his manners, for his bold stare perused Adalia, making her uncomfortable. The tall man followed suit.

"And who, pray tell, is your lovely friend?"

"She's not my— This is Miss Adalia Winston." Emerald waved her fan toward Adalia.

"Charmed." The man took Adalia's hand and placed a kiss upon it. "I am Richard Sharpe."

She tugged from his grip.

"And this is Melvin Sharpe, my nephew."

"A pleasure." Adalia smiled, peering behind them for any sign of Morgan.

"Would you care to dance, Miss Winston?" Mr. Sharpe asked. "That is, unless your card is already full."

The hair bristled on Adalia's arms. She glanced at the men, then at Emerald, then over the dance floor. "No, thank you, Mr. Sharpe. Though I am flattered at the invitation."

Mr. Sharpe frowned. Miss Emerald's eyes flashed with understanding. "Miss Winston is not accustomed to dancing. Isn't that so, Miss Winston?" She tapped Adalia's shoulder with her closed fan as if christening her a bumpkin.

Adalia bit her lip and lowered her gaze, suddenly wishing she could melt into the floor.

Mr. Sharpe ran a finger over his mustache and leaned toward her. Too close. The smell of cedar oil made her feel suddenly nauseous. "I'd be happy to instruct you," he said.

"Don't be silly," Miss Emerald chirped. "I doubt Miss Winston wishes to embarrass herself. Isn't that right, Miss Winston?"

Not knowing what to say and too angry to reply, Adalia merely gave her a tight smile.

"Besides." Miss Emerald fanned her face. "Miss Caroline and I are quite available."

"Very well." Richard Sharpe grinned. "Come, Melvin." He held out his hand for Miss Caroline while Emerald slid her arm through Melvin's. Emerald cast a look of victory over her shoulder as the couples swept onto the dance floor, leaving Adalia alone—alone and wounded like a bird that had just been attacked by wolves. No sooner had one pack left but another made their approach in the form of three more gentlemen.

She was about to make her way to the door and leave when Morgan and Mr. Drayton returned, drinks in hand.

"Away, away, gentlemen. The lady is with me." Morgan elbowed away the pesky carnivores and handed her a glass of lemonade.

His words and protective manner surrounded her like a battlement, easing her fears.

"Where on earth did Emerald and Caroline go?" He glanced around, saw them on the dance floor, then shrugged and downed the extra drink in his hand before sipping his own.

Mr. Drayton did the same.

"Would you care to dance, Miss Winston?" Morgan asked.

Adalia nearly choked on her lemonade. She coughed, tightening her lips lest she spray it all over his fine silk waistcoat. That would surely be the perfect ending to the evening's disastrous start.

"Mr. Rutledge," she began, wondering how to tell him of yet one more reason in a long list of reasons she shouldn't have accepted his invitation.

"Call me Morgan. I hate Mr. Rutledge."

"But that is your name. . . . Oh, never mind. Morgan, I must tell you something."

"Ah, a secret." He sipped his drink, his eyes twinkling at her from above the glass. Then leading her aside, he stepped closer. His spicy masculine scent filled the air between them.

Adalia ignored the mischief in his eyes. "I'm serious."

"Why ever for, Miss Winston? You have a lovely smile."

"I cannot dance," she huffed. There, she had said it.

Still he waited as if there were something else she would add. One tawny brow arched.

"Not a single step," Adalia added with emphasis. "Well, I did learn a reel with my father when I was young. Very young."

He laughed and fingered the cultured whiskers on his chin. "You are ever a delight, Miss Winston.

"This is no laughing matter, sir."

He stopped laughing, but his amused smile seemed permanently attached to his lips. "Then we will only dance a simple country set. Besides I didn't bring you here to dance."

"Why *did* you bring me here?"

"Don't you know, miss?" He leaned toward her, his mouth a mere whisper from her ear, his breath sending shivers across her neck. "Just to be near you."

❧

Sensing her tentative mood, her nervous reaction, Morgan watched Adalia as she followed his steps in the country dance. The last thing he wanted was to embarrass her or make her uncomfortable. He did his best to lead her through all the steps, and indeed, she was doing a remarkable job. His admiration for her rose yet another notch among the many that had risen since he'd picked her up at the doctor's home. He'd been concerned at her reaction to his friends' bombastic behavior, but she seemed unaffected by it. He'd heard the ladies belittling her gown, and still Miss Winston had held her head up with more class than either of them possessed. Now, she risked society's scorn by attempting an unfamiliar dance.

She gave him a nervous smile as she placed her gloved hand on his outstretched one and they spun about. He found her simple gown refreshing. Simple and alluring like her. The tiny flowers in her hair only enhanced her ebony curls as they bounced across her neck. She didn't need jewels or pearls or silk to enrich her beauty. Her loveliness shone through her eyes and in her lustrous skin. It exuded from her in an innocent charm he'd felt from no other lady.

As soon as the dance was over, her grip on him relaxed. They made their way to the refreshment hall for cake and libation. Though he tried to encourage his friends to engage her in conversation, they seemed intent on discussing their favorite topic—themselves—while ignoring her altogether. Yet, when he glanced her way, she didn't seem to care. Instead, she moaned with ecstasy over each bite of cake as she gazed across the room with such wonder and delight, he would have thought she was in the midst of St. James's Palace in London she was so enchanted. Her eyes roved over the gold-gilded mirrors hanging on floral wallpaper, the bouquets of roses scattered across the mahogany buffet tables laden with all manner of sweet cakes and puddings, the Turkish carpet set before a massive marble fireplace, the mantle, which held antique china figurines. With wide eyes and open mouth, she was like a child seeing the world for the first time.

Adoring all the opulence that had become so droll to him.

He found it utterly charming.

Emerald tapped him on the shoulder and fluttered her thick lashes his way. "Morgan, you've not danced with me all evening." Her bottom lip protruded in a childlike way. A plethora of ivory curls framed her face. She was indeed a beauty. And one sought out by most every man in the city. Then why did Morgan feel nothing when she cast her attentions his way?

"Surely you can leave little Miss Healer for one dance."

Morgan's jaw tightened. "Her name is Miss Winston."

"Yes, yes." She faced Miss Winston. "Do forgive me. You know I'm teasing you. I truly do admire your skill."

Miss Winston gave her a cursory smile and returned to admiring her surroundings.

Out of the corner of his eye, Morgan winced at the sight of Lord Demming approaching. The beastly man stopped, his body as rigid as a mast, before Morgan and lifted a quizzing glass to examine Miss Winston. "Morgan. I shall be utterly insulted if you do not introduce me to your guest."

Morgan released a sigh. "Lord Demming, may I present Miss Adalia Winston. Miss Winston, Lord Demming. He is the speaker of the General Assembly and a descendant of the Earl of Demming." Though Morgan heard he was the younger son of the late earl and therefore had no right to the title "lord." But such things were tolerated in America.

The man's chest swelled at the introduction. "I have not seen you before, Miss Winston. Newly arrived in town? I dare say, I normally hear word of any gentry settling among us."

To her credit, Miss Winston did not falter beneath the man's inquisition. "Yes, newly arrived, your lordship."

"And where, pray tell, is your father's land?" He studied her once again through his quizzing glass.

Morgan cringed and sipped his drink. He needed to intervene. Distract His Lordship from his line of questioning. Protect Miss Winston. "Lord Demming, I heard an additional ten men were added to the city guard?"

His Lordship shot Morgan an annoyed look.

Miss Winston lifted her chin and swallowed. "I have no father, your Lordship. I am an orphan."

"Indeed?" Lord Demming lowered his glass. "Then an uncle or brother perhaps?"

Morgan must find an excuse to leave before Lord Demming unleashed his pretentious screed upon the unsuspecting Adalia. Yet part of him wished to see how this courageous lady would stand up to the most pompous man in town.

Miss Emerald touched Lord Demming's arm, drawing his gaze. "Perhaps you have not heard, My Lord, but Miss Winston is Doctor Willaby's new assistant." Her tone gloated.

Morgan's anger simmered.

Lord Demming's brows drew together forming one long row of bristling gray hair. "Morgan, may I have a word?" He dragged Morgan aside.

∽

With the cake turning to pebbles in her stomach, Adalia watched the way the elderly man spoke with Morgan like a schoolmaster scolding a child. His livid glances in her direction allowed her no doubt as to the content of his rant. Miss Emerald lifted her nose in the air and excused herself, while a gentleman claimed Miss Caroline for a dance.

Only Mr. Drayton remained. He sipped his drink, swaying slightly on his feet. Adalia resisted the urge to ask why he too was not repulsed by her company.

"You do not seem as joyful as your friends, Mr. Drayton."

"Indeed. I loathe these idiotic affairs." His voice was nearly as dark as his mood.

Adalia studied him. If it weren't for the scowl on his face, he'd have been quite handsome—tall, commanding, with dark, short-cropped hair, cultured sideburns, and gray eyes that swirled like a tempest. "But surely you do not have to attend such events if you do not wish."

He sighed. "As heir to the Drayton fortune and son of Samuel Drayton, my wishes are of little consequence." He sipped his brandy.

"I do not understand."

He looked at her as if she'd told him his hair was on fire.

"Refreshing indeed." He gave her a sideways grin. "We must put on airs, you see, Miss Winston. We must be out and about in society, mingling with those in power. It comes with our status, for not only do we rely on our wealth, but on the good opinion of others to keep our position."

As he spoke, Adalia sensed a hopelessness about the man. As if he were bound by chains heavier than the ones that had shackled her ankles. "It seems a ridiculous requirement to me." She set her empty cake plate on the tray of a passing servant.

"Humph. It does, doesn't it? In truth, I am bored of it all." Mr. Drayton glanced over the sea of bobbing silk, feathers, and jewels. "The parties, horse races, plays. It all seems so trite and useless."

Though these lavish entertainments were indeed trivial in importance, they were also luxuries many people in the world never had a chance to experience. Wasn't it just like the wealthy to not appreciate what they had? "Perhaps you should be grateful for God's blessings." Adalia cringed at her harsh tone.

He laughed. "God?" He waved his drink over the crowd, sloshing brandy over the side. "God has nothing to do with any of this, miss." For a moment she wondered if he was right.

Morgan's brother approached, ending any chance Adalia had at rebuttal.

"Are you enjoying yourself, Miss Winston?" Hadley asked.

Aside from the charming grin he now regaled upon her, Hadley looked nothing like his brother. Where Morgan's hair was light, Hadley's was coal black. Where Morgan was thick muscled, Hadley was thin. Where Morgan's attire was within the boundaries of refinement, Hadley's was a garish display of silk and lace.

She smiled. "Indeed. It is a grand party. And you, Mr. Rutledge, are you enjoying yourself?"

"Hadley lives to see and be seen." Mr. Drayton drained his cup.

"Don't be so droll, Joseph. What is there not to enjoy?" Hadley winked at a passing lady.

Adalia sighed. Well at least one of these pampered fops seemed pleased with his lot in life. Though perhaps a bit too pleased.

Morgan excused himself from Lord Demming and finally approached. The anger lining his face softened when his eyes met Adalia's. He proffered his arm. "I believe this is our dance."

A Scottish reel drifted in from the ballroom. Adalia shook her head. "No, I cannot."

"Nonsense. Just follow me. It is quite easy." He led her onto the floor, and they lined up within a circle of other dancers. Adalia's chest heaved. She glanced behind her, seeking an escape, but instead saw Miss Emerald, Miss Caroline, and a few other ladies hunched together, claws drawn, and catlike grins on their faces as if waiting to pounce on her first mistake.

The partners bowed, took hands, and spun in a circle. They stopped, and a lady and gentleman to Adalia's right performed a set of fancy steps then twirled around each other. Adalia's mind grew numb. A third person joined their jig. Across the way, Morgan winked at her. A man stepped into the center, and the group held hands again and spun in a circle. The cake in Adalia's stomach rose into her throat.

The group halted, and a man faced her, shifting his feet on the floor. She froze, her eyes seeking out Morgan, who gave her an encouraging nod. She copied his steps, clapped, and then took his hands as he twirled her around. Laughter burst from the pack of felines on the edge of the floor.

Mortified, Adalia felt a flood of heat redden her face. More laughter pricked her from behind. Morgan was before her then and whirled her around. "Ignore them," he said as he passed, so graceful, so cultured in his steps, he put her to shame.

She tripped over someone's shoe, stumbled, and nearly fell. If not for Morgan's arm around her waist, she would have fallen—would have plopped to the floor, skirts sprawled about her, or worse, hiked immodestly above her ankles, looking much like the boorish bungler she was. Without hesitation, Morgan led her from the floor. Laughter followed them all the way to the foyer, where she tore from Morgan's grip.

"I wish to leave."

He drew her to the side and lifted her chin with his finger. "Why? Because you misstepped on the dance floor?" Admiration poured from his eyes.

"No, because I don't belong here. Please, Morgan, Take me home."

❦

Emerald stood beside Hadley, watching as Morgan escorted Miss Winston away. Inside, her stomach felt as though it had been twisted and wrung like a washed garment. Outside, she pasted on a smile. "What on earth does Morgan see in that common tart?"

Hadley clicked his tongue. "Jealousy does not become you, my dear."

"I'm hardly jealous," she spat. "I'm ten times the lady she'll ever be. More beautiful, educated, refined. . .wealthy."

"And don't forget simply delectable." He gave her a steamy look.

She slapped him with her fan and smiled. "You are incorrigible."

The dolt must have taken her playfulness as encouragement, for he leaned in closer. "If Morgan's infatuation with the girl doesn't fade soon, you could always take me up on my offer."

Emerald pushed him away. "Hadley, you are as handsome and charming as ever, but you know I've set my cap for Morgan, and I intend to have him."

He sighed and tugged on his cravat. "You wound me, dear lady. Am I never to have a chance? Am I always to be alone, brokenhearted?"

"You hardly pine away from lack of affection." She nodded toward Miss Sordenson, who was eyeing Hadley from across the room.

Hadley shrugged. "Either way, this Miss Winston will simply not do for a brother of mine. He's an absolute fool. Bed her if he must, but bring her into society? Egad, she behaved like a barbarian at court. A sheer embarrassment."

Pain spiked through Emerald at Hadley's comment. She turned it into anger. "My word. She couldn't even dance a simple reel. Clumsy, ill-bred chit. She's no doubt after your family's fortune."

"My thoughts exactly. If Morgan continues this behavior, he will besmirch the Rutledge name."

"Then, we will have to put a stop to it."

"How, my dear?"

"Easy. We will ruin her, of course. We will make Morgan see her for who she really is—a shameless, wearisome hussy."

Hadley grinned. "That's what I love about you, Emerald. Your devilish heart."

Chapter Nine

Adalia clung to Morgan as he shoved his way through the horde crowding the porch. If not for the strength and warmth of his arm beneath her fingers, she feared she would not be able to restrain her tears. A noxious cloud of cigar smoke joined fumes of alcohol in an assault on her nose. Coughing, she clutched her skirts and allowed Morgan to lead her down the stairs, battling his way through besotted partygoers until finally they exited the front gate. A fresh breeze from the bay swept away the stink of fustian excess. She wished it would sweep away her humiliation as easily. She wanted to disappear into the darkness. To sink into the mud beneath her feet. Anything to drown out the laughter trickling from the stately house as if everyone within was sharing a joke at her expense. Drawing in a deep breath, she batted a runaway tear from her cheek.

Morgan placed his hand on hers in a gesture so tender, it threatened to unleash more tears. "I'll call for the carriage."

She looked down, not wanting him to see her shame. "I'd rather walk, thank you."

"Very well." He led her down the street.

But she wanted to be free of him. She didn't want his pity. Never wanted pity from his kind. Adalia tore her hand from his arm and faced him. "Go back to your party, Mr. Rutledge. I'll be quite all right."

He leaned toward her and raised his brows. "That worked out so well for you last time."

She tightened her lips as a shiver followed the memory of Aniston Mulberry's assault on her nearly a week ago. With a huff, she slipped her gloved hand into the crook of Morgan's elbow once again.

He'd left his hat, and the evening breeze spread fingers through his hair even as moonlight stroked selected strands in gold. He smelled of brandy and spices.

Gravel crunched beneath their shoes as the sounds of revelry faded behind them. "I'm sorry they laughed at you," he said.

She tried to respond—to tell him it didn't matter, but her throat tightened.

"I shouldn't have forced you to dance."

She swallowed. Despite the behavior of his friends and associates, Morgan had been kind to her all night. A perfect gentleman, in fact. "I can hardly blame you, Mr. Rutledge." A landau passed; the rattle of wheels, the *clip-clop* of horses' hooves, and laughter spilling from within rose in a melodious tune.

They turned down Church Street. The scent of Mrs. Dither's famous rose garden swirled around Adalia, helping to ease her nerves. Nerves that shouted to her that she'd had no business attending the soiree tonight. What had she expected? That Charleston society— families who owned every plantation beyond the city, whose members sat on the City Council, whose grandfathers and great-grandfathers had been the Lord Proprietors of the realm—would welcome a simple woman like her with open arms?

Morgan drew a deep breath and glanced down the row of houses. "My friends behaved like stuffed prigs. I am ashamed of them."

"They behaved as they were trained to behave." Adalia felt the muscles in his arm tighten.

He gazed at her. "How so?"

"I know my station, Mr. Rutledge." Adalia stepped over a loose brick that had fallen from a garden wall. "I have no esteemed pedigree, no education, no fortune. I am but a common worker—a tradeswoman. I'm sure Lord Demming informed you as much."

Halting, Morgan faced her. "I care not what that bloated buffoon says."

"Well, you should. If you wish to stay in the graces of society. . ." She blinked at the intensity firing from his eyes. "At least that is what Mr. Drayton informed me."

Morgan snorted and gazed into the darkness. "Drayton knows nothing but how to dampen everyone's mood."

Without thinking, Adalia reached up to straighten his troubled cravat but quickly withdrew her hand. "Surely you can see the damage any courtship between us would bring to your standing." *Drat*. Had she actually said the word *courtship*?

She must have, for Morgan smiled and lifted her hand to his lips. "If you'd wish to discuss a courtship, you have my attention, milady."

"Do not call me that." She tugged from him. "I am anything but." If he only knew who she truly was, he wouldn't be speaking to her. Touching her. Making her entire body quiver. Another reason to end their association. That and the fact that he was a slave owner. Or at least the son of one. "I assure you, your standing would become vastly important to you should it be in jeopardy."

He shook his head, his lips slanting in that alluring way of his. Yet he did not deny her statement. Adalia tore her gaze from the adoration in his eyes—adoration that would be her undoing if she gave it any encouragement. Adoration she didn't understand. She started walking. He joined her, head bowed and hands clasped behind his back as if deep in thought. They walked in silence. A comfortable silence—odd for two people who were but strangers. Music from a nearby theater floated on a chilled breeze. Yet she was anything but cold walking beside this man.

They turned the corner. He touched her elbow to help her cross the street. Their eyes met in the light of a lantern, and she thought she saw a hint of sorrow in them. He smiled and she took his arm again and proceeded, implanting each precious second within her memory—the final seconds of her fairy-tale evening. For all except the final dance, it *had* been a fairy tale. But soon the clock would strike midnight, and she'd wake up a mere servant girl, an ex-slave, not the princess she saw reflected in Morgan's eyes.

Up ahead, Dr. Willaby's house came into view. The charade was at an end. Now, all Adalia wanted was to crawl into bed and hide beneath her coverlet—forget what a fool she'd made of herself tonight. Forget this charming man beside her, who made her insides melt and who treated her as though she were precious. At the gate, she stopped and faced him. Better he did not escort her to the porch. Better to end things here.

He rubbed the dark whiskers on his chin, so at odds with his light hair. "I hope you do not let tonight's events trouble you any further, Miss Winston. I shall never allow anyone to treat you with such dishonor again. You have my word."

"You cannot promise that, Mr. Rutledge." For some reason, she longed to reach up and caress his cheek, to see if his jaw felt as firm as it looked, to feel the bristle of his whiskers on her glove, to brush that rebellious strand of hair from his face. Instead she lowered her gaze.

"We don't have to attend any more silly parties," he said. "I tire of them anyway."

"Those parties are your world, Mr. Rutledge. They will never be mine."

"They are not my world. They are an obligation I grow weary of. Besides, they don't have to—"

She placed a finger on his lips. His breath warmed her skin through her glove, sending a thrill swirling in her belly. She withdrew her finger before the feeling inflamed her hand, her resolve, and caused her to touch his cheek, as she so desperately longed to do. "Thank you for your kind invitation. I truly did enjoy the soiree. Well, the décor and the food at least." She tried to smile, but in light of what she knew she must do, it faltered on her lips.

Morgan's grin slipped from his face as well, as if he could sense her next words.

Adalia swallowed and gripped the iron gate for support. "Mr. Rutledge, I must insist that you never call on me again."

❧

A mortal blow struck Morgan. He lowered his eyes, not wanting her to witness the pain—the weakness—on his face. He ran a hand through his hair and stomped his boot on the dirt, trying to shake it off. Two night guards marched by, tipping their hats at Miss Winston.

During their walk home, Morgan had tried to curb his anger toward his friends and Lord Demming, but at her dismissal it rose with renewed fervor. How could they have been so cruel to this precious creature? If they hadn't spurned her, if they'd accepted her, she wouldn't be tossing his affections aside.

He gazed into her eyes—dark and luminous like the sea at night. "My friends' opinions are of no consequence to me."

"It's useless, Mr. Rutledge."

His heart shriveled at her determined tone. "Please call me Morgan."

Releasing a sigh, she lowered her lashes. They fluttered like black silk over cream. Then squaring her shoulders, she gripped her skirts, spread them out, and released them. "I have no proper gowns. I cannot dance, and I am not skilled in the art and nuances of society's repartee."

Morgan wanted to grip her arms, shake some sense into her. But he

91

dared not lest this beautiful bird take flight. Desperation set in. He felt it clench his stomach, squeeze the life blood from his heart. Adalia was the only bright spot in his otherwise dismal existence. He could not let her go. He took her delicate hand and rubbed her fingers through the cotton. "That is what I admire so much about you, Miss Winston. You are nothing like them." He reached to touch her cheek. She flinched, her eyes shifting between his. He eased his fingers over her skin. Soft. So soft.

She jerked back as if he'd branded her. Why did she fear him? "You find me fascinating because I am different." Agony tainted her voice. "But you will tire of me soon enough."

"Never." How could he make her understand? He stepped closer, gazing at her lips, longing to know if they were as delicious as they looked. Moonlight turned her skin to glistening honey, her hair into trickles of obsidian. Everything within him longed to take her in his arms, love and protect her forever.

"I am but a momentary distraction to you." She met his gaze.

He leaned toward her ear and whispered, "If so, then let me be distracted forever."

She closed her eyes. And he could stand it no longer. He pressed his lips close to hers. But instead of the expected slap and retreat, she let out a soft gasp and received him, tentative at first, hovering, brushing against his lips, landing and then retreating as if a mere testing was enough. Her sweet breath puffed over his chin.

Morgan's body responded, and he drew her close, trying to deepen the kiss. She trembled and let out a tiny shriek. He released her.

Struggling from his embrace, she backed away, eyes wide and chest heaving. "Stay away from me, Mr. Rutledge." Then turning, she dashed down the pathway and up the stairs to the side of the house.

The sound of the door slamming drove the last nail in the coffin around his heart.

❧

Adalia dropped onto her bed and stuffed her head beneath her pillow to muffle her sobs. Why, oh why, had she allowed him to kiss her? Well, it wasn't really a kiss, was it? More like just a press of their lips. Still, why had she not been stronger? Run from him when she had a chance? She pounded her fists on the mattress, angry at herself, angry at the unfairness of life. After a few minutes, her tears spent, she sat and ran the back of her hand over her moist cheeks, plucking the wilted flowers from her hair. Moonlight angled over them as they lay in her palm. Several buds were missing. The rest were shriveled, their beauty but a memory. Like Adalia. Like her dreams.

Like Morgan's kiss.

No, more than a memory. Its effect still lingered on her lips, stirred a pleasurable warmth within her. She'd never kissed a man before. Willingly at least. Never wanted to kiss a man. After Sir Walter, courtship, marriage, and children seemed out of her reach—reserved for someone worthy of love, someone pure. Besides, the thought of any man touching her caused every muscle to clamp in revulsion.

Yet she'd enjoyed Morgan's touch, hadn't she? Just thinking of it sent delicious waves through her. Was that how love was supposed to feel? "Oh Lord." She grabbed her Bible, slid the wilted flowers inside, and closed it against her chest. "You have blessed me so much. Please help me to accept the path You have placed me on." She gazed out the window, where moonlight coated leaves in liquid silver. "And please help me forget Morgan Rutledge."

༖

Adalia took her seat beside the doctor at the dining table. Her stomach grumbled as Joy brought in platters of fried fish, garlic grits, and greens. The young slave stumbled, and a portion of fish slid onto the tablecloth, eliciting a frown and a "clumsy girl" from Doc Willaby.

No doubt used to the insults, Joy's expression reflected no offense. Adalia winked at her as she exited, wishing the doctor would allow her to join them. But dining with a Negro was akin to gnawing on a bone with a pack of dogs.

Or so she'd inferred from the doctor's attitude.

If he only knew the truth about Adalia. Part of her relished in the deception, in the sweet revenge it offered her people against all men who believed Negroes were ignorant beasts fit only to serve.

Part of her regretted the lie.

Regardless, she'd been pleased to accept the doctor's frequent invitations to dinner. And though conversation flowed awkwardly at first, she soon grew accustomed to his mannerisms and rather enjoyed their meals together. For the first time in years, she felt as though she were part of a family. Well, almost. Aside from his prejudice, the doctor was a good man. His gracious behavior toward her helped dull the pain of her own father's absence.

Dr. Willaby bowed his head, and Adalia followed suit as he blessed the food, never failing to do so at every meal. So unlike Sir Walter, who would wave away the servants and dive into his repast without a moment's hesitation. Occasionally, when he found himself in a particularly jovial mood, he would insist Adalia don her finest gown and join him—evenings that bore the fruit of her nausea well into the night. But most of the time she stood against the wall, awaiting his next command and watching him devour his food like an uncouth vulture.

"Amen," she parroted Dr. Willaby and passed him the platter of fish. The doctor began discussing his recent medical cases, delighting Adalia with his interest in her opinion. She had accompanied him on several calls recently and had been more than pleased when he asked her advice on treatment using her herbs.

"You have no doubt heard the Rutledge girl is ill." He dabbed his napkin over his mouth.

"The Rutledge girl?" The name she'd tried to keep from her mind these past two weeks came charging back, leading a band of shameful memories and a tingling she could still feel on her lips.

"Yes. Elizabeth, the youngest." The doctor bit into a biscuit, washing it down with a gulp of barley water. "I believe she's not yet seven years old."

Memories of Morgan's affection for the young girl filled Adalia's thoughts. "I had not heard. Have you been called to tend to her?"

"Oh, goodness, no. They called for Doctor Richardson. But the man declares he has no idea what is wrong with her. Some strange tropical fever and an odd rash on her arms and legs."

Adalia laid down her fork. "How horrible. Perhaps you should see her?"

He shook his head and shoved a spoonful of greens into his mouth as if completely unconcerned about the little girl's welfare. "What can I do that Doctor Richardson could not?"

"You are a brilliant physician. Perhaps there is something Doctor Richardson has overlooked."

He flashed her an impatient frown. "I only informed you because of your association with that family. Though"—placing an elbow on the table, he leaned toward her—"I am very pleased you have seen the light in regard to Morgan Rutledge."

She longed to ask him why he loathed the Rutledges, but she didn't want to pry. "I told you it was just a silly party. Nothing more."

"Indeed, you did." Reaching across the table, he patted her hand. "Never fear, I'm sure the young girl will be fine. No doubt one of these winter chills."

Adalia hoped so. Elizabeth had seemed like such a sweet, innocent child. Clearly she had captured her brother's heart. Why, oh why, couldn't Adalia get the man out of her mind? As well as the humiliation she'd suffered at the party. And worse, their kiss. She'd come to hate herself for enjoying it so much. And for wondering why he'd not made any attempts to see her since. Though she'd told him not to, of course. It was all too confusing. She pined for him one minute and was angry at him the next. Finally, she grew furious at herself for having ever entertained his affections. He was a man outside her class. And a slave owner! The latter should be enough to wipe away any happy memories of their time together.

Hours after dinner, Adalia stood at the window of her chamber, brushing her hair, when a rap on the front door echoed through the house. Moments later, Joy knocked and entered carrying a box.

A box that moved. Jerked and jiggled, in fact. And purred.

"A man dressed in a footman's livery dropped this off for you, miss."

Setting it on her bed, Adalia untied the strings, and before she could open the box, a kitten leapt from the folds in a tumble of wheat-colored fur.

Both Adalia and Joy said "aw" at the same time. Gathering the bundle into her arms, Adalia cradled the purring kitten, who promptly scrambled up her arm and settled on her shoulder, batting and nuzzling the strands of her loose hair.

Only then did Adalia notice the folded piece of paper attached to the side of the box. She pulled it free.

Dear Miss Winston,

It would seem when you met Snowdust, she had recently birthed several kittens. I hope you'll accept this gift with my apologies for your unpleasant evening the other night. I've named him Morgan. Hadley says he resembles me. I hope he'll bring you joy and comfort.

Yours,
Morgan Rutledge

Adalia drew in a deep breath. What a thoughtful gift. The man certainly knew how to soften her heart.

"From Mr. Rutledge?" Surprise lifted Joy's voice. "He sent you a kitten?" She giggled, and Adalia joined her.

"Silly man. What am I to do with it?" Yet even as she said the words, the precious creature purred in her ear and began nibbling on the lace of her nightdress.

"He is so cute, miss." Joy ran her fingers down the kitten's fur.

"Joy, where is my tea?" the doctor's voice bellowed from downstairs, startling Joy and sending her scrambling out the door, flinging a quick, "Excuse me, miss" over her shoulder.

Adalia released a heavy sigh at Doc Willaby's harsh ways with the girl.

The kitten leapt onto her lap and starting batting one of the buttons on the front of her nightgown. Holding the purring fur ball up to her face, she examined it. Two green eyes peered at her from within a fluff of tawny fur. "Morgan indeed. Now, how am I ever going to forget him?"

CHAPTER TEN

Morgan wrapped a line around the belaying pin then stood and stretched an ache from his shoulders. A stiff ocean breeze slammed into him, loosening his hat. He tugged it farther down on his head, wishing the wind would sweep away the foul mood that had clung to him ever since Miss Winston's rejection. The brig climbed a rising swell. Morgan balanced over the heaving deck. Salty spray showered him, and he took a deep breath. Yet even the scent of the sea could not shake the gloom from his heart. Nor did this trip to deliver a hold full of rice to Boston. The sea had always been his refuge, his escape from a life he abhorred. But thanks to Miss Winston, even that respite had been taken from him.

He leapt onto the quarterdeck and made his way to the stern, where the wake spread out like a lacy fan over azure waters. Yet, even that sight reminded him of the ruche decorating Miss Winston's collar.

Captain Bristo appeared beside him. "You haven't been yourself this past week. Something troubling you?" The captain clasped his hands behind his back and scanned the horizon.

"You know me too well." Morgan huffed.

"If I had to guess, I'd say a woman."

"Not just any woman."

"No, I wouldn't expect so." The captain gazed at the muted line betwixt sea and sky as the setting sun stroked the waves in crimson and gold. "This woman, she turned you down?"

"Asked me never to call on her again." Saying it out loud did nothing to ease Morgan's pain.

"Hmm. Troubling indeed." Captain Bristo quirked a brow. "Yet, surely there are a dozen ladies behind her waiting for one glance from you."

Morgan snapped the hair from his face and gripped the railing. "None like her. She's different. A healer. Kind, humble, honest."

"Good heavens! A commoner?" Bristo's sarcastic tone grated over Morgan.

"Yes."

The captain chuckled. "Morgan Rutledge taken with a commoner? I never thought I'd see the day. Are you sure you're not pursuing this lady simply to anger your father?"

Morgan blinked. He'd never considered the extra benefit. "I could care less what that man thinks."

"Indeed. Which is why you sneak away to sail with me." The ship creaked and groaned over a wave, adding a bite to the captain's taunting remark.

Morgan tightened his grip then shoved off the railing, crossing his arms over his chest. "Were I to take up a trade, I would be ostracized by society, by my family. I'd lose everything."

"And yet what would you gain?" Wisdom lurked behind the spark of playfulness in Captain Bristo's eyes.

Morgan ignored it. "Right now, I'd settle for the company of a certain lady."

"Perhaps it is just your pride that has been pricked. I sense you are not accustomed to rejection by the fairer sex."

Of course he wasn't. Morgan rubbed his eyes. This wasn't about his pride. Was it? A parade of comely ladies marched through his thoughts. Some he cared for but had grown bored with, most he had no feelings for at all, some he used, and some he hurt. "She haunts me."

"That's how I felt about my Lucia."

Lucia, the captain's wife. The one who, along with their child, had died in the hurricane of '04. "Do you regret marrying? After you endured the agony of losing her?"

"Not one minute," Captain Bristo did not hesitate to answer. Though he hesitated now. Clearing his throat, he looked away. "She was God's gift to me. An angel not fit for this world."

The sails thundered above them. Captain Bristo turned his back to the sea and surveyed the brig. "Perhaps this woman is God's gift to you."

"God has never given me a gift."

"Life itself is a gift, my young friend." He slapped Morgan on the back. "You have been born to privilege and wealth. What do you intend to do with them?"

Morgan shrugged, bracing his feet on the staggering deck. "What is there to do with them? They simply exist."

The captain's gaze drifted upward. "Furl topsails, Mr. Granger!" he bellowed across the deck. The boson repeated the order, ending it with an, "Aye, aye, Captain" as sailors leapt into the ratlines and clambered aloft.

Captain Bristo faced Morgan. Only brushstrokes of gray at his temples gave away his age of three and forty. Years of sun had left his face tanned and healthy, not cracked and lined like most seamen's. And though of common birth, he held himself with a dignity and honor lacking among many of Morgan's friends.

"I believe God has a purpose for each of us," he said. "He puts us in certain homes, certain circumstances, good or bad, that lead best to that purpose."

Morgan clenched his jaw. If God had given him a father like Franklin and a life of such emptiness, then He certainly wasn't anything like the kind, loving God Captain Bristo often spoke of. "And what is *your* purpose, Captain?"

"Sailing my ships. Privateering if war breaks out with Britain, as it appears it might." Excitement lit his eyes. An excitement that made Morgan jealous. "Search your heart." He poked Morgan's chest. "God places His desires, His plans for you, deep within us."

Morgan squinted against the setting sun. "And what of this lady? Is she my purpose?"

"Only one way to find out."

Sea spray showered over Morgan. He shook it off and gave Bristo an inquisitive look.

"Pray for God's will. Then pursue her. Don't give up. Continue to woo her until you are sure there is no chance." Shielding his eyes, he glanced toward the growing shoreline. "Mr. Hanson," he addressed the quartermaster at the wheel. "Two points to starboard, if you please."

"Two points to starboard, Cap'n," the man parroted, turning the wheel.

Morgan clung to the railing as the ship canted.

"Some things are worth fighting for, Morgan," the captain said. "Some things are worth working hard for. As you have done with your sailing."

A spark of hope ignited within Morgan for the first time in weeks.

"Now, let's go home, shall we?" He gripped Morgan's shoulder and shook him.

Morgan nodded his thanks as they took their positions to ready the ship to enter the harbor. Soon the brig slipped between Sullivans and Morris Islands, and with all sails furled and anchor dropped, she slowed to a halt in Charleston Bay. After bidding Captain Bristo adieu, Morgan headed for the Rutledge townhome, where he and Hadley stayed during the season. No sooner had he entered the door when his steward rushed up to him, his face a mottled twist of anxiety.

"What is it, Mr. Mobley?"

"It's your sister, sir. She is deathly ill."

❧

Adalia paced across her chamber, piece of vellum clutched in her hand. She reached her dressing bureau and spun around. The wooden floor creaked. Her nightgown tickled her ankles. A crisp breeze stirred the curtains at her window and showered goose bumps over her arms. The scent of brine and honeysuckle tickled her nose. She halted at the window and glanced into the darkness. Moonlight coated the plants and trees in a soothing milky white that defied the torment she felt inside. Opening the note, she spread it out next to the candle on her desk and read it once again.

Miss Winston,

My sister is gravely ill. None of the doctors can help her. You are our last hope. Please come quickly.

Morgan Rutledge

Folding the paper, she hugged herself. She'd received the note early that morning. Her first thought was to rush to the plantation as quickly as possible, but Doc Willaby insisted there was nothing to be done—that he'd heard from several of his colleagues and the illness was apparently some strange tropical fever beyond the help of modern medicine.

So, tucking the note away, she'd gone about her duties. Yet the desperate words called to her all day long from the pocket of her apron—the pleading, the wailing of a sick, desperate child. What if there was something she could do to help this poor girl? Having been raised in the tropics, Adalia had often come in contact with unusual fevers.

She plopped onto her bed, where M lay coiled in a ball, sleeping. She could not force herself to call him Morgan for the memories the name evoked, so M would have to suffice. Yet what did it matter? Either way, the Rutledge son was forever planted in her thoughts. The kitten opened his eyes, stretched out his front legs, and yawned. He rose, crawled into her lap, and curled into a ball again. Adalia stroked his fur. "Lord, tell me what to do." She spoke the same prayer she'd uttered all day. And the answer she kept hearing was still the same. *Go.*

༄

Pulling a chair to his sister's bed, Morgan sat down and dropped his head into his hands. He felt like crying, but he didn't dare. Rutledge men didn't cry. Didn't show emotion. Unless it was anger or pride.

Lizzie had been ill for nearly a month. The ravages of disease were evident on her frail body: sunken, hollow cheeks; purple shadows beneath dull eyes; and breathing that rattled as though the air passed through a sieve. He took her hand and caressed her tender skin, so hot to the touch. Too hot for a body to be for so long. Three doctors had attended to her. They'd bled her twice and placed leeches on her belly—Morgan shivered at the memory. One doctor had insisted she keep her bare feet in a tub of fresh milk for a day. Another rubbed lard over her legs and arms. But she kept getting worse. In truth, none of them knew what was wrong with her.

Lizzie was the only good thing that had come from his parents' union. Her sweet, kind spirit filled the house like the fresh scent of the sea. Just the sound of her laughter bubbling from room to room gave Morgan hope to go on each day. A reason to return to the plantation from town. And, oh, how she loved to sing. Already at age six, she had the voice of an angel. He eased his fingers over the bumps on her arm, red, swollen sores that gnawed away at her flesh like the leeches that had sucked her blood. If God took her home—if God stole her from Morgan—the final brick would be laid on Morgan's wall of belief that the Almighty had no good plans in mind for him at all.

A sliver of gray squeezed through the closed curtains as dawn broke. Morgan could still see his mother's anguished face as she'd paced before Lizzie's bed all through the night. She would still be here if not for Franklin, who'd stolen her away, insisting she partake of breakfast with him. Yet, if her stomach was as curdled as Morgan's, she wouldn't be able to consume any food. In the corner of the chamber, Hadley slumped into a velvet chair, his chin on his chest. His snores melding with the muted trill of birds outside.

Morgan dropped his forehead onto Lizzie's arm. "Dear God. Please don't take her away from me," he whispered his first prayer in years.

Lizzie's raspy breathing was his only reply. Each pant of her chest, each puff of breath escaping her lips, tightened a cinch around his heart in fear it would be her last.

༄

Upon rising early, Adalia dressed, grabbed her medical bag, and took the doctor's horse out to the Rutledge plantation. Regardless of her desire to stay away from Morgan, as well as Doc Willaby's incessant warnings, she couldn't ignore a plea to help a sick child. Even if there was nothing she could do, she could offer comfort to the family. She left Joy at home, not wanting the poor girl to suffer as she had the last time they visited the plantation. Yet, now as Adalia stood at the massive oak door, with its beveled glass windows, her knees began to quake.

The same black woman answered the door.

"I'm here to see Miss Elizabeth Rutledge. Mr. Morgan Rutledge called for me." Adalia lifted her satchel, hoping to dispel the confused look on the woman's face.

"Who is it, Mavis?" A male voice, as deep as Morgan's yet much harsher, preceded an elegantly rugged man with thick dark eyebrows and long gray hair tied behind him. With every clip of his boots over the ceramic tile floor, Adalia's nerves strung tighter. *This must be the infamous Franklin Octavian Rutledge, Morgan's father.* Behind him, a slender woman in her forties slid into the room as if she skated on ice. Though a bit disheveled, her golden curls and crisp blue eyes belied her age—deep, turbulent eyes that reminded Adalia of Morgan. Her gentle smile did much to loosen Adalia's nerves.

"A woman to see Elizabeth." The maid lowered her gaze and backed from the room.

"Humph." Mr. Rutledge eyed Adalia from head to toe. "I sent for no servant girls. Who are you?"

Adalia swallowed and opened her mouth to answer him when Morgan's voice shot down the stairs. "She is Miss Adalia Winston, Father. Aide to Doctor Willaby."

Mrs. Rutledge's face brightened. "Oh, my dear." Approaching Adalia, she gathered Adalia's hands in hers. "I have so desired to make your acquaintance. I've heard much of your herbal healing."

Stunned, Adalia took a step back beneath the woman's exuberance. But it was Morgan who drew her gaze. A wrinkled, stained shirt hung loose around his brown trousers. Strands of light hair escaped his queue and swayed over his stubbled jaw with each tread he descended. But it was the dark blotches shadowing his red-rimmed eyes that nearly broke her heart.

"Mumbo jumbo, if you ask me," Mr. Rutledge barked. A familiar shiver etched through Adalia at his degrading tone—the tone of a man who had the power of life and death over others. "You may leave, Miss Winstone." He dismissed her with a wave.

Mrs. Rutledge's joy of only a moment before slipped from her face.

"*Winston*, Father," Morgan reached the bottom step and gazed at Adalia as if she were the answer to all his prayers. "I invited her to see if she could do anything for Lizzie."

"Balderdash! What can this mindless servant do that three skilled doctors could not?"

Mrs. Rutledge faced her husband, hands clasped together. "Please, Franklin, allow her to at least try. What have we to lose?"

"Our reputation for one. When news gets out that we've allowed a witch doctor into the house"—he tugged on his white neckerchief, his face reddening—"we'll be the laughingstock of the entire county, not to mention invoke the scorn of the clergy."

Adalia clutched her satchel until her fingers ached. Anger and fear battled a war in her belly. She should leave. But the look of pleading in Morgan's eyes forbade her. He stepped between her and his father. "Is our precious status worth more to you than Lizzie, Father?"

The older man narrowed his eyes—eyes that were sharp, yet vacuous.

"Please, Franklin." Mrs. Rutledge laid a hand on her husband's arm.

With a huff of disgust, he jerked from her and stomped from the room, grumbling about living with a bunch of loutish imbeciles.

Shocked at the man's treatment of his family, Adalia nearly jumped when Morgan touched her. He set her hand in the crook of his elbow and comforted her with a smile. "Don't mind him," he said as he led her up the stairs. "It's his way."

"He means well." Mrs. Rutledge's voice followed behind them.

Morgan's grip on Adalia's hand tightened.

She swallowed, overwhelmed by the rising pressure to help this little girl. What if she failed? What if Elizabeth died? Terror consumed her, blurring her vision so that she barely noticed the winding marble staircase, the exquisite oil paintings of relatives lining the walls, the Ming vase, crystalline chandelier, the gold-fringed tapestry that greeted them on the second floor. Barely.

However, when she saw the shrunken little girl, scarcely a sliver in the middle of a huge bed, all the trappings of wealth around them faded. What was all this worth if they lost this precious child? The putrid smell of sickness filled her nose, her lungs, and hovered in the dark corners. Tears burned behind Adalia's eyes as she eased onto the bed and felt the girl's skin. Clammy yet feverish. She tested the muscles in her arms and pressed on her abdomen. Swollen liver. She gazed into her mouth, nose, and ears and examined the sores on her skin. Dread forced Adalia's heart into her stomach. *No, Lord, not this.* "Has she eaten?"

Morgan sank to a chair on the other side of the bed. "Not in days." The agony in his eyes as he gazed at his sister threatened to release Adalia's tears. His mother stood behind him, rocking on her feet, hugging herself, her eyes locked upon her daughter as if the invisible band of love between them would keep her among the living. The little girl moaned and shifted on the bed. Adalia made her way to the window, flung open the curtains, and lifted the pane. A breeze swept into the room, bringing with it the fresh scent of morning and the happy twitter of chickadees.

"The doctors said to keep the window closed, my dear."

Adalia hated to contradict such a stately lady as well as a bevy of doctors. "The fresh air will do her good, madam. Please trust me. And sunshine too, as long as you keep her warm. Also, she must drink as much fresh water as possible."

The woman nodded, her concerned look shifting back to her daughter.

A growl spun Adalia to the left. Morgan's brother, Hadley, sat up in his chair and scrubbed his face with his hands. His sleepy eyes scanned the room, as he squinted at the sunlight streaming through the window. They widened upon seeing Adalia. "Scads! What is she doing here?"

"She's helping Lizzie." Morgan circled the bed to stand between them. A protective act that warmed her heart.

Hadley let out a groan of displeasure and grabbed a bottle of amber-colored liquid from the table beside him. He took a swig, wiped his mouth with his sleeve, then settled back into his chair.

"Can you do anything, Miss Winston? What ails her?" Mrs. Rutledge's voice brought Adalia's attention back to the girl. Lizzie tossed her head back and forth over her pillow. Her damp curls matted to her cheeks.

Adalia had seen this type of ailment before. Stomach cramps, restricted breathing, high fever, and an inflamed rash. There was nothing she could do except give her something to lessen the fever, comfrey for her rash, and eucalyptus to ease her breathing. But it would not stop the illness. Soon her lungs would fill with fluid, the rash would turn into festering sores, and the fever would become an inferno. She'd seen too many die in Barbados from the same disease.

But how could she tell this woman that?

"I can try to make her comfortable, Mrs. Rutledge, but I'm afraid the doctors are right. There is naught to be done."

Throwing a hand to her mouth, Mrs. Rutledge began to sob. She stumbled, and Morgan caught her and led her to a chair. Hadley moaned and took another swig of whatever devilish brew he imbibed.

Pray.

The words spoken, yet unspoken, drifted around Adalia. Morgan dropped to his knees beside Lizzie and grabbed her hand, caressing her fingers. Agony thundered across his features.

Adalia's eyes misted. "However, I can pray for her."

Morgan squeezed his eyes shut. Hadley chuckled. Mrs. Rutledge looked numbly up from her chair. "That would be lovely, Miss Winston." Her tone dragged with hopelessness.

Adalia's hands grew moist. What was she doing? They'd invited her here to heal their daughter, not offer a prayer. Perhaps it had been silly to even suggest it. But no. She had prayed over many of the sick children under her care. Some had recovered. Some not. Yet, God would have His way in the end. Prayer was just a means through which His power flowed, through which His will was done.

Easing to her knees beside Morgan, she laid her hand on Lizzie's arm. Hot, searing flesh met her fingers. Adalia swallowed and drew a breath to settle her nerves. She gazed at the little girl, still fidgeting beneath the fever, only a shadow of the precious golden-haired child Adalia had seen in town. A shadow of agony now reflected in Morgan's eyes. Glassy and pained, they shifted to Adalia, begging her without words to save his sister. She remembered the way he had swept Lizzie off her feet and showered her with affection, the love that saturated the air around them both. *Oh Lord. Please.* Adalia wiped the moisture from her eyes and bowed her head.

"Father in heaven. I rebuke all sickness and disease in this precious girl. Cast from her the source of this illness. Restore her to full health and vibrancy that she may glorify You with her life. In the precious name of Jesus. Amen."

"Amen," Mrs. Rutledge added.

When Adalia opened her eyes, Morgan gazed at her with astonishment. He rubbed his face and stood, helping her to her feet.

"Thank you, Miss Winston." He swallowed and forced a smile.

"I wish I could do more." Adalia cringed at the lack of faith infused in her statement.

Lizzie gulped in a breath, drawing everyone's gaze. Her mother darted to the bed. The girl wheezed as if desperate for air then turned her head to the side.

Adalia flung her hands to her mouth as trembling overtook her. *Oh no, Lord. Please don't let her die!*

CHAPTER ELEVEN

Morgan closed his eyes. He didn't want to watch his baby sister die. Couldn't watch her die. But slowly, instead of the rasp of fading life, the sound of steady breathing drifted past his ears—like the calm caress of waves on a sandy shore. At first, he thought he was hearing things, that he'd invented a pleasant sound to drown out her death throes. But when he lifted his gaze, it was to Lizzie sleeping, her chest rising and falling in a harmonious rhythm beneath the coverlet. No more wheezing. No more gasping. No more thrashing.

His mother drew in a shuddering breath.

Tears spilling down her cheeks, Adalia dropped to her knees and took Lizzie's hand in hers.

Morgan's legs gave out. He grabbed the bedpost. Could God have healed his sister? Impossible. When had God ever answered one of Morgan's prayers? Or any prayer, for that matter?

"That's the first time she's slept so peacefully in weeks." His mother's voice was full of amazement. And something else he hadn't heard in a while.

Hope.

Hadley's boots thumped over the floor toward them. Suspicion darkened his brow. He took another swig from the bottle, and his gaze bounced from Adalia to Lizzie and back again. "This has nothing to do with her prayer," he spat, gesturing toward Adalia. "Pure coincidence."

Adalia stood and wiped her face. She withdrew a pouch and a tin from her satchel and handed them to Morgan's mother, who remained frozen by Lizzie's bedside as if one movement would disrupt the happy turn of events. "Prepare some tea with these yarrow leaves. It will help relieve her fever. And rub this comfrey salve on her rash." She glanced down at Lizzie. "But allow her to sleep as much as she wants. When she awakes, try to get her to eat something. Just chicken or beef broth at first."

His mother nodded, her eyes welling with tears. "I don't know how to thank you, Miss Winston."

"I didn't do anything. Truth be told, I still don't know if she'll recover." She glanced at Morgan. "But I do believe God touched her."

Hadley rolled his eyes. "Gullible fools!" He stomped out, taking his brandy and bad attitude with him.

Bending over her, Adalia wiped Lizzie's damp hair from her forehead. Her shoulders rose in a sob as she placed a kiss on the girl's hand. She truly did care. Even after his father had been so rude. And his brother behaved the cad. What a wonder this woman was.

She straightened and snapped her satchel shut. "I should be going."

"May I walk you out?" Morgan asked.

She smiled and nodded. As they descended the stairs, her steps faltered, and she trembled. Morgan gripped her elbow, wondering if it was the shock of Lizzie's recovery that caused it, for he felt equally unsettled.

"Thank you." She tucked an ebony curl behind her ear. "I suppose I'm a bit out of sorts."

"I'm quite amazed myself."

"That God heals or that He would use someone like me to do so?" Her tone was sarcastic, playful even, as she continued downward.

The butler opened the door, and Morgan escorted her onto the porch to a blast of sunshine and cool air. "No, milady, that God cares enough to answer prayers at all."

"Please don't call me that." Her lips pursed, and she glanced over the scenery. "I'm sorry you have such a poor opinion of God, Mr. Rutledge."

"Morgan."

She snapped her eyes to his—dark velvety eyes. "Like my cat?" she asked.

"So, you *did* receive my gift." He grinned and followed her down the porch stairs to the footman who was holding her horse's reins.

"You should not be giving me gifts." She clipped her satchel onto the saddle.

"It couldn't be helped."

"Of course it could, Mr. Rutledge." Her brows folded into an adorable pinch. "You simply learn to control your impulses. It is what separates man from beast."

"When it comes to you, I fear that is a hopeless endeavor."

"Separating yourself from a beast or learning to control your impulses, Mr. Rutledge?" One brow rose.

He smiled. "The latter. Although the former is a matter of dispute among certain circles."

She gave a sigh of frustration and looked away.

The horse snorted. Morgan wanted to join him. Why did this woman not respond to his charms?

He grabbed the reins, dismissing the footman with a wave. "If you wait but a minute, I'll saddle my horse and accompany you."

Withdrawing riding gloves from her saddle bag, she began tugging them on, jerking the leather over her fingers with determination. "I will be quite all right, Mr. Rutledge. You are not my protector."

"Indeed. But one can hope."

She grinned, feeding his hope. His gaze fell to her lips—lips the color of brandywine and every bit as delicious. Despite the chill of the day, his body warmed at the memory of how soft and moist they were and how responsive she had been. Her thoughts must have taken the same path, for a ruddy hue crept up her neck. She shifted her gaze over the plantation, her eyes locking onto some slaves in the field.

"What is your opinion of slavery?" she asked, facing him again.

Morgan ran a hand through his hair, wondering at the odd change in topic. He wanted to say the right words, anything to erase the disdain emerging at the corners of her eyes. But, in truth, he hadn't given the topic much thought. "I suppose it's a necessary evil."

Obviously he'd said the wrong words because that disdain instantly covered her eyes in a fuming glaze. "If it is evil, as you say, then why is it necessary?"

Morgan glanced at the slaves, their bare backs leveled to the sun. Lud, this woman challenged him like no other! Why had he not considered the right or wrong of forcing others to work against their will, of keeping them imprisoned on the plantation like animals? "You are right, Miss Winston. It does seem unjust."

"Then why not free them?"

"They are not mine to free. This is my father's plantation."

"But you do not even stand up for them! You do not question your father."

Her anger nearly sent him reeling backward. He'd never encountered such opinions. "To my shame, no, I have not." He sighed, frustration and confusion bubbling within him. "I grew up with slavery. I was told the Negro was incapable of caring for himself."

"Do you believe that?" Her tone was clipped.

He shrugged. "I had not considered otherwise."

She turned to leave. He touched her arm, halting her. "Until now, Miss Winston. You have given me much to consider."

The fire left her eyes. She searched his as if seeking the truth of his words.

"Why does it interest you so?" he asked.

She hesitated, bit her lip. "God has given me a heart for all those oppressed."

"It is a heart that puts mine to shame, miss." He took her hand in his and kissed it tenderly, thrilled when she allowed him.

The horse sidestepped, nearly bumping them. Morgan grabbed the halter and nudged the beast aside.

"There's a new play at the Charleston Theater opening this Saturday night. I wasn't planning on going due to Lizzie's illness, but if she begins to recover in the next few days, would you do me the honor of accompanying me?" He glanced over the scenery, bracing himself for rejection.

Her hesitation gave him hope. He met her eyes. The look within them prodded him on. "It will be dreadfully dull without you, Miss Winston. It's only a play."

"That's what you said about the soiree." She settled a straw hat on her head and took the reins.

"A play requires no dancing, miss. Nor much need for skill in the art and nuances of society's repartee, as you put it."

"What would your father think?" She snapped her head toward the house. "His scorn of my station is evident."

"I care not. Nor do I care what anyone else thinks." He gave her his most charming grin then leaned closer if only to get a breath of her sweet scent. "Do say you'll come."

Grabbing the horn, she mounted the horse with ease. After adjusting her skirts around her, she gazed down at him. He could see the shield soften in her eyes before she spoke. "Very well, Mr. Rutledge." She gave him a coy smile. "Only if your sister recovers."

"Of course. I wouldn't want to go otherwise."

This seemed to please her. "Do let me know how she fares."

"I will. And I'll send word when to expect my call on Saturday."

She studied him for a moment. A pleasant sort of perusal that stirred his soul more than his body. Then she nudged the horse and galloped away in a flurry of blue cotton and luxurious black hair.

☙

With Joy's help, Adalia lifted the young boy from his pillow and coaxed him to take a sip of rosemary tea. "This will help settle your stomach, Samuel." She laid him back down. He held his midsection, pain wrestling his features. Joy pressed a cold compress on his head. A light footfall and pleasant sigh brought Adalia's gaze over her shoulder to Father Mulligan, the priest of St. Mary's and the man in charge of the orphanage. Adjusting the stiff collar of his cassock, he smiled. "You're so good with the wee ones, Miss Winston. You have such a caring nature. God has truly given you a gift." He winked at Samuel. "It doesn't surprise me that God used you to heal Elizabeth Rutledge."

Joy snickered. Too faint for Father Mulligan to hear.

Heal? Was the little girl truly healed? Adalia still found it hard to believe God had used her to perform a miracle. Yet Morgan had sent word that after only two days Lizzie's fever and rash were gone and she was eating again. "Then you believe me?" she asked Father Mulligan with a grin.

"Why wouldn't I?" He lifted both his hands. "God heals, Miss Winston. It only baffles me that people are so shocked when He does."

"He heals white children," Joy mumbled.

Father Mulligan laid a hand on the girl's shoulder. "He loves all children. No matter their color."

Adalia took Samuel's hand in hers. A tiny smile broke through the discomfort on his face. "It's man, not God, who makes one nation or culture greater than another."

"I quite agree, Miss Winston." Father Mulligan strode to the other side of the cot. "He's healed many of these orphans. Sometimes God uses people, sometimes medicine; sometimes He has to act quickly, as in the case of Miss Elizabeth."

"What 'bout them that don't get healed?" Joy asked, keeping her gaze on Samuel. Adalia had often wondered the same thing.

"We must trust His plan, for He knows all things."

Joy grunted. Adalia knew the platitude sounded trite, but to her ears it was the sound of her father's voice when she was a child, strong and protective, telling her to trust God no matter what. Telling her to be like Job, who refused to curse God when everything was taken from him. To walk on water through the storm like Peter.

Adalia had learned that lesson the hard way when her parents died. It had become all the more real to her when she and her sister became slaves. Then when Delphia was taken from her, Adalia longed to turn her fury against God, longed to run away from Him forever. But the vision of her father kneeling before her and her sister in the dark, as the winds and rain and tree branches crashed against their small house, kept her focused on the truth.

"No matter what happens, girls," he had said, "remember God loves you, and all things work out in the end for your good and His glory. You must trust Him." Those were the last words he'd ever said to them. Then after stopping at the door for one last glance at his family, he sped into the violent tempest to save his fishing boat. When he didn't return in an hour, their mother went searching for him.

They never saw either of them again.

Adalia was twelve. Delphia only eight.

Joy helped Samuel sit up while Adalia coaxed him to take another sip of tea. "Doctor Willaby didn't believe my story about Elizabeth Rutledge. He believes all miracles ceased after the last of Jesus' disciples died."

"Sounds to me like you have proven him wrong, lass."

"If only I could convince him. It would be a shame for him to miss out on one of God's most important attributes."

"I fear there are many who agree with him." Father Mulligan frowned.

The *rat-tat-tat* of drums shuddered the windowpanes, where darkness beyond lurked like a predator.

Joy leapt to her feet. "Miss, I have to go." Her lip quivered. "It's nine o'clock."

Adalia stared at her, bewildered. "Do you have an engagement?"

"No, she has a curfew." Father Mulligan cast a harried glance out the window. "City ordinance. No Negroes on the streets after nine, Miss Winston. Or they'll be tossed in jail and whipped."

Adalia shook her head. "I've never heard such nonsense."

"I quite agree, but the city is afraid of an uprising since there are far more Negroes here than whites."

Handing the cup to Father Mulligan, Adalia glanced once more at

Samuel, but the sweet lad had drifted off to sleep. "Have Mrs. Charlotte give him some more tea when he wakes up, will you, Father?"

"Of course. You better leave, Miss Winston." He set the tea down and gave her a worried look. "I'd escort you, but I'm the only one here at the moment."

"I understand, Father." Adalia grabbed her satchel, their shawls, and scurried out into the dark night. Flinging Joy's wrap over her shoulders, Adalia took her arm and sped down a back alleyway to a road less traveled. Fortunately, by the sounds of revelry drifting up the streets from every direction, the Charleston elite were well into their parties for the evening, leaving very few people wandering about. Poor Joy hurried along, head down, jerking at every shifting shadow. Her fear spilled onto Adalia, and she found her heart leaping at each silly flutter of leaves or croak of frog. The more she thought about the curfew, the more her fear turned to anger. By all accounts, she shouldn't be out after nine either.

A few minutes later, they entered the doctor's foyer, slamming the door on the insane and unjust law.

Joy's sigh of relief was clipped in midair by the doctor's shout from the sitting room. "Is that you, Miss Winston? Joy?"

"Yes, sir." Adalia shrugged off her shawl.

"Joy, you should not be out this late! Go get me a fresh pot of tea at once."

Joy exchanged a glance of dismay with Adalia before gathering her skirts and hurrying down the hallway.

Hanging her shawl on the hook, Adalia entered the sitting room to find the doctor reading his Bible. She shook her head in astonishment. How could anyone read such holy words while using such a harsh and demeaning tone with another?

"Sit down, my dear. We need to talk." Without looking up, he gestured toward a chair across from his.

Normally Adalia didn't mind his fatherly tone, but tonight it bordered on commanding. And she'd had enough of being commanded.

She slid into a seat as Joy entered, service tray clanking in her hands.

The doctor slammed his Bible shut and laid it aside. He waited until Joy had poured them tea and left the room before picking up a small card from the table. Taking off his spectacles, he held it out to Adalia. "Do you know what this is?"

She had no need to examine it. She recognized the expensive paper, the fancy writing. "Yes, it is Morgan Rutledge's calling card."

"His footman said to remind you of the play this Saturday. Eight o'clock, I believe he said?"

❧

Willaby studied his young assistant.

"Yes, thank you." Miss Winston set down the card and picked up her teacup. Was that a hint of defiance he detected in her voice?

He forced down his rising temper. Miss Winston was beautiful, cultured, smart, kind, and generous—all the qualities he could ever hope for in a daughter. All the qualities he would have wanted in his own.

Had she lived.

When Adalia had come to stay with him, he'd thought God had answered the prayers of a lonely old man. Now he had someone to love, someone to guide, nurture, someone to share his life. Of course he wanted the best for Adalia. He certainly didn't expect her to stay with him forever. He wanted her to marry and have children—perhaps even allow him to be a part of their lives. He prayed she would find a suitable husband—an honorable, godly man who would treat her well. But her infatuation with the Rutledge snipe was simply beyond the pale! How could she not see that family's depravity? Why could she not see that by responding to Morgan's attentions, she was putting herself in grave danger?

But he knew not to push her as he had his dear sweet Sarah. He had handled things badly. Prayed for a second chance. And now that he had one, he would not ruin it. He forced a smile. "Do you think attending the play with him is wise?"

She set her tea down. "I know you don't approve of the Rutledges, Doctor, but I have found the youngest son, Morgan, to be quite agreeable and charming. I doubt he would do anything to harm me."

"Charming. I'll give you that. But listen to what the Good Book says about flattery." He opened the Bible to where he had marked it and scanned the page, seeking the verse he'd read just moments before. "For there is no faithfulness in their mouth; their inward part is very wickedness; their throat is an open sepulchre; they flatter with their tongue."

She listened as she always did when he quoted Scripture. But was any of it taking root in her soul like the good seed in Matthew thirteen? *Oh God, I need Your help.* He could not allow this precious creature to be ruined by that monster.

Speaking of monsters, a *me-ow* sounded, and in bounded a spinning ball of tawny fur. The cat flew through the air and landed on the back of Miss Winston's chair, digging its claws into the velvet upholstery. "Oh my," Miss Winston said as she extricated the feline's paw from the fabric and placed the animal in her lap, but the furry fiend leapt from her arms onto the floral drapes and scrambled to sit atop the rods.

"I'm so sorry, Doctor." Miss Winston stood and began scolding the wayward kitten.

"Where on earth did it come from?" Willaby studied his drapes in horror, hoping the beast wouldn't rip them to shreds. Reaching up for the cat, Miss Winston mimicked meowing sounds to entice the creature down.

Despite the mayhem, he smiled at the sight.

"It's a he. And he was a gift. His name is M," she said, her voice straining as she stretched to grab the cat. Finally the furry imp dove into her arms, and Miss Winston drew him against her cheek.

"An odd name—M?" Willaby asked.

Miss Winston shifted uncomfortably, her gaze not meeting his. "I'm sorry. I should have asked your permission to bring him into the house. I promise I'll keep him in my chamber." She kissed the kitten's head.

"No, 'tis all right." Tears blurred the doctor's vision as he watched Miss Winston stroke the animal with such affection, causing another scene to appear before his eyes. This time it was his wife, Ruth, with their cat perched upon her shoulder, batting a loose curl across her neck. She nuzzled against the feline's face just as Miss Winston was doing now.

Miss Winston's voice snapped him from the memory. "If you don't mind, Doctor, I'm rather tired. Can we discuss this at a later time?" She peered toward him, concern tightening her brow. "Are you all right?"

He looked away. "Yes, yes, quite all right. Of course, Miss Winston. Good night to you."

"Good night, sir."

He watched her leave then rubbed the tears from his eyes and picked up his Bible again. He spread his hands gently across the sacred pages. No, he would not make the same mistake twice.

He would not lose another daughter to the Rutledges.

CHAPTER TWELVE

On the arm of the most handsome man in Charleston, Adalia Winston braced herself for the scorn of society as she entered the Charleston Theater. Why, oh why, had she accepted Morgan's invitation? Especially since she had vowed to never put herself through this again. But she knew why. Morgan had been so honest with her at his plantation, so forthright about his attitude toward slaves. How could Adalia blame him for an opinion impressed upon him since childhood? At least he had been willing to consider the wrongs of slavery. And that, alone, had given her hope. Not for any long-term relationship, but for her ability to influence him. Perhaps that was why God had brought them together—the most ill-suited, unlikely couple in Charleston! In order for Adalia to open Morgan's eyes to the horrors of slavery and perhaps change the opinions of the next generation. Or maybe even to bring Morgan closer to God. He certainly needed a relationship with the Almighty. If she could achieve the latter, God would certainly convince him of the former.

Yet her deception gnawed away at her insides. Morgan had never asked her about her heritage. She had told no lies. Then why, as she entered the magnificent foyer, did she feel that she had perpetrated the greatest hoax ever attempted on Charleston society?

Is it pride, Lord? Pride that she could mingle so deceptively amongst a crowd who would clap chains around her ankles if they knew her true identity? Or was it simply delight she felt? Delight because she'd never attended a play and she so desperately wanted to enjoy one from the advantage of a society box before they discovered her ruse and condemned her to the pit with the commoners.

She drew a deep breath. The sting of spirits, cigar smoke, and beeswax blasted over her as her eye was drawn immediately upward to the fresco of angels adorning the domed ceiling. She lowered her gaze to the glittering chandeliers, and then to the mahogany tables framing the room, laden with all sorts of pastries and wine. Those patrons who weren't busy sampling the delicacies or engrossed in conversations snapped their gazes toward the newcomers. Yet instead of snobbish dismissal, some of the glances held interest—perhaps, dare she hope, even approval.

Approval she still fought to obtain from Morgan's companions, who were following behind them. Although Miss Emerald had smiled at her more than once in the carriage, her denigrating whispers regarding Adalia's gown at the last party still thrummed in Adalia's ears like the curfew drums for Negroes, telling Adalia she was not worthy to be out with such a noble crowd. Before or after nine o'clock. It made no difference.

Yet, at the moment, that noble crowd continued to stare at her. She glanced down at her plain skirts. Joy had aided her in adding a lace trim to the festoon of beads at the hem and neckline, and she wore a different sash, but she doubted that was the cause of their interest. In fact, wearing the same gown twice in a row was no doubt a glaring *faux pas* among this country set. Nevertheless, as Morgan led her farther into the room, the elite swarmed around her like butterflies of silk and satin.

"Good evening, Miss Winston."

"So nice to see you."

One particularly rotund lady with red plumes protruding from her stately coiffeur raised a lorgnette to her eyes and studied Adalia as if she were a specimen. "We heard of your miraculous healing of young Miss Elizabeth." She smiled at Morgan. "Good day to you, Mr. Rutledge."

He dipped his head. "Mrs. Rennard, how lovely you look." But the woman's eyes remained on Adalia.

Adalia swallowed. "It wasn't me—"

"Oh, do give us the details," the woman insisted.

"Yes, pray tell," an older, distinguished gentleman on her right said. "Did you learn charms and chants from the natives on Jamaica?"

"Of course not!" Adalia was appalled at the insinuation. Yet still the mob pressed in, curious gazes and questions assailing her from all around. The smell of expensive perfume and cedar oil tickled her nose, and she feared she'd sneeze all over them. That would certainly put a stop to their inquisition. Yet despite the exuberance of the few, Adalia did not miss the looks of aversion cast her way from those standing afar off, including Lord Demming, who spat out the words "witch doctor" for all to hear. Behind her, Miss Emerald whispered something to Caroline while Hadley and Mr. Drayton snuck away to the refreshment table. Thankfully, Morgan remained by her side, seemingly pleased with the attention she was receiving.

Adalia scanned the myriad eyes alighting upon her as if she were a princess—as if she had something of value to say. And if she were forced to admit it, her shoulders rose a bit beneath their approval. Yet her conscience quickly stabbed her like a thorn clawing her blooming pride. She must tell them it was God, not her, who healed Elizabeth. No doubt that would extinguish their regard as quickly as snuffing a candle.

"Hush now." Mrs. Rennard silenced the mob. "Let the girl speak."

When their chatter dwindled to a whisper, Adalia smiled. "I fear you are mistaken, Mrs. Rennard. It was God who healed Miss Elizabeth, not me."

The lady rolled her eyes and tapped Adalia's shoulder with her closed fan. "Oh, how modest she is. Wherever did you find her, Morgan?"

"Come now, how *did* you do it?" a young man to her right asked.

"I didn't—"

But further questions flooded her, muffling out her declaration.

Finally, Morgan slipped in front of her and held up his hands. "Now, now, let Miss Winston breathe, if you please."

A young lady with a pointy chin and nose to match leaned toward her from the side. "We are pleased to have you with us, Miss Winston."

Her genuine smile warmed Adalia.

An announcement that the play would begin in five minutes did more to disperse the crowd than Morgan's attempts. He swung around and raised his brows. "Seems you have become quite the talk of society."

Mr. Drayton and Hadley returned with drinks in hand.

Miss Emerald fingered a curl of her alabaster hair. "Rubbish, Morgan. You know how fickle these people are." She gazed over the departing mob, still whispering and casting glances at Adalia over their shoulders. "Miss Winston is an oddity. She brings a temporary amusement. That's all."

Though she knew it was true, the barb cut Adalia. Her gaze sped to Morgan, wondering if his obsession with her was merely a passing amusement as well. What did it matter? Tonight—for just one night—she would relish in the attention. Nobody, save her parents, had ever treated her as though she were special. And never had she been accepted into such a distinguished assembly.

Morgan frowned. "Must you always be so cruel, Emerald?"

Emerald laid a hand on Adalia's arm. "I meant no insult, my dear. It is just the way of things."

Mr. Drayton grunted. "I quite agree with Emerald. I wouldn't put too much stock in their attention, Miss Winston. Next week it will be someone else who captures their heart. And one of us could be cast away."

Adalia forced a smile. "Then it is a good thing I've never been much for the opinions of others."

Morgan cocked his head, his green eyes approving and proud. Her heart flipped in her chest. Not that it needed much incentive. She'd been having trouble settling it ever since she'd laid eyes on him earlier in the evening. He had a way of dressing that was both cultured and refined yet not pretentious or foppish. Or perhaps it was the way the tailored fabric clung to his muscular frame. It mattered not whether it was cotton or wool or silk-jersey—as were his waistcoat and pantaloons this night—his attire seemed only to accentuate his masculinity. Add to that his tawny hair drawn back in a queue, the dark whiskers crowning his chin below a rakish grin, and the man could melt an iceberg in the Arctic.

"Ah, Joseph, don't be so morose." Caroline slinked her arm through Mr. Drayton's. "These people are our friends. You've known them since childhood. Why, there are the Hydes, the Cravens, the Coopers, and the Carterets—all families hailing from the first settlers of this land. We are indeed privileged to be accepted among such a noble group."

"If, as in your case, Caroline, that is all you aspire to, then I quite agree." Mr. Drayton's voice carried no criticism, but Caroline's face fell nonetheless.

Hadley sipped his drink and gave Mr. Drayton a sardonic look. "What would you do without your position and money, Joseph?"

Mr. Drayton scanned the crowd. "I wonder."

Emerald stared at Adalia's hand still clinging to Morgan. A glimmer of spite sharpened her eyes before she gripped Hadley's arm. "Shall we go in before we miss the play?"

❧

Morgan watched Adalia's eyes light up like a little girl's in a pastry shop as she took her seat in the Rutledge box. Every smile she sent his way lifted his heart a bit higher until he felt it would leap through his throat. He'd been more than pleased that some of his acquaintances had accepted her into their tight circle. And equally pleased that Adalia seemed to enjoy their attention. Now, as the lights were doused and the actors came on stage, she clapped her gloved hands together with glee as if she'd never attended a play before. Perhaps she hadn't. Though he could not imagine how such a lovely lady could have avoided being swamped with invitations from admirers. Had she even had a coming out? Being a commoner, most likely not. He glanced behind him to where Caroline and Drayton had taken seats—Drayton looking as bored as ever—then over to Emerald, who slid into a chair beside Hadley. The beauty smiled his way before her eyes shifted to Adalia and iced over. Her jealousy baffled him, for he'd never given her any encouragement. Yet something in her look gave him pause. He would have to keep his eye on her. He wouldn't want her to ruin his evening with Adalia.

Speaking of keeping eyes on things.

If anyone had asked Morgan what the play was about, he wouldn't have been able to say. His gaze lingered around Adalia, watching her every gasp, moan, every lift of her lips and widening of her eyes as she engaged in the story being played out before her. What a charming, fascinating lady. So full of life. So appreciative of everything and everyone around her. It was as if God had opened the heavens and allowed one of His precious angels to escape. God. There Morgan went again, thinking of God. Something that had become a common occurrence since he'd met Miss Adalia. And especially after his sister recovered. How else could he explain it? If God had indeed intervened and healed Lizzie, surely it was this precious lady who drew His attention downward.

Soon the lanterns circling the theater were lit, the orchestra began playing, and the actors bowed to the applause of the crowd. Adalia clapped and cheered with fervor, then graced Morgan with a smile.

"Most pleasurable, Mr. Rutledge. Thank you so much."

"It is not over yet, Miss Winston. This is only the intermission."

"Oh my." She looked away, obviously embarrassed, her gaze scanning the two tiers of boxes forming a semicircle above the wide room—boxes filled with ladies and gentlemen in their finery and fripperies. So at odds with the plain garb of the people sitting in the pit. As if reading his thoughts she said, "I feel like a princess sitting so high above everyone else."

"You *are* a princess."

Her eyebrows dipped together and she gestured toward the masses below. "I belong with them, Mr. Rutledge. As you well know."

"Not while you're with me."

She looked at him for a moment, her eyes shifting between his before she lowered her lashes and ran her fingers over the velvet upholstered seat. "I feel like I'm intruding upon a dream."

Emerald rose to her feet. Morgan did not miss her whispered, "Indeed," but thankfully, it appeared Adalia had.

"Please." He stood, offering his elbow. "Join me for refreshments in the lobby." They started toward the back of the box when Emerald dove between them, weaving her arm through Adalia's and drawing her away.

"You can't monopolize Miss Winston all evening, Morgan. Come, Adalia, all the women gather in the orchestra garden during intermission to talk about our men. I guarantee you'll hear all sorts of delicious gossip." She gave Morgan a coy look.

Uncertainty shadowed Adalia's face, but then she smiled politely and conceded, reassuring Morgan that she would be all right.

He watched Adalia disappear behind the curtain, wondering if he should have left her alone with Emerald. He'd only invited his friends to join them, hoping that once they grew to know Adalia, they would love her as much as he did. Certainly this time alone with Emerald would aid that cause.

Hadley leaned against the wood railing of the box, glancing at the long drop below. "Scads, little brother, have you gone mad?"

"Whatever do you mean?" Morgan faced his brother with an indignant huff.

"I see the way you look at her. Like a slobbering mongrel. It's pathetic. You aren't serious about this girl, are you?"

"What is it to you?"

"Mother and Father will never accept her. You know that."

Of course he knew that. He'd been pushing that thought from his mind ever since he'd met Adalia. "I never say anything about your many trysts, Hadley. I advise you to stay out of mine."

"I would be happy to." Hadley crossed his arms over his chest. "As long as you swear to me that Miss Winston is no more than just that, a passing tryst."

❧

Emerald tried to focus on what the tart was saying in response to her feigned interest in Miss Elizabeth's healing, but the woman went on and on about God this and God that. It was beyond annoying. Besides, she spotted Morgan descending the stairs in all his glorious virility, Hadley fresh on his heels. By the scowls on their faces, Emerald assumed Hadley's little chat with his brother had not gone well.

On to plan B. As cruel as it was.

Morgan's approach gave her more impetus to put that plan in motion as his eyes sought out Miss Winston like a ship to a lighthouse— oblivious of the dozens of young ladies sending him coy looks from behind fluttering fans. Oblivious even to Emerald. The insult was beyond atrocious! Hadn't she been able to capture his attention before? Hadn't she seen the same intensity in his eyes when he'd gazed at her?

That was before this uncultured hussy came to Charleston.

Now, the man she loved, the man she'd hoped to marry, laid a hand on Miss Winston's back in a possessive gesture that splattered Emerald's insides with the color of her name.

Emerald slid her arm through Hadley's, if only to keep from plucking the woman's hair out strand by strand. "Allow us to get you both refreshments," Emerald said. The smile she forced nearly cracked her skin.

Suspicion darted across Morgan's eyes before he shrugged and faced Miss Winston, then leaned in to whisper something in her ear.

Spinning Hadley around, Emerald headed for the sideboard. "What happened?"

"What do you think?" Hadley snorted.

"You better do something. And fast. The fool is becoming more besotted with her by the moment."

"Indeed. But what can I do about my bird-witted brother?" He chuckled, fondling her hand.

Tugging from him, Emerald opened her reticule and pulled out a vial.

Hadley drew her to the side, out of the way of prying eyes. "What, pray tell, is that?"

She grinned. "Something that will cause that chit so much embarrassment, she'll never show her face in society again."

Hadley's grin became maniacal. "Indeed, you are a devilish sprite, my dear."

❧

"Miss Winston. I brought you some lemonade. I remember how much you enjoyed it at the last party." Emerald's smile was sweet—almost too sweet.

Adalia took the glass, shrugging off her vague suspicions. It was too pleasant a night to entertain unsettling thoughts. "Thank you, Emerald. How thoughtful of you." The sweet lemony smell taunted her taste buds. The lovely lady certainly seemed to be making an attempt at kindness. She included Adalia in conversations—had even asked about Lizzie's healing. Perhaps Emerald had changed her opinion about her, after all. Perhaps she was trying to befriend her.

"And some wine for you, brother." Hadley took one of the glasses in his hand and gave it to Morgan.

Morgan seemed less inclined to believe the best of his brother and his friend as he studied them both curiously.

Caroline slipped beside Adalia, drawing out her fan and waving it around her. "It's so warm in here, isn't it? Oh, lemonade." She eyed Adalia's glass. "I'm simply parched."

"You're welcome to my glass, Caroline. I haven't touched it yet." The poor girl looked like she needed a drink more than Adalia.

"Truly? How kind of you." Caroline took the glass and drew it to her lips.

CHAPTER THIRTEEN

Miss Emerald's gasp brought all eyes her way. She covered her mouth and took a step back. Dumbfounded, Adalia gazed at her, wondering if the woman had overindulged in wine. Then seemingly embarrassed at her outburst, she waved a gloved hand through the air, begging the apology of the curious crowd, who promptly went back to their merrymaking.

"Whatever is wrong with you, Em?" Caroline swallowed another gulp of lemonade and studied her friend. Her lips puckered. She stared at her glass. "A bit tart this evening."

Hadley exchanged a look of apprehension with Miss Emerald that set the hairs on Adalia's arms bristling. What were the two of them up to? Morgan must have had the same thought, for he chuckled and said, "Perhaps you two should step outside for some fresh air."

"I'll go get you another glass of lemonade, Miss Winston." Hadley scurried away before Adalia had a chance to tell him not to bother. Emerald cast a scathing glance after him before she faced forward, a spurious smile on her face.

Caroline sipped more lemonade then waved her fan about her face.

But it was the dainty man sauntering up to the group that drew Adalia's attention. The same man who had stared so hatefully at Morgan at the soiree now stopped before them, one hand holding a drink high in the air and the other settled coyly on his waist. This time, however, his spiteful glance barely swept over Morgan before his smile landed on Adalia. "Good day, Morgan. I dare say, do introduce me to your fascinating friend."

Morgan huffed. "What is it you want, Fabian?"

"Alas, I have told you." He gave Morgan an innocent look and shifted his hips. "Surely you cannot deny me an introduction."

"But to what end?" Morgan asked, eyeing the man.

Drayton grinned. "Another request for a duel perhaps?"

Mr. Saville flung a hand in the air, the lace at his cuffs covering his sleeve like an exposed petticoat. Adalia restrained a chuckle at the sight.

"I find it incorrigible that you refuse me the chance to win back my honor," he announced with flourish.

"I refuse you the chance to die, sir. That is all."

"Afraid you will lose?" He raised an eyebrow and placed his delicate hand on one hip.

Morgan laughed and fingered the whiskers on his chin.

Emerald's gaze shifted between Fabian and Morgan. "Oh, leave Mr. Saville alone, Morgan. Perhaps he simply wishes to meet society's current fancy."

The way she said it made Adalia feel as though she were a ship passing in the night.

Caroline pressed a hand on her stomach.

"Very well," Morgan said with impatience. "Mr. Fabian Saville, may I present Miss Adalia Winston. Miss Winston, Mr. Saville."

Slick black hair crowned a well-shaped head, high rosy cheekbones, and gray eyes flecked in brilliant red that made them seem like fiery embers. He took her hand and bowed to place a kiss upon it. "Charmed, Miss Winston."

Adalia's stomach turned. What was it with the men of this elite class? If they weren't shunning her, they were devouring her with their eyes.

Much like Morgan was doing to the man now—only his devouring was more that of a cougar about to pounce on dinner.

"You cannot keep this treasure all to yourself, Morgan." Mr. Saville said without taking his eyes off of her. "I insist you accompany me to the horse races this Saturday, Miss Winston."

Drayton snorted. "A fitting event for a man who can barely mount a pony."

Mr. Saville's eyes inflamed. "I am much improved upon a horse," he ground out through glistening teeth.

Though flattered that another accomplished gentleman wanted to escort her, Adalia's skin crawled at the man's invitation. "Well, I—"

"She's otherwise engaged, Fabian." Morgan tugged her hand from his. For the first time since she'd known him, Mr. Drayton smiled. So did Emerald, but her smile was more of the devious kind than stemming from mirth.

Mr. Saville thrust out his chin. "Your lack of civility does you no credit, sir."

"Then pray, trouble yourself no further over it and go find someone else to be civil with." Morgan waved him off, but his eyes were on Caroline, whose face had gone pale.

Emerald's gaze flitted from Caroline then around the room and back to Caroline again like a sparrow looking for a solid place to land. Adalia shook her head. Had Morgan's friends gone mad? And where had Hadley run off to?

Mr. Saville straightened his shoulders. "I do protest, Mor—"

A soul-grinding moan came from Caroline's direction. All eyes shot to her as she bent over, gripping her belly. The lemonade slipped from her hand and crashed to the floor, spewing its golden liquid amidst a shower of broken glass.

The huge room, which only moments before was abuzz with laughter and gossip, grew deafeningly silent. A servant ran up to clean the mess while Adalia tore from Morgan's grasp and threw an arm around Caroline. Emerald stood staring at her numbly.

"Caroline, what's wrong?" Adalia asked as Morgan stepped to her other side to assist the poor lady to a chair.

"I don't. . .know," Caroline managed to utter before another groan rumbled from her throat. She lifted her head and scanned the flock of eyes—some curious, some alarmed, others annoyed—that took her in as if she were the intermission entertainment. Terror stung her eyes. "Please get me out of here," she begged Adalia.

"Of course." Adalia exchanged a look of concern with Morgan as, together, they helped Caroline toward the front entrance.

"Oh no. Oh, heavens no!" Caroline moaned. Suddenly, her chest heaved. Tearing from their grasps, she stumbled toward the door, one hand on her stomach, one hand pushing people aside as she wove through the crowd. One final groan emerged from her throat before she stopped, bent over, and tossed the contents of her stomach into a brass spittoon.

❧

Morgan ordered their coach brought around while Adalia and Emerald hovered over a sobbing Caroline. Well, more like Adalia embraced the lady while Emerald stood by staring at them as if she hadn't a clue what to do.

Or she felt responsible, somehow.

"Terrible business," Hadley commented. "Poor girl. Such a sudden illness."

"Sudden, indeed." Morgan eyed him. When had his brother ever cared for the feelings of others? And when had Emerald ever offered to get refreshments? And why was Caroline fine one minute and ill the next? After she drank the lemonade. Lemonade that was meant for Adalia. He didn't want to think so poorly of his brother and his good friend, so he kept his accusations to himself. For now. Instead, he ground his teeth together as the coachman brought their carriage around and the footman leapt down, dropped the step, and opened the door.

Adalia assisted the hysterical Caroline to the carriage as Emerald walked stately by their side, shooing away onlookers as though they were pesky flies.

"It will be all right." Adalia embraced Caroline before helping her up the step. The poor woman slid onto the seat and gazed out the window, anguish raking her features. "How will it ever be all right?" Her glance took in the surrounding throng. "They will never forget."

"It doesn't matter what they think," Adalia said. "Go home and rest. Call on me if your stomach still pains you tomorrow."

Caroline nodded and dabbed her eyes with her handkerchief as Emerald joined her in the carriage. "Come along, dear. I'll see you home." Her tone held a hint of remorse, so unlike Emerald. "Enjoy the play. I'll take care of her," she said to Morgan through the window once they were seated.

"Very well." He turned to the driver. "Blaney, see that the ladies get home safely, and then you may retire as well." The footman closed the door and leapt onto the back of the carriage, a lightness in his step, no doubt at the early release from his duties.

Morgan faced Adalia, her concerned gaze still on Caroline as the carriage lurched, then trundled, down the street.

"I believe I'll join Drayton for the rest of the play." Hadley raised a brow and gestured toward the theater. "Morgan? Miss Winston?"

Morgan proffered his elbow for Adalia.

She faced him with a sigh. "I'm rather tired. Would you mind if we missed the remainder?"

"Not at all."

"Good night to you, then." Hadley bid them adieu and disappeared into the theater.

They walked in silence for several minutes, the sounds of the crowd and the music diminishing. A carriage rattled by. Across the street, a group of people strolled along, their joyous chatter carried on the wind, which also brought the scent of the bay to Morgan's nose. He hadn't been on the brig for weeks, and the longing to be upon the sea swelled within his heart until he felt it would burst.

"Poor Caroline," Adalia finally spoke, her voice breaking.

They passed beneath a streetlamp. Flickering light glistened over her ebony curls and transformed her skin into shimmering silk. Yet that silk now folded in concern for a lady who had barely given her an ounce of attention. Beautiful on the outside. And on the inside.

"She will recover," Morgan said.

"From the illness. But not from the embarrassment."

Morgan nodded. She was right, of course. Society rarely forgot such a social blunder, regardless of whether the act was unavoidable. They would eventually accept her back, but it would be the endless whispers behind her back, the biting taunts that would forever brand her as somehow less than they.

"Caroline seems obsessed with their approval," Adalia said.

"It is the lot of the landed gentry, I'm afraid. Especially those who wish to make a good match in marriage."

"Perhaps." She sighed. "I cannot imagine what brought on so sudden an illness. I must discuss this with Doctor Willaby."

Morgan would like to know as well. Of course Adalia would never consider any nefarious activity. But Morgan was not so naive. He'd known Emerald since they were children. And Hadley a lifetime. Though he could not imagine either of them being so cruel, their behavior tonight pricked his suspicion. If what he surmised was true, it would have been Adalia suffering now, not only from indigestion but also from chronic humiliation. And it would most likely have ended her willingness to join him in any further society events.

To join him at all, in fact.

And that scared him more than anything.

❧

Adalia took a deep breath and attempted to scatter her thoughts about Caroline. There was nothing she could do to ease her pain, save pray. And that she intended to do as soon as she got home. Perhaps God could use Caroline's shame to bring her into His loving arms, where she would find comfort and acceptance and freedom from the opinions of others.

They turned down Chalmers Street, and despite the disturbing event with Miss Caroline, Adalia found herself suddenly wishing the night would never end. She could think of no other evening that equaled this one. The Charleston elite had accepted her as one of their own! All save a few. *And all because of You, God. All because of Your healing of Elizabeth.*

She longed to spread out her skirts and twirl in the street, as she had done when she was a girl and her father would sing and clap and call her his little princess. She had felt like a real princess tonight. The magnificent theater, the play, the gowns, the jewelry, the gentlemen in silk lutestring suits—the opulence. Everyone's eyes on her. And Adalia on the arm of the handsome man beside her—handsome and charming. Just like a prince.

Surely, she must be dreaming. Only in her dreams would she ever be a part of this fairy-tale world—a world she had, until recently, only glanced at through a window like a hungry, ragged child standing out in the cold rain—a window made of impenetrable glass.

But Morgan had opened the door and invited her in. She smiled up at him now, drawing his gaze, along with his grin.

Sharing a bottle of liquor, two men stumbled toward them. They belted out a ribald ditty then stopped when they spotted Adalia and Morgan. One of them fumbled to remove his hat. She stiffened. Morgan slipped an arm around her waist and led her by them, directing a warning at them with his eyes. A thrill spiraled through her at the protective press of his hand on her back.

Morgan glanced over his shoulder, no doubt to ensure that the men continued on their way, when a man dressed in a white cape crossed in front of Adalia. No. More like he drifted across her path, glancing at her in passing. His face, so calm and serene and perfect, stole the gasp from her mouth.

"For all that is in the world—the lust of the flesh, the lust of the eyes, and the pride of life—is not of the Father but is of the world," he said, his voice soothing yet commanding like the deep rumble of waves on a shore.

She blinked and turned toward Morgan, asking if he knew the man, but when she looked back, he was gone.

Morgan faced forward. "What man? Those two sots?" He thumbed over his shoulder. "I wouldn't worry about them."

"No." Adalia scanned the dark cobblestone street. Save for pyramids of light beneath the streetlamps, all was dark. "A man wearing a white cape."

"I think I would have seen such a gaff of fashion." He chuckled as they approached the doctor's home. Light danced over the garden from the side window where Dr. Willaby, no doubt, still read his Bible in the sitting room.

Once again, Adalia found herself standing on the first step of the porch, facing a pair of green eyes that were as enchanting and mysterious as a forest at dusk.

"Thank you, Mr. Rutledge. . .Morgan," she said, dipping her head.

"Finally." He flashed a grin and took her gloved hand in his, caressing her fingers.

"I had a marvelous time at the play."

"Your first?"

"Was I that obvious?"

"Nothing about you is obvious." He moved closer, still rubbing his thumb over her hand. She could feel his warmth, smell the scent that was Morgan. Any closer and his whiskers would scratch her forehead. He exuded a masculinity, a protectiveness that reached invisible arms around her, making her feel safe. . .yet, at the same time, raising an alarm that screeched through her, alerting her to danger—a strength that could subdue her without hesitation.

Tugging her hand from his, Adalia took a step back.

He rubbed his chin and frowned. "Why are you frightened of me?"

"Not you." She shook her head. She could never tell him what had happened to her. "I simply don't like to be touched."

He cocked his head, probing her with his gaze before his brows knit. "Someone hurt you."

Blast the man's perception. So uncommon for one raised in narcissism. But she could not lie to him. Instead she lowered her chin.

With a touch of his finger, he lifted her to face him. "I would never hurt you, Adalia. And I will kill anyone who does."

The look of sincerity and intensity in his eyes sent her heart pounding. He ran his thumb over her jaw. Waves that felt like the heat of a tropical sun spread down her neck. Why was she reacting like this? What were these powerful, inescapable feelings? In an attempt to ignore them, she gave him a coy smile. "Such gallantry, sir."

"Have I finally convinced you that I am no monster?" He placed one boot atop the step. "You did allow me to kiss you once."

"Not a monster. Perhaps merely a rake. And it was not a kiss."

"My lips touched yours, if I recall. I believe that counts."

"I was taken off guard. You pressed your advantage."

"Yet you did not resist." He leaned toward her ear, his face inches from hers. "Shall we attempt another, milady? If only to prove to you that I pose no threat?"

Adalia's breath whipped in her chest. No, she couldn't possibly. It was one thing to have his lips graze hers and quite another to purposely kiss him. For one thing they were not courting, for another the look in his eyes. . . Oh my, the look of desire in Morgan's eyes! She'd seen it before.

Images of Sir Walter intruded into the moment. Visions flashed like morbid vignettes, illustrating her life, her past—who she really was. The malicious folds of his face, his lips dripping with desire. His hands pawing her skin.

She swallowed away a shudder and shot a defiant glance toward Morgan. But his eyes no longer reflected raw desire. Now they gazed at her curiously, tenderly, as if he were gazing at a masterpiece—a precious painting he had no intention of harming. It did much to dissolve her fear. And much to heighten her desire to be loved, cherished, and protected. Seconds passed as he awaited her answer. Seconds in which her mind waged a battle between right and wrong, dreams and reality, fear and hope. Finally, her thoughts abandoned her altogether as he dropped his gaze to her lips. The way he glanced at them as though they were coated in sweet cream drew the strength from her knees, from her resolve. She opened her mouth to say no. She would absolutely not allow his kiss! But another word barged its way to her lips—"yes."

CHAPTER FOURTEEN

Morgan's lips touched hers. A jolt of pleasure spun through Adalia, swirling from her belly, down her limbs, and tingling in her toes until she was forced to lean on him, lest she fall. His whiskers brushed her cheek as he caressed her lips with the tenderness of a man handling a priceless vase. He wrapped an arm around her back and pressed her against him, his passion growing as he drank her in. He tasted of wine and salt and Morgan.

Adalia's head spun in a tempest. A storm that clouded her reason, her senses. A storm she never wanted to cease. He let out a passionate moan that pricked her memories and resurrected her fears. What if she couldn't stop him? What if all men, once they started on a sensual journey, could not retreat? She pressed a palm against his chest.

He withdrew, his mouth hovering over hers. She felt his body tense. His tight chest heaved beneath her hand. Reaching up, he caressed her jaw, her neck, and placed the gentlest of kisses on her cheek.

"Adalia," he breathed into her ear. "Sweet Adalia." A quiver ran down her.

"Morgan, we mustn't." She took a step back. He allowed her, but kept his arm around her waist.

"Why not?" he breathed out, his tone impassioned. "You enjoyed it as much as I did." His gaze fell on her lips again, and he started his descent.

She pressed her fingers on his mouth, halting him, embarrassed that her pleasure had been that obvious. "We are not courting."

He took her fingers and kissed them. "Easy to rectify."

The way he looked at her caused her body to warm all over again.

She looked away. "We hardly know each other."

"Another matter easily rectified." This time he smiled, the lantern light glinting off his ivory teeth.

What was she doing? Her intent had been to convince him of the ills of slavery. To draw him into God's arms. Not her own! Besides, if he knew who she really was, he wouldn't be standing here. He wouldn't be kissing her. Or even speaking to her. Would he? She wanted so much to believe that her race would not make a difference to him. Hadn't he told her she'd given him much to consider?

He kissed her hand again, gazing up at her in playful seductiveness.

Her heart sped. This was madness. But if so, perhaps sanity was greatly overrated.

"You'll have to try harder if you wish to dissuade me from pursuing you, milady."

"Don't call me. . ." She stopped, hopelessly lost in his charming smile. "What am I to do with you?"

His brows arched. "I have a few ideas."

The sensual gleam in his gaze sent her leaping backward out of his grasp.

He sobered, concern lining his eyes. "I've frightened you again. Forgive me." A breeze played with a loose tendril of his hair. He glanced down for a moment. "I must leave town. . . . I mean I must spend a few days on the plantation. Please say you'll attend the horse races with me on Saturday."

"I don't gamble."

"Neither do I, mil—" He stopped himself. "It's quite the grand affair. I assure you, you'll find it enjoyable."

Adalia had no doubt. Besides, what harm could it do? Perhaps she could discuss slavery with him, or even talk about God. Certainly attending these affairs granted her more time to do both. And she could not deny that deep within her a tiny bud of hope had sprouted—a hope that Morgan wouldn't care about her past or her race. That someone like him could love someone like her. Now, as he gazed at her with such longing, and with the effects of his kiss still storming through her, weakening her knees, she began to believe that dreams did come true.

"Saturday then," he answered her non-response. Kissing her hand one last time, he retreated down the path, never taking his gaze from her. He stumbled over an uneven flagstone, caught his balance, and smiled at her like a boy caught stealing a piece of pie.

"Good sleep to you, fair maiden." He bowed, and just like the prince in her dreams, he disappeared into the darkness.

Leaving Adalia feeling like she was tumbling into that darkness alongside him. A darkness that was both pleasurable and dangerous. A darkness from which there was no escape.

৯৲

Planting his boots on the foredeck of *Seawolf*, Captain Bristo's brig, Morgan thrust his face into the wind. Warm air, spiced with tropical flowers, filled his lungs. He breathed it in like an elixir that would heal all his ills. All but one. Only a certain lady with silken black hair had the cure for that affliction. He rubbed his lips where he'd sampled her particular elixir two nights ago—his mind and body still reeling from the effects.

Adjusting his cocked hat, he stared at the sun high in the sky. Perhaps he shouldn't have taken advantage of her without a formal understanding between them. But she'd looked so alluring standing there in the moonlight, her skin as lustrous as pearls, her hair spirals of precious ink, her lips so full and inviting. He'd lost control. And he wasn't sorry for it. Not until he'd frightened her. Her response to his kiss had once again inflamed his senses. So much so, he'd pressed her too far. Taken a step too close. And like a rare, exotic bird, she flitted away. But not too far. He smiled. That she harbored feelings for him was obvious. That he so desperately needed her affections terrified him.

The ship swooped over a white-capped wave. He gripped the railing. Clearly someone had hurt this precious bird in the past. His knuckles whitened at the thought. Perhaps someday she would tell him about it. But for now, he'd be gentle. He would approach her with patience. For he never wanted to frighten this bird away.

"You must be thinking of a lady." Captain Bristo startled Morgan as he slid beside him and scanned the horizon.

Morgan chuckled, squinting toward his captain. "Guilty as charged."

"The same lady?"

Morgan rubbed the back of his neck. Had he gone through women so quickly that his captain needed to ask such a question? The thought brought him shame. "Yes. Miss Adalia Winston."

"So you took my advice and pursued her?"

"That I did."

"And your charm won out." It was more of a statement than a question.

"Did you have any doubt?"

The captain chuckled and shook his head. "God help this poor woman."

"Apparently, He does." Morgan snapped the hair from his face. "You'll be happy to know she's a godly woman."

Sails thundered above as they shifted in the wind, drawing Captain Bristo's gaze. "Indeed. God does answer prayers."

"If you've been praying for Miss Winston to accept my suit, I thank you."

The captain clasped his hands behind him and smiled.

"And thank you for taking me on board at the last minute," Morgan added. "This quick trip to Savannah is just what I needed."

Turning, Bristo found the boson on the main deck. "Trim the sails to the wind, if you please, Mr. Granger." The man tipped his hat and spit a string of orders, sending sailors into the ratlines.

"You're welcome to sail with me anytime. You know that."

"How fares the merchant business?" Morgan asked.

"I'm thankful to be able to sell this hold full of corn and dried beef." The captain shrugged. "But I'm still recovering from Jefferson's embargo. Not to mention Napoleon and England's trade restrictions. Blast it all! How is a merchant supposed to survive?" He released a heavy sigh as the ship canted to port. "And with the constant threat of the British impressing Americans into the Royal Navy, it's been hard to find decent sailors who'll risk leaving shore."

"Do you think we'll go to war?"

"Perhaps. God help us if we do." Bristo stared over the sea.

Morgan doubted God had much to do with men's wars.

"If war does break out, I hope to become a privateer." The captain's brows rose. "Say you'll join me, Morgan."

At his invitation, a thrill stabbed Morgan, injecting him with life. He would love nothing more than to sail the seas, preying on British merchantmen in defense of his country. Finally his life would have purpose and meaning! And with Adalia waiting for him at home, his happiness would be complete. But there he went again, allowing his dreams to get the better of him. His momentary joy quickly dissolved in light of the impossibility of the first and improbability of the second. He stared at the glittering azure waters, anywhere but into the confident, determined gaze of the man he most admired in the world. "You know I can't."

"I know you choose not to." His voice brimmed with disapproval. "And what of this lady? If I remember, she's a commoner. Would your parents accept her as a suitable wife?"

"I don't know." But of course he did. They most certainly would not. Morgan clenched his jaw, angry at the change in topic. Angry at himself for his weakness. Angry at God for teasing him with the vision of a life and a woman he could never have.

The brig dove into the trough of a wave, sending foam over her bow and showering Morgan with salty spray.

Captain Bristo looked at Morgan with concern. Not condemnation. Never condemnation from this man. "Until you find out whether your parents will approve and until you decide what you would forsake to be with her, perhaps you should not toy with her affections."

Morgan shook the droplets from his face and frowned. He'd been so intent on capturing Adalia's heart, he hadn't thought about what he'd do after he obtained it. Normally, after a lady gave herself to him, he would grow quickly bored and move on to the next conquest. Though he'd never once thought that was possible with Adalia, he'd also never given much thought to what their future held. A philosophy by which he normally led his life. Always rushing into things, basing decisions on his feelings with no thought of consequences. Like sailing.

Yet perhaps that frivolous way of life would no longer do. At least not when it came to Adalia. For the first time in Morgan's remembrance, it mattered to him what a lady felt. It mattered to him that she never be hurt.

With a slap on the back, Captain Bristo marched away, shouting orders to the crew. Morgan hung his head, staring at the foamy, inverted V the bow sliced through the blue water. He pondered Captain Bristo's words. He pondered the course of his own life, but most importantly he pondered the biggest question of all.

If he continued his pursuit of Adalia and things turned out as he hoped, would he be willing to give up everything to be with her?

ॐ

Kneeling on an old kitchen rag before her garden, Adalia poked another tiny hole in the dirt then set the spade aside. She adjusted her bonnet to better shade her face against a noon sun that warmed both her back and the rich soil with a promise of spring.

"Joy?" She held out her hand, palm up. "The chamomile please?"

Joy knelt beside her and placed the tiny seeds in her hand. Adalia smiled at her maid before she scattered them in the holes dotting the freshly turned soil. After covering them with dirt, she brushed her hands and surveyed her garden. The smell of rich earth and dogwoods filled her nose. "Now, the sage, if you please."

Joy held out a handful that looked more like tiny gnats than seeds. "You sure know what yer doin', miss, for a white lady."

Adalia smiled. "My mother grew herbs and vegetables every year." She dumped the seeds into the divots, remembering how the scent of rosemary, sage, peppermint, eucalyptus, and basil had combined in an ethereal perfume that swept through their brick home. The memory of those scents brought Morgan to mind, though his scent was more spice and salt.

Drat! Why was she thinking of him again? Though he'd been gone for two days, his kiss still lingered on her lips, taunting her, pleasing her. And condemning her. She shouldn't have allowed him such liberties. What he must think of her! What she thought of herself. After Sir Walter, she had vowed never to allow any man to touch her again, let alone kiss her. But Morgan's kiss had been so different. So unexpected in its tenderness and affection. Her body did not tighten in alarm. She did not cower in disgust at his passion. Quite the opposite, in fact.

It both shamed and elated her. Nevertheless, after a long night of repenting before God, she decided to inform Mr. Rutledge that such favors would not be offered again.

Not unless they were properly courting.

Surely that wasn't even a possibility! From the way his father had treated her, he would never agree to such a match for his son. Unless. . . dare she entertain a speck of hope from society's recent acceptance of her? A fly buzzed about her head, and she batted it away. And her fanciful thoughts with it. Thoughts she must not entertain. Dreams she must not allow to grow. Dreams led to hopes, and hopes led to disappointments.

She would maintain a friendship with Mr. Rutledge. A friendship and nothing else.

She leaned over to cover the seeds when a bundle of tawny fur tumbled onto the dirt, halting on all fours as if frozen beneath a predator's gaze. "Oh, M, not my garden," Adalia whined, but before she could grab him, the rambunctious kitten began digging in the spot where she'd just planted the chamomile. "Stop that, you little imp!" She pounced on him, but he slipped away, her palms thumping the dirt.

Joy giggled.

Adalia jumped to her feet. Wiping her hands on her apron, she surveyed the yard. Rustling sounded from a shrub to her right. She crept toward it. "Come here this instant, you little minx!" Just as she reached the bush, M sprang from the leaves, bounding toward her. She leapt for the wayward kitty, but her hands met air as the feline darted past.

A man's groan filled the air. "Of all the—!"

Joy's laughter faded.

Adalia knew before she turned what she would see.

Doctor Willaby with paw prints of mud running up his trousers, over his coat, and a look of censure lining his face. And M, licking his paws, sitting on the branch of a hickory tree behind him.

Adalia threw her hands to her mouth. "My apologies, Doctor. He got away from me."

"I am a man of great patience, Miss Winston." The doctor examined his soiled attire, then began brushing the spots, finally giving up when he saw that he was making the stains worse. "But I am not a man of *infinite* patience. If you are to keep this beast, you are to contain him." Though he frowned, a smile peeked from the corner of his mouth.

Joy rose, lowering her gaze to the ground.

"Yes, sir. Forgive me. I promise to do better," Adalia said.

M dove from the tree and slunk around her ankles. Adalia picked him up, cradling him against her chest. "Thank you for allowing me to plant an herb garden, Doctor."

The hint of a smile forced its way to his lips. "Oh, I nearly forgot. Miss Emerald Middleton is here to see you."

Adalia must have heard incorrectly. "Miss Emerald?"

"She's a lovely lady from a good family. A churchgoing family," Doc Willaby added. "It's good to see you making such friends."

Friends. She would hardly call Emerald that. Even so, the man's criteria for social approval seemed somewhat jaded. Morgan was a far more honorable, generous person than Miss Emerald. Wasn't he? Suddenly she found herself questioning her own judgment. What did she know about such things when she'd been locked up as a slave for seven years?

The doctor turned to leave. "Very well, then. I best go attend to my attire."

Joy exchanged a tremulous look with Adalia.

Drawing M to her cheek, Adalia snuggled against his soft fur. "You're just like your owner. Wild, impetuous, and naughty." The thought sent renewed warmth through her, and she handed the kitten to Joy with a huff. She needed no reminders of Mr. Rutledge. "Can you please put M in my chamber, Joy? We'll finish the garden tomorrow."

"Yes, miss."

A moment later, Adalia entered the sitting room, suddenly realizing, in light of Miss Emerald's impeccable appearance, that she too should have changed her attire. She dared a glance at the dirt stuck beneath her fingernails and staining her sleeves. Quickly she clasped her hands behind her back.

Miss Emerald's lips slanted. "Oh, my, my, my, this will never do." She shook her head, scanning Adalia from head to toe.

Only moments before, frolicking in the garden, Adalia had felt alive like a fresh sprout in spring. Now, beneath this woman's perusal, she wilted like a flower in the bright sun. "What a pleasure to see you, Emerald. Shall I have some tea brought in?"

"Tea? Oh no, dear. I don't intend to stay." She glanced around the room as if spending any more time in the place would somehow corrupt her. Sashaying to the window, she eased aside the curtains and gazed down into the garden.

Adalia forced down her annoyance. "What may I do for you, Miss Emerald?"

"For me?" Emerald laid a gloved hand on her chest as a grin rounded her painted lips. "I believe the question is what may I do for you?"

"I don't understand."

"I know we got off to a rather"—she hesitated—"disagreeable start. I am sorry for that. Morgan considers you a friend, which makes you my friend as well." Though the ice hardening in her eyes told a different story. "And as my first act of friendship, I thought how fun it would be to go shopping. For a proper gown, of course. Now that you're part of society, you must look the part, don't you agree?"

Adalia clenched her fists behind her back. How dare the woman intrude upon something so personal? Was she truly trying to befriend Adalia or bring attention to the fact that Adalia would always be in a class far beneath Morgan?

Emerald tilted her head, sending one of her snowy curls dangling over her neck. "Besides, you don't want to embarrass Morgan, now, do you?"

Adalia hadn't considered that. Did she shame him with her common attire? Horrified at the thought, she wasn't sure quite how to respond.

Emerald raised her cultured brows and released a sigh. Golden sunlight swirled around her, making her appear like a dazzling ivory statue.

And Adalia paled by comparison.

She did have some money saved. And she had been thinking of buying a new gown anyway. What harm would it do to allow someone as refined as Emerald to assist her? Before she knew it, she had accepted the woman's help.

Two hours later, after purchasing yards of magenta silk and streams of lace from the drapers, Adalia stood before a massive dressing mirror at the tailors waiting to be measured. Emerald, who'd been nothing but courteous and chatty since they'd left the doctor's, stood off to the side, examining a wardrobe full of the latest fashions from Paris. Adalia could not fathom the change in the lady. Though Emerald had offered Adalia a modicum of kindness at the theater, her sudden interest put Adalia's suspicions on full alert. Yet, as the afternoon waned and Adalia could think of no malicious motive for Emerald's behavior, she'd asked God's forgiveness for her uncharitable thoughts and responded to Emerald's kindness, excited about the new friendship.

A young woman entered the back room, measuring tape in hand. "Now, Miss Winston, if you'll remove your skirts and petticoats, I'll measure you for your new gown."

Adalia's heart crammed in her throat. They would see the scars on her back. Why hadn't she thought of that? How could she explain what were obviously stripes from a whip? "Can you measure it through my gown?"

"Don't be ridiculous, dear." Emerald approached and began unbuttoning Adalia's dress from behind. "Such modesty." She clucked her tongue.

"That isn't necessary, really." Adalia attempted to extricate herself from the flurry of hands, tugging, untying, and loosening, but before she knew it, she had been stripped down to stays and chemise. Jerking away from their prying fingers, she swerved about, frantically tearing pins from her hair and allowing her ebony curls to tumble down her back in an effort to hide her shame.

The tailor's assistant fumbled with her gown and petticoats as if she hadn't seen a thing out of the ordinary.

But not Emerald. Instead of shock, instead of pity, instead of concern, the woman's blue eyes sparked with malicious delight.

CHAPTER FIFTEEN

Snipping off one last Peacock flower, Adalia laid it atop the others in her basket and glanced across the Miles Plantation. She breathed in the moist air fragranced with hibiscus and gardenia and lifted her face to the sun. Sir Walter so rarely allowed her outside that when he'd asked her to collect flowers for the front parlor, she'd not hesitated to obey. He hadn't even shackled her ankles as he always did when she left the house.

Not shackled her ankles?

She glanced down at her bare toes, peeking out from beneath her skirts, and took an oversized step forward. Nothing restricted her movement. A daring, wonderful, incredible thought sped through her mind. She surveyed the sugar fields, empty of workers in the noonday heat. She was all alone. No one watched her. No foreman or footman or master was in sight. And Sir Walter was probably napping in his favorite wicker lounge on the veranda as he always did when the heat became oppressive.

Heart throbbing, she inched past the smokehouse, then the tool shed, past the vegetable garden, pushed through some thickets until there was nothing but open field between her and the stone wall marking the boundary of her prison. Thankfully, some of the sugarcane had been recently harvested, leaving an open stretch of ground. Clutching her skirts, she bolted across the field, her feet slapping the mud. Spears of severed stalks cut into her skin. But she didn't care.

The wall grew closer, each stone more defined in her bouncing vision, empowering her legs and hailing her with freedom's call. Sweat streamed down her back. Her lungs crashed against her ribs. Could she make it?

Then the thump of horses' hooves drummed in her ears. She glanced over her shoulder to see Sir Walter atop his favorite steed, a maniacal look of joy on his face as if he'd expected her to run. In his hand, he gripped a long, coiled rope.

She faced forward, alarm choking her. She stumbled on a rock. Landed facedown in the dirt. Got up and darted off again.

"You can't escape me, my pet. Never!" His laughter stabbed her back, bringing tears to her eyes.

Thick, braided hemp cinched around her chest, jerking her backward and slamming her to the ground.

Sir Walter's face hovered above her, shadowed by a halo of sunlight. Hoisting her to her feet, he dragged her behind his horse like a prisoner of war. Then tying her to a tree, he tore the gown from her back as the vacant eyes of slaves and servants looked on, forced to watch.

The crack of the whip. *Thwack!* Sir Walter's deranged laughter. Pain like a thousand hot knives scored her skin.

Crack!

Searing heat. Her legs staggering.

Thwack!

Adalia jerked upright in her bed, a cry on her lips. She gulped for air. Shapes formed in the darkness, her dressing bureau, desk, wardrobe. She was in her bedchamber at Doctor Willaby's.

Not on Sir Walter's plantation.

Not in the room where he had taken her after the whipping. Where he had rubbed salve on her wounds and told her the lashing was for her own good. That he hadn't wanted to punish her. That he was sorry for her pain. That she must face the fact that she was his forever.

Before he made it so with his body.

Shoving aside her coverlet, Adalia flew to the corner and vomited in her chamber pot. She wiped her mouth and dropped to the floor in a heap, sobbing.

M nudged her leg. "Me-ow."

Adalia placed him in her lap and stroked his fur. "I'm sorry, M. I'll be all right. Just a bad dream." He crawled up her arm to his favorite spot on her neck, where he nestled against her cheek. A shaft of moonlight drifted over her from the window. Grabbing M, she cradled him in her arms while she allowed the milky glow to bathe her, wishing it would wash away her memories.

"Thank You, Lord, for delivering me from Sir Walter. But I still bear the shame. The scars. Inside and out." She hung her head as tears filled her eyes.

By My stripes you are healed.

The soft words twirled around her atop wisps of silver light. Adalia batted away a tear. Yes, indeed. How could she have forgotten? Her Lord was also whipped. Scourged beyond recognition. And all for her. Somehow, it made her feel closer to Him.

I bore your shame.

Adalia nodded. "But it still remains, Lord." It clung to her in the pink tracks on her back—stigmas of disgrace. Forever marking her as a slave, as less than human. And now, Miss Emerald had seen them as well. No doubt she would tell Morgan.

Adalia could already hear the first strike of the clock at midnight, could already feel the fairy tale dissolving around her. She supposed it was for the best. But oh, how she had loved being treated like a princess! How she loved being swept into a world that until now had only existed in her dreams. Accepted, valued, adored.

Not rejected, scorned, and hated.

M swiped at the ribbon hanging from her nightdress, caught it in his paw, and began gnawing on it. Drawing him to her face, Adalia kissed his wet nose. "You'll always love me, won't you, M? No matter what my race or pedigree?" M responded by nuzzling his face against hers. She took that as a yes. A wonderful yes that helped soothe her sorrow. Too bad the furry scamp reminded her so much of Morgan. For if the truth came out, Adalia must put Morgan out of her thoughts. And her heart. Rising, she sat on her bed and opened her Bible for her morning reading. "Lord, please help me to forget. Help me to be content with the wonderful freedom, the wonderful life, You have given me."

⁊

Morgan closed his eyes, wishing the woman away. Wishing he could close his ears as easily.

"You don't believe me?" Emerald's voice was incredulous.

Morgan gripped the bridge of his nose and glanced over the race track, an oval of sun-bleached sand surrounding a manicured plot of grass. A few yards away stood the massive wooden grandstand in which Charleston society fluttered like a flock of caged birds. Indeed, they cackled and prattled much like birds, some reclining on cushioned chairs, others prancing about in anticipation of the race. Plumes fluttering atop both the men's and ladies' hats only confirmed Morgan's assessment. A bevy of servants and slaves scrambled to the refreshment booths and tables outside the course where they retrieved all manner of drinks, liquors, cakes, sweets, and even mock turtle soup for their masters. A live band to the right of the stand regaled them with spirited tunes. His gaze landed on Adalia sitting up front beside Drayton and Hadley.

"No, I do not believe you." He speared Emerald with his gaze.

She pursed her lips, a red hue rising over the creamy skin of her neck. "Why would I lie about such a thing?" She stamped her shoe onto the dirt and adjusted her parasol. "She had whip marks on her back. I tell you. Whip marks!" Her chest rose and fell beneath her lacy fichu like an angry bellows. "Which can only mean that Miss Winston has been whipped."

"Your deductive reasoning is impeccable." Yet even as Morgan joked, he cringed at the thought of anyone hurting Adalia. "Only slaves and criminals are whipped."

"Precisely."

"So since she clearly isn't Negro, you're saying she's an outlaw?" he all but growled.

"She is hiding something. I know it."

Morgan raked a hand through his hair. "This jealousy is beneath you, Emerald. Most unbecoming."

The creamy skin of her face erupted in blotches of maroon. "Then ask her yourself! If she is such a saint, surely she will not lie."

"I will not dishonor her with such a ridiculous question. I'll hear no more of it." Before enduring Emerald's angry retort, he swung on his heels and made his way to the grandstand. Her groan followed him. As did the patter of her shoes. Whipped, indeed. Surely a woman as resourceful as Emerald Middleton could come up with a better accusation. Ludicrous! Adalia may be a commoner, but she had come from a good family, an honorable farming family in Jamaica.

Whinnies and neighs brought his gaze to the horses approaching the starting line. The animals snorted and pawed the sand, barely able to restrain their energy. His jaw stiffened beneath his own mounting tension. How dare Emerald make such a scathing allegation? If she were a man he'd call her out to a duel immediately. As it was, he had to contain himself with the reins of propriety, much like the thoroughbreds were being restrained now before the race.

Morgan mounted the steps into the shade of the grandstand and took a seat beside Adalia, instantly rewarded with her smile. She'd seemed a bit uneasy when he'd appeared at the doctor's to escort her to the races—even shocked. But thankfully, she had settled into her usual joyful, awed appraisal of everything around her.

She sipped her cool tea and lowered her gaze, fingering the tassel of a gold cord wrapped about the waist of her sprigged muslin gown—a gown he had not seen before, a gown that opened down the front to show a lacy petticoat beneath. And though he had seen a thousand petticoats before, the sight of hers sent a heated cyclone through him. A welcoming breeze danced through the ebony curls at her neck, and he longed to run his finger through one. Instead, he leaned forward, elbows on his knees, and clutched his hands together, hoping the spring air would cool his passion.

Mr. and Mrs. Richard Singleton passed in front of them. "Good day to you, Morgan, Miss Winston." Morgan returned their greeting as Adalia nodded with a smile. Though some people remained at a distance, several had greeted her as if she were one of them. Their acceptance of her warmed him. If only Morgan could convince his father of the same.

Shouting from the commoners crowding the other side of the track drew Adalia's gaze. "Why must they endure the hot sun while we sit in the shade? They don't even have chairs or refreshments." Her voice edged with concern and bewilderment.

Morgan rubbed his chin, astounded by her question. Astounded that he'd never considered the why of such a thing. He shrugged. "That rabble? They are tradesmen, dockworkers, merchants. Where should they sit? Certainly not here with us."

She looked at him as if he'd told her to throw herself on the track to be trampled beneath the horses.

Horses that now charged forward as the crack of a pistol split the air. Hadley pushed to his feet, glass of wine in hand. No doubt he'd placed a large sum on one of the thoroughbreds. Drayton set his glass on a passing servant's tray and grabbed another one. Emerald swept past Morgan, chin in the air, and took a spot beside Hadley.

The band's tune ceased in mid-note as cheers broke from the crowd on both sides of the track. Thankfully, the excitement drew Adalia's attention to the race, instead of remaining on Morgan's blunder. Setting her glass down on the table, she slid to the edge of her seat, her eyes sparkling like glistening onyx as they followed the horses around the track.

"I am one of your so-called rabble," she said without facing him.

Morgan cringed. "I meant no disrespect. It is simply the way of things. I have good friends who are tradesmen."

The horses sped past again, their hooves thundering, showering the onlookers with dust and the smell of horse flesh. Ladies plucked out their fans while gentlemen shouted encouragements to their favorite riders.

"Indeed?" She arched a brow of disbelief. "Who?"

Morgan huffed. Well, perhaps only one friend. "A merchantman. Captain Kane Bristo. He's like a father to me." Even as he said it, he wondered why he'd disclosed something that he had never told anyone else.

"A merchantman? So, there is more to Morgan Rutledge than you have let on. You must tell me about him sometime."

She looked at him with such coy delight, he was sorry he hadn't told her before.

"Regardless, Morgan"—oh, how he loved hearing his given name on her lips—"all men, and women I might add, are created equal in God's eyes, regardless of class, wealth, or education. Or color," she added emphatically.

"Perhaps in God's eyes. But not in society's."

"Which means society dares to defy God's design and His love for all people."

Love? Morgan coughed into his hand as he muffled a snort. He'd always pictured God much like his father, a cruel overlord whom he could never please. "Or perhaps God's love is not strong enough to restrain the strictures of society."

She gave him such a look of disapproval he feared he'd stepped beyond the boundaries of her tolerance. But then her lips lifted on one side. "What am I to do with you, Morgan Rutledge?"

He leaned toward her, her rosemary scent sweeping away the odor of horses and perfume. "I have some ideas if you'd care to hear them."

She must have sensed his intention, for she turned her face away. She was right, of course. He could expect no further affection from a woman like Adalia without an understanding between them. And though his heart ached to initiate a formal courtship, Morgan could make no promises without his father's approval.

An approval he needed to maintain his current style of living. An approval he must obtain before his heart was so firmly anchored to

Adalia's, that he would never survive being wrenched from her.

He glanced across the field at the boisterous men, women, and children in tattered garb standing in the hot sun. He had never known anything but privilege. He'd never known want. He'd never had to worry about food or attire or shelter. The town mayor, members of the council, even visiting senators from Columbia tipped their hat at him on the street. And why? Simply because his family had money. Prestige.

Despite his boredom with it all, he could not imagine how much worse his life would be without the privileges of his class. Better to be bored in luxury than bored in poverty. Though he wouldn't be bored as a merchantman... But he might be poor, he reminded himself, for how could he be assured of success at sea? What if he couldn't earn enough to keep his ship? Then what would he do? Beg on the street?

৵

Adalia watched the horses as they thundered past again. She'd never seen animals so magnificent, so fast!

"They have one more lap until the end of the first heat," Morgan said, snapping his fingers at a passing slave and ordering a lemonade. The boy darted off toward the refreshment booths.

Adalia stared after him. He could be no more than twelve, the age when she'd become a slave. In fact, at the first sight of all the slaves serving the crowd, Adalia had almost spun about and told Morgan she'd find her way back to the doctor's house alone. But that wouldn't do anyone any good. The slaves would still be here, and she would have missed out on her last afternoon with Morgan. For, from the disdainful looks Miss Emerald cast her way, Adalia had no doubt that the woman planned to inform Morgan of Adalia's scars. What was she waiting for? To accuse Adalia in front of all of Charleston society? Yet, unless she were to strip Adalia in public, Emerald could provide no proof of the scars and, even then, no proof of their origin. Though the mere unveiling would ban Adalia from society.

Adalia sighed. Still it was inevitable. But would Morgan believe Miss Emerald? She had been a loyal friend to him for years. Of course he would. Oh, it was all too much to consider! Adalia clasped her gloved hands in her lap so her trembling would not be obvious. She could handle being ostracized from society. But she doubted she could handle the look of scorn that would surely fill Morgan's face. A face that now gazed upon her with a depth, a growing bond, an affection that clawed at her heart, knowing its eventual demise.

Earlier in the day, Adalia had all but resolved that she would not be attending the races—that Morgan had learned of her stripes and come to a conclusion that forbade any further association. So she was surprised and delighted when he appeared in the doorway looking as dapper and handsome as ever! How could she resist one last outing with such a man? One last chance to speak to him of God and the evils of slavery.

"What is a heat?" she asked him by way of sweeping away the morbid gloom that had consumed her thoughts.

"A set of specific races in a series." He pointed with his glass at the horses who darted across the finish line. "These horses are racing two four-mile heats," he yelled over the din of cheers and curses at the outcome.

The boy brought Morgan's lemonade and then stood before Adalia, eyes lowered, as if waiting for her to ask for something. She grabbed his arm, making him jump. "You need get nothing for me that I cannot get myself." Placing a finger beneath his chin, she raised his gaze to hers and smiled. Eyes darting to Morgan as if expecting punishment, the boy bowed and dashed away.

When she faced Morgan, he stared at her as if she'd sprouted the wings of an angel. Finally, he stood and held out his hand. "Would you care for a stroll, milady, while they prepare the horses for the next heat?"

As they wandered through the crowd mobbing the track, Adalia was quite taken in by the variety of entertainments available. Jugglers; a colorful bird that reminded her of those on Barbados that sang hymns perfectly; public auctions; tables filled with all manner of luxury items all for sale: jewelry glittering in the sun, vases, figurines, snuff boxes, canes, even hats and bonnets. Beneath one large tent, magnificent horses were being sold—thoroughbreds recently imported from England, Morgan had told her. Several gentlemen in top hats gathered around to place their bids.

Adalia stopped at a small corral where a huge pig, aptly named "Learned Pig" performed tricks such as grunting yes and no when asked questions put to him by the audience, tapping out answers to arithmetic problems on a fence post, and rolling over in the mud on cue. She couldn't contain her giggles as they wandered away.

"Even a pig delights you." Morgan placed her arm in his, his eyes aglow with admiration.

"Why, of course. I've never seen such a thing as a learned pig." She laughed. "What an enjoyable afternoon."

Morgan squinted over the track, the crush of people, the wares and refreshments for sale. "I suppose. I have no idea why it hasn't the same effect on me."

"Because you're accustomed to it. You expect it."

"It is all I've known, my father's world."

"But is it yours?" Adalia bit her lip. "Is it the world God has for you, the life God has for you?"

He frowned, his boots stirring up dust with each thump on the ground. "God has for me? Ah, Miss Winston, God has nothing for me. Nor do I believe He notices me at all. If He did, I doubt He'd be too pleased with what He found. But you, on the other hand, you are worthy of His attention."

"You do not know Him. He is no respecter of class like. . ." She hesitated.

"Like I am?"

She smiled. "He loves both poor and rich, slave and free, privileged and destitute, and He has a plan for each if they'd but give their lives to Him."

"I give no one, man or God, my life, Miss Winston. If I'm going to make a mess of things, I'd rather own up to it myself."

"But God is nothing—"

"Come, the last heat is about to begin." He tugged on her, cutting off further conversation and leaving Adalia feeling sorrowful, despite the joyous day. At the grandstand, they stepped over a snoring Drayton and took their seats.

The horses whizzed past, but Adalia could no longer focus on them. She felt time slipping from her, stripping away the fripperies of her charade, sweeping away the opulence and gaiety surrounding her. She glanced at Miss Emerald sitting beside Hadley. The spite in her icy stare sent a shiver down Adalia before the lady pasted on a smile. Adalia faced forward. What had she ever done to her? But then again, what had she ever done to Sir Walter, save be tainted with the blood of a Negro?

Soon, the race ended. Hadley cursed and stamped off. Drayton woke up from his drunken stupor, and Emerald glared at Adalia before she pranced away.

Ladies clapped. Men cheered, while others growled. The chink of money and flap of notes filled the tent as the band blasted a jaunty tune. But all the noise faded into the background as Morgan led Adalia down the stairs and onto the track. She smiled and greeted those around her with as much poise and style as she could, trying to enjoy every last minute she had with Morgan—every last minute she played the princess in this fairy-tale charade. Before Miss Emerald revealed her secret and this bourgeois pack turned on her like hungry wolves.

❦

"Whatever has you in such a foul humor, Emerald?" Hadley sipped his drink. "At least I have a good reason for my despair. I just lost twenty dollars."

"You can afford it, Hadley." Emerald snapped. "What I can't afford is your brother's growing infatuation with that bedeviled harridan." She stared at the couple as they sauntered across the track, arms entwined.

"I told you he wouldn't believe you about the scars. Not sure I even believe you."

"You Rutledge men. Blinded insensible by a beautiful woman."

He kissed her cheek. "If you are referring to yourself, I have indeed lost all reason."

She batted him way. "Don't. People will think we are courting."

"An atrocious prospect."

Emerald waved her fan about her face, fluttering her curls over her neck and cooling the sudden heat rising on the tide of her anger. She would not lose Morgan to that base strumpet. She would not!

Hadley sipped his drink then glanced over his shoulder and leaned toward her. "I have the solution to your problem, my dear."

Emerald released a sigh, bracing herself for another of Hadley's amorous proposals. "Unless it's to rip her gown from her back so everyone can see her scars, I can't imagine what we could do."

"Nothing quite that crude, I assure you."

She studied him, noting the malicious glaze covering his eyes. "Why would you help me, anyway? You want me for yourself."

"That I do, my dear. It pleases me you have noticed."

"I'd be a fool not to, Hadley. But I've told you, I've set my sights on Morgan. I must have him."

"And I want your happiness, Emerald. It is all I want, even if it means losing you." He kissed her hand. "Perhaps someday you will see that it is I, not Morgan, who loves you."

Emerald met his eyes, shocked by the sincerity in his tone, shocked more by the longing in his eyes. "Hadley Rutledge, putting someone else ahead of his own interest, it is too much to believe." She tugged her hand from his with a chuckle. "But of course, could it also be that you don't wish your brother to marry a commoner."

"That is true. It would ruin our family name." Disappointment flattened his voice.

"Now, what is this scheme of yours?" Emerald prodded, desperate to change the subject.

"Part of my brother's foolish attraction to this woman is that he lifts her up as some pristine goddess. If he should discover that she, shall we say, has less than scrupulous morals, or perhaps a sordid past? I have no doubt it would dissuade him from further advances."

Emerald's rising hope crumbled. "And if Morgan should discover that we are prying into her past or meddling in her affairs, he will hate me. Besides, apparently her morals are impeccable. And her past naught but dull and uneventful."

"We don't know that for sure. But I know someone who has connections and who would be happy to find out." He gestured behind him where Fabian Saville was leaning on a post, glaring after Morgan and Miss Winston with even more malevolence than Emerald had been.

"I do believe our dainty friend, Fabian, would do just about anything we asked, as long as it did Morgan harm."

Emerald felt her first smile of the day begin to creep over her lips.

Chapter Sixteen

A breeze whipped up from Charleston Bay, fluttering Adalia's hat ribbons beneath her chin. They tickled her neck as the scent of fresh fish, salt, and sodden wood filled her lungs. A bell rang, accompanied by the lap of waves against pilings and the clamor of voices: peddlers hawking their wares, dock workers, customs officials, merchants, and servants hustling to purchase supplies before the heat of the day made their errands unpleasant. Halting, Adalia squinted against the rising sun and gazed over the glittering waters of the bay where a ship had just arrived. Joy slipped beside her, carrying the wrapped bundle of fresh cod Doc Willaby had sent them to purchase.

"Do you know that ship, miss?" the maid asked.

Adalia shook her head. "No, but it reminds me of a ship I sailed on once." The ship that had saved her from Sir Walter and brought her to freedom in Charleston. And even though she'd suffered from *mal de mer* most of the voyage, the sea would always hold a special place in her heart. With its fathomless depths and ever-turbulent waters, it formed a shark-infested moat between her and her past. Between her and Sir Walter. For a brief moment Adalia wondered what the vile man was doing. Had he accepted that she was gone? Was he looking for her, or had he moved on to his next victim?

Her insides clenched at the thought.

Commands aboard the ship sent the anchor crashing into the bay as sailors scrambled to lower a boat. A fisherman passed by, tipping his hat in her direction.

Clutching her reticule, she turned and continued down Bay Street, wishing all her memories of Sir Walter, of her past, would remain on the other side of that moat. A tremble ran through her. From the chilly morning or thoughts of Sir Walter, she didn't know which.

Shifting her thoughts to more pleasant things, Adalia allowed her excitement to rise for the coming evening. "I must stop at the tailors before we head home."

"Another gown, miss?" Joy's dark eyes were playful.

Adalia chuckled. "Yes, apparently, it is quite the breach of etiquette to wear the same gown to more than one event."

"Seems a waste to me, havin' all those gowns." Joy glanced down at her own gray skirt, the hem of which frayed like jagged teeth.

Shame struck Adalia. How thoughtless she had been. Only three months ago, she possessed only one gown, not much better than Joy's. Truly, God had blessed her. Though why, she could not imagine. She wove her arm through her maid's as they darted across the bustling road and headed down Market Street. "Perhaps we shall have you fitted for a new gown someday."

"What do I need a new gown for, miss?" Joy smiled, not an ounce of envy tainting her voice.

Along Market Street, doors of shops flung open, anticipating the day's business while vendors set up displays to lure people inside. Soon the cobblestone street grew abuzz with servants, slaves, tradesmen, and workers. High society wouldn't be out and about for hours. Even though Adalia had spent two months in their company, she still felt more comfortable among these commoners. Joy let out a dreamy sigh. "It must be excitin' to attend all them parties and balls."

"Indeed, it is." Comfortable or not, Adalia was having the time of her life. "Morgan, I mean Mr. Rutledge, is escorting me to an orchestra concert tonight at Dillon's Inn." Last week she'd enjoyed the horse races. This week, she'd already attended dinner at the Sign of Bacchus and a ball at the Rhetts' estate. Fond memories of each event brought a smile to her lips even as a pinch of unease slithered through her. She'd fully expected never to see Morgan again after the horse races, but apparently Miss Emerald decided not to tell him about Adalia's scars. Perhaps the woman possessed some kindness after all.

And of course, Adalia was thrilled to accept all of Morgan's subsequent invitations. Each moment with him gave her more opportunity to discuss God and slavery, not to mention feed her hope for a possible courtship should his parents agree. Oh, to think it might be possible! Could God perform such a miracle?

As Adalia allowed her heart to soar at the thought, Joy's face folded in a frown. The young girl stumbled over the uneven ground. "I thought we were helping at the orphanage tonight."

Adalia's steps grew heavy. They passed the open door of an inn, where the scent of fresh baked bread and buttery grits made her stomach grumble. How could she have forgotten the orphanage? She'd never forgotten those precious children. But she'd promised Morgan. He'd been so gallant and kind and attentive the past week, how could she resist?

"We shall go to the orphanage tomorrow," she said curtly, forcing down her guilt.

Joy gave a weak smile in reply. "I guess I don't blame you, miss. Mr. Rutledge is a fine-lookin' man. An' wealthy too. You must feel like a queen."

A wagon filled with sacks of rice clanked over the cobblestones, rattling Adalia's conscience. Queen? Or intruder? One of the Charleston elite or a black slave? How long could she hide the truth? How long before everyone saw through her disguise? And why did it matter so much what these people thought of her? Taking Joy's arm, Adalia led the way across the street, side-stepping a fresh pile of horse droppings.

Covering a yawn, she hurried past the mercantile and boot maker's shop, turning down Meeting Street. Coming home late on multiple nights this week had not afforded her the rest she needed, particularly when she had to rise early to accompany the doctor on his rounds. She could certainly see why the Charleston gentry did not have time or energy to labor during the day. Their nightly soirées were both time consuming and exhausting. So much so that Adalia found herself longing to be free of employment, longing to have the luxury of time that wealth afforded. But that was ludicrous. She should be thankful for the lodging and position God had provided for her with Dr. Willaby.

As they approached the Bank of Charleston, a modishly attired gentleman emerged from the door, his back to them, and headed to his right in quite a hurry. A pouch fell from within his black coat, dropping to the cobblestones with a heavy clank. Yet, he continued onward, oblivious that he'd lost something. Stooping, Adalia picked it up, loosened the strings, and peeked inside. Sunlight glinted off more gold coins than she'd seen in a lifetime.

Joy's jaw dropped. "Oh, miss. It's a fortune."

"Sir!" Adalia shouted after the man, but he darted across the street without a glance behind him.

"That would buy a hundred gowns. An' fine jewelry too." Joy voiced the thoughts shouting in Adalia's head. Yet still the man strutted down the street, completely unaware of what he'd lost.

Joy glanced after him. "He looks to have more 'an enough, miss."

"It doesn't matter, Joy. It isn't our money." Adalia would not entertain another second of dreaming about what these coins would buy her. She had never stolen anything in her life, and she wasn't going to start now.

"Follow me," she ordered as she gathered her skirts and wove through the carriages, horses and people now crowding the street. Two blocks away, she spotted the gentleman and made a dash to catch him before he disappeared again. Finally her touch on his arm turned him around.

"Oh, Mr. Saville. I didn't realize it was you." Startled for a moment, Adalia merely stared at him.

"Miss Winston, we meet again." The smile he gave her bore none of the charm it had when he'd approached her at the playhouse.

"You dropped this, sir." Adalia handed him the pouch, her voice clipped as she caught her breath. Joy rushed up to them, halted, but stepped back beneath the man's imperious gray eyes.

A flash of disappointment, maybe even disgust, rolled across his face before he took the pouch. "Such honesty, miss. How can I ever thank you?"

Yet Adalia got the impression the man harbored anything but gratitude.

"No need. Good day to you, Mr. Saville." She swerved about, clutched Joy's arm, and hurried down the street, away from the odd man with the stormy eyes—eyes that reminded her too much of Sir Walter's.

One glance over her shoulder told her he remained in place staring her way. Shrugging off the eerie feeling, she rounded a corner. Up ahead, Adalia spotted Mr. McCalla, the mayor, his wife on his arm. Tugging from Joy's grasp, Adalia continued onward, stepping in front of her maid. It wouldn't do for the couple to see her servant walking beside her in such a familiar manner. Her acceptance into society was tenuous at best. She had appearances to maintain if she were to ingratiate herself further. For Morgan's sake, of course.

"Good day, Miss Winston." The mayor tipped his top hat in her direction. His wife smiled as they sauntered past. Their acknowledgment landed on Adalia shoulders like an inaugural cloak of acceptance as she made her way forward. It wasn't until she entered the tailor's that she remembered Joy. Turning, she found the girl waiting outside the shop, her chin lowered. Adalia's heart shriveled. Chastising herself for her thoughtlessness, she went and stood before her maid. No, not her maid, her friend. "I'm so sorry, Joy." She laid a hand on the girl's arm. "Can you ever forgive me?"

Joy flashed her a pained look. "I understand, miss. I knows my place."

"Your place is beside me. We are friends. I honestly don't know what came over me." She'd never cared about what others had thought of her before. Shame and remorse stripped away her ill-fitting cloak as she silently repented of her behavior. "Now come, let's have a look at my new gown." Looping an arm through Joy's, they entered the shop together.

❧

Leaning back into the upholstered Queen Anne chair—one of four that circled the small table at Dillon's Inn—Adalia listened to the orchestra play Beethoven's Second Symphony. She'd never heard such mellifluous harmony before. Not even at the balls she'd thus far attended. The pleasant sound flowed from a full band—complete with percussion, brass, woodwinds, and strings—perched on a dais at the far end of a large oblong room dotted with tables and chairs. Light from several lamps and sconces flickered over the scene, dancing in harmony with the music.

Closing her eyes, Adalia attempted to drown out the muffled whispers of the Charleston haut ton, including Emerald and Caroline, who sat at the table with her, and tune her ears to the delicate peaks and plummeting valleys of notes that sent her on a pleasant voyage to a distant world. A world without cruelty and class and slavery. She was almost at the gate of that distant haven when a man's voice jerked her back to reality.

"We meet again, miss."

Not Morgan's voice. He had gone with Drayton to get refreshments for the ladies. This voice was higher, slicker, reminding Adalia of expensive oil. She opened her eyes to see Mr. Saville, holding a steaming china cup.

He bowed elegantly before her, but not before he shared an odd glance with Miss Emerald. "I must thank you again for your honesty today, Miss Winston." His gaze dropped to her hand as if he wished her to raise it for his kiss. Which she could not bring herself to do.

"I have brought you some tea. A small token of my appreciation." He slid the cup onto the table.

"That is too kind of you, sir, but Mr. Rutledge is bringing me something to drink." Adalia peered through the crowd in search of him, suddenly longing for his presence—his protection.

Mr. Saville fingered his mustache then drew his lips into a pout most inappropriate for a man of his class and maturity. "It is a special brew you'll only find here at Dillon's and only on certain occasions, miss. I had it made just for you."

Steam rose from the dark liquid, bringing the scent of almond and vanilla to Adalia's nose. "I thank you, sir. I shall try it then."

The man bowed. Then turning on his heel, he sashayed into the crowd, one lacy hand in the air, and disappeared like a smoky apparition. Picking up the tea, Adalia warmed her hands on the cup, allowing the soothing scents to calm her heightened nerves. Mr. Saville was just being kind, she told herself. He could not help that he made her uneasy. She sipped her tea. A pungent, yet sweet flavor set her tongue on fire. But the warm liquid slid down her throat and loosened the knot in her belly. And the ones in her nerves.

The orchestra stopped for a break, and the crowd rose from their seats and flitted through Dillon's Inn, partaking of tea cakes, apple pie, madeira, and the latest gossip. Adalia turned to face Caroline. "I'm so glad you joined us, Caroline." It was the first time Adalia had seen her at any event in weeks.

Caroline cast a wary glance over the room. "It would seem, aside from a few snickers, that my embarrassing incident is all but forgotten."

"As I told you it would be." Emerald patted her friend's hand then shifted to Adalia. "I do believe you've made a new admirer, Adalia."

"He is not an admirer. He is merely thanking me for—"

"How nice." Emerald twirled a finger around one of her curls and surveyed the crowd. "Mr. Saville doesn't offer his special tea to just anyone. I hope you appreciate it."

Adalia studied the woman, such a dichotomy of emotion and intention. One minute cruel, the next doting. One minute her words carried a bite; the next her tone was innocuous. Adalia had no idea which to believe. Was the lady friend or foe? Adalia's scars had never been mentioned, yet they lingered in the air between them, taunting Adalia with whispered threats and spreading an ever-widening gulf of distrust between the two ladies.

Regardless, Adalia determined to return Miss Emerald's scorn with kindness. She took another sip of tea. "I do appreciate Mr. Saville's generosity. The tea is delicious." But what were the ingredients? Vanilla, almond, perhaps a bit of cocoa, honey, but something else that added a sharpness, a warmth to the brew. A warmth she was beginning to feel all the way down to her toes. She wiggled them within her satin evening slippers as tension cracked and slipped from her shoulders. She would have to discover the secret of this tea. Perhaps she could use it as a sedative for her patients.

Morgan and Drayton returned, drinks in hand. Morgan's brows rose as he set the lemonade on the table and eyed the tea in Adalia's hand. "I see you grew tired of waiting."

"A gift." Adalia adored the look of jealousy crawling across his eyes.

"I should have known not to leave such a lovely lamb alone among wolves."

A faint snort sounded from Miss Emerald's direction as Drayton handed them drinks and dropped into one of the chairs.

Morgan proffered his elbow. "A turn about the room, Miss Winston?"

Adalia rose. The room tilted. Tables canted like ships in a storm, candle flames swirled around her. Even Morgan seemed about to topple over. Then the scene leveled again.

Shaking her head, Adalia clung to his arm as they began their stroll.

"Are you feeling well?" he asked.

"Yes, quite." Aside from a bit of dizziness, she felt more relaxed than she had in years. Relaxed and something else—uninhibited, liberated. Free to allow her bold gaze to wander over Morgan as they walked. To enjoy the way candlelight braided gold through his hair that was strung tight in his queue. To enjoy the way his forest-green eyes purveyed the scene with authoritative aplomb. The way his satin waistcoat strained beneath his thick chest.

But most of all, she enjoyed the way she felt protected and cherished by his side.

He caught her staring at him. His perplexed look transformed into one of delight as he leaned toward her. "You look lovely tonight, Adalia. But then you always do."

"Do you like my new gown?" She gazed down at her evening dress of black velvet trimmed with gold cord and nearly tripped. She tightened her grip on his arm.

"Yes, and apparently I'm not the only one."

Adalia's glance took in the myriad male eyes latched upon her. Heat suffused her face.

Weaving through the crowd, Morgan stopped before one of the bay windows. Lanterns flooded the gardens of Dillon's Inn as people mingled about in search of fresh air. He drew close until she felt his breath on her neck. "You don't know how beautiful you are, do you?"

A thrill sped through Adalia. Before she'd met Morgan, she'd never felt beautiful. An object of desire, yes, but never beautiful. "That you find me so is all that matters." The words tumbled from her lips like rebellious sprites.

These were not the words of a friend. Not the words of a lady trying to keep her distance. Trying to win this man's heart for God.

Morgan's grin told her he had not missed the ardor in her voice.

Thankfully, the orchestra began to play, and he escorted her back to their table. Steam rose from the tea cup she'd left empty. Or had she? She sipped it as she allowed herself to once again get swept away in the music. What delightful tea! It warmed her all over, ushering her into in a dreamlike state that sent her worries scurrying into hiding. Miss Emerald should have some of this tea. It would do much to liberate her from the irritation that seemed to plague her. She needed to relax, enjoy the music. Adalia offered her some, but she declined.

The concert came to an end. Flashes of glittering gowns and tailcoats of fine velvet passed before Adalia like images from a heavenly mirage. The honeyed notes that only moments before had sweetened her ears dissolved beneath the clamor of nonsensical chatter.

Feeling suddenly flush, Adalia rose to her feet. The room spun. An uncontrollable giggle spilled from her lips as she toppled backward. If not for Morgan's strong arms, she would have surely landed on the floor in an embarrassing exposé of lace and petticoats. Oddly the thought sent another giggle to her lips instead of the horror she would have expected. A flood of disapproving eyes brought yet another chortle tumbling from her mouth.

"Good heavens, I do believe Miss Winston has had too much to drink." Emerald's smile reminded Adalia of a panther on the prowl.

"Don't be absurd." Morgan steadied her. "Adalia doesn't partake of spirits." The blur that was his face defined into a pair of concerned eyes.

"Of course not." Adalia hiccupped then covered her mouth and plopped into her chair again.

An unusual smile spiked one side of Drayton's lips. Caroline fixed her gaze in her lap as Emerald's satisfied smirk oscillated in Adalia's disobedient vision. Why could she not focus on anything? She gazed across the room. Tables, chairs, the musicians mulling about the stage, patrons, and even the flickering oil lamps, all joined in some sort of perverse country dance. "Are we on a ship?"

Grabbing her teacup, Morgan raised it to his nose. "Jamaican rum." His voice was belligerent. "What did you do, Emerald?"

Adalia put a hand on his arm. "Don't be cross, Morgan. It's too fine a night to be angr. . .angee"—oh drat, now her voice was rebelling as well—"angry," she finally managed.

Emerald stood and lifted her chin. From Adalia's viewpoint, it resembled the jagged edge of an iceberg. "How dare you, Morgan! I had nothing to do with this."

"She said the tea was a gift. From you, perhaps?"

The words seemed muffled, distant, drifting through Adalia's mind and evaporating before she could make sense of them. Or even care what they meant.

Morgan slammed the cup down and continued arguing. Drayton's voice joined the fray, but Adalia was staring at a man dressed in white who emerged from the crowd and drifted toward her. A familiar expression of serenity glowed from his face.

"For you are God's workmanship, created in Christ Jesus unto good works, which God hath before ordained that we should walk in them."

Though he did not shout, his words slashed a trail through her thicketed mind.

"Do you see him?" Adalia pushed to her feet, staggered, then faced her friends.

"See who?" Morgan took her arm.

"The man in whi—" Adalia turned to find that he had, once again, vanished.

Chapter Seventeen

Fury raged through Morgan. "Come, I'll take you home, Adalia."

"Oh, must we?" she cooed. "I don't want to go home. It is far too early." Her glassy eyes breezed over Drayton, Caroline, and Emerald as if to elicit their agreement, before landing on Morgan—buzzing around Morgan would be a better description.

Though her inebriated state angered him—mainly because it was not her doing—Morgan had to admit he found this joyful, unfettered side of her quite adorable.

Emerald gave a sordid chuckle and glanced at Caroline, whose look of sympathy transformed to one of languid mirth.

Drayton leaned back in his chair and waved a jeweled hand through the air. "Ah, let the lady stay, Morgan. I must say, I'm quite enjoying this side of her."

"She is not here for your entertainment." Morgan seethed. Then placing an arm around Adalia's waist, he led her out of the inn. Beaded coiffures dipped behind fans. Whispers floated in the air as gentlemen's glances followed them down the street. Morgan waved off his coachman in favor of walking. The night air would help clear Adalia's head. Not that he was all too sure he wanted it to clear as she caressed his arm and placed her chin atop his shoulder to stare at him.

"You have the most beautiful hair." She reached up to finger a strand that had loosened from his queue.

Morgan had not thought it possible that he could blush. Surely it was the warm night that caused heat to swamp his face. He tugged at his silk neckerchief, loosening the knot. Music drifted to his ears from another party down the street. Adalia began to play with the lapels of his coat.

He took her hand and raised it to his lips, then placed it back on his arm. If the woman didn't restrain herself, Morgan couldn't be sure of his own self-control. The scent of rum swirled about him, reminding him that she was not culpable for her actions. Which also reminded him that someone had played a cruel joke on her.

If it wasn't Emerald, then who?

"Adalia, dear, who gave you the tea?"

"Ah, the tea." She faced forward again. "Marvelous stuff. I simply must have the recipe." She thrust a finger into the air before breaking into a song.

"I smile at love and all his arts
The charming Cynthia cried
Take heed for love has piercing darts
A wounded swain replied."

Morgan ushered her forward away from prying ears, an unavoidable grin on his face. Even deep into her cups, the woman was an absolute delight.

"And who gave you this marvelous tea?" He tried again.

Her brow furrowed. "That man who doesn't like you. Mr. . . . Mr. . . . ."

"Mr. Saville?"

"Yes, that's the one."

Morgan clenched his jaw. Of course.

"Why doesn't he like you, Morgan?" She leaned on his shoulder and smiled up at him.

He nearly laughed at the childish look on her face. "An incident, a few years ago. I challenged him to a horse race, knowing he couldn't ride, knowing he was a bit of a namby. His horse bolted out of control, and I was forced to rescue him. He landed in a mud puddle in the process."

"Is that all?"

"I humiliated him in front of society. You know, we men must be proficient at riding. To be seen so incompetent was an insult to his manhood."

"Surely that wouldn't be enough to cause such lasting hatred."

"One would think. Yet his intended, a young lady from Savannah, witnessed the entire episode and broke off their relationship. Besides, I have denied him his revenge, his chance at restitution."

"By not dueling with him?"

"He's desperate to prove his virility to all of society, to prove he's no limp-wrist." Yet now, Morgan just might give him the satisfaction for getting Adalia besotted. But no, the dandy wasn't worth it. Morgan would find another way to extract his revenge.

Adalia seemed satisfied with his answer and began humming again. They turned down Queen Street. "That was such a beautiful concert, Morgan." Sidling up to him, she leaned her head on his shoulder once again.

Two gentlemen across the street winked in his direction. Their nods of approval showered him with shame. How many nights had he escorted an inebriated woman to his townhome only to take advantage of her weakened condition? Consensual, of course, but nonetheless inexcusably dishonorable. Yet wasn't that expected of men of his station? Men who wore their amorous conquests like plumes in their hats. Even his own father? But as he gazed at Adalia, the idea of her becoming anyone's plume ripped his gut open. Even his own plume. She was an innocent dove amidst a pack of licentious hounds. He must protect her.

Tightening his grip on her waist, Morgan vowed to do just that. Even it if meant from himself as well. As if to weaken his resolve, her warmth melded into his side, showering him with her scent of rosemary and vanilla. His body responded. He loosened his cravat further.

She stopped humming. Thankfully because her voice was terribly off-key. Suddenly jerking from his grip, she swerved to face him. Light from a streetlamp trickled streams of silver over her, setting her ebony curls sparkling.

"Do you want to know a secret?" She fingered the whiskers on his chin and ran her gaze over him. "I think you are the most handsome man I've ever seen." She smiled. Not the smile of a seductress, but the pleased smile of a little girl who'd reached some grand conclusion.

The admission sent his heart reeling. "Shall I share a secret with you?" He tapped her on the nose.

"You find me attractive too? That's no secret, silly. You've told me that before." She gave him a coy smile and began walking again, dancing, in fact, holding out the folds of her skirt and drifting over the sandy street like a swan on a lake.

She tripped and Morgan dashed to catch her.

She folded into his arms and squeezed his biceps. "Hmm. So strong.

I feel so safe with you." She cuddled against his chest.

A chest that now expanded beneath her admiration. Morgan found himself suddenly thankful he'd had nothing to drink, or he'd surely succumb to her charms.

She looked up at him. Her glistening eyes flitting between his. "Morgan, are we friends?"

He brushed a curl from her face. "Of course." Though he wanted much more than that. Though he'd been hesitant to push her. Unsure of her feelings. Until now.

She backed away. "I've tried to be your friend."

"Is it that difficult?"

"No." She smiled.

"We can be more than friends if you'd like."

"That wouldn't be right." Mischief winked from her eyes. "You don't know who I am."

"I know all I need to know."

She gave him a puzzled look then grew sad. He took a step toward her, longing to wipe her sorrow away, replace it with the glee of only a moment ago, but she turned and sped forward. "You can't catch me."

Laughing, Morgan darted after her, reaching her side without difficulty. She glanced over her shoulder and giggled. Several of her curls loosened from their pins and tumbled down her back like silken ink. Morgan swallowed. He stopped her with a touch, and they strolled onward, arm in arm.

They approached Doc Willaby's home, Adalia dancing down the path. She jumped onto the first porch step and turned around. "Aren't you going to kiss me?" She tapped her moist lips with her finger then leaned toward him, closing her eyes.

Morgan groaned inwardly and licked his lips, remembering her sweet taste, longing for it as a man longing for a drink after a long voyage. But no. He could not take advantage of her in this condition.

He rubbed his thumb over her jaw, searching for strength to resist this morsel freely offered to him. "Go inside, Adalia. Get some sleep."

She popped her eyes open, disappointment stealing their sparkle. "I rather enjoyed our last kiss." A tiny furrow formed between her brows. "I suppose I shouldn't tell you that. It's rather shameless of me, isn't it?" She fingered the wooden post and leaned her head against it. "Did you enjoy it?"

Was she jesting? "Very much."

"It felt like lightning in my stomach." She spun her fingers over her belly.

Morgan's heart lurched. Did that mean she had feelings for him? Or was it simply a physical reaction?

She leaned toward him and whispered in his ear, "You make me feel strange things, Morgan Rutledge."

Strange, wonderful things, he hoped, as her words and the breath that carried them were making him feel right now. He cupped her face. "Good things?"

"Far too good." She hovered her lips over his. Rum and vanilla assailed his senses, weakening his restraint.

He withdrew. "You are very special to me, Adalia."

The trill of a whip-poor-will floated on a breeze that eased a strand of hair across Adalia's cheek. She snapped it away, studying him as her eyes misted. "I care very much for you, Morgan." She looked away. "Sometimes it hurts."

Morgan took her hand in his. "It shouldn't hurt."

"We are from two different worlds. Worlds too far apart." She spread her arms out then dropped them to her side, her voice breaking. "But I cannot seem to let you go."

"Then don't." Placing a finger beneath her chin, Morgan brought her eyes to his. And what he saw within them thrilled him down to his soul. Despite the alcohol, or perhaps because of its ability to loosen her inhibitions, true affection burned in their depths. She cared for him! The realization sent his heart soaring and his mind spinning with possibilities. Could he hope to possess such a precious woman?

If only his father got to know her, perhaps he'd be willing to overlook her common birth. Only one way to find out. Morgan would invite her to the annual Rutledge party at their plantation. There, he would formally introduce her to his parents and declare his intentions to marry her.

❧

An army marched through Adalia's head. Not only marched but also fired round after round into her brain. Throbbing pain jarred her awake. Her thoughts scrambled to attention in a haphazard formation—a scattered row of clipped memories that mocked her with a shame she knew she should feel but had no idea why. Where was she? She reached up to rub her forehead when a tiny *me-row* preceded the stretch of a warm ball of fur curled on her chest.

"M," Adalia could barely squeak out the single syllable from a mouth stuffed with sand.

The cat nestled against her chin, bringing her a moment's comfort that quickly dissipated beneath the visions flashing through her wakening mind: her at Dillon's Inn enjoying a concert; exotic tea that made her tingle all over; strolling about the room on Morgan's arm. But then the memories became distorted: Morgan's concerned face, his friends laughing at her, the man in white, disapproving glances, a walk home in the dark.

A kiss. . .

Adalia sprang up, instantly regretting it. M let out a whine of complaint and leapt from the bed while Adalia's stomach bubbled like a witch's brew. Holding it, she nearly gagged, trying to catch her breath, trying to sort through shifty memories. Had she kissed Morgan? Rays of sunlight speared her eyes. She squeezed them shut. What had she done? No. Not a kiss. She would remember that.

With difficulty, she swung her legs over the side of the bed. Who had turned her head into an iron ball? It fell into her hands. She moaned, forcing down a burst of nausea. Foul breath curled her nose. Her breath? Had she partaken of alcohol?

Impossible. And yet. . .

The tea. That wonderful, devilish tea. From that slippery man, Mr. Saville. A trick. A cruel joke. But why?

M jumped into her lap and plopped down with a yawn.

"I fear I made a fool of myself last night, little one." She scratched between his ears, his favorite spot. Purring rose as snippets of her conversation with Morgan broke through the surface of her murky mind. Adalia declaring her affection for him. Asking him, no begging him to kiss her! Admitting how his touch affected her.

She moaned and ran her fingers through her tangled hair, only now noticing that she still wore her gown. Her new gown, now hopelessly wrinkled and omitting a rather disagreeable odor.

Morgan had not kissed her. Though she'd all but begged him to. Shame sent a wave of heat up her neck even as her admiration for the man swelled. He'd not taken advantage of her. . .her condition. What sort of man would do that? A good man. An honorable man. A man who cared for her.

Struggling to rise, she hobbled toward her dressing bureau and poured a glass of water from the pitcher. The cool liquid did nothing to assuage her thirst. And everything to cause her stomach further discomfort.

How did people drink such horrid stuff night after night? She never wanted another sip of alcohol again.

Her closed Bible stared at her from her nightstand. The precious Word of God that had sustained her through the past seven years—had comforted her and instructed her and strengthened her to endure what no woman should have to endure. She'd never failed to read it every morning before she began her daily tasks. When had she stopped?

Leaning her forehead on the top of the bureau, she bit her lip against the agony raging through her head and creating a maelstrom in her belly. "I'm so sorry, Lord. I've neglected You. I've been so caught up in the busyness of life." She sighed as tears spilled from her eyes, some plopping on the wooden floor below, some dribbling down the front of her dresser. "And I'm sorry I was foolish enough to trust a man I didn't know. Forgive me. And please help Morgan to forgive me."

Would Morgan forgive her? She could remember no hint of disdain from him last night. No disgust at her condition. Quite the opposite, in fact. Oh, why had she behaved the besotted carp when she'd wanted to tell Morgan of the goodness of God, of the joy one received when following Him? Good heavens! What a terrible witness she was! Her father would be mortified. She banged her head against the wooden bureau, increasing her pain. But it wasn't enough punishment for what she'd done.

Opening her top drawer she reached behind her handkerchiefs and chemises and pulled out the pouch containing her mother's pearls. Lowering onto her bed, she spilled them into her hand as M crawled into her lap and began batting the precious beads. "No, no, M." She set the pesky feline on the floor. With pink nose in the air, he leapt onto the windowsill and stared outside, wearing much the same smug expression she'd seen among Charleston gentry. Smiling, Adalia leaned over and pressed the pearls to her forehead as she closed her eyes. The cool beads rolled over her skin, calming her throbbing pulse.

"Mama, I wish you were here. I wish I could talk to you, tell you everything that has happened to me since you and Papa went to heaven. I've gone from an orphan to a slave to a princess, Mama. From poverty to living like a queen." At least when she was with Morgan.

Yes, so much *had* changed. Adalia couldn't imagine ever going back to the life of a slave. And if she were truthful, not even the life of a mere servant. She had gained the respect of society, the love of a wealthy land owner, the privilege of attending elaborate parties. How could she ever go back? She stared at the pearls. Sunlight caressed them in sparkling grays and lustrous blacks. Beautiful, exotic, precious. Just like her mother.

Yet the people of this town would not see those qualities. They would not find Adalia beautiful or precious if they knew Negro blood flowed in her veins. It didn't make sense. Wasn't right. But what could Adalia do to change it? She slid the pearls back into the velvet pouch and tied it tight, hiding them away, wishing they were white and lustrous like most pearls...

And then hating herself for the thought.

Her mother would understand. She would love to see Adalia so happy, so adored and accepted.

Wouldn't she?

A tap on the door exploded like rifle shot in Adalia's head. Stuffing the pouch back into her drawer, she closed it and spun around. "Yes?"

Joy poked her head inside. "Are you all right, miss?"

Except for her pounding head, queasy stomach, and parched mouth? "Yes. Just getting a late start today."

Slipping into the room, Joy set a basin of steaming water on the dresser and eyed Adalia's disheveled gown with confusion. "The doctor's been askin' 'bout you. He has a patient he wants you t' see."

Adalia sank back onto her bed. Today of all days.

"Miss, you don't look too well." Joy approached, wiping her hands on her apron.

"I don't feel very well, I'm afraid. It was a rather...eventful evening."

"Did you enjoy the concert?"

"What I remember of it." Adalia rubbed her temples then glanced up into a pair of curious brown eyes. "It's a long story." It would do Adalia no credit to share the shameful tale with her maid. The thought stopped her—when had she begun to think of Joy as a maid and not a friend? When had Adalia become accustomed to even having a maid?

The precious girl inquired no further. Nor did an ounce of censure appear on her face. Instead Joy gave her a sympathetic look. "I'll tell the doc you are ill today, miss. You needs t' rest."

"No, don't." Adalia's harsh command stopped Joy short. She softened her tone and pasted on a smile. "I'll be all right. Thank you." She must attend to her duties. She must remember she was a tradeswoman, not one of the Charleston nobility.

"I'll have Cook make you breakfast."

"No." Adalia cringed as her voice blared like a gong in her ears. "I mean, that's kind of you, but I'm not very hungry." At the girl's wounded look, Adalia rose and folded her in an embrace. "Forgive me, Joy. I'm not myself this morning."

The girl's body stiffened. "Oh miss, you don't smell so good." She pushed away from her, eyes lowering. "I's sorry, miss. I shouldn't have said that."

Despite her shame, despite the fact that Adalia felt as though a dozen carriages had ambled over her body, she could not help but laugh at the girl's honesty.

The fear faded from Joy's eyes, and she joined Adalia's laughter, sending tension fleeing from the room. "Let me hep you freshen up and get dressed."

Twenty minutes later, after splashing water on her face and arms, drinking some peppermint tea Joy had brought her, and donning fresh undergarments and a gown, Adalia headed downstairs. She turned to shut the door, and her glance landed on her Bible atop her nightstand.

Still closed and unread.

Batting away the conviction, she promised to do her readings and prayer later. When she had more time. Down in the foyer, instead of giving her medicines, instructions, and sending her on her way as she had hoped, Dr. Willaby beckoned her into the sitting room.

"Please." He pointed toward a chair, his eyes never meeting hers.

The hairs pricked on her arms at the condemnation pouring from him. Squinting at the sunlight angling through the windows, Adalia eased into the chair, set down her medical satchel, and folded her hands in her lap.

"Forgive me for rising late, Doctor. I—"

"I know very well why you had trouble leaving your bed this morning, Miss Winston." His voice stung with disappointment and something else—fear? "I'll not hear your excuses."

Mortified, Adalia remained quiet, praying the man would stop shouting.

"Can you deny that you partook of some sort of vile alcoholic brew last night?"

Her stomach lurched, sending a clump of bitterness into her throat. How did he know? She closed her eyes as faint memories of him standing in the foyer as she entered the house sifted through her mind.

"The Good Book says"—he tapped the pages of his open Bible—"be not drunk with wine, but be filled with the Holy Spirit." Sharp eyes stabbed her from above wire spectacles.

"I can explain, sir." She sent him a look of appeal.

"I hope so, Miss Winston, for I will not offer a room in my home and a position in my employ to an unscrupulous woman." He slammed his Bible shut and set it aside, his bottom lip curling. "I understood you to be a chaste, godly woman."

"I am. . ." She hesitated. "Unbeknownst to me, someone slipped alcohol into my tea last night."

"Someone?"

"A man. At least I think it was him." A crisp breeze stirred the curtains. The smell of roses helped to revive her jumbled thoughts. "I assure you, Doctor, I have never partaken of alcohol before. Nor shall I ever again if I have any say about it."

He frowned, still gazing out the window, where the rattle of carriages sounded more like the frontline of a battle. "And these are the friends you keep?" Disdain rang in his tone.

"Most are kind, sir. I don't know why this man or anyone would do such a thing." Unless it was to get revenge, to embarrass Morgan.

The doctor rose, adjusted the gray coat he always wore, and walked to the window. "Just for the fun of it, no doubt. These pampered brats are so bored, they find their amusement at the expense of others." He faced her, more fear on his face than castigation. "Don't you see how they are infecting you with their wickedness? No proper lady should be gallivanting about town at all hours of the night."

Adalia forced down her rising anger. "I am hardly gallivanting. I'm merely attending concerts, plays, and balls. Nothing immoral or illegal. Morgan is kind to me."

"Humph." He pulled out his pocket watch, the gold chain glimmering in the sunlight. "The Rutledges. Scoundrels all, if you ask me." Gazing at the time, he snapped it shut and returned it to his coat.

Adalia squeezed the bridge of her nose. The action seemed to relieve some of the pressure attempting to burst through her skull. "What do you have against them, sir? They are a well-respected family."

His gaze lowered to the garden outside the window. The lines on his face deepened and seemed to sag. "I had a daughter once," he said sadly. "Sarah."

Emotion rose to join the nausea burning in Adalia's throat. From a few comments the doctor had tossed around, she had suspected as much. And from the sorrow that continually lingered around the edges of his kind face, she also suspected that something terrible had happened to her.

"She was beautiful, kind, intelligent." He gave Adalia a forlorn smile. "Much like you. Although with golden hair and eyes the color of Spanish moss." He faced the window again. "Like her mother."

A palpable sorrow filled the room, misting Adalia's eyes. Several silent moments passed as the doctor seemed lost in his memories.

"What happened to her?" Adalia dared ask.

He snapped from his daze. "Hadley Morgan happened to her." He cleared his throat. His eyes narrowed, still staring out the window. Cast in bright sunlight, he suddenly looked much older, the lines on his face more defined, his gray hair thinner. "He courted her, charmed her. Much like his brother is doing with you now." He stopped, obviously choked up, coughed into his hand. "When she informed him she carried his child, he denied it was his and never spoke to her again."

Adalia gasped.

"Nine months later, she died in childbirth."

Chapter Eighteen

Saying the words "died in childbirth" out loud for the first time in years stabbed Willaby's heart with as much pain as if the disaster had just occurred.

"I'm so sorry, Doctor." The tears in Miss Winston's eyes touched him, drawing out the rest of the tragic tale. Surely if she knew the truth, she would call an end to her foolish liaison with Morgan Rutledge.

He clasped his trembling hands behind his back, afraid to utter the words that had sealed the tomb on his happiness so long ago. But they must be said. For Miss Winston's sake. "My wife could not bear to lose Sarah. Though I did my best to comfort her, she died of grief shortly afterward." He faced her, his jaw clenching so tight, it hurt. Anger was the only way to force back the pain. "Can you see now what monsters those Rutledge boys are?"

She drew a handkerchief from her sleeve and dabbed at her eyes. "How horrible. What you must have gone through." Her brow wrinkled in agony. "I agree that Hadley is quite possibly the monster you believe him to be. But not Morgan. He is nothing like his brother."

Willaby's face grew hot. "He has deceived you. He's all charm and wealth and looks, but he comes from the same seed, Franklin Rutledge. The man is known for his many trysts in town."

He saw surprise roll across her face. Perhaps he was getting some-where. "You must not see Morgan again, Miss Winston." He gripped the back of a chair, forcing urgency into his tone. "You must call off the relationship. Can't you see that he will drag you down into a pit of evil? That he will destroy you? As he did my precious Sarah."

Willaby fought back the moisture filling his eyes and turned away.

Back toward the window, where the sunlight defied the darkness growing in his heart. He must give Miss Winston time to think, time to absorb this shocking news, time for the revelation to sink into the rational, godly part of her mind.

But when he turned around, no resignation, no concession appeared on her face. Instead, her brow furrowed again as she gazed down at her folded hands. "You do not have much faith in me, Doctor, if you believe I would allow anyone to do that to me."

Confound it all! Why wasn't she seeing reason? Willaby slammed his hands a bit too hard on the back of the chair, but at her flinch, he drew a deep breath, trying to contain himself. "It's not you I am questioning. It's the Rutledges and all those like them."

She rose, drew a hand to her temples, and winced as if in pain. "I promise that will not happen. I will not let it. I believe there is a divine reason for my friendship with Morgan—to help bring him and perhaps his entire family to God."

Willaby had not expected that argument. Clever girl. Using God as an excuse. Weaving around the chair, he approached her. Yet as he neared, he found no deceit in her eyes. He hesitated. "A worthy goal, Miss Winston. But perhaps a task not meant for someone as innocent as you. The Good Book says to flee temptation. As Joseph did when Potiphar's wife threw herself at him." He smiled. "Sometimes God requires us to run."

"Morgan isn't a temptation, Doctor. Why even last night he did not take advantage of my, my"—she lowered her chin—"situation when he could have. He is honorable."

Willaby saw the same look in her eyes that he'd seen so often in Sarah's. The same mesmerized glaze as if the Rutledges had cast an evil spell on her. Must he endure this nightmare all over again? Outrage bubbled in his gut, threatening to erupt in a tirade of accusations, biblical admonitions, and imposed restrictions. But he wouldn't let it. It hadn't worked with Sarah—may have even driven her further into Hadley Rutledge's arms. Oh, the guilt! Willaby strode to the fireplace. "Why will you not listen to me?"

"You never informed me that restrictions on my social life were part of my employment. I hope they are not, Doctor. I need you to trust me. Trust my judgment. And trust that God will protect me." Her voice, so defiant, so confident felt like needles stabbing his back.

Despair dragged all hope from Willaby. Just like Sarah, he saw now that he would not be able to convince Miss Winston with arguments or punishments. He sighed.

"Very well." He waved her off. "Have Mr. Gant take you to the Beauford residence. Mrs. Beauford's gout is acting up again, and she requested you bring her more of your black sage tea."

Miss Winston's skirts swished. Yet she didn't leave. She slipped beside him and squeezed his hand—a gesture that brought him a modicum of comfort. "You can count on me, Doctor. I promise you, I will be careful with Morgan. You have nothing to fear." She gave him a sweet smile then excused herself, leaving Willaby alone.

Alone to stew in his anger, his fear, his absolute terror that Miss Winston. . .Adalia would soon find herself in the same predicament as his precious Sarah.

He walked back to the window and glanced down into the garden. The myriad greens and colorful reds and yellows of spring flowers blurred in his vision. And for a moment, a rare, precious moment, he saw Rachel, his wife, and Sarah dancing among the blooms, chasing butterflies and giggling with delight. His precious, innocent daughter.

Until she had met Hadley Rutledge.

Willaby fisted his hands. He would not allow that to happen again. He could not.

Marching from the room, he hastened up the stairs as quickly as his aged legs would carry him and entered Adalia's chamber. Closing the door quietly behind him, he scanned the surroundings. The silly kitten curled on the bed pried one eye open and gave him an uninterested glance before going back to sleep. Starting at the dressing bureau, Willaby began opening drawers and rummaging through Miss Winston's belongings. He hated to lower himself to such despicable measures, but he had to know what she was up to—if she was lying to him about the depth of her relationship with Morgan or about the drinking. As Sarah had done on so many occasions. What he was looking for, he didn't know. A bottle of rum or wine perhaps to prove her propensity to drink or a love letter from Morgan exposing their affair. If Miss Winston were lying, he must toss her from his home. Before he got too close to her. Before he cared too much and was devastated as another loved one was ruined by the Rutledge's licentious appetites.

Shifting his gaze away from her undergarments, he sifted through the drawer carefully. Nothing. Nothing in any of the drawers but a pouch of black pearls. Odd. No doubt they were of sentimental value to her. He moved to the bed stand, searched through her Bible, petted the infernal cat, then headed to the wardrobe, where he inspected her gowns and knelt to examine her extra pair of shoes. Relief swept through him. There was nothing here that would lead him to believe she was lying.

Sunlight drifted through the window, shifting over something stuffed in the back of the wardrobe. A valise. Dragging it toward him, he reached inside, surprised when his fingers struck a hard, cold object. He pulled out an iron band and examined it. It appeared to belong to a pair of shackles, though the chain had been severed at the edge. He turned them over. Engraving on the side drew his gaze. Holding it up to the sunlight, he read the words.

Miles Plantation Barbados

Too stunned to even think, Willaby shoved the valise back in place and headed downstairs. The band seared like hot iron in his hand as he pondered the reasons Adalia would possess such a thing. He wandered in a daze into the sitting room and sat upon the cushions by the bay window, holding the heinous object up to the light. Perhaps they belonged to a slave Adalia's family had owned—a beloved slave, no doubt. But hadn't she said her parents were simple farmers? Besides, they lived on Jamaica, not Barbados.

So lost in his thoughts, Willaby failed to hear the knock on his front door, failed to hear the housekeeper open it, and didn't realize he had a visitor until Miss Emerald Middleton sashayed into the room.

"Miss Middleton to see you, Doctor."

Willaby set the band down and stood, attempting to mask his confusion with a smile. "How nice to see you again, Miss Middleton. But I'm afraid Miss Winston is not here at the moment."

"Oh." She pouted and Willaby couldn't help but notice how lovely she was. How wonderful that Adalia had become friends with such an upstanding lady.

Her blue eyes shifted out the window then down onto the band, gleaming in the sun. She moved toward him. "I was so hoping to ask her out to tea. When will she return?"

"I'm not sure, Miss Middleton, an hour or two, perhaps?" Willaby said as her eyes snapped once again to the band. She halted before him and pointed a gloved finger at the ring of iron.

"Whatever is that you have there?"

"It's nothing, miss. Just something I found."

"In Adalia's chamber?" She offered him a sweet smile.

Willaby blinked. "Why do you ask? Has she confided in you?" Perhaps he could glean some information from Miss Middleton that would aid him in his cause.

"Yes, she confides in me about many things." She strolled about the room, running a finger over the furniture. "In fact, did you know she has scars on her back? From a whip. She showed me. I wouldn't tell you except the sight of them caused me great concern. For her welfare, of course."

"Whip marks? Unheard of. Where did she get them?"

"I cannot tell you, Doctor."

A thud sounded above stairs. Odd. No one should be up there. Intending to excuse himself to check it out, he started for the door when Miss Middleton touched his arm.

"I am happy we have this opportunity to speak privately, sir. I've been quite concerned for Adalia, you see. It's Morgan Rutledge."

"Concern?" She had his attention now. Perhaps he had found an ally in his quest to protect Adalia.

"He is not suited for her, Doctor. I fear his intentions are not honorable."

Willaby could almost hug the lady. "I quite agree! I've been trying to tell her as much."

"She won't listen to me, either, I'm afraid."

"No, she's quite stubborn." He smiled.

"Perhaps if I examined that"—she gestured toward the band again—"whatever it is you found, I could help you. If we could figure out more about Adalia, perhaps we could find something that will dissuade Morgan's attentions."

"I don't see how a. . ." But Miss Middleton had already scooped up the band and was studying it in the sunlight.

Only then, when a sinister gleam appeared in her eye, did Willaby feel a pinch of unease.

❧

Fabian burst out onto the street, brushing off twigs and leaves and cursing under his breath. He found Emerald waiting for him, an impatient look in her eyes.

"I found nothing," he said. "Nothing at all that would incriminate her in any way. Though I was tempted to steal her pearls."

"Pearls?" Emerald shook her head. "Oh, never mind. I discovered something far more valuable." She smiled, wove her arm through his, and yanked him down the street, filling him in on her next sordid plan.

Early the next morning, adjusting his hat against the stiff breeze, Fabian waited for a coach to pass then dashed across Bay Street to Union's wharves. Dodging around workers, he drew a handkerchief to his nose as the smell of fish and rotting produce assailed him. Several yards off the edge of the quay a brig rocked lazily in the murky waters. Was it the one he sought? Two small boats, weighed down with goods, were tied to the end of the dock where a man stood, papers in hand, surveying the line of incoming supplies.

Fabian marched toward him, his buckled shoes clapping over the sea-worn planks. The wind nearly tore his plumed hat off his head. Holding it down, he patted the letter secure in his waistcoat pocket and approached the man, who barely gave him a glance above his ledger. "Mr. Saville, I presume?"

A worker, crate perched on his massive shoulder, bumped into Fabian. Without even a word of apology or a by-your-leave, he knelt and handed the crate to a man in the boat, who stacked it atop the others.

Amazed at the ill-mannered brute, Fabian brushed his coat and stepped to the side. "Yes. I am Mr. Saville." His gaze swept to brig, the name *Endeavor* on her hull now clear in his sight.

A slave struggled by, a large barrel on his back. Lowering it with difficulty, he left it on the edge of the dock before ambling away.

"Well, where is it? I haven't got all day." The man made a mark on his papers.

Neither his demeanor nor the smell emanating from his ragged attire fostered much confidence that Fabian's task would be completed. Nevertheless, he reached into his coat, drew out the letter, and handed it to him. "Can you assure me this will arrive at its destination?"

Stuffing the papers beneath his arm, the purser held out his other hand. "As long as you pay me what we agreed."

With a huff, Fabian unclipped a small pouch from his belt and handed it the sailor. *Greedy and uncouth.* The man did nothing to change Fabian's opinion of seamen.

Opening the moneybag, he counted the coins with his eyes. Then, satisfied, he stuffed the pouch in the pocket of his loose trousers and stared at the letter.

"Miles Plantation, Barbados, eh? Yes, I'll make sure it gets there. You can bet on that."

Chapter Nineteen

Taking Morgan's hand, Adalia climbed into the brougham. She slid onto the leather seat as he leapt inside and sat across from her. Excitement bubbled within her at the prospect of being formally introduced to his parents at the annual Rutledge party. It wasn't the introduction that excited her as much as the realization that Morgan wanted to take their relationship a step forward, toward a formal courtship.

Of course, before any permanent understanding could be reached between them, Morgan would have to renounce slavery. He wasn't to inherit the plantation anyway, but Adalia must ensure that if he ever did, the slaves would be set free. For she could never marry a man who enslaved others. *Oh Lord, could this be Your will all along? To use me to free the Rutledge slaves?* And from there, who knew? It was too much to consider! But right now, all she could think about was that Morgan Rutledge was quite possibly the prince Adalia had sought her entire life.

He tapped the hood, sending the brougham rumbling on its way. Sunlight stroked his hair, tied behind him in a stylish queue. He shifted his wide shoulders beneath an elegant black tailcoat and met her gaze. There came that grin that sent her heart fluttering. They had not spoken since the night of the orchestra at Dillon's Inn, and she knew from the mischievous sparkle in his eyes that he was thinking of their walk home.

Her face heated, and she drew out her fan, waving it about her neck. "It is most improper for us to ride in a covered carriage without benefit of escort."

"We have the footmen. Besides, I'm afraid everyone is already at the party, so I suppose you'll have to trust that I shall behave the gentleman." He raised his brows.

"That won't be too difficult"—she gave him a sincere smile—"since you have already proven that to me beyond all doubt."

He seemed pleased at her approbation. "You refer to your overindulgence in rum, no doubt?"

Despite his teasing tone, indignation gripped her. "You scamp." She tapped his leg with her shoe. "You know that was not my fault."

His wide grin told her he did.

Adalia sighed. The *clip-clop* of horses' hooves settled over her in a soothing cadence. "Still, I thank you for your honorable behavior."

"I assure you, milady, it was no easy task. Especially when you all but begged me for a kiss." He chuckled.

"Do not call me—I did not beg you!" Her anger quickly dissipated beneath his playful grin. She glanced out the window at the passing homes. Honeysuckles, magnolias, and bougainvilleas splashed color across the front gardens. "I suppose my behavior was beyond shameless."

"I quite enjoyed it." He shifted his boots on the floor and leaned forward on his knees. "But it was more your words that stirred me."

Taken aback by the intense look in his eyes, she giggled nervously. "What credence can you give to drunken ramblings?"

"You don't remember what you said?" His voice was playful.

"Some." She looked down.

"I've come to know that words spoken with the aid of spirits are often truthful."

"Oh, you have, have you? I assume you have much experience in such matters?"

"Enough." He grinned.

She stared at the fan splayed in her lap.

Crossing the distance between them, he slid beside her and took her hand in his. Her breath clambered in her throat. "You have made me a happy man." He kissed her fingers. Even through the cotton gloves, she could feel his warm lips. His spicy scent spiraled around her, sending her senses reeling.

She scooted away from him, remembering what Doc Willaby said about being deceived by his charm. "I must speak to you of something."

"Anything."

"Did your brother court a lady named Sarah Willaby?"

A breeze, ripe with the smell of the sea, wandered through the carriage, sweeping away the jaunty mood. Morgan frowned. "Ah, I see the doctor has finally told you why he hates me so." He released her hand. She felt the loss immediately.

"Yes. Hadley was very much in love with her."

Love her? "Then why did he abandon her in her"—Adalia snapped her fan shut—"condition?"

The carriage jostled, sending them bouncing. Morgan gripped the edge of the seat and looked down. His jaw clenched. "Hadley had every intention of marrying the lady, but Father forbid the union. Said he would disown Hadley and leave him a pauper on the street."

Adalia's chest grew heavy. What a tragic tale. So much loss. So much pain. But anger soon pushed her sorrow aside. Anger at Morgan's father. Anger at Hadley for not doing the honorable thing, no matter the cost. Anger that the young lady had paid such a huge price.

"Are you aware of her tragic end?" Her tone was livid.

Morgan nodded. "It nearly destroyed Hadley. I don't think he's ever been the same. For one thing, he's never listened to Father again. They've been at odds ever since."

She studied him as the impact, the tragedy of the story, turned inward, becoming personal. Like a disease, growing and devouring her dreams. Would Morgan do the same thing? If his father forbade their courtship, would Morgan abandon her?

The carriage rattled to a halt before the Rutledge home. A row of servants framed a stone pathway to the open front door from which spilled ladies and gentlemen in fashionable array. A footman opened the brougham and lowered the step. Sliding her hand into Morgan's, she stepped down before the elegant estate, brimming with music and laughter—the plantation home she'd first approached three months ago with such fear and trepidation.

With such reproach.

As she stood there gazing at the scene, feeling every nerve spark in excitement as well as dread, the truth clawed its way to the forefront of her mind. She couldn't settle for a mere friendship with Morgan anymore. She loved him! She wanted to be a part of his world. Of him. And the realization frightened her to death. Especially since the power to make her dreams come true rested solely in the hands of Franklin Rutledge, a man who at her initial acquaintance had dismissed her as being beneath his attention. Her knees grew weak at the prospect of another rejection. Yet wouldn't it be better to face the man's verdict on their courtship sooner rather than later? Squaring her shoulders, she allowed Morgan to lead her up the steps and into the house. A house that suddenly felt like a viper's lair.

A crush of people mobbed the foyer, spilling from the sitting room and dining room on either side. Greetings hailed them above the clamor of voices as the sound of an orchestra drifted through the house atop a hearty breeze.

"Morgan, ole chap. Good of you to make an appearance at your own party!" one foppish gentleman said.

"Good afternoon, Miss Winston." Mrs. Pickney, one of society's most esteemed matrons, dipped her head.

Delighted at the woman's acceptance, Adalia returned her smile as Morgan acknowledged salutations tossed his way.

The scent of perfume, tobacco, and smoked pork filtered through the house as Morgan led her into the back gallery before exiting onto the veranda overlooking the garden. Dozens of servants skittered among guests who were clustered beneath moss-draped oak trees. Cushioned chairs dotted the lawn as children wove threads of laughter through the chattering mob. To the right an orchestra filled the spring air with soothing music.

Excitement gripped Adalia at the scene. Even Sir Walter's occasional evening galas were no match to the extravagance spread before her.

Sir Walter. Why had she thought of him now? When she wanted to enjoy her day, cherish the moment, not remember her past. Yet as Morgan escorted her to a refreshment table covered with bowls of fruit, assorted hors d'oeuvres, lemon cakes, and punch, she couldn't help but focus on the myriad servants, some obviously slaves, who moved among the crowd with vacant eyes.

At the party but not a part of it.

Experiencing the same music, laughter, and luscious scents, yet not enjoying a moment of it. Adalia stared at a young Negress who passed before her, carrying a tray of empty glasses, hoping to make eye contact, hoping to offer her a smile, but the girl's eyes remained fixed forward.

Memories brought her back to the times when Sir Walter had forced her to serve at his parties. Times before she had matured into a woman and he had put her on display. Times when just like these slaves, she had moved about through the array of glittering figures as if she were a ghost. Amazing how people could grab a glass of wine or pluck a morsel of food from a tray and never once acknowledge the person holding it. Anger transformed into guilt and finally into shame before Adalia's knees weakened. Truly, she had no right to be here at all. She tightened her grip on Morgan. He halted before the table and gave her a concerned look. "Are you all right?"

She smiled her response.

"Nervous about meeting my parents?"

"You forget. I have met your parents."

He selected a glass of sweet punch from the table and held it out to her. "No, I haven't forgotten. It will be different this time."

"Morgan, you devil!" Hadley slapped him on the back. "I quite feared you would leave me all alone to entertain Father's stodgy guests." His glazed eyes brushed over Adalia. "Though I see now this day will be anything but dull."

Adalia knew he didn't refer to her interesting company. And by the manner in which Morgan slammed an entire glass of wine to the back of his throat, she wondered if he weren't as nervous as she.

"Father has softened," Morgan said.

Hadley chuckled. "Has he?" He glanced around as if looking for someone then snapped his fingers at a servant. "Brandy." He faced Morgan. "You'll have to drink a lot more than one glass of wine if you are to convince yourself of that."

"It would seem you've had enough for the both of us," Morgan said.

Drayton joined them, drink in hand. "Miss Winston, you've braved the lions' den once more, I see."

Adalia sipped her punch. "I have found most of the lions in this den do not bite, sir."

"And yet you have not encountered the most ferocious one." His eyes flashed above a grin that harbored more warning then glee.

Caroline slid her arm through his. "Oh, leave her alone, Drayton. Don't let them frighten you, Adalia. They are simply jealous." The stunning brunette leaned toward Adalia. "I must say, you continue to keep the Charleston elite quite astir."

Drayton snorted.

Adalia swept a gaze over the crowd. Though some Charleston gentry still snubbed her, she found several pairs of eyes drifting her way. Because of God's healing of Elizabeth? Or had they heard of her shameful drunkenness? Either way, she hated being on display.

Miss Caroline sighed. "I suppose I must perform some miraculous feat in order to gain the notice of society."

"I did not—" Adalia began.

"Why do you care what this fickle lot thinks, Caroline? Really." Drayton's outburst stole the lovely smile from the lady's face.

The slave returned with Hadley's drink. Grabbing it, he waved the man off and took a sip.

"Where's Franklin?" Morgan asked.

"Our illustrious father? Ah, he's around somewhere"—Hadley gestured with his drink, spilling some over the side—"hobnobbing with those from whom he can benefit the most. Yet never fear, as soon as word gets out *whom* you have brought"—his sordid glance toward Adalia made her toes curl—"he'll no doubt seek you out."

Adalia pressed a hand over her gurgling stomach, the punch bubbling into her throat.

"Come now, Hadley, you're scaring the poor girl," Drayton offered.

Morgan gave her a reassuring look.

Regardless, Adalia found her fear rising with the afternoon heat. Hadley downed his brandy then squeezed the bridge of his nose. "I do believe I need to sit down." Turning, he stumbled off.

An hour passed as Morgan led Adalia through the crowd, engaging in small talk that evidently, from his polite nods and short answers, bored him to tears. Whenever a gentleman approached, Morgan placed his hand possessively at the small of her back, thrilling Adalia at his protectiveness. Yet, as the afternoon waned, she sensed his muscles tensing along with hers.

A breeze swept over her, cooling her neck and tossing her curls. She drew a deep breath and glanced at the people lining up for a country dance beneath a massive tent just beyond the gardens. The bubbling splash of a fountain blended with the orchestra in a lively tune. It was far too charming and beautiful an afternoon to be so anxious. She must remain calm and put things in God's hands.

Drayton joined them again just as a glimmer caught the corner of Adalia's eye. She turned to see Miss Emerald, dressed in a gown of creamy satin with a velvet sash, gliding their way, smiling and waving off the gentlemen clamoring for her attention. Adalia wondered why she had not swooped down on Morgan the minute he had arrived.

"Morgan, darling." Her blue eyes latched upon him as sunlight set her curls aglow like pearls. "You're needed in the house. I'm afraid it's Hadley."

"What has he done now?"

"Why, he's passed out on the sofa in the foyer, making quite a spectacle of himself."

Morgan frowned. "Very well." He took Adalia's hand, but Emerald stayed him with a touch. "We will keep Miss Winston company while you're gone. No need to involve her in your family affairs."

"Indeed, Morgan," Drayton added. "I'll remain with her. She'll be in good hands until you return."

Morgan's wary glance shifted over them, but at Adalia's nod of assent, he kissed her hand. "Don't accept a drink from anyone," he said, eyes shifting toward Emerald. "I'll return momentarily." Adalia watched him walk away, admiring his confident gait, the lift of his shoulders, and the way the sunlight streaked his hair. When she faced her friends, she saw she wasn't the only one admiring Morgan.

Clearing her throat, Emerald fluttered her fan about her face. "Now, what shall we talk about? Hmm." She laid a finger on her chin as if searching for some topic that would not be above Adalia's comprehension.

Refusing to be insulted, Adalia feigned interest as the lady began to ramble on. Something about the weather and the atrocious gown Miss Walker was wearing, and when the latest fashions from Paris would arrive in town—all things that only thickened the glaze over Drayton's eyes while benumbing Adalia's mind. Emerald even complimented Adalia on her gown. "It looks lovely on you, Adalia. I told you that color would suit you." She smiled.

What was wrong with the lady? Did she take Adalia for a fool? The last time Adalia had seen her, she'd done nothing but stare at her with contempt. Why, now, this pretense of friendship?

Still, where was Morgan? One glance over the garden did not reveal his handsome face. Instead, the brilliant glow of a white satin suit caught Adalia's eye. Sunlight filtered through the oak trees above and dappled the man's coat in sparkling snow as he skated before her—more like a radiant blur than a physical presence. Excusing herself, she followed him, weaving through the chattering crowd and ignoring Drayton's call to return.

As if sensing her behind him, the man in white turned. "Charm is deceitful and beauty is passing, but a woman who fears the Lord, she shall be praised."

Though he spoke softly, his words thundered within her. They barely had time to sink in before he slipped through the crowd and disappeared. Grabbing her skirts, Adalia tore after him, determined to discover the strange man's identity. And why did he quote Scripture? Was he some kind of ethereal evangelist? If so, why was he wasting his time with her? She was a Christian! She loved God!

Craning her neck to see over the feathers, flowers, and beads floating atop the sea of hats, she threaded through the mob, nudging people aside while begging their pardon and inquiring after the man in white. All she received in return were frowns, snorts, and concerned looks as if she'd gone mad.

When she reached the edge of the garden, the man in white was nowhere to be seen.

The only place he could have gone was into the house. Adalia rushed up the stairs into the back gallery, empty now since most of the guests had vacated the house for the cooler breezes outside. Resounding voices drew her down a hallway to her right, where a door stood ajar. A quick glimpse of bookshelves told her it was the library. Not wanting to intrude, she turned to leave when Morgan's voice halted her and lured her back to listen.

☙

"Father, I love her." Morgan stood before Franklin and met the man's hardened stare. When he'd gone to help Hadley to his chamber, he'd found his father standing over him, staring at his eldest son in disgust. Instead of helping Morgan carry him upstairs, Franklin had dismissed Hadley with a wave and dragged Morgan to his library. After lighting a cigar and pacing before the bay window overlooking the garden party, Franklin had faced his son, the usual look of scorn riding high on his brow, and demanded to know how Morgan could have brought that baseborn woman into his home.

"Love. Pishaw!" Franklin huffed. "Believe me, boy, it's only lust you feel. And that will pass. Trust me on that."

That he probably spoke of Morgan's mother, not to mention all his various affairs, only increased Morgan's fury.

Franklin puffed on his cigar. "Besides I didn't bring you here to discuss your trysts."

"Adalia is not one of—"

"I want you to take over the running of the plantation." His father's brisk declaration surprised Morgan. The man had never expressed an ounce of confidence in either Morgan's brains or his ability.

"But what of Hadley?"

"You saw your brother. He's a drunk and a gambler. And no matter how hard I try to steer him down the right path, he refuses."

Morgan hadn't recalled any steering by their father. And especially not down a good path. "Your opinion of him must have indeed taken on new depths for you to come to me."

"I'm done with him." Franklin blew out a puff of smoke and watched it dissipate as if it were Hadley himself. "Let the boy waste his life away if he wants." His eyes narrowed on Morgan. "You'll do just fine, boy. With a bit of hard work, that is. I should have seen that from the beginning."

A compliment. At last a compliment from his father! As jaded as it was. Yet Morgan found he could not absorb it. Found that the casing around his heart forbade it entrance. He crossed his arms over his chest. "You always told me I was good for nothing."

"Trying to spur you on." Franklin huffed, pointing his cigar at him. "Encourage you to do better."

"Rubbish."

"Ah, good. You've finally grown a spine. Believe me, you'll need it to run this place." Franklin marched to his desk and glanced at a group of papers. "We'll start with the books first thing tomorrow morning."

Morgan swallowed down what felt like a brick. It landed in his belly like ballast in a ship's hold. Running the estate would keep Morgan landlocked, imprisoning him in a life worse than death. A life of ledgers and planting and harvesting and managing and lording it over a swarm of slaves and servants who would hate him for his position and power.

He shifted his stance and gripped the back of the chair. This was the first time his father had displayed an ounce of confidence in him. Part of Morgan came to life beneath his approval.

And part of him felt as though he was about to make a pact with the devil.

Speaking of the devil, a devilishly grand idea occurred to Morgan. For the first time in his life, he may have the upper hand with his father. He lengthened his stance and met his father's critical glare. "I came here to discuss Miss Winston. I intend to court her formally."

Franklin stared at him as if Morgan had asked to marry a horse. "She's comely, I'll give her that. So bed her and get her out of your system. But courting? Marriage? Impossible! Miss Emerald has always been our choice for you. She has every quality benefitting a man of your pedigree and status. Not to mention a substantial dowry. We cannot risk tainting our blood with a woman we know very little about or even who her parents were." His face folded in his usual disapproving frown. "Marry Miss Emerald, and keep this tart on the side if you must."

Blood surged into Morgan's fists. "Do not speak of her in that way."

Franklin chortled, a wicked sort of incredulous chortle. He stood to his full imposing height, planting his knuckles on his desk, leaning toward Morgan. "If you marry that commoner, you will never see a penny of the Rutledge fortune."

❧

Standing on the front porch of the Rutledge home, Emerald handed Hadley a glass of cool tea. "Here, drink this. Perhaps it will dilute the alcohol in your blood."

Taking the glass, Hadley set it down and slouched back in the chair, his eyes closed against what he claimed was the worst headache of his life. "Never fear, Emerald, once my father rejects Miss Winston, that will be the end of her."

The sorrow in his voice reminded Emerald that much the same thing had happened with Hadley's infatuation with Miss Sarah. Perhaps he was right. Perhaps Morgan would not be willing to forsake everything for the petty chit. But the man had been acting so befuddled lately, she couldn't take the chance. She must follow through with her plan.

Turning, she gazed over the oaks lining the front drive, watching the Spanish moss sway in the breeze.

"Enjoying the scenery?" Mr. Saville's sudden appearance beside Emerald gave her a start.

"Where have you been?" she snapped.

"Good day to you as well." He gave a mock bow.

Emerald sighed. "Have you heard back from the Miles Plantation?"

"It's far too soon." He shrugged and ran a finger over both sides of his mustache. "And I can find nothing incriminating about the woman either. She is a saint. She won't steal, she works hard, she has no lovers, and she won't drink unless fooled." His voice was incredulous, as if the very idea of not partaking in at least one of those vices was beyond his comprehension.

"What about her past? Surely there's something."

"All I can discover is that she came here from the islands. Jamaica, they say." He withdrew a handkerchief and dabbed his neck. "But my inquiries have come up empty. Apparently her family was not prominent, for no one on the island recalls the Winston name."

"Well, of course, her family was not prominent. That's the bloody point." Emerald huffed, feeling her insides tangle into a hopeless knot. "Nothing seems to work. I try to make her sick, and her kindness causes me to poison my friend, Caroline." Guilt pinched Emerald once again for the unfortunate incident. "She returns your money, Fabian, and Morgan's admiration for her rises. She drinks too much, and Morgan protects and defends her. Everything I do, every plan to separate them, only draws them closer."

"Perhaps you should stop trying," Hadley mumbled.

She gave him a venomous look, but his eyes were still closed.

"Are you sure this new plan will work?" Fabian asked, leaning back on the porch railing.

"I have no idea. But I won't waste the opportunity."

"But we've sent the letter." He shrugged, running a finger through the lace at his sleeve. "Perhaps that is all you need."

"Who knows if anything will come of it?" Emerald gave him a look of disgust. For goodness' sake, did he or did he not want to punish Morgan?

Fabian pursed his lips. "You know I'd do anything to get back at Morgan. But poor Miss Winston—I have no beef with her."

"Don't be such a ninny, Fabian. She will not be harmed."

Hadley chuckled.

Emerald found her patience wearing thin. "Just hide behind the dressing screen. If she doesn't disrobe, you know what to do."

"How will you get her to follow you?" Fabian shifted his hips and wiped dust from his coat. "She doesn't exactly trust you."

"Caroline will help. She does whatever I ask."

"Hmm, must be nice." He gave a devilish grin.

"You just do what you're told, and I'll bring Morgan along at the right time." Then turning on her heels, she headed into the house.

Chapter Twenty

Adalia threw a hand to her throat to stifle the shriek rising to her lips. Morgan's father had certainly made his feelings clear. Heart hammering in her chest, she hesitated at the door, listening, waiting to hear Morgan's answer. Waiting—with her heart in the balance—for him to tell his father that his wealth and position meant nothing to him if he couldn't have her.

But only silence slunk from the room. That and the light notes of the orchestra and the prattle of the partygoers drifting in from outside. The paneled hallway began to spin, and she leaned her head on the wall when the door jerked open, and Morgan stormed out of the library down the hall, his face bunched tight in anger. He hadn't seen her.

And she didn't want to see him right now. He had not countered his father's threat! He had not stood up for her. Tears blurred her vision as Adalia tore down the hallway, pushing her way past servants and guests, with one thought on her mind. Leaving. She had to get away from this place—this world where she didn't belong. From Morgan. She'd been a fool. A complete and utter fool! Wiping her face, she barreled around the corner toward the front foyer.

A figure leapt from the side. Miss Emerald plowed into her with a shriek. Orange liquid splashed over the front of Adalia's gown. She gasped and stared down at the mess as Caroline hurried up to her, a horrified look on her face.

Emerald clicked her tongue. "My, my, my, look what you have done. Well, at least you didn't spill any on me. Caroline, would you take Miss Winston upstairs to Mrs. Rutledge's dressing room and try and salvage this lovely gown?"

"No, that's quite alright." Adalia refused Caroline's outstretched hand. "I'm very sorry, Emerald. This was all my fault. But, I must go." She tried to push past the ladies, hoping they hadn't seen the tears in her eyes.

"Nonsense, Miss Winston." Emerald looked truly alarmed. "This fabric will stain if you don't take care of it immediately. It will only take a moment."

Caroline looped an arm through Adalia's and smiled, tugging her toward the stairway. "Come along. It will be all right."

"I'll send up the chambermaid," Emerald called after them.

Though suspicion rankled across Adalia's mind at what Emerald might be up to, she had no reason to doubt Caroline. Besides, Emerald was right. There was no sense in ruining her new gown. And she could use the time to gather her emotions before she saw Morgan. Now that her mind had stopped reeling, she realized she had neither horse nor carriage to take her home.

She depended entirely on the man who'd just ripped her heart in two.

Still in a daze, Adalia allowed Caroline to lead her upstairs and into a room at the far end of the hall. Thick velvet curtains draped elegantly around windows through which sunlight streamed onto a Turkish carpet. Paintings of ladies in finery hung above dressing screens and vanities littered with powders and perfumes.

Caroline closed the door and started unbuttoning Adalia's gown.

"What are you doing?"

"I'm going to remove your gown, so the maid can treat it properly."

"No, please." Adalia spun around. "I'll keep it on."

Caroline gazed at her curiously. "Don't be shy. It will be far easier with it off."

A knock sounded, and an older lady entered, wearing a plain dress and a mobcap and carrying a rag and some jars in her hand. "Oh, my goodness," she said as she approached.

"She wants to keep her gown on," Caroline stated.

"Very well, I'll do what I can. Have a seat, miss."

Adalia slid onto one of the cushioned chairs, glad to take the weight off of her trembling legs. Still trembling from anger and sorrow. She wiped the remaining moisture from her eyes and drew in a deep breath while the maid went to work.

"Powdered starch and vinegar should do the trick," the woman said as she fluffed out Adalia's skirts and sprinkled white powder on the stains. "But you'll have to wash it properly when you get home."

"Are you all right, Miss Winston?" Caroline knelt to look up at her. "You seem out of sorts, and your eyes are red." She took her hand. "It was only an accident. Nothing to be overwrought about."

Muffled voices came from the hallway. One of them male. And it sounded like Morgan.

Adalia's heart caught in her throat. Movement behind one of the dressing screens in the corner drew her gaze. Fabian Saville stepped out from behind it, his eyes on the door and, his face tight.

The maid gasped. Caroline jumped to her feet. "What are you doing here, Fabian? Get out at once!"

Ignoring her, Fabian, a determined, nearly frightened look on his face, dashed toward Adalia and just as the door opened, grabbed the collar of her gown and tore it down her back. The force of his wrench ripped her petticoat and chemise as well, leaving her back exposed for all to see.

❧

Morgan entered the room, Emerald on his heels. His quick glance shifted over Adalia, Caroline, and finally Mr. Saville. "What is the meaning of this?"

Mr. Saville grinned.

Morgan stormed toward him. "What are you doing in a ladies' dressing room, Fabian? And with Miss Winston and Miss Caroline?"

Saville backed away and held up his hands. "Just showing you the truth."

Emerald, her face aglow with delight, rushed over to Adalia and pointed at her back. "See, Morgan! See the stripes on her back?"

Adalia tried to stand, but her legs gave out. She attempted to shift her back away as Morgan's gaze bounced from Emerald to Adalia. Finally, he cornered the chair she sat upon and studied the bare flesh on her back. Lowering her face, she closed her eyes, not wanting to see his expression, not able to stand the disgust, the repulsion she knew would be there.

"What?" was all she heard him say. But then something unexpected proceeded from his mouth.

"Did you tear her gown, sir?"

"I did."

"And you! You forced me up here to see this."

Emerald groaned. "I tried to tell you, Morgan, but you wouldn't listen."

"This means nothing!" Morgan huffed.

Adalia opened her eyes, wondering if she were hearing things. Her gaze met his, and the concern she saw in them took her aback. But then that concern turned to fury as he faced Mr. Saville.

"Tearing a lady's gown! You have gone too far, Fabian!" He slowly made his way over to the fop, anger seething in the air around him. "Spiking a lady's drink and now this. . .this I cannot let pass without repercussion."

One cultured brow rose. "Grand! A duel, perhaps?"

Clutching the man by his cravat, Morgan dragged him out of the room. Mr. Saville's protests and groans faded down the hall.

With a tight purse of her lips and a lift of her chin, Emerald followed after them. The maid finally rose and began muttering under her breath.

Caroline turned to Adalia, a stricken look on her comely features. "I'm sorry, Miss Winston, I didn't know what they had planned." She handed her a shawl.

Adalia smiled. "I believe you." Yet she didn't know what to believe about what had just happened. No time to think now. She had to stop Morgan from killing Fabian. Swinging the shawl over her shoulders, she grabbed Caroline's hand and darted from the room.

૭૨

Morgan slammed his fist across the man's jaw, sending him flying over the porch railing into a huckleberry bush.

Emerald let out a tiny shriek.

Hadley, who had been sitting in a chair on the porch when Morgan dragged Fabian outside, chuckled and rubbed his forehead.

The other guests mulling about turned to stare.

Morgan thundered down the steps just as Fabian rose from the bushes, curses shooting from his lips and twigs littering his fine coat.

Grabbing his lapels, Morgan plucked him from the shrubbery. "You are a cad, sir."

"Only trying to help, ole chap. Since you are obviously too beef-witted to believe the truth." Fabian smiled at the crowd growing around them.

Incensed, Morgan drew back to strike him again, but Fabian

slammed his fist into Morgan's belly. Doubling over, Morgan tumbled backward, allowing the pain to feed his anger.

Adalia appeared on the top step. "Stop it this instant!" She stomped her foot.

Fabian shook his hand, wincing, though a smirk remained on his face. Morgan started for him, but strong arms held him back. Hadley blocked his way, one hand on Morgan's chest, one hand rubbing his temples. "You should settle this like gentlemen."

"As I have been telling him." Fabian flung a hand in the air, his tone victorious.

The fiend was right. For once. "Indeed, you shall finally have your satisfaction." Jerking from his brother's grip, Morgan wiped the sweat from his brow and narrowed his eyes. "You have insulted Miss Winston. I demand reparation. Pistols or swords?"

"Why, pistols of course." The confidence in Fabian's tone ignited Morgan's alarm. Why had he given him the choice? Morgan was much more proficient at swords.

"Then I shall see you at dawn."

Chapter Twenty-One

Weaving around a newly arrived phaeton, Adalia headed down the driveway, ignoring the stares that followed her. No doubt the elite were anxious for their daily entertainment from the lowly maid who'd forced her way into their formidable circle.

A duel? The thought of it, the thought of anything happening to Morgan, caused the blood to race from her heart. Foolish man! Foolish, wonderful man! One minute he was unwilling to lose his fortune for her, the next he was willing to lose his life. Nothing made sense anymore. She didn't know whether to be furious with him or love him all the more.

Good heavens, he had seen her scars! What he must be thinking. Tears trickled down her cheeks, and she wiped them away. She had been so looking forward to this party, to this day, and now everything was ruined.

Boot steps pounded behind her. She hastened her pace.

"Adalia. Please stop."

"Go back to your guests, Morgan."

"Adalia." Gripping her arm, he swung her about.

Gone was the charming smile that graced his lips. In its stead, a mixture of panic and remorse thundered across his face. "Why are you leaving? If it's because I fought, I had to defend your honor."

"But a duel, Morgan? You could die."

"I won't. Fabian is a featherhead."

Yet Adalia saw the flicker of doubt in his eyes.

"Besides, he's been begging me to duel for years."

"It's far too dangerous. Go tell him you won't do it. I'm not worth it."

Morgan grabbed her shoulders. "What are you saying? Of course you are."

She jerked from his grip. "Worth dying for but not worth losing your fortune over!"

Confusion muddled his face for a moment before he spiked a hand through his hair and glanced down. "You heard."

"I did."

"I'm sorry."

"No more than I." She started down the path. "Now, if you please."

"Do you intend to walk all the way back to Charleston?"

"If I have to."

"Allow me to call for my carriage." He blocked her path. "I'll explain everything on the way back."

"I'd rather walk." She skirted around him.

"Please, Adalia." He clutched her arm again then led her to the side of the drive beneath an elm tree. Grabbing her hand, he caressed her fingers. She wanted to pull away, to slap him for hurting her, to hug him for coming to her defense, but the confusion of it all prevented her from doing anything but stand there.

Even so, this might be the last time she felt his touch. The last time she watched the wind tease the tips of his tawny hair, loosening a strand over his cheek the way it always did. The last time his spicy scent filled her senses.

"I'm sorry for my father's cruel opinions," he said, still holding her hand.

Her anger returned. "It was not his opinions that upset me. But your lack of them." She watched him melt beneath her livid tone. He tightened his grip on her hand as if he feared she would run away. "I was too angry to answer him."

"Or perhaps you had no answer." She tore from him, fighting back tears. She must remain strong. She must not give in to the tender, pleading look in his eyes. "You misled me. I am not some tart, as your father put it, to be toyed with and discarded."

"You don't understand." His jaw tightened. "I never meant to. . . I love you, Adalia. I do. I cannot help it." He stepped toward her, his eyes misting.

She turned away. "But the cost is too high."

He sighed and shoved the wayward strand of hair behind his ear. "What would I do without money? How would I survive?"

Not the answer she expected. But an honest answer, nonetheless. And one that shredded the last remnants of the fairy-tale veil covering her eyes. It had been fabulous these past few months. Like living a dream. But the dream was over now. She knew that by the look of defeat and fear on Morgan's face. The way he glanced over the plantation as if he could never escape it. As if he were shackled to it like one of his slaves. And suddenly Adalia realized Morgan was as much a slave as she had been. Maybe even more. Despite her anger, her heart went out to him.

"How would you survive?" she said. "You would work like the rest of us. Find a trade. You're smart, resourceful."

"But there is such risk. If I fail. . .I will starve." Pain burned in his gaze. "We will starve. How can I expect you to endure that with me?"

A breeze flapped the hem of her gown and quivered the leaves in the tree above her, making them sound like a thousand whispers, cheering her on.

"Life is full of risk, Morgan. It's what makes life exciting." She searched his eyes for any sign of understanding, but uncertainty still reigned. "The true measure of a man is not in his fortune or status. But in his courage, wit, and honor."

The crack of a whip drew her gaze to the fields beyond the house. A slave bent over in pain before one of the taskmasters. He struck the man again, and Adalia felt the fire on her own back. She tightened the shawl around her.

"You saw my scars."

Morgan studied her. "You were whipped. I can see that. It doesn't change anything except that it made me want to kill the man who did it."

"Don't you want to know why I was whipped?"

"It doesn't matter." He took a step toward her, turmoil burning in his eyes. "It makes no difference in my affection toward you. It's not like you are a slave!" He let out a sordid chuckle.

She backed away from him, suddenly chilled.

No matter how honorable, how kind, how romantic Morgan was, he was still a slave owner. Somehow in all the glamour and romance, she had forgotten that—had hoped she could change that fact. But his unwillingness to part with any of his wealth and the incredulous tone of his last words proved the impossibility of her task.

"Whether we ever see each other again or not, I beg you, Morgan, do not allow your father to rule your life. If you do, you are no less a slave than those men in the fields." She hugged herself to keep from touching him. "You must step out and trust God."

Yet even as she said it, she wondered if she had been trusting God. She couldn't remember the last time she had truly spoken to the Almighty, save in passing or at meals.

Morgan lifted his hand to caress her cheek, but she stepped out of his reach. She swiped away a tear. "Marry Emerald."

"I don't love her." He swallowed, his chest rising and falling as if he'd just realized the inevitable. "I don't want to lose you, Adalia."

Yet, his tone carried a hopelessness that sealed their destiny. "You can't have it all, Morgan." Wiping her face, she lifted her chin. "Now, if you don't mind having your footman drive me home. . ."

When his only response was to order the man to bring the carriage around, the last shred of Adalia's heart crumbled in her chest.

And the fairy tale faded into oblivion.

ॐ

As Morgan watched Adalia drive off in his brougham, he felt as though his life, his hopes, his dreams rode off with her. She was right, of course. He knew she was right. He couldn't have both her and his fortune, his status. Not if his father had anything to do with it. He watched until the carriage disappeared behind the curtain of Spanish moss hanging from the trees then turned and trudged back to the house. What should have been a happy occasion—the announcement of his and Adalia's courtship—turned out to be the worst day of his life.

He'd certainly expected opposition from Franklin. He certainly expected to put up a fight. But he hadn't expected the stubborn man to be so cruel as to not only disinherit his son but also disown him. Yes, he'd threatened the same with Hadley and Sarah, but Hadley was his wonder boy, the favored son upon whose shoulders rested the future and hopes of the Rutledge family.

Not Morgan. Never Morgan. Until today. Why, of all days, did his father decide to make Morgan his heir apparent today?

He'd wanted so much to tell him he could take his fortune and position to the grave, but fear had clamped his tongue. Then when Adalia had looked at him with those fathomless eyes brimming with tears, it was all he could do not to take her into his arms and tell her he'd forsake everything to be with her. But his fear rose again like a Carolina crocodile snapping its jaws on his determination and courage. He hated to see Adalia hurt. Hated that he'd been the cause. But wouldn't he hurt her more if he married her without two coins to his name? How many times would they go to bed hungry before that sparkle in her eye would dim? Before she would no longer look at him with admiration and love. But instead with disgust and disdain. She deserved better. She deserved a life of opulence and ease.

A life he could easily give her if only his father would agree.

He rubbed the sweat from the back of his neck as he ascended the front steps, spewing curses upon each tread. He should have known better. He should have thought things through, foreseen the inevitable outcome, instead of plunging headfirst into unchartered seas. Now, he had broken not only Adalia's heart but his own as well.

Yet, there had to be a way. He fisted his hands. He must think of something. Some way to convince Franklin, blackmail him if he had to.

That was, if he didn't die tomorrow in a duel.

CHAPTER TWENTY-TWO

Daddy, Daddy, look at me!" With hands spread out at her sides, ten-year-old Adalia spun around, staring up at the hundreds of leaves framing a cerulean sky. She felt the lacy hem of her new gown tickle her ankles as she twirled barefooted over the sandy dirt.

Clapping and cheering filled the air, and she stopped and smiled at her father, who was sitting on a bench before their humble home, cleaning a fresh catch of fish.

"Am I beautiful, Daddy?" Adalia adjusted the sprig of flowers her mother had pinned in her hair and held out the folds of her gown. Her first and only formal gown—a luxury promised to her on her tenth birthday. She would wear it to the yearly harvest festival, where all the local farmers gathered to celebrate God's bounty.

Her father dropped the fish he'd been cleaning back into the bucket. His adoring gaze took her in as if she were diamonds and jewels, not a simple farm girl. "You are the most beautiful girl in the world," he answered with all sincerity.

Adalia dashed and melted against him. Protective Daddy arms enveloped her like thick wings, covering her, shielding her. The smell of fish curled her nose, but she didn't care. It was the smell of her daddy.

Nudging her back, he kissed her forehead. "You'll always be my little princess."

Feeling every bit like royalty, Adalia skipped and danced around the clearing, admiring how the sunlight frolicked in patches of shimmering light over her gown. "Now, all I need is a prince, Daddy." She stopped before him again.

"Someday, my precious one"—he tapped her on the nose—"God

will send you a prince who will love and cherish you."

Adalia giggled with delight. "Do you promise, Daddy?"

He nodded. "You deserve no less." Cupping her face in his hands he kissed her cheek, and Adalia closed her eyes, her heart soaring.

Then the rough hands grew soft and smooth, and the touch pinched instead of loving. Instead of fish, bergamot stung her nose, sending her heart hammering against her chest.

She opened her eyes to see Sir Walter's flaccid face inches from hers. Rage and a touch of madness whirled in his dark eyes. Releasing her with a jerk, he backed away. "Princess, you say?" He chuckled.

Adalia rose from where she'd been kneeling in prayer in her chamber. So caught up in the presence of God, she hadn't heard Sir Walter enter. Heat flushed through her. He'd heard her petition to someday become a princess, to find her prince.

"Slaves only become princesses in fairy tales, my dear. And fairy tales never come true."

Adalia glanced out her barred window, where a moonless light dripped ebony over the Miles Plantation. When she met Sir Walter's gaze again, candlelight flickered over a rising maniacal grin. He only came to her chamber at night for one thing.

Adalia woke with a start. Sweat beaded on her neck. One glance out the window told her it was still night. Thank goodness she hadn't overslept. She hadn't decided whether to attend the duel when she'd retired. She'd been far too distraught. She hadn't been able to think straight through all the tears and the heartache. But sometime during the night, amidst all the nightmares, all the pain, terror for Morgan's life overcame her anger and her grief. Not that she could do anything. But she must try to stop them.

Flinging the covers aside, she quickly donned her underthings and gown and headed downstairs.

Urging Doc Willaby's horse to a gallop, Adalia reached the edge of town within minutes and headed down the muddy path edged with hickory and pine. Dawn's blush pinked the horizon, barely pushing aside the shadows of the night, giving her just enough light to see her way down the moss-entangled trail and out onto a lush field where she'd heard Hadley say the duel would take place. She wondered why they chose a spot much closer to town than Rutledge Hall, but then again, dueling was frowned upon in most circles. She doubted Morgan had even informed his father of the event.

She reined the horse to a stop. He snorted and pawed the mud as she scanned the area. Gray mist swirled in a chaotic dance around spindly grass. In the distance, shadows of looming trees rose like guardians of the night. No sound reached her ears save the croaking of frogs and the distant gush of a creek—muffled, yet magnified in the dank air. A chilled breeze clawed her cloak and scattered goose bumps down her arms even as an eerie feeling of foreboding struck her. It was the perfect place to act out such an obscene play.

Although dueling was not outlawed yet, there were rumblings among the legislature and sermons from the pulpit against such barbaric traditions. Adalia quite agreed.

Something caught her eye at the far end of the field, and she galloped in that direction, her medical satchel bouncing over the saddle. Fighting the exhaustion tugging at her eyes, she forced her gaze beyond the tree line, where she could make out blurry shapes moving about. Crashing through the foliage, she dismounted and tied her horse beside six others then marched toward the men with one thought in mind.

To end this madness.

She spotted Morgan straight away, leaning casually against a tree as if he hadn't a care in the world. Absent a waistcoat and cravat, his white shirt flapped in the morning breeze as he shifted one booted foot across the other and yawned. Across the clearing, Mr. Saville puffed upon a cigar, unimpressed by Morgan's courageous display. Hadley and another man, whom Adalia assumed was Mr. Saville's second, stood to the side examining a pair of pistols. Two other men whispered amongst themselves.

"Morgan Rutledge, I insist you stop this tomfoolery at once!" She barreled toward him. His face registered shock, but his features quickly tightened in concern. He took her arm and led her aside as the other men glanced their way.

"What in the blazes are you doing here?"

Her anger faded into dread at his closeness. His touch. His scent. The look of love in his eyes.

"Please, Morgan. This isn't necessary."

"Ah, if it isn't the marked woman." Mr. Saville's voice oozed over her back. "Come to bid adieu to your beau?"

Morgan stiffened, his eyes locking on Mr. Saville like cannons on a target.

Adalia ignored the buffoon. "Please stop this. For me?"

He lowered his gaze, his expression softening. "That's why I'm here. For you, milady."

"Don't call me that." Tears filled her eyes.

He cupped her chin, brushing his fingers over her jaw. "I told you, I love you, Adalia. And if I must, I will defend your honor to the death."

"But what purpose will it serve? We can never be together. Walk away," she pleaded. "Just walk away. What is the honor of a common woman worth?"

He looked at her as if she'd asked him the value of a chest full of gold. "Everything."

The other men approached, Mr. Saville among them, his eyes cold and lifeless.

Morgan released her and faced his opponent. "This is your last chance to apologize to the lady."

"The lady, you say?" He avoided Adalia's gaze and instead leveled the full force of his contempt at Morgan. "No one is whipped but a slave or a whore."

Jaw grinding, Morgan started for him. He didn't get far before Hadley's arm held him back.

Too shocked by Mr. Saville's vulgar statement, Adalia merely stared at him, wondering at the depths of his hatred, wondering if this was all part of Emerald's plan to win Morgan. If so, would she rather see him dead than in the arms of another? And where was she, anyway? If she cared so much for Morgan, she should be here to witness the fruits of her labors.

Morgan ceased struggling against Hadley's grip and ran a hand through his loose hair. "Please leave, Adalia."

"Yes, I do insist," one of the other men interjected. "Women should not be present at duels."

"I am here on business. To help the injured."

This brought several snorts from the men, but finally, much to Morgan's obvious dismay, they agreed. More, Adalia surmised, because they were in a hurry rather than that they wished to appease her.

Grabbing her satchel from the saddle, Adalia took up a spot on the edge of the small clearing. Her legs dissolved into pudding as the two men moved to choose their weapons. She leaned on a tree and spoke her first prayer in a while, "Oh Lord, please do not let Morgan die."

❧

Turning away from the desperate look in Adalia's eyes, Morgan faced his opponent. He cleared all thoughts, all emotions from his mind and focused on the business at hand.

"Very well, then." Hadley opened the wooden box containing the French dueling pistols. Mr. Richards and I have checked the weapons thoroughly and found them equally sound. They are both loaded and ready to fire."

Selecting one, Morgan checked the priming, noting the elaborate engraving running down the barrel from the hammer. Mr. Saville, with a rather bored look on his face, plucked the other one and held it up in the muted light.

Hadley snapped the box shut.

Mr. Richards gave Morgan a look of pity before he spouted the rules. "We will count ten paces, as agreed, then at my command, you may turn and fire. You have one shot each."

One shot to shut the mouth of this swaggering popinjay for good. Morgan gave the man a grin that belied the twisting in his gut. He hadn't known when he'd challenged Mr. Saville that the dandy was an expert marksman. Morgan's own skill with pistols had much to be desired. Swords was another matter. He should have insisted on swords.

But it was too late for that.

Hadley slapped him on the back then leaned in to whisper. "Do be careful. I would hate to lose you, brother."

"I'm touched." Morgan took his position at the center of the small clearing. Unfortunately, he faced Adalia. He hated that she would witness this. Hugging herself, she leaned against a tree. Her wind-blown hair tumbled over her shoulders and down her gown like raven silk. Her cheeks were flushed. Her eyes pools of tears. He knew he'd hurt her by not standing up to his father. Sweet, sweet Adalia. He must find a way to make her his wife.

If he survived.

Fabian took his position behind Morgan.

"Ready," Hadley shouted.

A stiff breeze cooled the perspiration on Morgan's neck and chest and swirled the mist around his boots.

"One."

Morgan took a firm step forward, staring straight ahead into the gray shadows, suddenly realizing this misty morning scene could be the last thing he ever saw.

"Two... Three... Four."

Three more steps and the gun slipped in his moist hands. He gripped it tighter.

"Five... Six... Seven."

His legs felt numb. The frogs quit croaking.

"Eight... Nine."

He took one last glance at Adalia—if only to forever imprint her beauty in his mind.

"Ten."

God, if You exist and You give a care, I could use some help.

"FIRE!"

Morgan spun around. Fabian's dark form took shape. He aimed his pistol.

Crack! The shot echoed through the mist. Smoke curled from Fabian's gun. He chuckled, but his smile soon faded when Morgan took a step toward him.

That was when the pain hit. Like a brand to Morgan's shoulder, it seared down his arm, then across his chest. Morgan glanced down to see blood dripping from his fingers onto the grass. Still he did not lower his gun.

Adalia screamed.

"You're hit, brother," Hadley exclaimed in a worried tone.

"I won. It's over." Fabian's voice lacked its normal swaggering tone. In fact, he sounded quite frightened.

"Morgan hasn't had his shot yet," Hadley remarked, his tone strained. Morgan turned to see him holding Adalia back from rushing to his aid.

Ignoring the pain in his shoulder, he leveled his pistol at Fabian's chest.

Yet, instead of crumbling into a whimpering ball, Fabian's eyes hardened. He straightened his spine. Morgan would have to give him credit for courage, at least. His finger twitched over the trigger. Just one push and the world would be relieved of one more villain. One more unscrupulous villain.

But Adalia's whimper struck him from behind. "No, Morgan. It's not right."

"Finish him!" one of the witnesses shouted.

"Apologize to Miss Winston at once, and I will forfeit."

"You cannot forfeit, Mr. Rutledge," Mr. Richards said as if he were presiding over a courtroom, drawing Fabian's angry gaze. "You must fire your pistol."

"Do you wish to live?" Morgan asked Fabian.

Fabian seemed to be pondering the question as his eyes bounced from Morgan to Adalia and over the other gentlemen present as if dying were a more honorable option than apologizing.

Blood trickled from Morgan's left hand onto his boots. His head spun, and the pistol shook.

Fabian watched the barrel waver over his chest, fear making an appearance in his eyes.

"Answer me or die, sir," Morgan demanded.

Fabian must have seen the determination in Morgan's eyes. Better yet, he must have believed it, for he released a ragged sigh. He glanced toward Adalia then lowered his gaze. "My apologies, miss."

Morgan fired his gun. As intended, his shot landed in the dirt beside Fabian, who stumbled backward, horrified, checking for wounds on his chest.

Mr. Richards chuckled.

Sunlight streamed into the clearing, chasing away the mist. The warble of birds filled the air. Adalia's beautiful face appeared in Morgan's vision. His last thought before he dropped to his knees and everything disappeared was that he must have died and gone to heaven.

CHAPTER TWENTY-THREE

Bring him in here," Hadley instructed two footmen as they carried Morgan up the stairway and into a chamber on the left. Keeping pace with the men, Adalia pressed a cloth to Morgan's bloody shoulder and squeezed through the door alongside his prostrate body. The servants laid him on a bed and then left the room, allowing two chambermaids to scramble in after them, their faces masks of alarm.

Opening her satchel, Adalia handed a pouch of nettle to one of the women. "I need hot water, clean cloths, bandages, and please boil these leaves," she ordered. "And have someone call for the doctor immediately." One nod from Hadley sent the maids scurrying off.

"Will he live?" Hadley peered down at his brother, his face pinched. Adalia couldn't tell if he was worried or just curious.

Sitting beside Morgan on the bed, she tore open his shirt and ripped the sleeve down his left arm, exposing the wound near his shoulder. Blood gurgled from the opening, and she placed the nearly saturated cloth back onto it. Morgan groaned.

Hadley did too. "I think I'm going to be sick," he said, holding his stomach.

"Then leave." Adalia hated to be curt, but she had no time for weakness. Especially when there was a circle of maroon advancing over the silk coverlet beneath Morgan's arm. She tried to lift him to check the damage, but he was far too heavy. "Help me, Hadley."

With face turned away, Hadley slid his hands beneath Morgan's side and raised him while Adalia looked beneath his arm then scanned the bed stand for anything she could use. Grabbing a stack of handkerchiefs, she stuffed them against the exit wound. "That's good.

206

Thank you, Hadley. The bleeding should stop soon."

Releasing his brother, he stepped back.

Lifting the bloody cloth, Adalia peered into the bullet hole. Relief sped through her. "The bullet went clear through him." She glanced out the door, anxious for her supplies, then back up at Hadley, whose face was chiseled in white. Perhaps he did care for his brother, after all.

"Don't vex yourself, Hadley, he will live. I'll do my best to clean and bandage him until the doctor arrives."

Hadley released a heavy sigh as the maids returned, pots of boiling water and cloths in hand. Adalia got to work, thankful Morgan was still unconscious. Within minutes, she had the wound cleaned, stitched, and a eucalyptus and nettle poultice spread over the opening. Somewhere in the middle of her ministrations, Emerald swept into the chamber and gasped in horror before flying to Morgan's other side.

"It's all my fault," she sobbed as she clutched his hand.

"What did you think he would do when he saw my back?" Adalia snapped.

"I thought he would dismiss you." Hate sparked behind her glassy eyes. "As he should have."

Adalia shook her head. The lady was all peaches and cream on the outside, but on the inside, nothing but rotting fruit.

"Will he live?" Emerald's voice caught as she gazed at Morgan.

"Yes."

Hadley made his way to a side table at the far end of the room, poured himself a drink, and then sank into a chair in the corner.

Two chambermaids remained at the foot of the bed gazing at their master with concern.

Adalia wiped the blood from her hands and sat back, watching the rise and fall of Morgan's muscled chest and the way his eyelids fluttered as if he were reliving the duel. No blood marred the white bandage she had just wrapped around his firmly sculpted arm. Good.

Emerald brought his hand to her lips, her eyes turquoise pools. "Why hasn't he woken?

"He lost a lot of blood." But he should be conscious by now. Adalia dabbed a damp cloth over his forehead. Surely she had done everything right—hadn't missed some scrap of bullet somewhere. Where was the doctor, anyway? *Come on, Morgan. Please wake up.*

Voices lured Morgan from his quiet repose. One angelic voice in particular tugged on his consciousness, bidding him wake. Trouble was, the more he attempted to reach it, the more pain coursed through his body. Finally, he opened his eyes and was rewarded with Adalia's radiant face leaning over him. She smiled, that adorable little smile of hers that sent his troubles scurrying like rats before the light. Not even the pain pulsating in his arm could keep him from basking in that smile.

"How are you feeling?" she asked.

"Like I've been run over by a carriage." His chuckle faltered on his lips.

Hadley's tall figure appeared behind Adalia. "Welcome back, brother."

Someone kissed his right hand, and he turned his head to see Emerald, teary-eyed and timid, giving him an adoring look. So unlike her. Not the adoring part. But the timidity and tears.

He faced Adalia again. "Where am I?"

"Our townhome in Charleston," Hadley answered. "You beat that blackguard, Fabian." He snapped his drink to the back of his throat with a proud huff.

Ah, yes, the duel. It all came back to Morgan now. The mist, the gray haze, the shadows, French pistols, Fabian's apology. It seemed like a chilling dream.

But the pain in his arm spoke otherwise.

"And me, fainting like a woman." Sudden embarrassment swamped him. He struggled to sit. Both Adalia and Emerald tried to help him, but he swatted them away. "I'm all right, ladies. Just a bit light-headed."

"You need your rest. You've lost a fair amount of blood." Adalia gathered the red-stained rags proving her statement and dumped them in the pot of water.

Ignoring the pain, Morgan propped himself up on his pillows and met her gaze. Her ebony hair splashed around her shoulders in waves that reminded him of the sea at night. Lips the color of brandywine flattened as she looked at him. And those eyes. Those dark, deep eyes he'd thought he'd never see again. They captivated him. Particularly with the look he saw in them now—a mixture of desperation, joy. And love.

"You saved me." He tried to reach for her hand, but pain shot through his shoulder.

She shook her head and looked down. "You were lucky—the bullet went through your arm. I only dressed your wound."

"Such a brave girl."

"Such a foolish man," she retorted. "You could have been killed."

Pulling his good hand from Emerald's grasp, he clutched Adalia's. "I would happily do it again for you."

A squeal slipped from Emerald's lips—barely discernable, but there nonetheless. Rising, she moved toward the door. Morgan knew he had hurt her, but it was time the woman understood where his affections lay. Besides, he couldn't tear his gaze from Adalia's eyes. Though now confusion rolled over them, clouding her affection. He supposed he couldn't blame her. "I've been a fool, Adalia. I will find a way for us to be together. I promise. I will make Franklin see."

Hadley let out a snort and made his way to Emerald, who appeared as though she would faint.

"Come, love. Let's leave them alone." Hadley's voice held more compassion than Morgan had heard in quite a while.

❦

Storming down the hall, Emerald tore from Hadley's grasp. "Everything I do—even this ridiculous duel—only brings Morgan closer to that. . . that. . .ill-bred, goose-witted slattern."

"Perhaps it's time to quit the game and count your losses, love."

"Never!" She reached the bottom of the stairway and faced him like an angry lioness. "We must think of something else."

Something else? Hadley had only gone along with her schemes to appease her, to befriend her, to make her see that he would do anything for her, that *he* was the man she wanted. Of course he had no desire to see his brother married to a commoner. It would besmirch the Rutledge name beyond repair! But hadn't he been in Morgan's shoes once upon a time? He knew the pain of not having the one woman he loved. Besides, he wondered if he wasn't doing himself a disservice in the long run. If Morgan's pursuit of Adalia ended, he'd be free to receive Emerald's advances. And where did that leave Hadley? Yet how could he turn her down? She'd hate him forever if he refused to come to her aid. He loved her. He would spend a lifetime making her happy. Why couldn't she see that?

"But what else can you do?" Hadley forced a sympathetic look that was lost on Emerald, who gazed up the stairs to where Morgan lay.

Grief and jealousy burned within him. After Sarah, he didn't think he'd ever love again. For months, regret and guilt had eaten away at his soul until he took to the bottle to dull the pain. He'd lost the one woman he loved because of his own stupidity. He would not lose another.

He knew Emerald well enough to know there was only one course of action that would keep him in her favor. He must continue to help her in her quest to separate Morgan and Miss Winston. And hope that her infatuation with his brother would fade over time. Perhaps when Morgan was free, he would continue to refuse Emerald's attentions. Either way, Hadley would be there to comfort her. He would be her rock, her knight. She would see that he was the only one who truly cared for her.

He leaned toward her, drawing her sea-blue eyes his way. "I said, what else can we do, love?"

❧

Taking Dr. Willaby's hand, Adalia stepped down from the phaeton. She clutched her satchel and waited for him while he ordered Mr. Gant to settle the horses for the night and stow the carriage. They'd spent the day making house calls, and Adalia was pleased when the doctor allowed her to administer her herbs and teas on more than one occasion. After witnessing the effectiveness of her remedies, he seemed willing to give her elixirs a try on less serious illnesses, especially when most of his patients adored her. For the first time in her life, Adalia felt worthy, useful, and productive.

Doc Willaby placed her hand in the crook of his elbow and led her up the stairs to the front door. "It's been quite nice to have you home these past few weeks. Especially at night." He gave her a curious look that begged the question she knew he wanted to ask.

Was she still seeing Morgan Rutledge?

But how could she answer him if she didn't know herself? She'd neither seen nor heard from Morgan in two weeks. Not since the duel. Not since he'd sworn he'd find a way for them to be together. Was it just the emotion of the moment? His gratitude for her medical care? Or had his father said something to him?

"It has been nice to be home," she answered the doctor, though she couldn't say that was entirely true. She missed the soirees, the concerts, the beautiful gowns—the attention, the approval she received from Charleston society.

Doc Willaby ushered her into the foyer, where Adalia quickly checked the silver platter on the front table for any calling cards or posts. Empty as usual. Seeing a flash of white down the hallway, she shouted for Joy.

Within seconds, the young slave came running, wiping her hands on her apron, her smile a half-moon of pearly white teeth. She stumbled over a porcelain planter, tipping it over and spilling dirt across the tile floor.

"Oh, of all the. . ." Doc Willaby grumbled as he hung his hat on the hanger.

Kneeling, Adalia helped Joy gather the dirt.

"Stupid, clumsy girl," the doctor exclaimed. "Adalia, no need for you to assist. Joy can take care of it." He took her arm and all but dragged her into the sitting room.

Why was he so kind one minute then so uncaring the next? Suddenly Adalia didn't feel like spending any more time with the doctor. Untying the ribbon beneath her chin, she removed her hat, her anger bolstering her courage. "You shouldn't treat Joy that way."

With a heavy sigh, he sank into his favorite chair. "She's always bumping into things."

"She's a human being with emotions just like us."

He gave her a perplexed look. "She's but a slave."

He might as well have said, "She's but a horse" or "She's but a cat" for all the value his tone implied. Staring at him, Adalia wondered what he would think if he knew he'd spent the day with a slave—entrusted his patients to a slave.

Feeling nauseous, she excused herself and went to her chamber to rest. Yet, she could find no rest. Instead, she paced across the room, the creak of the floorboards thrumming a rhythmic tune that only ceased when she stopped long enough to gaze out the window at her herb garden below. Which was doing quite nicely now that the weather had grown hot.

High temperatures meant "the season" in Charleston was nearly at an end and soon the elite would scamper back to their plantations and estates to ride out the sweltering heat at home. She wondered if Morgan would stay away from town as well. Of course he would. It was what was expected of his class. And Morgan seemed quite obsessed with maintaining the respect of society.

She sighed and twirled a curl dangling about her neck. Soon there would be no more cotillions, concerts, plays, or horse races—or at least very few. The thought dampened her mood. Not that she would be able to attend any more of the extravagant functions without Morgan.

His silence could only mean one thing. That he had not yet been able to convince his father to allow their courtship. Or worse, his father had refused again. But why hadn't Morgan sent word?

Sudden dread clenched her stomach. What if his wound had become infected? What if something horrible had happened to him? Would his brother alert her? Probably not. Nor would his parents or Emerald, or even Drayton.

Dashing to her looking glass, she adjusted the pins in her hair and dabbed some beet juice on her lips. Then donning a lacy pelisse, she grabbed her medical satchel and headed downstairs. One peek inside the sitting room revealed the doctor snoring with Bible spread across his lap and spectacles sliding down his nose. Good. She wouldn't have to make an excuse for her improper behavior.

She crept outside and gazed at the lowering sun. She had just enough time to go to the Rutledge townhome, check on Morgan, and be home before supper. Yet as she slipped out onto Calhoun Street, she suddenly felt like a fool. It was highly improper for her to call on a gentleman. Only wanton women visited men in their homes alone. But it couldn't be helped. She must know if Morgan was all right. And if so, she must know his answer. She must know in what direction her future lay. For to be suspended thus between two worlds was nothing but torture. If Morgan rejected her, it would be better to find out now and be done with it. And give her heart time to heal.

If that was even possible anymore.

She made her way through the busy streets of Charleston, weaving among the throng of both workers and slaves. The heat of late afternoon had driven most of the gentry inside, but a few greeted her as she passed. The smell of fish rose from an open market where an old fisherman hawked his daily catch, flooding her with happy memories of her daddy. A slave crossed in front of her, his eyes downcast and a heavy crate weighing down his back. Adalia glanced at him in sorrow and then pressed on. A lady, decked in a satin walking dress and fringed parasol, sauntered past, a package-laden servant scurrying behind her.

An odd feeling gripped Adalia. All three of her worlds, her happy childhood, past slavery, and hopeful future took on scent and form and drifted before her on this bustling street. Each one having nothing to do with the other. Separate and distinct. As if even acknowledging the other's presence would cause a catastrophe.

Somehow Adalia had a sense they were all about to collide. But like oil and water, sweet and sour, black and white, she doubted they would mix well.

Halting before the Rutledge townhouse, she tried to settle her thrashing heart. The three-story building that sat gable-end to the street was much more elaborate than Doc Willaby's home. She hadn't given it much notice when they'd brought Morgan here after the duel. But now it ascended like a palace out of the sand. The great double piazza attached to the southern walls, enclosed with ivory balustrades that matched the window grilles, and the intricate *R* surrounded by wrought-iron buds and flowers on the main gate did nothing to settle her nerves and more to make her feel like a pauper begging a prince for a favor.

Squaring her shoulders, she ascended the steps and knocked on the door. After a few moments, the butler answered, looked her over, and then stuck his head out the door to see if anyone else was with her.

"I'm here to see Morgan Rutledge," she said.

He raised his bulbous nose. "I'm afraid he is not home at the moment."

"Do you know where I may find him?" At the man's petulant attitude, Adalia tapped her foot.

Before he could answer, a slender hand adorned with a massive ruby curled around the edge of the door and swung it farther open. The surprise in Hadley's eyes faded into a twinkle.

"Ah, Miss Winston. Do come in. That will be all, Mr. Lane." He waved the butler away with one hand while he raised a drink to his lips with the other.

Was the man ever without his alcohol? "No thank you. I'm looking for Morgan."

"He is not here."

"So your butler declared. Where may I find him?"

"Hmm." He pressed a finger over his chin and glanced both ways out the door as if he were looking for his brother. "Well, I cannot be entirely sure."

A gust fluttered the hem of Adalia's gown and brought the scent of brandy to her nose. She sighed her impatience at the man's theatrics.

"He could be at Miss Dianna's or"—he frowned—"at Miss Silvia's."

Adalia shook her head, the names carried away with the wind. "I beg your pardon, who did you say?"

Hadley leaned on the door frame and crossed one foot over the other. "Well, I can't be sure which one. You see, he has so many."

"So many what?" Needles pricked down Adalia's back.

"Paramours, of course. Lovers, if you prefer the more candid term."

Those needles now punctured her lungs, releasing the air. It bubbled from her throat in an unladylike grunt.

"Oh my, look at your face! You didn't know, then? I thought you understood about us Rutledge men. We marry women we don't want and bed women we can't marry." He chuckled as if he'd uttered a grand adage.

Adalia felt the blood drain from her face.

He pointed his jeweled finger at her. "Which is probably why you find yourself standing here. Morgan hasn't called upon you since the duel, has he?" Hadley clucked his tongue in feigned disgust. "You see our beloved father once again denied Morgan's request to court you."

The needles moved to stab her heart. Adalia took a step back and nearly stumbled on the steps. She grabbed the post.

"Don't despair, Miss Winston." He slammed the last of his brandy down his throat. "I'm sure he meant to tell you. It was no doubt too painful. But since he can neither marry you nor bed you, well, that is most likely the reason for his absence."

Chapter Twenty-Four

"Ah, there you are." Doc Willaby's voice startled Adalia. She quickly wiped the moisture from her cheeks and turned her face away. "Whatever are you doing out here in the dark?" He eased onto the stone bench beside her.

Adalia tried to collect her wits. And her voice—strained from hours of sobbing.

Leaning forward, the doctor peered at her then laid a gentle hand on her arm. "When you didn't join me for supper, I worried. But when you didn't appear for our evening Bible reading, I knew something was wrong."

"I fear I'm not suitable company."

"You are always good company, Miss Winston." He paused. "What brings you out to the garden at this time of night?"

Adalia drew in a deep breath and gazed over the yard, so bright and lustrous in the light of day, but in the darkness, nothing but clusters of shadows lit by moonlight diffused through clouds. Still, it had been the only secluded place where she could pour out her agony undisturbed. Or so she had thought. "I needed to sort through some things."

"You sound distraught, my dear. Is there something wrong?" The concern in his voice brought more tears to her eyes. She raised a hand to her nose. "You were right about the Rutledges." Though she hated to admit it. Though she hated to even say it out loud. For doing so made it all the more real. But of course it was real. She'd heard it from Hadley's own lips. And, unlike Emerald, he had no reason to lie.

Morgan had lovers. A bevy of them from the sound of it. At first, she had refused to believe it, but then she remembered that Morgan had spoken of a lascivious past before he'd met her—of multiple lovers, of certain expectations of men of his station. He had spoken of it with such disgust that she'd thought he was done with it, that he regretted his actions, that he wanted to start anew with Adalia. But perhaps his father's refusal of their courtship had, indeed, forced him back to that life, if only to dull the pain. She wished she had some way to lessen her own agony.

Thankfully, the doctor did not expel a litany of "I told you sos." Instead, he let out a heavy sigh and took her hand in his. His warm squeeze brought her a modicum of comfort. "I'm sorry, Adalia."

"I've been such a fool."

"You're not the first woman to be taken in by the Rutledge charm, my dear. But at least no damage was done. There *was* no damage done?" His tone was worried.

It took a minute for Adalia to realize what he meant. "Of course not!" She took her hand back then regretted her harsh tone. "The damage is merely internal, for I believe death would be less painful than this ache in my heart." An ache that throbbed with the thought of never seeing Morgan again, never feeling the touch of his hand on her back, her arm. Never feeling his embrace. Never seeing that rakish half-smile of his, the adoration in his green eyes. The way he made her feel like a princess. It was all over. This was one fairy tale that did not have a happy ending.

෪

A lump formed in Willaby's throat. He didn't know what to say to cheer the poor girl. Instead, he sat in silence and allowed her to spend her tears. Her sobbing woke memories he preferred to keep dormant. Memories of his precious Sarah sobbing much like Adalia was doing now. Only her wails had been far louder and more violent and had continued for days. No amount of consoling by either him or his wife had brought her comfort. As a doctor, he'd never felt more useless and weak. He could fix almost anything that ailed his precious daughter.

Anything but a broken heart.

After weeks of such desolate melancholy, he'd had to force food down her to keep her alive—her and the baby she carried. Hadley Rutledge's brat. In the months that followed, she wandered around the house at all hours of the day and night like a homeless specter. A soulless person with dark circles beneath her vacant eyes and her skin pale and languid.

That was when his wife, Rachel, became ill.

Adalia's sobbing stopped, jarring Willaby from his morbid memories.

"Forgive me, Doctor." She wiped her face and gave a stuttering sigh. "I have forgotten myself."

"There's nothing to forgive, my dear. I wish I could bring you some comfort."

She stood and pressed down the folds of her gown. "You have. Just by listening." He thought he saw a glimmer of a smile in the darkness. "I should retire," she added.

Willaby rose to his feet. "If there's anything you need, please let me know."

He barely saw her nod before she faded into the shadows and disappeared in the house. Bowing his head, he lifted up a prayer for the girl he'd grown to care for as his own. "Oh God, please heal her broken heart. Please do not allow her to wilt away like my Sarah."

Guilt tugged at his conscience. He wished he hadn't betrayed Adalia's confidence by snooping about her chamber. Wished he hadn't been so foolish as to allow Miss Emerald to see the band he'd found. The lady was up to something. What, he couldn't imagine. But why else would she lie about whip marks on Adalia's back? Preposterous! Yet nothing had come of her seeing the band. Perhaps she had forgotten all about it or, even better, found no link to Adalia. Even still, he should have allowed matters to work out on their own, knowing the Rutledges would show their true colors eventually. He should have trusted God.

❧

Morgan caught himself whistling. Whistling? He hadn't whistled in years. But of course he knew the reason. The past two and a half weeks his father had kept him at the plantation—time in which Morgan proved to his father that he possessed a mind for business—had paid off. More than paid off! He'd finally convinced Franklin to allow a courtship with Adalia. Of course there was a price to be paid. A huge price. Morgan would slowly begin to take over the running of the Rutledge estate: managing their ten employees and sixty slaves, inspecting crops, purchasing equipment, maintaining all the buildings, looking after their collection of rare Marsh Tacky horses, and keeping the books. Just listing all the tasks caused a sick feeling to well in his belly. He'd rather be a swabby out at sea than be landlocked with such mind-numbing duties.

But Adalia was worth it.

Which was why he was sauntering down Calhoun Street in his finest attire with a bouquet of fresh flowers in his hand and a song on his lips. Not to mention, gathering quite a few curious glances as he went. Today, he would make his relationship with Adalia official. And after a respectable courtship, he would make her his wife. His wife! He could hardly believe it. The most beautiful, kind-hearted, intelligent, courageous lady in the world would soon be his.

With an unavoidable smile on his face, he opened the gate to the Willaby home, took the stairs in two leaps, and knocked on the front door. Their man, Mr. Gant, answered, the flat line of his lips sinking into a frown at the sight of Morgan.

"Miss Winston, please."

The tall, lanky man adjusted his neck cloth as if it had suddenly grown tighter.

"Who is it, Mr. Gant?" the doctor's voice blared from inside.

"It's Mr. Morgan Rutledge to see Miss Winston, sir."

The doctor's footsteps thudded, and Mr. Gant's face relaxed, as if he'd been relieved of some heinous duty. Shoving the man aside, Doc Willaby scowled at Morgan. "How dare you show your face here, sir!"

Morgan blinked, unsure if he had heard the man correctly. He knew the doctor didn't care for him, but he'd never been so belligerent before. "I have something urgent to discuss with Miss Winston. Is she here?"

"Haven't you done enough damage?" Hatred and disgust sparked across the doctor's eyes.

Igniting Morgan's anger. "To what do you refer, sir?"

"Never mind." He straightened his coat. "Miss Winston does not wish to see you. Now nor ever." He waved him away.

Morgan shoved the flowers forward. "At least give her my flowers and tell her I called."

His answer was the door slamming in his face.

Bewildered, Morgan stepped back and slowly descended the steps. He rubbed the back of his neck and gazed over the garden to the street beyond. What just happened? Perhaps he'd caught the doctor at a bad time. Perhaps the man had just received some tragic news. Or worse, he'd decided to keep Adalia away from Morgan because of what Hadley had done to Sarah.

Morgan began to wonder if Adalia had received any of the notes he'd sent her the past few weeks, telling her where he was, what he was doing. That his father forbade him to ride into town. Morgan laid the flowers on the porch railing and made his way to the street. The good doctor couldn't keep her locked inside that house forever. Sooner or later she'd emerge to see a patient or run some errand. Somehow she would discover that Morgan had come to call, and she'd figure out a way to see him.

Yet another week passed, and Morgan had not heard a peep from her, nor had he caught a glimpse of her in town. At least not alone. Never without the doctor. One time when he'd seen her sitting next to the doctor in his carriage, he'd dashed out into the street to hail them, but Doc Willaby snapped the reins, and the carriage sped down the street. Morgan had made a spectacle of himself running after it until the ache in his legs and strain of his lungs forbade him to go farther. In fact, he seemed to have ascended the throne of Charleston's latest gossip. Everywhere he went, members of society and even servants snickered at him behind their hands.

"Ditched by a common woman, he was." "Making a fool of himself for a woman below his station." Their snide quips assailed him. Though they grated on him, he knew their interest would shift elsewhere soon.

So, he'd done the only thing he knew to do. He sent dozens of posts, flowers, and gifts to Doc Willaby's home. He had no doubt the man tossed them in the refuse, but surely Joy would see to it that one of the gifts would sneak through to Adalia. One of his posts begged her to meet him at a specific time and place. Yet, she did not come. No notes of thanks. No explanation. Not even a "Please, leave me be!"

He had done everything he could to contact her. But to no avail. He foresaw months, even years passing in which she continued to ignore him. He couldn't let that happen. Nor could he think of anything he'd done to deserve such treatment.

Though Miss Emerald attempted to hide her utter glee over this recent turn of events, she remained at a distance—like a predator biding her time, waiting for the opportune moment to pounce. Caroline accused Emerald of being the cause of Miss Winston's absence, while Drayton merely shrugged and declared that women were fickle creatures.

"She was never right for you, brother. Marrying her would ruin the Rutledge name." Hadley propped one boot atop the marble hearth in the sitting room of their townhome. "You'll get over her soon enough. Why, I know of a ravishing lady with both pedigree and fortune who is dying to make your acquaintance."

Morgan crossed his arms over his chest and gazed out the window at the passing horses, people, and carriages. "Not interested." He rotated his sore arm and stretched his shoulder, where an ache reminded him of the bullet wound Adalia had dressed so expertly. It had healed perfectly. Perfect like her. No other woman could ever take her place. If she truly didn't care for him, if she truly never wanted to see him again, that was one thing. He would honor her wishes, of course. But he must hear it from her own lips. Not the lips of a man who hated his family and would do anything to keep them apart.

He must find a way to speak with her alone. To gain an audience with her where she couldn't run away. Where he could hold her captive until he'd had his say. *Captive.*

"Well, I dare say, do you plan on being celibate the rest of your life?" Hadley gave a chuckle as if such a thing were possible. "For I don't see that there's anything you can do about Miss Winston."

Ah, but there was. Morgan rubbed his whiskers as a devilish idea formed. "That's where you're wrong, brother." He spun around, noting the surprised look on Hadley's face as Morgan passed him on the way out of the room. "I know exactly what I'm going to do."

&

Drawing the covers over her head, Adalia curled into a ball and prayed for God to dry up her tears. She'd cried herself to sleep every night for over three weeks. And she was tired of it. Good heavens, the cad was not worth so much grief. No doubt he was right at that moment in the arms of another woman. Loving her, whispering in her ears the same enchanting things he used to say to Adalia. The thought caused yet another sob to rise in her throat.

M poked his head under the covers and then slid beneath the quilt and nestled against Adalia's chest. His purring rumbled in the small space. *Drat!* The darned cat did nothing but remind her of Morgan. She should get rid of him, but she'd grown quite fond of the furry imp. Much as she had grown fond of Morgan. Yet the cat was nothing like its master. M was kind and affectionate, tender, and loving, and most of all—loyal. Adalia could always count on the kitten to curl up beside her, or on top of her, or around her neck, and bring the comfort and warmth of unconditional love. In fact, she couldn't imagine her life without him.

Renewed tears filled her eyes. They slid over her nose and her face and onto her pillow as she stroked M, eliciting a new round of purrs.

At least the cat enjoyed her company.

"Father God," she said, trying to pray, but further words escaped her. God knew she was hurting. Why didn't He comfort her? Why had He allowed this to happen? She sighed as M yawned and rolled onto his back, stretching his paws to her face. But she knew the answer. God had not allowed this. She had. She'd allowed herself to get swept up in the opulence, the glamour of high society—swept up in the arms of a man who treated her like a princess. Like the princess her daddy told her she was. Somehow, she had convinced herself that Morgan loved her, that she had a chance to be a part of his world. "Oh God, I thought I was a princess."

You'll always be My princess.

The soft words settled inside her, reminding her of her earthly father. Did God love her as much as her daddy had? Why had Adalia spent so little time with Him recently? Her Bible had grown dusty these past months sitting atop her nightstand. Though she knew she should read it even now, knew it would bring her comfort, she couldn't bring herself to open its holy pages. She couldn't bring herself to read the truths that would surely convict her for her recent actions. She was miserable enough as it was. In fact, she couldn't do anything but cry. Was it true that anger always came after sorrow? She hoped so. The sorrow was unbearable.

She could handle anger.

M laid a paw on Adalia's chin, alerting her that she'd stopped petting him. She began caressing his belly once again until, finally, her heavy heart dragged her into a fitful slumber.

❧

Morgan made his way down Bay Street. Dressed in his sailor attire and under cover of night, he felt confident no one would recognize him. Excitement buzzed through him like an agitated hive, for he felt every bit like the rapscallion his reputation declared him to be. In fact, it took all his control not to run all the way to Doc Willaby's home, but he didn't wish to draw any unwanted attention. Not that there was anyone of note about at two in the morning, save drunks, thieves, and the night watchmen. The latter being the only ones he needed to avoid.

Slinking around the corner of the doctor's house, Morgan made his way to the back garden. He knew the slaves and servants would be quartered below stairs, and that only the doctor and Adalia occupied the upstairs chambers. But which one was Adalia's? He gazed up at the two open windows gaping at him like suspicious eyes and chose the smaller one facing the garden. Stretching his injured shoulder, he leapt into the large oak beside the home and climbed up its thick branches with ease, thankful for his training as a topman on board Captain Bristo's ship.

The tree's branches were close to the house, affording him a slight view inside the window. At least as much as the moonlight allowed. There she was! His sweet Adalia, covers over her head, and her dark hair sprawled over the pillow above her. He'd recognize those silken black locks anywhere.

Grabbing the branch, he swung down and inched closer. The wood scraped his fingers and creaked beneath his weight. The screech of a night heron sounded. Sweat trickled down his back. He started to leap when a wheat-colored cat appeared on the window ledge, eyeing him curiously. Adalia had kept his gift. That thought alone brought him a modicum of hope.

Gathering his strength, he swung his legs and soared across the distance. He grabbed the window ledge. His body slammed against the outside wall. But it was the pain in his shoulder that made Morgan cry out. Biting his lip, he pulled himself up, flung himself through the window, and landed on the floor with a thud.

Adalia shrieked. The cat pounced on Morgan's chest. Shoving it aside, he lunged for the bed and eased Adalia down as he covered her mouth with his hand. Her wild gaze darted over his face. "Shhh, Adalia."

The cat let out a pitiful meow and darted into a corner.

Arms flailing, Adalia struck him and tried to shove him from the bed with her legs. He could think of no other recourse but to throw his body atop hers. It worked. His weight pinned her down. But it also sent a swirl of desire in his belly as he realized that naught but her thin nightdress and his clothing separated their bodies.

She thrashed beneath him. Morgan groaned. Each move sent hot blood coursing through him. "Adalia. Please, sweetheart. Be still." His face was inches from hers. Her sweet scent filled his nose, his lungs, teasing him. "I will not hurt you."

Her chest billowed against his. The breath from her nose dashed over his hand, tight on her mouth. The crazed look in her eyes softened before resignation set in. She stopped struggling.

Morgan jumped off her, keeping his hand on her mouth. "Adalia,

I'm not going to hurt you. I simply wish to talk."

Wide-eyed, she stared at him, her chest heaving, her hair ribbons of ebony over her pillow.

"I'm going to take my hand off now. Please don't scream."

She didn't scream. She clamped her teeth into his palm. Pain etched into his fingers. "Ouch!" Snagging his hand back, he waved it in the air.

Adalia shoved off the other side of the bed, grabbed her coverlet and clutched it to her throat. "How dare you barge into my chamber at night!"

Too loud. He held up his hand to motion her to silence as he slowly circled the bed. "Apparently it is the only way to gain an audience with you."

Her brow furrowed in confusion at his statement. "Other women may swoon in your arms beneath such brutish tactics, but I am not impressed." Though her stance was defiant, her voice quavered.

"Adalia." He reached for her, but she backed into the shadows. He halted. "You know me. I would never force myself on you."

"I don't know who you are anymore."

Morgan took another step toward her. Why would she say such a thing?

"Get out of my chamber at once, or I will scream."

Morgan cringed. "You're already screaming. And I only ask for a few minutes of your time."

"It's hardly appropriate here in my chamber with me in my nightdress." She paused, shifted in the shadows.

"Then meet me tomorrow."

Shuffling noises sounded from within the house. Morgan walked to the door and listened, then returned to her. He had to hurry.

ᘒ

Adalia slunk further into the corner. What was the scoundrel doing? Trying to win her back? But by such inappropriate means! The man was incorrigible. He'd scared her nearly to her wits' end. He was either besotted or he'd gone completely mad. She smelled no alcohol on him, so it was obviously the latter.

Swallowing, she pressed a hand over her still-thrashing heart. If she screamed again, eventually the servants would wake. Not Dr. Willaby, though he was just down the hall. The man slept as sound as a hibernating bear. He'd never heard Adalia's screams from her nightmares. But Joy would hear. Joy would come.

M's eyes peered at her from beneath the bed. *Traitor!*

Morgan shifted his stance, confusion wrinkling his brow as awkwardness came over him. Moonlight silhouetted his muscular frame. Perhaps in her heartache, in her desperate longing for him, she only dreamed he was here. But no, she could still feel the press of his hand on her mouth—gentle, but firm. She could smell the spicy scent that was Morgan and taste his blood on her lips.

Part of her longed to forgive his intrusion and into his arms, kiss him, and tell him she loved him. But Hadley's words rose up like a barrier between them, keeping her frozen in place and barricading her heart in steel.

✑

Morgan approached her. "Adalia. I don't know what's going on here, but I love you. My father has granted permission for our courtship."

Adalia tried to skirt around him. Not the response he expected. He grabbed her arm, jerking her to a stop. "What is wrong with you? Did you hear what I said?"

"Then why haven't you sent word in three weeks?"

"Keep your voice down." His seething whisper filled the air.

A creak sounded from below.

"I don't believe you. Let me go!" Adalia tugged in his grasp.

"Why don't you believe me? And why are you so angry?"

"I want you to leave, Morgan."

"I don't have time for your stubborn theatrics. Will you or will you not agree to meet me tomorrow, so we can discuss this?"

"There's nothing to discuss." Turning her back to him, she headed for the door. "I'm calling Mr. Gant."

Every fiber within Morgan screamed in frustration. If she called the footman and they tossed Morgan from the house, he'd never have a chance to talk with Adalia again. He'd never know why she was so angry. Never know what he had done. Never convince her of his love. The doctor had done a great job of keeping them apart for the past three weeks. Morgan had no doubt the man could keep him from Adalia indefinitely. No, he could not wait another day, another week, another minute to set things straight between them. "I'm sorry, Adalia."

She reached for the door handle. "For which offense?" Her voice was curt. "For—"

He spun her around in midsentence and stuffed a handkerchief in her mouth. "For this."

She groaned and kicked him in the shin. He grimaced. "And for this." Tightening the coverlet around her, he hoisted her over his shoulder without effort, opened her chamber door, and halted on the landing, listening. After peering into the darkness, he began descending the stairs. Another sound filtered from the servants' quarters below. The creak of a tread. Someone was heading up to the main floor. Adalia squirmed and moaned and pounded her fists on Morgan's back. He hated to do this to her, but she gave him no other choice. Pressing her legs against his chest, he darted down the remaining stairs, tore open the front door, and carried her into the night.

CHAPTER TWENTY-FIVE

Unusual sounds penetrated Adalia's slumberous mind. Unusual, yet somehow familiar. Creaks and groans and the *swoosh* of water. She must be dreaming. If she was, her bed just tilted. And her mattress was hard as a rock. Something pricked her cheek. A splinter? She moved her fingers, praying she would feel her soft coverlet. Or perhaps M's fur. Nothing but rough wood met her touch.

She bolted upright. Her heart cinched in her chest. Her glance took in the small room: a table and chair bolted to the floor; a large trunk; a cot extending from the wall; a tiny oval window through which sunlight streamed. And her, perched on the floor. No, not a decent floor but rough wooden planks that looked as if they hadn't been swept or polished in years. Reaching up, she plucked a splinter from her cheek and rubbed her aching head.

That was when the sounds shot through the fog of sleepiness, pinching memories awake—memories of being on a ship at sea. She struggled to rise and stumbled to the window, nearly tripping on the coverlet dangling at her feet. Nothing but blue met her gaze. Blue sea and blue sky, distinct only in hue and intensity. She'd been kidnapped! Ignoring her queasiness, she rushed to the door and tugged on the handle. Locked.

The deck canted. Adalia's knees wobbled, and she sank onto the cot. Shock forbade her to believe her awakening memories—the sight her eyes were now seeing. Yet even her tortured mind could not invent a story so incredible. Or so completely insane! Visions sparked in her mind: Morgan, hoisting her over his shoulder like a sack of rice, carrying her across Charleston, depositing her in a boat and rowing her out to a ship, then carrying her down a ladder and tossing her in this cabin. After removing her gag and untying her hands, he'd tried to reassure her of her safety before he stormed out. Adalia had banged her fists on the locked door until they were red and aching. She'd screamed and wailed and paced and fretted until she had dropped onto the floor and fallen asleep.

But what she hadn't anticipated was that the ship would sail. Was Morgan still aboard? Had he discovered her heritage and sold her back into slavery? Surely if that were true, she'd be chained up below in the hold, not in this cabin.

Her questions were soon to be answered as the click of a lock, followed by the clank of a latch, rang through the cabin. Only then did Adalia realize she still wore her nightdress. Grabbing the coverlet from the floor, she held it up to her chest as the door opened to reveal a kind-looking, elderly woman carrying a bowl and pitcher with a gown flung across her meaty arm.

"Good morning, Miss Winston." She set the bowl and pitcher down on the table and faced Adalia. Bright eyes and sun-kissed cheeks brought beauty to a face lined with age and surrounded by a mass of tight gray curls.

Dumbfounded, Adalia could only stare at her.

"Ah, still a bit scared, are you now?" Laying the gown and petticoats across the chair, she turned and poured water into the basin. "I don't blame you. 'Twas a frightful way to be brought on board."

"Who are you, and why am I at sea?"

The lady chuckled. "Do forgive my manners. I am Mrs. Wallace, wife to the purser aboard this ship." She set the pitcher down and gave Adalia a curious stare. "As to the second question, you'll have to ask Mr. Rutledge about that."

"Morgan? He is on board?"

"Why, of course. What would be the purpose of bringing you on this voyage if he weren't coming along?" She laughed as if the question were ridiculous. "Now, I've brought you water for washing and some underthings and a fresh gown." One gray brow rose as she glanced over Adalia's thin nightgown. "I can see Mr. Rutledge was correct when he said he had to rescue you rather quickly."

"Rescue?" Adalia fisted her hands at her hips, dropping the coverlet. "He didn't rescue me. He kidnapped me!"

If she expected to find a mother's comfort or sympathy from

the weathered old woman, Adalia discovered she was mistaken. Mrs. Wallace gave her a look of reprimand before she shrugged. "Well, you'll have to take that up with him, miss."

"How can I do that when he keeps me locked in this cabin?"

"You need not worry about that. Mr. Rutledge informed me that he locked you in here for your own safety during the night, since you are so afraid of sailing and all. He was worried you might wander above and fall into the sea. Such a thoughtful man." She smiled a dreamy smile as she headed toward the door. Adalia growled inwardly. Obviously Morgan's charm worked on women of all ages.

Mrs. Wallace stopped at the door and turned. "He said you'd be a bit out of sorts this morning, miss. Especially after all that crying and whining last night. But don't vex yourself. After you've had a bit of food and fresh air your mind will clear. I'll bring your breakfast in a minute."

But Adalia didn't want any breakfast. In fact, her stomach rebelled at the thought of it. Instead, she quickly donned her undergarments and gown and left her cabin in search of Morgan. Ignoring her queasiness, she followed the light to a ladder leading upward, and in moments, she emerged onto the main deck to a blast of wind that tugged at her hair. Squinting in the bright sun, she scanned the deck. Sailors stopped their tasks to stare at her but soon returned to their duties. The snap of sails drew her gaze above, where white canvas was bloated with wind and more sailors shuffled over the yards like monkeys. The sound of Morgan and another man conversing on the deck above her spun her around. At least she thought it was Morgan. With his back toward her, he looked more like a pirate in his tight breeches, white shirt, and cocked hat.

"Mr. Morgan Rutledge!" Clutching her skirts, she darted up the ladder and charged toward him.

He faced her, his momentary look of terror fading into exaggerated aplomb. "Ah, milady, you're awake. Sleep well?"

"No, I did not sleep well." Adalia halted before him, glancing at the other man, who stared at her with a most peculiar look on his face. A young face that belied the graying at his temples. A strong jaw, short-cropped brown hair, and blue eyes that matched his coat completed a look that was more cultured than most seamen.

"May I introduce Captain Kane Bristo." Morgan gestured toward the man. "Captain, this is Miss Adalia Winston."

"A pleasure."

When Adalia did not offer her hand, the captain simply bowed. "Are your quarters to your liking, miss?"

Was everyone aboard this ship mad? "No, they are not to my liking!" Adalia pressed a hand over her churning stomach.

"I told you she was a bit cantankerous, Captain." Morgan took her arm to lead her aside.

Adalia tore from his grasp and stormed back to the captain. "If you do not turn this boat around and take me back to Charleston at once, I will charge you and your crew with kidnapping!"

He flinched and glanced at Morgan. "First of all, it is a brig, miss. Secondly, you are here as Morgan's guest, are you not? Did he not rescue you from your abusive employer?"

"Abusive. . ." Adalia slowly faced Morgan. She clenched her fists, her nails stabbing her palms. Morgan, however, seemed to be having trouble meeting her gaze. Instead, he shifted his boots over the deck and glanced aloft.

"Why, you unscrupulous, debauched, lying, swaggering, worthless muck-rake!" She pushed him with all her might. But he didn't budge. Pointing a finger his way, she turned to the captain. "This man stole me from my bed in the middle of the night."

Sailors stopped to listen. Some of them chuckled. Others whispered amongst themselves.

The ship plunged over a wave. Salty moisture showered over Adalia as she held out her arms to catch her balance.

The captain's eyes narrowed on Morgan. His jaw bunched. "In my cabin. Now!"

ல்

"By all that is holy upon the seas, what is the meaning of this?" Captain Bristo stormed toward the stern windows then spun around. Rage battled across his face. His eyes sparked like cannon fire.

Morgan couldn't remember ever seeing him so angry. Blast that Mrs. Wallace! Morgan had instructed her to inform him when Adalia awoke. That way he could speak to her before she met the captain. And he wouldn't be standing before the captain's desk about to lose his position aboard the ship.

"I can explain, Captain." Morgan's voice betrayed his guilt. There really was no logical explanation—none an honorable man like Bristo would accept.

Captain Bristo planted his knuckles on his desk. "Did you kidnap that poor woman?"

"In a sense, I suppose, but—" The captain's upraised hand halted Morgan's tongue. Bristo took up a pace behind his desk, crossing through spears of sunlight that stabbed through the window panes. "Do you know what this means? You have made me party to a crime. Even if I return to Charleston immediately"—he shot Morgan a seething glance—"which my schedule does not permit. I could lose my ship. I could be tossed in jail." With each word, his voice grew louder and louder.

"I made sure that would not happen," Morgan said. "Before we set sail, I told the constable what I was doing and why. As long as I bring the lady back unscathed, he will ignore any charges she might bring against us."

Captain Bristo gave him an incredulous snort. "And why would he do that?

"Because he knows me. He knows I mean her no harm. And because I am privy to information"—Morgan wouldn't divulge that the constable had a tryst with the mayor's wife—"that could ruin him."

"Kidnapping *and* blackmail. This gets better and better!"

Morgan sighed and lowered his gaze.

Captain Bristo circled his desk. "And what of her employer? Surely he will notice her missing? Was he abusive at all? Gad's fish, you lied to me!"

"I had no choice." Morgan met his gaze, hoping his friend would see the sincerity in his eyes. "You wouldn't have let me bring her on board, otherwise."

"No, I wouldn't have."

"But I did send Doc Willaby a post telling him where she was and not to worry."

Bristo gave a sordid chuckle. "You sent him a post? Are you daft, man?"

"Quite possibly."

"Why would he believe anything you say?"

"Because I signed it from Miss Winston."

Shaking his head, Bristo picked up a pistol from his desk. "Now we add forgery to the list."

Morgan wondered if he intended to shoot him. Faith, this was not going well.

"That's why she was pounding on the door, then?" Bristo ran a finger over the engraving on the barrel of the gun. "She wasn't suicidal.

She didn't want to toss herself into the sea. . ."

Morgan swallowed.

"I cannot believe you lied to me." The anger fled Bristo's voice, replaced by sorrow.

The man's disappointment stabbed Morgan like a blade in the gut. Until this moment he hadn't realized how much he valued Bristo's approval—lived for it, in fact. Morgan's heart plunged. "I had no choice. I had to speak with her."

"And this was the only way you could think of? Why not simply call on her like a normal gentleman?"

"She wouldn't see me."

"I hardly blame her now that I see what you are capable of."

"Come now, Kane, you know me." Morgan hoped the use of his given name would remind the man of their deep friendship. "I've told you of my feelings for Adalia. I was desperate. Doc Willaby was keeping us apart, probably feeding her lies. I know it was rather rash of me, but I had no recourse."

"Other than to kidnap her? By thunder, Morgan. When will you learn to think"—he tapped his skull—"before you act? This sort of behavior may be acceptable in your frivolous circles, but it will not do here. Nor, I imagine, will it do much to engender the lady's affections."

Morgan suddenly regretted his brash actions. And the lies that had gone with them. He hadn't considered the impact it would have on his dear friend. He raked a hand through his hair. "I promise she will calm down after I speak with her."

Captain Bristo leaned back against his desk. "Well, there's naught I can do about it now. I must get this cargo of rice and indigo to Wilmington, or it will rot in the hold. You'd better have the best of intentions, Morgan. If I hear you have mistreated Miss Winston in any way. . ." He clenched his jaw.

"How can you say such a thing?" Morgan wilted beneath the man's lack of faith. "I love her. I would never harm her."

A flicker of pain crossed the captain's blue eyes. "I never would have thought you would have lied to me either." He set the pistol down.

"I was wrong. I should have told you."

Captain Bristo crossed his arms over his blue coat. "When are you going to stop trying to run your own life and rely on God?"

Rely on God? Morgan bit back a bitter chuckle. "God takes no care for the likes of me."

"Indeed? Have you asked Him?"

"What? If He cares for me?" Morgan did laugh this time. "I've disappointed Him too much for him to pay any notice. . .even if He does exist. Besides, I find His standards too high, His strictures too confining."

"Then you don't know Him at all." Captain Bristo gave him a sad smile. Morgan hoped he was done proselytizing.

"Very well." Bristo sighed, then his gaze hardened. "You should know that I will deny any knowledge of this should charges be brought against you."

"Of course. And I will tell them you had nothing to do with it."

The captain nodded, squeezing the bridge of his nose. Morgan noticed a white sheen covered his face.

"Are you feeling all right, Captain?"

"Yes, just a bit tired. Back to your duties, Morgan." He gestured with his head toward the door.

Morgan turned to leave.

"And, Morgan?"

He spun around.

"She's lovely." The captain grinned. "A bit spirited with a rather sharp tongue, but lovely, nonetheless."

❧

Groaning, Adalia lay back on her cot and pressed a hand over her belly. Darkness consumed the cabin, but she hadn't the strength to get up and light the lantern. She prayed the ginger Mrs. Wallace had brought her would begin to work soon. She'd only recently discovered that the poor woman also suffered from *mal de mer* and had a ready supply of the soothing herb on hand. If only Adalia had spoken with the lady earlier. Instead, she'd spent the entire day in her cabin alternating between bouts of singing into her chamber pot and swaying in dizziness on her cot.

She had not seen Morgan since he'd followed his enraged captain below deck. She hoped the man locked him in the hold or better yet, keelhauled him. A fitting punishment for his crime. Not only in kidnapping her but also in forcing her to endure such agony. And why was he on this ship, anyway, looking more like a seaman than a spoiled aristocrat? Did his father own a merchant fleet? If so, Morgan had never spoken of it.

Part of her was curious to hear the reason for his temporary madness.

Part of her didn't want to know. There would be no explanation, no justification, nothing that would open her heart to a man who'd flown into the arms of other women so quickly.

Or who kidnapped women in the middle of the night from their beds.

He had said his father agreed to their courtship. He had said he loved her. Yet everything she had recently discovered about him, everything she knew about his father, stood against the truth of his words.

The door creaked open. Morgan entered with a lantern. Light bathed the room, shoving the darkness aside.

"Go away."

He closed the door and set the lantern on the table. "Not until we talk."

"If you have an ounce of mercy within your lecherous body, please leave me be. I'm ill." She turned over in her cot, facing the wall.

She heard him take a seat on the chair. "Mrs. Wallace informed me that you refuse to eat."

"I cannot eat. Thanks to you."

"I didn't know you got seasick."

"I was given no opportunity to inform you."

"And I was given no opportunity to ask since you refused to speak to me."

"I don't speak to libertines or kidnappers."

"Lib. . ." He huffed. "I only kidnapped you so I could speak to you uninterrupted."

The squeak of the chair and thump of his boot told her he'd risen. She peeked at him through her lashes then struggled to sit. She would meet this man face-to-face, not lying down. She regretted the action instantly. Both because her stomach rebelled but also because Morgan looked more handsome than she'd ever seen him.

Gray breeches molded to his muscular thighs before disappearing within knee-high boots. A cream-colored shirt, ruffled at the cuffs, lay partially open on his chest. His windswept hair was tied behind him, cavalier style. The sword strapped to his thigh winked at her in the candlelight. She remembered the feel of him on top of her. All muscle and steel. Heat rose to her face. She hated that she reacted to him so. "You look like a pirate," she spat.

"Thank you."

She gazed up at him. *No, no, no. Anything but that grin.* But there it came, curving on his lips and sending her heart thumping. "It wasn't a compliment."

"Too late to recant."

She frowned. "What do you want?"

"To tell you once again that my father has agreed to our courtship." The words flew from his mouth as if he feared she would interrupt him again. Still they refused to penetrate the shield around her mind. Or her heart.

She gave an unladylike snort. "And now you lie to me."

He planted his hands on his waist. "Why would I lie? And more importantly, why won't you believe me?"

"Because I heard your father's opinion of me. He would never agree to a courtship. And because for three weeks I have not heard a word from you."

"I was at the plantation for over two weeks. My father refused to let me go until. . . Well, it doesn't matter. But I sent you a post nearly every day. Flowers and gifts as well. And after I came into town, I called on you several times."

Adalia closed her eyes against the urgency in his voice. She rubbed her temples. Why couldn't everything stop spinning? The cabin, her head—her heart. Posts and gifts? Could Morgan be telling the truth? Yet, where had they gone?

Doc Willaby. His concerned face arose in her vision, the sad tale of his daughter swirling in her memory. But he was a godly man. A godly man wouldn't steal and lie, would he?

Opening her eyes, Adalia gazed at Morgan and saw nothing but sincerity in his green eyes. Either he was an excellent liar or he meant what he said. She mustn't believe the latter, for that would mean engaging her heart once again in a game she was sure to lose. She struggled to rise—lifted a hand to stave off his advance—and made her way to the window. A night breeze tossed her hair behind her as it filled her lungs with the scent of brine and wood. Her stomach began to settle. Thank God. The last thing she wanted was to be sick in front of this man.

"Adalia, tell me what I've done to deserve your scorn. The last time I saw you, you were dressing my wound and looking at me"—he paused—"well, looking at me quite adoringly."

Adalia spun around. "I suppose that's what all your women do."

The ship rose over a swell. She staggered and started to fall. In two steps, Morgan slipped an arm around her waist, steadying her. "What are you talking about?"

Heat inflamed her skin beneath his touch. The scent of him nearly broke down her resolve. She wrenched from his arm and sauntered away, her back to him again.

"I know about your affairs, Morgan."

"Oh, you do, do you?" His voice rang with sarcasm.

"Yes." She leaned a hand on the chair to steady herself. "Hadley told me, so there's no use denying it."

"Hadley what?" His tone was incredulous. "Scads, woman." She heard the shuffle of his boots on the deck. "I swear to you I have not touched another woman since I met you."

Something in his voice, his tone, a ringing of truth, brought her around. She had to look at him to know for sure. He always showed his true emotions through his eyes. And there it was, burning in the center. Sincerity, honesty. It stunned her. Shamed her. Threatened to moisten her eyes with tears. But she could not let them flow. Not yet.

A knock on the door broke the trance between them. "Morgan!" An urgent voice penetrated the wood.

Morgan hesitated, groaned in frustration, then opened it, never taking his eyes off of Adalia.

A young lanky sailor stood on the other side.

"What is it?" Morgan asked.

"It's the captain. Mrs. Wallace sent me to tell you he's quite ill."

Chapter Twenty-Six

Morgan stood at the taffrail, gazing at the waves of foam-capped sapphire fanning from the bow of the ship. Waves that were restless and turbulent like his nerves—like his heart. The rising sun blanketed his back and cast golden spires over the water, transforming the blue into glittering peach. The *Seawolf* pitched over a roller. Spray showered over Morgan, and he gripped the railing. Despite the beauty before him, he hung his head. He'd certainly made a muck of things. Why did he always dash into action without considering the consequences? Was he so spoiled, so self-serving, as Adalia had once called him, that he never thought of how his actions might affect others? Now, he'd disappointed—no, betrayed—his good friend and one of the few people whose opinions Morgan valued the most. And for what? Quite possibly nothing. For after all his efforts, all his explanations, Adalia remained unmoved.

Why she believed Hadley's word over his, Morgan could not fathom. He'd never been unfaithful to Adalia, never even glanced at another woman since he'd met her. A blast of wind tugged his hair from its queue and jarred memories loose along with it. Memories of how he'd been disloyal to nearly every woman he'd courted. How he'd been unwilling to restrict himself to just one of the lovely ripe fruits of Charleston society, but instead had partaken of the entire bowl at once, leaving a crop of spoiled half-nibbled produce behind.

Shame weakened his knees, and he nearly toppled over as the *Seawolf* climbed a rising swell. He'd well earned—and deserved—his reputation around town. A debased reputation that surely had made its way to Adalia's ears. And though he had not betrayed her, he was

236

reaping nothing but the seeds he had sown.

Yet, he wasn't the cad he used to be. Was he? Not since he'd met Adalia. Hope still flamed in his heart that she would believe that—believe in him. It had been two days since the captain took ill. Two days since Morgan had explained everything to Adalia, since he thought he'd seen a weakening in her eyes before they'd been interrupted. Then why was she avoiding him? Though she had been busy attending the captain, he'd seen her on deck more than once, but every time he'd approached her, she scurried away. Why, she barely even looked his way on his many trips below to check on the captain's health.

He shouldn't have brought her here. He had no right to take her from her home. Blast it all, he was a swaggering oaf! He'd been so confident in her affections, so sure that once he'd spoken to her, she would fall into his arms with complete and utter glee and agree to their courtship, that the alternative hadn't even occurred to him.

Pushing from the railing, Morgan growled and fisted his hands on his waist, wishing he could shove one across Hadley's jaw. Dash it! What was his brother thinking, telling Adalia such lies? This went far beyond a childhood prank. It was unforgivable. And Morgan intended to set things straight when he returned. But for now, all he wanted was for Adalia to believe him—to look at him with those deep, adoring eyes once again.

A sail snapped above, reminding him of her sharp tongue—a tongue sharp enough to lash a man into submission. He chuckled. She had pluck, he'd give her that. He pictured her sashaying about her cabin in that lilac gown that clung to her in all the right places, her raven hair tumbling down her back in wild abandon, one hand pointed at him in accusation, while the other pressed her nauseous stomach. He grinned. It had taken all his control not to take her into his arms. Well, that, and the fact that he didn't particularly relish being clawed to death. He would wait until the wildcat becalmed and began to purr again. If she ever did.

The brig slid into a trough, and his hopes plummeted with it. He could think of only one reason she avoided him. The reason he dreaded the most. That she didn't love him—that it was over between them forever.

"Land away!" came the shout from above. Morgan plucked the telescope from his belt and raised it to his eye.

A ribbon of land rose to float atop the horizon. The American coastline. They'd be in Wilmington before noon. He'd better get below and see if the captain would be well enough to direct the ship into the harbor and see to the off-loading of the goods. If not, Morgan felt confident he could handle things. At least that would give him a chance to see Adalia.

Leaping down the companionway, he headed aft toward the captain's cabin. At his quiet knock, the door creaked open to reveal her beautiful face. Instead of fading to a frown, her gentle smile remained as she allowed him entrance.

"How is he?" he asked, glancing at the bed, where Captain Bristo appeared to be fast asleep.

Mrs. Wallace glanced up from a chair beside the bed where she was whittling a piece of wood.

Before Adalia could answer, the captain's cracked voice filled the room. "I'm quite all right, Morgan. No need to whisper."

Adalia approached the bed, gazing at the captain with concern. She had attempted to pin up her unruly curls, but they escaped here and there, spilling onto her shoulder. A sheen of perspiration lined her forehead and neck, and exhaustion weakened the spark in her eyes. But still, she was the most beautiful thing Morgan had ever seen.

"I just wish I had my medicines here," she said.

Captain Bristo lifted a hand then dropped it to the mattress as if it weighed a ton. "It is nothing. Just a slight fever. If you weren't here, Morgan, I'd be up on deck commanding the ship."

"From your back, no doubt," Mrs. Wallace added with a wink.

"Good to hear, Captain," Morgan said. "I've come to report that we will be in Wilmington by noon."

The captain pried his eyelids half open, though even that small action seemed to pain him. "Ah, good. I shall be up in a few hours."

"You will do no such thing, Captain," Adalia retorted. Picking up a pitcher, she poured water into a glass. "You are far too weak, and your fever might return."

Mrs. Wallace glanced down at the pile of wood shavings at her feet. "If you'd eat something, you might recover sooner."

Adalia lifted the cup to Captain Bristo's lips. He gulped the fluid then turned his ashen face toward Morgan. "This is why women should not be allowed on board ships. If I'd wanted a nursemaid, I would have remained at home with my mother." His laughter turned into coughing, giving Morgan pause.

"Rest, Captain," Morgan ordered. "I can take care of things above."

The captain's eyelids fluttered then sank shut. "Perhaps you're right. Take the helm, then. I trust you."

I trust you. The words fell sweet upon Morgan's ears, especially after his recent betrayal. But then Captain Bristo had always been quick to forgive and slow to judge. One of the many things Morgan admired about him.

The captain's deep breathing soon filled the cabin. While Mrs. Wallace continued her whittling, Morgan dared a glance in Adalia's direction. She'd been staring at him, but now she shifted her gaze away.

"Will he be all right?" he asked, longing to bring her eyes back to his.

She nodded. "If he rests, yes. In fact, he is much improved over yesterday."

"Good." Morgan hesitated, listening to the soothing creak and groan of the timbers. "May I speak with you in the hallway, Adalia?"

She bit her lip and glanced at Mrs. Wallace, but still she would not meet his gaze. "I'm needed here, Morgan."

Mrs. Wallace bounced a glance between them, seemed ready to say something, but then thought better of it and continued her work.

Morgan's heart felt as though a cannonball had been strapped to it. It was over between them. He knew it. She simply didn't have the heart to tell him.

☙

Adalia emerged onto the main deck, bracing herself against the thrust of the wind. She'd attempted to pin up her hair with some of Mrs. Wallace's pins, but she could see now the effort had been in vain as strands whipped around her face. Shielding her eyes from the sun, she spotted a line of sandy shore and sparse trees off the bow and a gaping mouth of water that must be the entrance to the river leading to Wilmington Harbor. The fresh air stole the odor of sickness that seemed to cling to her even as it filled her lungs with the salty smell of life. She pressed a hand to her belly. Either the ginger was working or she'd gotten used to the constant movement of the ship. At least she had one thing to be thankful for.

In truth, she had many.

Morgan's voice bellowed from above, and she slunk to her usual spot in the shadows beside the quarterdeck. From there, she'd been able to watch Morgan command the ship these past few days without him knowing. At least until he'd noticed some of the sailors gawking in her direction.

Yet, for two days, the confusion spinning in her mind and heart forbade her to speak to the man who was the cause of her turmoil. She'd needed time to think things through away from his charm, away from the way he made her feel. So, she'd spent the past two days pondering his words, sorting through the maze of thoughts, feelings, lies, memories, even the man's rakish reputation, only to realize that the man she'd fallen in love with could never do the things Hadley claimed. Now, as his commanding voice swirled about her, she found the pain in her heart had disappeared. Mended and healed.

She longed to tell him so, but now was not the time. He had a ship to navigate into Wilmington and duties to attend. She would wait and content herself with hearing his voice, watching him command the ship as if he'd been born on deck—born to be a captain. Born to be at sea. His authoritative yet kind tone sent the sailors scurrying to do his bidding. Respect for him and his leadership shone in their eyes. Even now as he directed the helmsman and called for topmen to furl tops and courses, there was a lift to his voice, a purpose and hope she'd never heard in his tone before.

As men scrambled aloft and lowered sails, the mad dash of the sea against the hull softened to a purl as the ship slowed and entered the mouth of Cape Fear. Adalia should go below and check on the captain, yet she found herself captivated by the way Morgan navigated the islands and shoals. Where had he acquired such skill? It seemed as though he'd been sailing for years. But how could that be?

Two hours later, Adalia moved to the larboard railing and leaned over to get a good view of the city. Buildings sprang from the wilderness like wolf pups from a den. People and horses hustled to and fro beyond docks that thrummed with workers.

A rather crusty-looking sailor stopped before her. He tipped his hat and glanced down at something. "Beggin' yer pardon, miss."

Adalia moved out of the way, and the man grabbed a line attached to a belaying pin. Choosing a position farther up the railing, she turned to look up at Morgan and found him staring at her with such longing in his eyes that emotion cluttered in her throat.

He swept a determined glance over the ship and spit a trail of rapid-fire orders, "Leadlines readied in the fore! Remove shot from saluting cannon! Guns squared and braced. All hands, bring ship to anchor!"

The men skittered to their tasks.

Boom! The fire of the saluting cannon caused Adalia to jump, though she'd seen the men hovering around it with the slow match. The fort at Wilmington replied, and soon the ship slid to a near halt in the harbor, and the anchor plunged into the sea. Adalia watched as the cargo was hefted from the main hatch by a crane rigged to one of the yards and then loaded into the boats. Morgan never hesitated in his command. Even when the crane jammed and they nearly lost a crate in the bay, he remained calm, in control, and decisive.

When he left on the final boat to settle accounts with the dock master and merchants, Adalia went below to check on the captain. She found him sleeping soundly.

"And he even ate some stew," Mrs. Wallace announced proudly. "Now you go on and get some rest, dearest. No need in both of us sitting here."

After thanking Mrs. Wallace, Adalia happily returned to her cabin, washed as best she could with some leftover water in her basin, and laid down on her cot. Within moments she was asleep.

A loud creak jarred her awake. She rubbed her eyes and tried to shake the fog from her head. Only then did she see that moonlight, not sunlight, filtered through the cabin. How long had she slept? Rising, she ambled to the window and peered out. A full moon trickled glittering silver over cobalt waters—not the waters of a bay but the waters of the open sea. They had left Wilmington, already?

After abandoning her hopeless efforts to press the wrinkles from her gown, Adalia made her way to the captain's cabin but found both Mrs. Wallace and Captain Bristo fast asleep, the former slumped in her chair, chunk of wood and knife still in her hands, and the latter snoring in his bed. After gently removing the knife from Mrs. Wallace's hand, lest she hurt herself, Adalia glanced at the clock hanging on the captain's wall. Five in the morning. *Five!* She'd slept for over twelve hours. Right through the raising of the anchor, the hoisting of sails, and the trip back down the river to the sea. She couldn't remember sleeping that soundly in a long while.

Adalia tiptoed out of the cabin and ventured on deck. Most of the crew would be asleep. Perhaps she'd have a chance to pray—something she hadn't done in quite some time. What she hadn't expected was to find Morgan awake. Yet, there he stood on the foredeck, a sinewy shadow against an oversized moon. She knew it was him by the confidence in his stance and the way the light streaked his hair in pearly bands. Excitement gripped her. Followed by apprehension.

She clutched her skirts, ascended the ladder, and slid beside him. He turned nonchalantly to see who it was then flinched in surprise. Before alarm tightened his features. "Is the captain all right?"

"Yes," she said. He instantly calmed and she added, "He's still sleeping." Adalia gripped the railing and gazed over the inky sea. So peaceful, so calm, yet with a slight crackle in anticipation of dawn. Much like the anticipation now causing her heart to leap. Leaning on the railing, Morgan faced the sea, his jaw chiseled stone. Had she waited too long? Been too stubborn? Damaged this man's pride too much?

Either way, she might as well get to the point and be done with it. "Morgan, I came to tell you that I believe you."

He slowly turned to face her, a quizzical look furrowing his brow. The moonlight accentuated the shadows beneath his eyes, deepening her guilt. Still he said nothing.

Adalia lowered her gaze. "I'm sorry. I just couldn't understand why Hadley would lie." She wrung her hands together. "I shouldn't have thought the worst of you. It didn't help that I hadn't heard from you in so long and that—"

His lips were on hers. Firm and warm and moist. Caressing. He cupped her face in his hands and deepened the kiss. A knot of warmth swirled in Adalia's belly. Her toes tingled, and she fell against him, returning his kiss with equal passion. His hand slid behind her neck as he drank her in, tasting her lips, her mouth, as if he'd been starved for far too long. Time suspended. Time and the world around her, for she could no longer hear the waves against the hull, the flap of sails, the creak of the ship. All she could hear was the thunderous beat of her own heart.

❧

Reluctantly, Morgan withdrew from the kiss lest he gave in to every impulse within him. He caught his breath then swallowed her up in his arms. Laying his chin atop her head, he felt tension drain from him as laughter rose to his lips. He'd nearly resolved himself to life without her. It was why he hadn't been able to sleep. Why he'd been pacing the deck all night trying to come to grips with his fate. Even now, he didn't want to let her go. Never wanted to let her go.

Nudging her back, he peered down at her. "I sent letters nearly every day telling you I was still at the plantation."

Adalia's eyes flitted between his. "I never got them."

Morgan raked his hair back and huffed. "I'm afraid the good doctor wanted to keep us apart more than you realize."

"I know he doesn't care for you, but—"

"Loathes me is more like it."

"Well, perhaps." Her smile lit the night.

Morgan raised a brow. He wouldn't tell her the man had slammed the door in his face more than once. In fact, Morgan cared not a whit about the doctor at the moment. For Adalia was once again in his arms, and life was suddenly worth living. As if in celebration, pink, orange, and gold christened the horizon.

"So you agree to my courtship?"

She hesitated, bit her lip, and gazed out to sea. Fear—or was it sorrow?—spiked across her eyes.

Morgan's heart wavered precariously on the edge of a cliff. One "no" from her would send it crashing into the abyss.

Finally, she faced him. "I would be honored." She reached up and brushed her fingers over his stubbled jaw, sending a new wave of desire through him. Amazing how one touch from this woman could affect him so.

"But how did you convince your father?" she asked.

"I told him I'd run the plantation in Hadley's stead."

She frowned. "But Mor—"

He laid a finger on her lips. "Not now." He didn't want to discuss it now. He didn't want anything or anyone to dampen this moment. He caressed one of her curls and longed to run his fingers through the rest. Cupping her face again, he gazed into her eyes. "I love you, Adalia."

A tear slid down her cheek—a liquid diamond over satin. She smiled. "I love you too, Morgan."

He brushed his lips over hers, breathing in her scent, hovering, caressing, as he swallowed her up in his embrace. Where he longed to keep her safe and loved forever.

The sun's glow crept over his eyelids. The start of a new day. A day he'd dreaded only moments ago. But now looked forward to with great anticipation. He withdrew, happy to see he'd left her breathless.

"Sail ho!" a man in the yards called.

Snapping from his daze, Morgan scanned the horizon. He yanked his scope from his belt and pressed it to his eye.

"Two points to starboard, sir," the voice confirmed what Morgan's eyes beheld. The night had betrayed their position.

Lifting a hand to shield her eyes, Adalia gripped his arm with the other. "Who is it?"

Morgan's chest tightened. "My guess? I'd say she's a privateer. And she's heading straight for us."

CHAPTER TWENTY-SEVEN

Morgan couldn't believe his bad luck. Of all the places for a privateer to turn up at the rise of the sun, it had to be straight off his starboard bow. And they had the weather edge as well. The joy of his reunion with Adalia quickly dissipated beneath his rising fear. Lowering the scope, he slapped it against his palm.

"But we aren't at war," Adalia said.

"Not yet. But that won't stop the British from boarding our ships and stealing our men."

"What are we to do?" He could hear the fear in Adalia's voice. Pasting on what he hoped was an unruffled expression, he touched her elbow and ushered her to the main deck. "I need to talk to the captain."

"Orders, sir?" the night watchman asked from the quarterdeck, his Adam's apple bobbing in his throat.

"Sound the alert, Mr. Granger, if you please. All hands on deck. Up tops and stays. Set all canvas to the wind!"

Morgan glanced over his shoulder at the oncoming predator, then up at the quartermaster standing steadfast at the wheel. "Adjust heading two degrees south by southwest, Mr. Hanson. Put as much distance between us and them, gentlemen!"

"Ayes" rang from both men as Morgan led Adalia below. He intended to escort her to her cabin, get her inside where it was safe, but his frenzied mind drove him straight to the captain's cabin. The clanging of the bell vibrated through the bulkheads as Morgan barreled inside, Adalia on his heels.

Mrs. Wallace glanced up from her seat by the captain's bed. The lines of her face twisted in worry.

Adalia rushed to her side. "What is it?"

"I'm afraid he's grown worse, miss. Woke me up with his groaning just a few minutes ago."

Adalia laid the back of her hand on the captain's cheeks and faced Morgan. He knew before she opened her mouth that the captain was in no condition to command a ship in battle. He appeared in no condition to even rise from his cot.

Mrs. Wallace wrung water from a cloth and dabbed it over the captain's flushed skin. "His fever has returned."

Terror held Morgan in place, threatening to strangle him, squeezing the breath from his lungs. It was one thing to command a ship through peaceful waters, or even to escape a pursuing frigate under Captain Bristo's watchful eye.

But quite another to engage a British privateer by himself.

Footsteps thundered on the deckhead. Shouts and curses filled the air above them. The men needed a leader. And they needed one fast.

Adalia looked his way, the fear in her eyes increasing when she saw his face. "What is it, Morgan?"

"Nothing." He found his voice and coughed. He would not reveal his terror to these women. He would not tell them of his inhibitions, his lack of experience, nor that the blood seemed to have escaped his legs. Sails rumbled as they caught the wind and the brig jerked, jarring those numb legs. He caught Adalia before she fell. Her dark velvet eyes skittered between his. "What will they do if they capture us?"

"Steal our money, our ship, and most likely force us to serve at the pleasure of His Royal Majesty's Navy."

Morgan regretted speaking the truth so openly, especially when terror overtook Adalia's face.

"And what of us women?" she asked.

Instead of answering her, instead of voicing his deepest fears, he swallowed her up in his arms. "I won't let them touch you." He nodded toward Mrs. Wallace, whose pudgy face had gone white. "Either of you."

He forced Adalia back. "Take care of the captain. And stay below." Then swerving about, he started to leave.

"You can do this, Morgan." Her confident tone turned him around. "I've seen your skill in command, the way the men look up to you."

He brushed his thumb over her cheek. How did the woman always know what to say?

"Captain!" Mr. Booker charged into the room. His frenzied gaze took in the captain's prostrate form before his eyes shifted to Morgan. "They're gaining, sir."

Morgan swallowed and faced Adalia. "Stay here." Then shoving his hat atop his head, he marched from the cabin, firing orders to the second mate. "Extinguish the galley fire; sand the top decks; run up the powder cartridges from the magazine; have the men arm themselves, pistols, swords, and boarding axes. Ah, and send the sharpshooters to the tops."

"Aye, aye, Cap'n. I mean, Mr. Morgan, sir."

The slip of tongue sent a sliver of confidence through Morgan as he stormed onto the main deck. A confidence that quickly melted beneath the torrent of self-doubt that assailed him from within. Trying to shake the voices off, he made his way to the quarterdeck, gave the helmsman a nod of assurance, and turned to face the enemy.

Worthless miserable mongrels! Morgan's father had shouted at his two young sons. *Why, I begin to wonder if you are my own flesh and blood.* At five years of age, that was the first time Morgan had been called worthless. A title he grew quite accustomed to in the years to follow. Insulting tirades from his father became a family ritual, much like holiday events, only more frequent and without the joy. Eventually, Morgan grew numb to them. Or had he?

The crew swarmed over the deck, arming themselves and manning the carronades. Sails thundered above, drawing Morgan's gaze to the sharpshooters ready to fire and the topmen adjusting canvas. The brig rose and plunged through the sea, sending foamy squalls over her bow.

A group of sailors gathered on the main deck, their anxious eyes locked on Morgan, awaiting his command. Beyond the stern, the privateer flew through the sea like a blade through pudding, cutting a swath of whipped cream. The Union Jack taunted him from the gaff.

God, help me. The silent prayer spun through his mind as his gaze landed back on his crew. He could not let them down. He could not let his captain down. He could not let Adalia down.

A jet of orange flame caught the corner of his eye, followed by the boom of a cannon.

"All hands, down!" Morgan yelled.

❧

Adalia dropped to her knees before the captain's bed and took his hand in hers. His skin felt as hot as the bed warmer Joy had often slipped beneath Adalia's covers on cold nights. Pressing his hand to her forehead, she closed her eyes and said a silent prayer for his recovery.

Mrs. Wallace returned with another pitcher of water and patted Adalia on the back. "That's a good girl. Praying is about all we can do right now."

Sweat lined the captain's face and slid onto his pillow. He moaned and his eyelids fluttered.

"I wish I had my herbs—my cassia and nutmeg."

The deck jerked to port, and Mrs. Wallace slid back onto her chair as the mad dash of seawater against the hull grew louder. "Is there something else we could do for him?"

Adalia shook her head and stood. "No. When he wakes, we must get him to drink as much water as we can. Besides that, try to keep him cool."

A thunderous roar boomed in the distance, and Adalia's wide eyes met Mrs. Wallace's. The older woman threw a hand to her throat. "Good Lord, help us all!"

Adalia didn't have to ask to know they'd been fired upon. Fear for Morgan, for the crew, sent her rushing for the door. "I must go see what is happening. Will you watch the captain?"

"Of course but you're not supposed—" Mrs. Wallace's admonition was muffled beneath the shouts and thumping of feet above as Adalia darted down the hallway and up the companionway ladder onto the main deck. Instantly, the ship angled to starboard, sending her tumbling to the railing. She gripped the moist wood until her fingers ached and the deck leveled. Sailors flashed past her in dizzying directions across the decks, some scrambling aloft, others carrying powder and shot from below, while others dumped sand over the wooden planks.

"We'll race to get windward of her and cut across her bow," Morgan's voice shot through the rush of wind that swirled around Adalia's ears. "At my command, prepare to tack aweather."

"Aye, aye, sir." Mr. Booker, the second mate, blared orders to a man on the main deck, who repeated them aloft to the topmen. Adalia wondered how they could hear so high above the deck with all the blustering wind. Yet they seemed to understand, for they moved about their tasks.

Another roar pummeled the sky. Adalia crouched, covered her eyes, and waited to be blown to oblivion.

"Just a warnin' shot, miss." A voice as rough as rope brought her an odd comfort.

Adalia opened her eyes to see Mr. Griggs, if she remembered his name, standing before her. Scraggly hair that looked as though it hadn't been washed in years flailed like thick twine beneath his hat. He scratched his prickly chin and gave her a look of reprimand. "Mr. Morgan insists ye go below, miss. Fer yer own safety."

But Adalia didn't want to go below. She was tired of being locked up against her will. "Tell me the truth, Mr. Griggs, am I any safer below?"

He flattened his lips with a snort. "At the moment, no, miss. But should we get close enough to fire our muskets—"

"If that happens, I promise I will oblige." At least above deck Adalia could see the incoming shots. Would have a few seconds to prepare—to say a prayer for herself and the crew. Below, she could be blown to bits without warning.

Instead of forcing her to obey, Mr. Griggs merely took a position beside her at the railing. Her curious stare caused him to add, "Mr. Morgan thought ye'd be sayin' that, so he asked me to keep an eye out fer ye."

Despite the harrowing circumstances, Adalia couldn't help but smile.

A smile that quickly dissolved beneath another resounding *boom!*

"Helm hard a port! Raise tacks and sheets!" Morgan commanded.

"Ye might be wantin' to hang on, miss," Mr. Griggs warned, though he made no move to do so himself.

Adalia gripped the railing again as the ship yawed widely to larboard. Yards and blocks creaked, and the eerie chime of strained lines filled the air, accentuated by the gush of seawater over the bulwarks. Her arms and legs began to ache with the sheer effort of trying to stay upright and not tumble across the deck, or worse, fall over the railing into the sea.

As soon as the ship leveled, Morgan leapt onto the main deck. "Bear off; haul your braces; ease sheets; starboard guns standby!" He bellowed the orders with such authority that if Adalia had known how to comply she would have dashed off to do his bidding.

Mr. Griggs eased her out of the way as gunners, stripped to their waist, with cloth stuffed in their ears, darted to the carronades lining the starboard railing. Sails thundered in a mad search for wind, then snapped when their appetites were satiated, jerking the ship once again.

Morgan glanced her way in passing as he plucked out his long glass. With loose hair blowing behind him and glinting in the sunlight, he braced his boots on the deck and studied the oncoming enemy. His jaw was determined steel, his shoulders a span of confidence as though he'd been fighting sea battles for years.

Her admiration for the pampered aristocrat rose. She'd never dreamed that behind that charming, polished facade lurked a man of such courage, skill, and valor.

She never dreamed she'd be in the midst of a sea battle either. Minutes ticked away like hours, each one drawing the ships closer together. A metallic taste filled her mouth. She didn't wish to die. She and Morgan had just declared their love. On their return to Charleston, they were to begin courting.

It would be so unfair to die now!

Boom! Boom! The air reverberated in a nightmarish detonation. Something heavy zipped past Adalia's ears with a ghostly whine. A splash told her it landed in the sea. But the sound of crunching, snapping wood and the eerie rip of canvas told her that damage had been done. She opened her eyes to find that one of the shots had punched the outer jib, leaving a rugged hole in the sail.

"Fire as you bear!" Morgan shouted and the gunners went to work. Moments later the simultaneous explosion of the ship's carronades staggered the brig from stem to stern. Mr. Griggs put an arm around Adalia—an arm she was thankful for since Morgan's next commands sent the ship veering to starboard. The deck vaulted upward. She clung to the railing with one hand and Mr. Griggs with the other. Gray smoke enveloped her. It stung her nose and stole the breath from her lungs. Coughing, she shrank against the bulkhead. Why had she decided to stay above deck?

Minutes later, the clearing soot revealed the privateer, her top foremast sail flapping idly in the wind. Gray smoke poured from a rent in her hull above the water line. Shifting her sails, she tacked about.

Was she leaving? Adalia allowed hope to rise. Yet after nearly an hour of maneuvering, in which Morgan matched move for move with his enemy, the privateer charged forward.

Morgan did the same.

Adalia's legs trembled. From standing on the heaving deck so long or from fear, she didn't know.

"Morgan, why are you heading straight for them?" Mr. Booker exclaimed. His harried tone caused some sailors to stop what they were doing and stare off the bow. They wiped sweat from their foreheads, leaving smudges of soot that made their eyes look like full moons against a dark sky.

"Because they won't expect it," came Morgan's confident reply.

"They're readying their larboard battery! That's the end of us," Mr. Booker shouted, dashing to the railing much faster than his corpulent frame seemed to allow. He cast a pleading glance over his shoulder at Morgan.

"Wait," Morgan said. A simple command, absent the urgency and fear that seemed to consume the crew. Instead, Morgan crossed his arms over his chest and braced his feet on the deck as the *Seawolf* flew across the water, rising and plunging through the rollers, sending spray over the nervous sailors.

"What are your orders?" Mr. Booker turned and gripped the hilt of his sword as if he would challenge Morgan there and then.

"Aye, what are we doin', Morgan? Have you gone mad?" the quartermaster yelled from his post at the wheel.

"Prepare the starboard guns, Mr. Booker. Fire on my order." Only a slight twitch in Morgan's jaw gave Adalia any indication of apprehension.

"They'll finish us off afore we have a chance."

Morgan flinched then stared at the second mate. "Do as I say," he barked.

Adalia swallowed and bowed her head. Oh, why hadn't she thought to pray before? What was wrong with her? "Father, please save us! Please give Morgan wisdom to defeat our enemy."

As if in answer, yellow flames speared out from the privateer. The sky bellowed like a giant demanding entrance from another world. Adalia slunk to the deck and cringed. A volcano of fire and metal burst upon them. The ship staggered beneath the blow.

෧෭

Morgan crouched as a scream pierced the air. Wood shattered, showering him with splinters. The smell of gunpowder and blood assailed him. A mixture of fear, purpose, and determination forced him to his feet. Forced him to scan the deck and see how badly they'd been hit. Had some of the crew been killed? Pain lanced through him, and he glanced down. A spike of wood protruded from his side. Yanking it out, he pressed a hand over the puddle of warm blood. Just a flesh wound. Darting to the railing, he peered toward the privateer. Her topmasts poked through a cloud of billowing gray smoke. She had taken the bait, become overconfident. And now she was blind.

But only for a moment.

"Helm hard a lee!" he shouted. The brig veered to port, presenting all her guns.

"Fire!"

Boom! Boom! Boom! Boom! Boom! The shots echoed across the sky. Then all went silent. Only the rustle of water and dash of wind sounded as the *Seawolf* finished her tack and brought the privateer up on her hind quarter.

Leaping on the quarterdeck, Morgan marched to the stern, heart in his throat. Either his plan worked or he had sealed the fate of the *Seawolf* and all on board.

The mist cleared. He scanned the enemy ship. He couldn't see her larboard side. But by the way the sailors were scampering across the deck and leaping below in a frenzy, he guessed his guns had hit their mark. Then in a stroke of providence, their top foremast cracked and toppled over like a felled tree, bringing her rigging and sails with it. Morgan smiled. His crew cheered. In moments, the privateer veered away, bidding them farewell with an impotent shot that splashed into the sea just short of the *Seawolf's* stern.

Morgan let out a sigh and stretched the taut muscles in his back. He had done it! He had defeated a British privateer! How, he had no idea. In the heat of action, something had shifted within him. A part buried deep within had emerged. A part he hadn't known existed. A part that shoved aside fear and self-doubt and took command. Turning, he made his way back to the main deck, where Mr. Booker met him, both surprise and exaltation rolling across his lined face.

"Damage report," Morgan said.

"Mr. Thompson got a splinter in his leg." He gestured toward two sailors who were carrying the injured man below. "We received two shots between wind and water, and our jib is damaged. Nothing that won't keep us from heading home straight away." Morgan had never seen the man's smile so wide.

"Let's hear it for Mr. Morgan! Hip hip hurray! Hip hip hurray!" one of the sailors shouted, and the men raised muskets and swords into the air and showered him with praises. His gaze landed on Adalia by the quarterdeck. The soot smudging her face and neck made her smile seem all the more bright.

He rubbed the back of his neck and shook his head. Lud, she'd stayed on deck. Through the entire battle! He'd only permitted her to remain because he assumed she'd scurry below at the first cannon fire. But there she stood, admiration spilling from her eyes. Then they widened in terror as she dashed to his side. "You're hurt."

Morgan followed her gaze to his blood-soaked shirt. "Just a scratch." He'd all but forgotten it. "Go tend Mr. Thompson first. I'll meet you later below."

At first she seemed unwilling to go but then nodded and followed the injured man down the companionway ladder.

"Good job, men!" Morgan scanned the crew. "Now, let's make all sail and head home." He slapped Mr. Booker on the back. The second mate gave him a salute before scurrying off. Warmed by the men's respect, Morgan made his way to the starboard railing. Gripping the damp wood, he gazed over the sea, set aglitter by the sun now high in the sky. They'd been at battle for hours. He should be tired, but his body was wound like an anchor chain. And his mind was no better off as chaotic thoughts spun too quickly to make sense of what had happened. Of what he'd done. He chuckled and lowered his gaze to the foamy water dashing against the hull.

"God, if You're there and You helped me, thank You. Thank You for saving us."

ॐ

"Take off your shirt and sit down." Adalia entered Morgan's cabin and set the basin of water on the table.

"It's barely a scratch." Morgan obeyed nonetheless. Tugging his stained shirt over his head, he plopped into the chair.

Adalia laid out bandages on the table, trying not to look at him. She knew she shouldn't be alone with him in his cabin, but the stubborn man had been busy with ship business until well after supper. She dipped a cloth in the water as silence stretched between them.

"How is Thompson?" Morgan finally asked.

"Well. His injury was minor." Adalia wrung out the cloth, staring at the shadows crossing the bulkhead from the lantern overhead. Not only was she alone with him, but he was also stripped to the waist! Her pulse raced, and she hoped the creak and groan of the ship would muffle her rapid breathing.

"And the captain?" he asked.

"His fever has abated." She dipped the cloth into the water again.

"I believe you've sufficiently drowned the poor rag." He chuckled.

Adalia felt her face redden. Squeezing the water from the cloth, she spun around. More heat flooded her face. Arms of sculpted bronze framed a chest that exuded power. Below it, a rippled firm belly caused a flutter in her stomach. She'd seen him bare-chested before. The first day she'd met him. But her reaction then had been nothing compared to now.

Avoiding his gaze, she knelt to examine the wound, unable to stop thinking about the way he'd commanded the ship during battle with such skill and authority. As if he'd been born to it. He was a true leader. Courageous and daring. She had fallen in love with the pampered aristocrat. But the pirate made her heart steam.

He must have sensed her discomfort, for she felt his smile upon her. That arresting smile that now drew her gaze upward to his eyes, the color of Spanish moss. He eased a lock of her hair behind her ear and ran his thumb over her cheek.

A wave of pleasure surged through her. She lowered her gaze. "We shouldn't be alone."

"Yet you're the one who came to my cabin." His tone was teasing.

"To clean your wound, you daft oaf." She blew out a sigh of frustration and pressed the cloth on the gash in his side—perhaps a bit too hard.

He winced but did not cry out.

"Sorry."

"Will I live?"

Adalia peered into the small tear in his flesh. No splinters. "Yes, you'll live."

She dabbed the cloth over the opening again, wiping up the blood. He lifted his hand to stroke her hair.

"Sit still."

"Yes, ma'am."

She tried not to notice the muscle twitching beneath her every touch—solid and hard. Confound it all, her body reacted again. She must divert the direction of her thoughts. "How did you learn to sail a ship?"

"I've been sailing with Captain Bristo since I was seventeen."

"But why? I don't understand." She gazed up at him.

"I met the captain in a tavern. He was recruiting men for a crew. I was young and already bored with life. So, I thought, why not?"

"But your father. Surely he disapproves."

"He doesn't know. He never will. I sneak away when Hadley and I come to town during the social season."

Adalia finished cleaning the wound and stood. Tossing the cloth into the basin, she grabbed the bandage. "But surely Hadley knows and would tell him."

"No, my brother thinks I'm off with friends or lovers. Besides he's foxed most of the time." He was staring at her with that look again—like he could see deep inside of her and delighted in everything he saw. "You are so beautiful."

The cabin seemed to close in on Adalia. Why did they make these rooms so small? Flushed yet again, she knelt and stretched the bandage around Morgan's back. His taut skin was just inches from her face. His scent swirled around her. Her head grew light. *Concentrate.*

"You always smell so sweet," he said.

Adalia's breath quickened. She cut the bandage and tied it in place. "There, that should take care of you."

She was about to stand, to put distance between herself and Morgan, when he placed a finger beneath her chin and lifted her gaze to his. The intensity in his eyes took her breath away and all restraint with it. He lowered his lips to hers. Every ounce of her responded as if she were a powder keg and Morgan the match. His kiss was gentle, brushing over her lips like the lapping of the waves against the hull. Each press sent off tiny explosions within her. When he withdrew, Adalia's strength withdrew with him, and she nearly fell backward. Would have fallen to the deck if he had not reached out and grabbed her.

"Forgive me." She stood and scooted away from him. "It's been a long day, and I'm tired."

He said nothing. Only grinned at her. Placing the rest of the bandage atop the table, she hugged herself and leaned against the bulkhead, knowing she should leave but unable to bring herself to do so. Why didn't the man put on his shirt? Instead he leaned back in his chair and gave her that look that said he knew how much he affected her.

She averted her gaze. "You are a natural-born captain, Morgan Rutledge."

He grunted and sorrow shadowed his face.

And then the realization hit her, and her own heart plunged. "When you take over the running of the plantation, you won't be able to sail anymore."

He leaned over, elbows on his knees. "Not very often, no."

"But you love it so much. I could see that today. Even in the midst of danger. You're different out here. You are alive. You have purpose."

His silence gave her the answer she sought. She knelt and peered up at him. "Then you must not accept your father's offer."

He brushed the hair from her face. "I will not give you up. Not even for this."

Tears filled her eyes. "Then why not have us both?"

"I cannot. Running the plantation requires my full attention." He gave an incredulous chuckle. "Why, I don't even own a ship. I'd be nothing but a common sailor."

"Are wealth and status so important to you that you'd rather be miserable than part with them?"

"I won't be miserable with you by my side."

"But this is what God meant for you to do. I know it. Are you so concerned with the opinions of others, the approval of an empty-headed bourgeois that you ignore your destiny?" Yet even as Adalia said the words, she realized that lately she'd been very much concerned with those same things.

Morgan stared down at his boots. "I cannot fathom being poor, being worried about from whence my next meal would come from, being snubbed by everyone on the streets, not attending society functions."

"Yet you never seemed to enjoy them overmuch."

"True, but my presence at those functions defines me. Places me in a position of respect, of value. Without that I'm simply. . ."

"Common like me?" Adalia gave a sad chuckle and lowered her gaze.

He caressed her cheek. "No. You are far from common, my love. And when we are married. . ."

Married? Her heart sped up. She rose to her feet, too stunned to speak, and took a step back.

Standing, Morgan took her hand and brought it to his lips, his eyes never leaving hers. "Will you marry me, Adalia?"

She could only stare at him in wonder before a small grin lifted her lips. "I do believe that was the shortest courtship on record."

"I cannot wait another minute to make you mine." Desperation filled his eyes. "This battle has made me realize how short life can be—how precious every moment."

He leaned his forehead against hers. Their breath mingled in the air between them, and Adalia felt like she was dreaming.

But when his lips met hers again, she knew she was not. He kissed her deeply then planted a trail of kisses down her neck. Adalia moaned.

"Are you still sorry I brought you on this voyage?" he whispered in her ear.

Gathering what shred of self-control she still possessed, Adalia pushed him away. "No, but if you ever kidnap me again, Morgan Rutledge, you will regret it."

"The next time I swing you over my shoulder it will be to carry you across the threshold of Rutledge Hall as my wife. You'll be the new lady of the plantation someday."

Lady of the plantation. A thrill began to spiral through Adalia. But it was instantly crushed as the word *plantation* landed like a boulder in her gut. This was all happening far too soon. She'd hoped to have time during their courtship to convince Morgan—to turn him against slavery. Until he did, she could never agree to marry him! Besides, she must tell him the truth of her heritage. It wouldn't be right to enter a marriage shrouded in deception. But how could she? He would reject her. Hate her. She couldn't bear it.

Firm and unwavering, she met his gaze. "I cannot abide slavery, Morgan. I simply cannot. I could never be mistress over slaves." She slid away from him and turned to face the bulkhead, overcome with loss and sorrow. Waiting for his rejection.

For a moment, he said nothing. Then his boots scuffed over the deck, and he gripped her shoulders from behind. She felt his breath on her neck. "Then we shall free them. Hire them on should they choose to stay."

She spun around, stunned. "Truly? But wouldn't that cut too deep into your profits?"

"So we won't be the wealthiest land owners in town." He shrugged. "Of course, I couldn't free them all at once or we'd lose everything. And I can do nothing until my father relinquishes all control to me."

"But that could be years."

"Perhaps. But in the meantime, as their mistress you could do much to increase their comforts."

"True." Adalia bit her lip, her mind spinning with conflicting thoughts. Her heart a torrent of emotions. Perhaps this was her purpose. To ease the burden of these people, remove their shackles, grant them more freedom, give them a life she never had with Sir Walter.

"Think of the good you can do for them," Morgan said as if reading her thoughts. Though he seemed sincere, Adalia wondered if he were only trying to appease her into saying yes.

"Why the sudden change? You've had slaves for years."

"My father has had slaves. I always accepted them as necessary to our livelihood. In truth, your repulsion of slavery gave me much food for thought. To my shame, I had never considered the injustice of it— hadn't really considered it at all." He scratched his whiskers. "But I have begun to see that your opinions have merit."

Adalia felt as though she were floating. "I can hardly believe my ears! I am so happy to hear it, Morgan. Tell me you are speaking the truth."

"I am." He took her hand in his, caressing her fingers. "You have my word, they will be freed over time."

Adalia smiled, but guilt stole it away. She should tell Morgan the truth. He would, no doubt, ask about the stripes on her back someday. She could make up a tale, tell him her father. . .no, wait. . .a master at the island school had whipped her for unruly behavior. But it would be a lie between them forever. Yet his eyes reflected nothing but love for her right now. How could she watch that ardor transform into disgust, even hatred? No, she couldn't tell him. She would lose him. And what good would that do the Rutledge slaves? They would have no advocate. No one to improve their station. No one to ensure their freedom someday. Surely God would overlook her deception for the greater good.

"What's wrong, sweetheart?"

She fell against him, wrapping her arms around him, soaking in his strength, his protection. Afraid to let go. Afraid the dream would evaporate. "Oh, Morgan, I'm so happy."

Nudging her back from him, he cupped her face. "The Brewton ball, the final ball of the season will be in two weeks. I'll announce our engagement then."

Though Charleston society had tolerated Adalia, now they would truly welcome her as one of their own. From poverty to wealth. From slave to princess. Just like her father had said. She could hardly believe it. Forcing down a niggling feeling of unease, she stood on her tiptoes and kissed Morgan.

Everything would work out fine. Like the perfect ending to a fairy tale, nothing could prevent her dreams from coming true.

❦

A knock echoed through the sitting room again. "Mr. Gant!" Willaby shouted. Placing his Bible on the side table with a huff, he rose and headed for the foyer, grumbling. "Where is that man when I need him?"

He opened the door to find Miss Emerald and a rather ostentatiously attired man standing on the porch. The lady handed Willaby a letter, its wax seal split open. Her caustic smile sent a chill down his back. "You may be interested in the contents of this post, Doctor, recently arrived from Barbados."

CHAPTER TWENTY-EIGHT

After a difficult farewell, Adalia watched Morgan saunter down the street until he disappeared from sight. Only then could she tear her gaze away from him. She hated to be separated—never wanted to be without him again. But for now, he must ride out to the plantation and inform his parents of their engagement. She hoped—no, she prayed, all would go well. But surely if they had already accepted their courtship, Mr. and Mrs. Rutledge would not have too much difficulty taking the extra step to allow them to marry.

Adalia smiled. She could hardly believe it herself! Turning, she opened the gate to Doc Willaby's home and made her way down the flagstone path. Wobbling slightly, she caught her balance. They'd just gotten off the ship, and her land legs had not yet returned.

Thankfully, by the time they arrived in Charleston Harbor, Captain Bristo was well on his way to recovery. Though pale and thin, he'd come on deck to guide the ship into the bay, amazed and delighted to hear the sailors' version of how Morgan defeated the British privateer. Several times he congratulated Morgan, sporting a confidence in him that seemed to raise Morgan's shoulders. Adalia could not help but see the strong bond between the men. Morgan chose his friends well, for there were many good qualities in Captain Bristo worthy of admiration.

Even though the captain insisted he was quite recovered, Adalia intended to ask Doc Willaby if he wouldn't mind checking on him just to be sure. That was, if the doctor was not too angry at her for leaving so suddenly. Morgan had told Adalia about the note he'd sent in her stead. She hoped the doctor had accepted it without too much angst.

Oh, what did it matter? She was far too happy to dwell on such things. Leaning over, she breathed in the sweet scent of a rose then gazed across the front yard. Morning sunlight reflected vivid yellows, blues, and pinks off the magnolias, jessamine, and bachelor buttons. Had the garden always been this beautiful? Clutching her skirts, she mounted the stairs then angled around the side of the piazza to the front door.

She froze when she saw her valise sitting on the porch beside the entrance. But it was the iron band perched beside it that caused her heart to cease pumping. Shock forbade her mind to make sense of the sight. She inched forward. The band was hers. She saw the Miles Plantation crest etched on the side. But what was it doing out here? With her things? Even if the doctor found it, how would he know...

Adalia's head spun. She gripped the post. The door swung open. Doc Willaby, his face a maddening twist of disgust and fury, stepped onto the porch. Adalia caught a glimpse of Joy standing in the foyer behind him, her hands clasped together.

"I see you have returned, Miss Winston." His voice was as sharp as his eyes.

Was it her absence that sparked his anger? "I beg your forgiveness, Doctor. The circumstances of my departure forbade me to inform you in person."

"Do you think I care a whit about that now!" She'd never heard him yell so loudly.

Adalia shrank back. Over his shoulder, Joy's trembling lips and wide eyes did not bode well for Adalia's future. Inhaling a deep breath, she faced the doctor. "Whatever is the matter, sir?"

"Whatever is the matter?" He seethed, his eyes sparking fire. His gaze landed on the iron band. "You are a Negro slave. That is what is the matter."

Adalia's heart folded in on itself. Thoughts spun like a tempest in her mind with nowhere to land. *This can't be happening.*

"And a runaway slave at that! Will you deny it?"

A fire ignited behind Adalia's eyes—in her throat. Her legs gave way, and she stumbled, gripping the post tighter. Her voice came out in a whisper of defeat. "How did you...?"

"Humph." Withdrawing a letter and his glasses from his waistcoat, he unfolded it and read. " 'Runaway five months ago from a Sir Walter Miles of Barbados.'"

Her blood froze as the implication of his words became all too real. "You contacted him?"

"No." A brief glimmer of sorrow crossed his gaze. "Someone else took the liberty. After I found the band to what I presume were your shackles." He snatched off his glasses. "And here I thought I was protecting you. Keeping you from consorting with those Rutledge miscreants. When all the time, you were deceiving me. Using me."

Adalia opened her mouth to say she'd never used him. That she'd never actually lied. But defending herself seemed of little import now in light of the news that Sir Walter knew her whereabouts.

"Do you know what you have done?" Her voice cracked.

"Yes! Because of you, I have taken a runaway slave into my home, given her employment. Even"—he looked away—"dare I say, treated her as my own daughter."

His sorrow caused Adalia's heart to sink. She had admired the doctor. Cared for him like a father. Stumbling toward him, she laid a hand on his arm. "I am still the same person."

He shrugged her off and backed away as if she had a disease. "I should alert the authorities and have you locked up until your owner arrives. But I have a reputation to uphold." He grimaced. "I would be the mockery of the entire town and perhaps even lose my patients should they discover I was duped by a mere slave." He waved her off. "I cannot stand the sight of you. You are to leave my home at once and never return."

The cruel command sent tears to Adalia's eyes. But it was the news that Sir Walter was on his way that threatened to crush her. The revelation dug into her soul, ripping out her recent happiness and putting dread in its place. "When should I expect him?"

"How should I know? He said he had some business to deal with first and then he would take the first ship to Charleston."

Adalia hadn't much time. She gave the doctor one last pleading gaze, hoping to find some measure of affection. But his eyes were iron. "Thank you for your kindness to me, Doctor." Tears trickled down her cheeks.

He turned on his heels and slammed the door in her face.

In a stupor, Adalia picked her valise and headed down the steps. Her world spun in a thousand horrifying possibilities. The sound of footsteps turned her around. Perhaps the doctor had changed his mind. But it was Joy who headed for her, arms open. Dropping her case, Adalia swallowed her up and rubbed her back, trying to settle the girl's sobs.

"I'll miss you so much, miss. Where will you go?"

"Don't worry about me, Joy." Adalia released her and wiped tears from the girl's face. "Do what the doctor says. Don't make him angry.

Be safe, dear one." She kissed her cheek. "Maybe someday we will both be free."

"Joy, come here this instant!" the doctor barked.

Joy gave Adalia one last hug and then darted inside.

Turning, Adalia dragged herself back down the flagstone path. Everything blurred before her. Even the flowers lost their luster. She should leave Charleston as soon as possible, but without food and very little money, she wouldn't get far. Country roads were treacherous and unsafe for a woman alone. She would never see Morgan again! She reached the gate and nearly crumbled at the thought. But she mustn't think of that now. Batting tears from her cheeks, she headed down the street. She must find a place to hide. Perhaps Father Mulligan would take her in and hide her away until she could get the funds necessary to purchase passage on another ship. She would have to find a way to get the money soon. If she didn't and Sir Walter found her, he would drag her back into a slavery worse than death.

𑁋

Morgan met his father's gaze with equal austerity. He would not cower beneath the man's bullying anymore. He would not lower his eyes, shift his feet over the woven rug in his father's study, or leave in a huff of rebellion. This was far too important. Out of the corner of his eye, Morgan saw his mother's worried look as she stood beside her husband's desk.

Franklin rose from his chair to his full, imposing height—a height Morgan nearly equaled. But one he had always found intimidating. Along with his father's menacing voice.

"You are what?" that voice now said.

"Engaged. To Miss Winston," Morgan repeated.

His mother gasped and glanced at her husband, no doubt expecting him to explode into one of his berating outbursts or worse, circle the desk and pummel his son.

Instead, Franklin huffed. "I only agreed to this silly courtship because I was sure you'd grow tired of the chit."

"Beware, Father, how you refer to your future daughter-in-law." Morgan crossed his arms over his chest, drawing from the confidence he'd gained aboard the *Seawolf*.

His father must have sensed it in his voice, for his eyes narrowed, and he studied Morgan as if he were seeing him for the first time.

"She's a lovely girl, Franklin, is she not?" Morgan's mother interjected. "Despite that she comes from common descent, she's intelligent and kind."

Without affording his wife a single glance, Franklin kept his hard gaze on Morgan. "She has no name, no dowry."

"We already have both, Father. What need do we have of more?"

"Preposterous. Simply preposterous! What will our friends think? The mayor, the councilmen, society?"

Morgan shrugged. "Their opinions should be of no account to us. Besides, they already adore her." A breeze wafted over him, and he glanced out the window at the sundrenched fields, feeling more in control than he'd ever felt in his father's presence.

Moving to the sideboard, Franklin poured himself a drink and tossed it to the back of his throat. The clock atop the mantle ticked away minutes that seemed as long as hours. His father growled. "There will be conditions."

Hope took root.

Conditions, Morgan could handle, expected, in fact. "Such as?"

"You will spend the majority of your time here on the plantation. You will obey my every command until such a time as I deem"—he pointed his empty glass at Morgan—"and *only* I deem that you are ready to take over the plantation. You will learn, study, and work hard. No more frittering away your time on frivolous pursuits. I don't want you drinking and gambling your life away like your brother. Is that clear?"

Morgan's jaw tightened. The sentence was passed. The judgment made. Morgan would never sail again. Nor would he command a ship, or even spend time with his friend Captain Bristo. Giving Franklin such power over him caused bile to rise in his throat. But it wouldn't be forever. There would be an end to his father's reign. Granted, when Franklin decided it would end. But it would come.

Adalia was worth it.

"After you turn over the plantation, I can run it as I please?" Morgan asked.

Franklin hesitated. "What's got into you, boy?"

"I've grown up."

He snorted as if that were not possible. "We shall see. We have an accord, then?"

"Oh, this is delightful," his mother said. "I may yet have some grandchildren."

Morgan leaned forward, hand outstretched. "We have a deal."

His father eyed his hand, hesitating, then gave it a firm shake.

And for the first time, Morgan had an inkling of what it felt like to become a slave.

Unfortunately, his form of slavery began right away. Franklin insisted he stay the week and assist with supervising the implementation of irrigation troughs from the river. Though Morgan found the task laborious and boring, he honored his side of the agreement. He missed Adalia. Time seemed to inch by without her, but soon the week was over and after his father released him, Morgan bathed, donned a clean suit, and headed into town to tell Adalia the good news.

৯১

Willaby studied the man who'd introduced himself as Sir Walter Miles just moments ago at the front door. A tall, imposing figure, dressed in the finery of his class, who seemed to absorb all the fresh air as he entered the sitting room.

"Won't you have a seat, sir?" Willaby gestured toward a chair.

"Ah, yes, thank you. It has been a long journey." Sir Walter ran a finger through his short-cropped hair, and Willaby wondered if he'd saturate his hand with the grease that slicked through the strands.

"All the way from Barbados?" Willaby asked.

"Yes, arrived only moments ago."

"I'm wondering how you knew to find me?"

"Ah, that would be the letter I received from a Mr. Fabian Saville, I believe his name was." His glance took in the room with a scowl before he slid onto the settee. "He informed me my slave resided at your house."

Ah, yes, the pretentious friend of Miss Emerald's. Yet it was the word *slave* that set the hairs on the back of Willaby's neck on end. Even after a week, he'd been having a difficult time thinking of Adalia in that way.

Joy entered the room and curtseyed.

"Some tea for our guest," Willaby ordered, noting the way Sir Walter's gaze absorbed the young girl. Licentious, lustful. Not until she left did he return his eyes to Willaby.

Taking his own seat, Willaby asked, "What can I do for you?"

"Why, sir, isn't it obvious?" The man gave an unbelieving snort. "I've come for my runaway, Althea."

"Althea?" Willaby flinched, momentarily confused.

"Ah, that's right. She's Adalia Winston to you." Sir Walter brushed a speck of dirt from the table beside him, then crossed his legs. "If you'll bring her to me, I'll be on my way."

"I fear I cannot do that, sir. She is not here."

Sir Walter's eyes ignited. "I asked you to detain her."

"I found I could not abide by your wishes," Willaby said. "It would do irreparable damage to my reputation."

"So you allowed another man's slave to go free?" Sir Walter shocked Willaby with his rage, but the man soon calmed himself. "I assumed"—he glanced around the room as if measuring the value of its contents—"after she deceived you, you'd want to see justice served."

Willaby forced a smile. "She could not have gone far."

Joy entered with a silver tea service and set it on the table. As she leaned to pour the tea, Sir Walter's eyes shot brazenly to her backend. Willaby was so mortified at the man's audacity that he was speechless.

Joy handed him a cup. His hand overtook hers in the exchange, and she leapt back. A smug look claimed his face as he sipped the tea. The girl passed Willaby his cup, and he quickly dismissed her.

"She's quite a beauty," Sir Walter said, his lurid gaze following Joy until she disappeared around the corner.

Willaby hadn't noticed. She was a mere slave. And a clumsy one at that. "I suppose."

"Just the sort of girl to keep your bed warm at night." He winked, and his smile reminded Willaby of a rat who'd just found a piece of cheese.

The tea sped a trail of revulsion down his throat. "I beg your pardon, Sir Walter. I do not consort with slaves. Nor with any woman to whom I am not married."

Seemingly unaffected by Willaby's castigation, the man's gaze landed on the Bible by Willaby's side. A slow, mocking grin spread across his mouth. "Ah, a religious man, I perceive. I meant no offense."

Willaby's stomach sank. What had this man done to Adalia? Sweet Adalia. Had he abused her? Taken advantage of her? Slave or not, Negro or not, she didn't deserve that.

No one did.

Sir Walter sipped his tea and set it down with a clank. "Nevertheless, where did Althea go?"

"I have no idea," Willaby lied, instantly begging God's forgiveness. He'd heard she'd gone back to that rat-infested excuse for an orphanage he'd found her in. But now, faced with the lecherous squab before him,

Willaby vowed to never divulge her whereabouts.

"You have no idea, sir? It's not that large of a town. How many places could a runaway Negress hide?"

Willaby set his own cup down, lest the tea add to the nausea brewing in his stomach. "Perhaps she has left town." He hoped she had left town.

A knock on the door brought a welcome interruption. Willaby rose to answer it but heard Mr. Gant's voice grow rather heated. Moments later, Morgan Rutledge plowed into the room, flowers in hand and a look of outrage on his face. "Why do you continually insist on forcing a wedge between Adalia and me, Willaby? I am her fiancé, and I will not be put off any more. Please inform her I have arrived."

Willaby cringed. Sir Walter rose, a blustering, bewildered look on his face. "Gadzooks, fiancé?"

Ignoring the man, Morgan directed a heated gaze to Willaby. "She didn't tell you? I am to announce our engagement at the Brewton ball in three days. And there's nothing you can do about it. Now, please summon her."

Sir Walter's outrage turned to laughter so uproarious he could hardly contain himself.

Willaby cringed. "She is not here." He needed to shut the man up before he blurted out where she might be! Facing away from Sir Walter, he gestured with his eyes toward the door. But Morgan only stared at him as if he'd gone mad.

"Mr. Rutledge." Sir Walter laid a finger on his chin, his laughter finally abated. "I've heard your name before."

"No doubt you have, sir. My father owns one of the biggest cotton plantations in Charleston."

"Indeed?" Sir Walter grinned and held out his hand toward Morgan. "I am Sir Walter Miles. I have the pleasure to own one of the most successful sugar plantations on Barbados."

"How nice for you, sir." Morgan shook his hand. "Forgive me, but I am in a hurry." His eyes met Willaby's again.

"As I said, she is not here, Mr. Rutledge." Willaby forced a look of alarm onto his face while tightening his lips. Perhaps the swaggering fool would take the hint this time.

Morgan hesitated, studying Willaby for several seconds, before he finally nodded.

Willaby ushered him into the foyer.

"If I do not find her, I will be back." Morgan laid the flowers atop the side table.

Willaby nudged him out the door, then stepped out after him. "Try the orphanage hospital," he whispered. Morgan eyed him with suspicion before he strode away.

By the time Willaby made his way back into the room, Sir Walter had collected his hat from Mr. Gant and was heading out. "I'll be staying at the Sign of Bacchus if the Negro minx returns. I trust you'll alert me."

"Of course." Willaby forced a grin.

Sir Walter slid his hat atop his head. "Very good. In the meantime I believe I know where to start looking. I thank you for your time, sir." He gave a mock bow and whistled as he bounded down the piazza steps.

Willaby could hardly walk back into the drawing room, his feet were so heavy. Nearly as heavy as his heart. How could he have been so wrong? Slavery itself wasn't wrong, was it? It was why God made the Negro—to serve, to obey. After all, slavery existed in the Bible. But then Adalia had entered his life. Sweet, caring, intelligent Adalia. He'd gotten to know her. Love her. *A Negress?*

He'd been so furious at her for lying to him that he'd lost his mind. All he thought to do was to cast her from his home. Teach her a lesson. Rid himself of a mistake that would forever scar his reputation.

Now, to discover the horrors she must have endured under the cruel and lecherous hand of the madman Willaby had just allowed into his home.

Sinking into his chair, he dropped his head into his hands. Why had he allowed Miss Emerald to see the iron band—to read the inscription? He should have been more careful. Should have thought things through. "Oh God, what have I done?"

CHAPTER TWENTY-NINE

Grabbing a glass of Madeira from a passing servant, Sir Walter scanned the crush of Charleston society flitting about the tavern's main hall. Fortunately for him, having a room in the most prestigious tavern in the city afforded him access to the upper crust and their soirees. A soiree like the concert happening here tonight.

He sipped his wine, savoring the sweet, pungent taste, and wove his gaze around silk and satin gowns and feathered hats in search of the object of his interest. A cluster of elderly women passed by, offering him pasted-on smiles and scrutinizing stares—no doubt to ensure he belonged among them. He smiled in return, but as soon as they moved from his view, the large frame and light hair of Morgan Rutledge focused in his vision from across the room. Sir Walter watched him for a moment, noting that the young buck seemed highly distraught about something. Quite animated in fact, as he spoke to a group of friends: a light-haired beauty, a rather dour-looking, yet handsome man, and a lanky fop who kept one eye on his friends and another roving over the passing females. Mr. Rutledge ran a hand through his hair and excused himself from the group. The sullen man followed him.

This was Sir Walter's chance. Making his way through the crowd, he halted before the fair-haired beauty, dipping his head at her and her companion.

She gave him a quick glance then sighed as her eyes wandered in the direction Mr. Rutledge had taken. The tall man studied Sir Walter as if he were a servant.

Sir Walter clenched his jaw and took another sip of wine to calm his anger. "If I may introduce myself, I am Sir Walter Miles."

This drew the lady's avid gaze. "Sir Walter from Barbados?"

"At your service, miss." He bowed.

She held out her gloved hand. "I am Miss Emerald Middleton. I am the one who found the remnant of shackles with your name on it, and this is Hadley Rutledge"—she gestured toward the tall man. "It was my friend, Mr. Saville, who sent you the post."

Taking her hand, Sir Walter kissed it while acknowledging Hadley. Indeed, fortune smiled on him tonight. "I owe you my gratitude, miss."

"We hadn't expected you so soon." Hadley sipped his drink.

"I just arrived this morning."

Miss Emerald touched his arm and leaned closer to him. "Did you find Miss Winston?"

Sir Walter did not miss the excitement in her voice. "As soon as I stepped off the ship, I went to see the doctor you spoke about in the letter, but he claims she no longer lives with him."

Miss Emerald forehead wrinkled.

"I fear I've come all this way only to discover that she has slipped through my fingers." Sir Walter sighed. "If there's anything you can tell me about her whereabouts that might help. . ."

The beauty twirled one of her pearly curls as the orchestra began tuning its instruments. "We have no idea where she is," she said with a huff. "Morgan can't even find her." She stared into the room where he had disappeared. Sir Walter knew she had found him because her eyes transformed into sparkling sapphire.

"That's quite disappointing. I had so hoped to take her far away to Barbados on the next ship"—he dipped his head close to hers—"with no chance of ever returning to Charleston."

Miss Emerald's smile nearly blinded him. Hadley shifted his stance and cocked a brow.

"Perhaps you could tell me about her time here in Charleston," Sir Walter pressed. "Did she make any close acquaintances? Besides Mr. Rutledge, I mean."

Miss Emerald's eyes hardened. "Well, she seems quite fond of that slave who's always following her around."

"What slave is that?"

"Doc Willaby's slave. Joy, I think her name is. Perhaps they are together even now."

Sir Walter pressed his hair back at his temples. Ah, this was getting better and better.

ॐ

Adalia dipped her pen in ink and leaned over the piece of foolscap atop her desk. Light from a single candle flickered ghoulish shadows over the paper, taunting her, daring her to write the letter she knew she must. But every time she began, her eyes flooded with tears, and her vision clouded until she could see nothing but nebulous shadows. Setting down the pen, she leaned back in her chair and glanced over her tiny chamber. Though small and cramped and hot, she was ever so grateful that Father Mulligan had taken her back into the orphanage. She had not told him why she'd returned. And he had not asked. He'd simply ushered her back into her old room with a kind smile. Of course they needed help with the sick children. And though they had never paid her before, this time, Father Mulligan offered her a small stipend each day. Perhaps he sensed her desperation, or perhaps God had told him of her need. Either way she was grateful, for she finally had enough to book passage on a ship.

And leave Charleston forever.

Hence, the reason for the letter she'd attempted to write two nights in a row without success.

It was to Morgan, of course. To tell him good-bye. To tell him that she would always love him. She owed him at least that.

Of course he'd discovered where she was. It wouldn't be too difficult since he knew she often volunteered at the orphanage. And for the past three days and nights, he'd been pounding on the doors of St. Mary's, begging Father Mulligan entrance. For one brief second, she thought of seeing him, asking for his help, but how could she with Sir Walter on his way? She would only be prolonging the inevitable. Thankfully, the father had honored Adalia's wishes and kept Morgan out. He would discover the truth soon enough. And any love he expressed to her now would just be a fanciful illusion.

She'd been such a fool.

She was a fool still, for she'd stayed far too long in Charleston. The past week and a half she'd done nothing but pray and cry, trying to find a way to marry Morgan—to have the life she dreamed of with the man she loved. But no amount of time or tears provided any solution other than the obvious one—she must leave town. And quickly. In all likelihood, Sir Walter had already arrived and was searching for her. She could only hope that Doc Willaby would not think to mention the orphanage to him. But why wouldn't he? And although she'd begged Father Mulligan to not tell anyone she was here, once Sir Walter explained the situation, the priest might very well decide that it was the right thing to return a slave to her owner.

Adalia's heart faltered at the thought. A sweat broke out on her palms. She rubbed them on her skirts, longing for M. The pesky cat always brought her such comfort. She hoped Joy was taking good care of him. She hoped the doctor would allow him to stay with them and not cast him from the house as he had done Adalia. For she couldn't bring him with her. The longer she stayed in town, the more dangerous it became. She must finish this letter and leave on the first ship sailing out of Charleston in the morning. To where, she had no idea. Some place where she could start all over again.

Re-dipping the pen, she made another attempt.

Dearest Morgan,

By the time you read this, I shall be gone. Please do not search for me. I cannot explain why I'm leaving, but suffice it to say it is for the best. Thank you for making this common lady feel like a princess, if only for little while. I love you with all of my heart. I always will. Be happy, Morgan. Follow your dream, and sail away to that exotic horizon.

Yours forever,
Adalia

There. She folded the paper and sealed it with wax from her candle. Short. Not overdone with useless sentiment. It was better that way. She would send it to the plantation since the season was nearly over. In fact, there was only one party remaining, the Brewton ball, which took place tomorrow night.

The ball where Morgan would have announced their engagement.

But by then, Adalia would be on a ship far away.

Rather than curl up and cry herself to sleep, like she'd been doing for so many nights, she flung her night robe over her shoulders, tied it around her waist, and headed out to the sick room to check on the few children she'd been tending the past week. Nothing serious. One had a simple cold, the other a heat rash. After finding them both fast asleep, Adalia gazed out the window at the open space between the orphanage and church. Moonlight tiptoed across the yard, leaving silver footprints in the sand.

Beyond, the white steeple of St. Mary's speared into the darkness like a beacon of hope. Movement tugged Adalia's gaze to the shrubbery edging the courtyard, where a man in white stood gazing up at heaven.

She clutched her throat. Darting to the door, she burst into the yard, drawing the man's attention. He lowered his gaze to hers. She inched toward him, holding up a hand, not wanting to frighten him off—praying he would not disappear as he always did. But he remained in place, staring at her with those eyes that looked like transparent pools the closer she came. And peaceful. They were so peaceful. She stopped within a few feet of him.

His gentle smile put her fears at ease.

"Who are you?" she asked.

"The fear of man bringeth a snare: but whoso putteth his trust in the Lord shall be safe," he said, and then he cocked his head and examined her as if he found her somewhat confusing. "You are highly favored and precious to the King."

His voice sounded like the purl of water across the hull of a ship. Soothing, authoritative. Before Adalia had time to consider his words, he turned, drifted over the courtyard, and disappeared within the church.

"Come back!" She ran after him. She needed to know who he was. Where did he come from? Why did he always speak to her and then leave without explanation?

The creak of the aged door filled the sanctuary as Adalia slid inside. Making her way through the inner door, she entered the sacristy. She wasn't supposed to be here. Only the priests could enter this way. Creeping forward, she emerged into the chancel, where the pulpit, lectern, and choir seats formed out of the shadows. Flickering candles lined the altar. Beyond them, darkness hung over the sanctuary. No sign of the man in white. Skirting the altar, Adalia descended the steps and swung to sit in a pew.

The smell of tallow, aged wood, and something else—a sweet scent—swept over her. She gazed up at the stained-glass windows surrounding the dark outline of a crucifix. The man in white's words filled her mind. *The fear of man bringeth a snare.* She remembered that verse from somewhere. Her childhood. Her father had often quoted it. The fear it spoke of didn't refer to a natural fear. It meant reverence. It meant something one held in awe, something one held above God. Her father's sun-bronzed face filled her vision. Adalia was helping him clean fish, and he was discussing Scripture as he always did.

"It means when you care more for the opinions of men than the opinion of God," he had said. At the time, Adalia had shrugged, not entirely understanding.

But that understanding fell upon her now like a death shroud, nearly smothering her.

That was precisely what she had done. She had cared more about what Morgan thought of her, what society thought of her. Cared more that she was accepted in their pretentious circles than she had cared to please God. She hadn't asked God if He wanted her to be a part of society. She'd simply forged ahead on the pretense she was helping Morgan draw close to God. But that was a lie. She'd relished in the pomp and glamour, in gentry's acceptance of her, feeding her need to be loved. Her need to be accepted, not outcast.

Like a slave.

She clasped the back of the pew in front of her. "What is wrong with wanting to be accepted?" she whispered. But she already knew the answer. Nothing, except when seeking that acceptance took the place of God.

She had made the approval of Morgan and the Charleston elite her god. And in the process she had shoved the true God into a corner.

Grief threatened to choke her. Shame pulled her down to a kneeling position. She dropped her head to the pew back and sobbed. "I'm so sorry, Father. I'm so sorry."

All the things the man in white had told her over the past months flooded her mind.

Charm is deceitful and beauty is passing, but a woman who fears the Lord, she shall be praised.

For all that is in the world—the lust of the flesh, the lust of the eyes, and the pride of life—is not of the Father but is of the world.

For we are his workmanship, created in Christ Jesus unto good works, which God hath before ordained that we should walk in them.

The fear of man bringeth a snare: but whoso putteth his trust in the Lord shall be safe.

She had not only feared the opinion of men but also denied who she truly was. She was Althea Claymore, daughter of Benjamin and Edith Claymore, and one-quarter Negro. She had lied, deceived, and hidden her true heritage all because of a society whose perverted ideas said she was worthless. She'd been embarrassed, ashamed of who God had made her to be. She was His workmanship, His masterpiece!

Created for good works. Ah, she had failed Him so!

Even worse, she'd mistreated Joy. She hadn't wanted others to see her friendship with the slave. Heaven help her, she'd even been willing to lie to her would-be husband about the stripes on her back—to own her own slaves for a time on the Rutledge plantation. After she knew the horrors of slavery firsthand!

"Oh, Father, forgive me." She sobbed. Tears streamed down her cheeks and plopped onto the wooden pew. "I turned away from You, and I didn't even know it." She'd stopped praying, stopped reading her Bible, stopped conversing with God.

And because of that, she'd made a mess of things. She'd caused people pain. Morgan, Doc Willaby, Joy. Herself. And now, she was on the run again.

The man in white. Who was he?

Adalia lifted her head and wiped her moist cheeks, glancing over the dark church. Still no sign of him. An angel perhaps? Whoever he was, God had sent him to draw Adalia back to the Lord. Each time she was about to slip a little further from God, the man in white had crossed her path with a Word from God. To warn her. But in her desperation to be accepted, favored, she'd ignored him completely.

Favored. Hadn't the man in white said she was favored? Precious?

Folding her hands on the pew, she gazed up at the cross. "Father, how can You think that after what I've done?"

You are forgiven, child. The words drifted by her in a whisper. Heard, yet silent.

"Am I still Your daughter?"

Each of the candles lining the altar flickered one by one as if someone walked by. But no one was there. *My princess.*

Adalia smiled. Closing her eyes, she raised her hands toward heaven. She'd been a fool. Had gotten swept up in a world that was nothing but smoke and ashes. The fickle opinions of men—based on their own twisted ideas of what made someone valuable. Why had she ever sought their approval? Now, as God's presence and love wrapped around her, filling her to near bursting, she couldn't imagine ever giving His acceptance up for such a worthless counterfeit.

Leaning her head back down on the pew, she prayed for Morgan. That he would forgive her and find happiness at sea. She prayed for Emerald and Hadley and Caroline and Drayton. For Doc Willaby that he would see the truth of slavery and let go of his bitterness—that God would comfort him in the loss of his wife and daughter. And she prayed for Joy to find freedom someday.

She prayed until a loud noise jerked her from her semiconscious state. Rubbing her eyes, she glanced up as sunlight lit the stained glass in a rainbow of sparkling colors—God's promise of salvation and mercy. She smiled and thanked Him for His unending grace. Shuffling sounded from behind the altar. Adalia rose and darted out the back door before anyone saw her. She made her way to her chamber, a new lightness in her step. She hoped she hadn't missed the early ships leaving the harbor. Donning her undergarments and a blue gown, she straightened the room, grabbed her valise, and headed out to say good-bye to Father Mulligan.

He met her in the courtyard, a paper in his hand. "I was just coming to see you," he said.

"And I you, Father."

His gaze landed on the valise, and a frown tugged away his usual smile. "You're leaving again?"

She nodded. "I'm afraid I must. You've been so kind to me, Father. A true example of Christ's love. I shall never forget you."

Her last statement brought sorrow to his eyes. "I have enjoyed your company, Miss Winston. And we have appreciated your care of the children. We will all miss you very much."

He stood gazing at her as if trying to figure out a way to make her stay. "Oh." He shook his head. "A post for you." He handed her the letter. When she began to protest, he held up a hand. "No, it's not from Mr. Rutledge or Doctor Willaby. Per your request, I have not accepted anything from them. But this man was so persistent. Especially when I told him I could not allow him inside the orphanage or the hospital. He said it was most urgent, so I took the letter and told him that if I saw you—and I did emphasize *if*—I'd make sure you got it. His name"—he examined the letter—"is Sir Walter Miles."

Adalia's blood chilled.

She clutched the letter, snapped the seal and read. . .

My dearest Althea, or should I say Adalia?

    Didn't I tell you that you could never run away from me? That you will always be mine? Such a shame you did not listen. Now, you have caused nothing but trouble and grief. For me and, apparently, for many others. But I have come to take you home.

*Yes, yes, I can hear you saying you will never leave your sacred
haven and come willingly with me back to Barbados. However
I believe you will. You see, I have something quite valuable to
exchange. I do believe you are familiar with a young girl, a slave
called Joy?*

Adalia's legs turned to mush. She would have collapsed if Father
Mulligan hadn't grabbed her arm. He peered at her, asking something, but
she couldn't make out the words. A fog had invaded her mind and muffled
her hearing. Though she didn't want to, though she wanted to tear up the
note, set it aflame and pretend it had never come, she read on. . . .

*Joy, what a luscious little treat. Why, she's aboard my ship
now, all ready to sail to Barbados with me in your stead. That is,
if you will not come. It seems she ran away from the good doctor.
Or that is the news about town. Lucky for me I was able to capture
her. Oh, and by the by, I would keep that between us if I were you.
If I hear that you've informed the doctor, I will set sail with her.
If I hear you've sent someone to alert the authorities, I will set sail
with her.*

In fact, I will set sail with her if you do not do exactly what I say.

*Tonight is the Brewton ball, I believe? Where you and
that prigged buffoon, Morgan Rutledge, were to announce your
engagement. . . Yes, yes, I know all about that.*

*In fact, I want you to attend as planned. Wear your best gown,
my pet, and join your friends. Once I see you, I will release Joy, and
you will come with me. Back where you belong.*

*Forever,
Sir Walter*

CHAPTER THIRTY

Lifting her chin, Adalia drew a deep breath and started down the pathway to the Brewton home. Music and laughter trickled from the open windows on both floors as candlelight spread a sparkling sheen over the elaborate gardens. Such beauty and gaiety.

A perfect disguise for the monster within.

Sir Walter was in that house—stalking her like a crocodile intent on dragging her to his dark lair. She shivered. Took a step forward. Her legs wobbled. Pausing, she waited for her heart to settle. It did not. A gentleman and lady strolling about the gardens greeted her. She smiled and took another step and then another until she had ascended the stairs and wove through the crowd on the piazza to stand before the entrance.

Trembling, she stepped through the front door. A footman took her shawl, and she slipped into the shadows beside the door, needing a moment to gather herself. Jewels, feathers, satin, and lace swam before her in dizzying waves of opulence. Adalia drew a hand to her head. *Please do not faint. Not now.*

Inhaling a shuddering breath, she pressed her gloved hands over the folds of her skirt. She'd chosen a cream-colored gown with bouffant sleeves tied with pretty ribbons. Sparkling beads lined the neckline and trailed down the front, which opened to a satin underskirt, trimmed in lace. It was her best gown. She would enjoy it while she could, for she doubted she'd ever have the opportunity to wear it again.

She glanced once more over the crowd. Would Morgan be here? She hoped not. For she didn't think she could bear to see his face when Sir Walter revealed her true identity. Which she knew was the reason the fiend had insisted she meet him here. To shame her. To expose her in front of all her new friends.

She lowered her hand to her mother's pearls strung about her neck. Black and lustrous—just like her mother. And just like Adalia. She'd been ashamed of them. She'd hidden them away, as she'd done her own heritage.

But not anymore.

God had revealed to her how precious she was. She'd been wonderfully and exquisitely designed before the foundations of the earth were formed. Holding her head high, she plunged into the crowd, nodding at those who greeted her from both sides. Despite her dire circumstances, the thought of how mortified these haughty snobs would be once they discovered whom they had allowed to infiltrate their elitist circles brought her some measure of satisfaction.

She no longer cared what they thought of her. No longer craved their acceptance. And now as she walked in their midst, she found the revelation quite freeing. Entering the main ballroom, she scanned the couples swaying on the dance floor, then moved her gaze to the people clustered about them in giddy conversation. Her eyes locked on Drayton standing beside Emerald and Hadley in the far corner. He lifted his drink toward her in greeting, surprise arching his brow.

She started for them, her heart thrashing against her chest. Morgan was nowhere in sight. Nor did she see Sir Walter. But he was here. She sensed him in the way her skin crawled the moment she entered the house. In the way acid now flooded her mouth. She fingered her pearls again, drawing strength from them as she approached her so-called friends and studied each of them with renewed understanding.

Drayton looked ever so morose as he nursed a drink and watched the dancers with vacant eyes. Trapped in a world he detested, the poor man was a slave to the expectations of his class. Hadley stood beside him. Depositing an empty glass atop a passing tray, he grabbed another and powered it down in seconds before shifting such a longing glace at Emerald that even Adalia was surprised. He didn't realize it, but he was nothing more than a slave to alcohol and to the whim of a woman who loved another.

Adalia's eyes shifted to Emerald, all shimmering alabaster and alluring smiles. She waved her fan about and fluttered her lashes at every passing gentleman, wielding her beauty like a sword to get what she wanted. Yet, in the process, her looks had become her master. Her homage to a comely appearance had prevented her from embracing the finer qualities of kindness, honor, and love.

Adalia took another step toward them, pitying them. She wove around a group of people as the sounds of merriment and music muddled together into a distant chorus. A chorus that announced Adalia's fate. She closed her eyes for a moment, seeking the courage she'd felt earlier that day. The courage that had emboldened her to do the right thing—to save Joy from that monster and deliver her own life up instead. To face the consequences of her lies and play the hand of humiliation and rejection Sir Walter would deal her. Then why, now, did the urge to turn and run away overpower her, begging her to flee?

She froze for a moment, pondering her options. Emerald's spiteful gaze snapped her way. Hadley's brows rose. They seemed none too pleased to see her. She could turn and run. She could remain free! But Joy's sweet face filled her mind—her heart. And Adalia realized she could never live with herself if she allowed Sir Walter to take the sweet child. Word about town was that Joy had, indeed, gone missing. Doctor Willaby had even posted a reward for her return, only confirming Sir Walter's threat. Adalia could only pray he had not touched the girl yet.

Be strong, precious one.

Releasing a deep breath, she proceeded forward as her thoughts shifted to Caroline, who, like Adalia, was enslaved by the opinions of others. And Doc Willaby, who lived in a prison of his own bitterness. And lastly, Morgan, trapped by a fear of failure that kept him from living the life God planned for him.

In a sense they all were slaves of something, weren't they? And the worst part of it was, they didn't even know it. Adalia shook her head. She had escaped her physical slavery only to willingly become a slave to people who were naught but slaves themselves. But God had set Adalia free yet again. And the freedom He offered was true freedom—the kind no one could ever take away.

Adalia halted before her friends. Drayton was the only one who smiled at her. Hadley barely glanced her way, and a grin of victory played on Emerald's lips. "I wondered if you would dare show your face."

Adalia lifted her shoulders, unsure of what the lady meant, but finding she really didn't care. "Then you need wonder no longer."

"Adalia," the voice was not the one she expected, not the nasally whine of Sir Walter, but the deep, masculine intonation of... "Morgan," she whispered his name on a breath of hope as she spun around to face him. . .absorbing him with her eyes.

Never wanting to forget.

He wore a black silk tailcoat over a waistcoat embroidered with silver thread. Skin-tight pantaloons disappeared within Hessian boots. A white stock about his neck complemented his clean-shaven face, save for the neatly trimmed whiskers he liked to keep on his chin. All but one rebellious strand of his hair was tied behind him.

But it was the look of joy and bewilderment on his face that melted Adalia's heart.

He took her hands in his and kissed them both. "Where have you been? I've looked everywhere for you." He searched her eyes, his own brimming with emotion.

Oh, how good it was to see him! To touch him! Adalia memorized the look of desperate love on his face, knowing it would soon be gone. Or would it? Perhaps he truly loved her. Perhaps the news of her heritage wouldn't matter to him. Perhaps he would fight to save her, purchase her, rescue her from this madman. Dare she hope?

As if to answer her question, a chill shrouded her like a mist in a dark forest. Sir Walter slipped beside Emerald, exchanging a smile with the beauty before he faced Adalia. "Ah, the lioness emerges from her den."

A shadow crossed Morgan's face. He tore his gaze from Adalia to face the intruder. "Sir Walter Miles, I believe?"

Sir Walter grinned and smoothed the slick hair at his temples. "We meet again, Mr. Rutledge."

As if by instinct, Morgan nudged Adalia behind him, and studied Sir Walter as if he were an annoying fly. "What is your business here, sir?" His tone was accusing—unfriendly as if he sensed the man's bestial character.

The brewing altercation drew Drayton's gaze while Emerald raised a hand to her mouth to hide her growing smile.

Adalia wished Sir Walter would get on with his deviant plan. She slid from behind Morgan to face her accuser. He hadn't changed. He bore the same malevolent eyes set too close on his wide head, the same greased-back hair, edged in gray, the same pompous stance and lecherous grin.

Her stomach shriveled as he undressed her with his eyes.

Noting the brazen look, Morgan charged toward him. "How dare you gaze at my fiancé in that manner?"

"Fiancé?" Emerald chuckled. "Oh, dear Morgan, if you only knew."

Morgan shifted confused eyes her way. "Knew what?" Quickly dismissing her, he faced Sir Walter again.

Emerald shoved between them, holding up a gloved hand. "He has something you need to hear, Morgan."

The orchestra stopped, and dancers spilled from the floor to mingle with the crowd. Blood rushed past Adalia's ears. She pressed a hand over her churning stomach. She could still leave. She needn't face this!

"Say your piece, sir," Morgan demanded. "Or I shall call you out." He clutched Adalia's hand.

His warm squeeze settled her nerves, gave her the courage to stay.

"Fiancé! Bah!" Sir Walter exclaimed. His loud bark drew the glances of those around them. "How can that be when she is my slave?"

Drawing in a deep breath, Adalia forced back tears as she kept her gaze straight ahead. She would not cower in shame.

"Rubbish!" Morgan ran a hand through his hair. "What madness is this?"

"Yes, yes, it is quite shocking, I'm sure. But this woman you call Adalia Winston is an imposter. Her real name is Althea Claymore. She ran away from my sugar plantation in Barbados nearly six months ago."

"Absurd!" Morgan shouted. "She is white, sir, in case you haven't eyes to see."

"Nay, I'm afraid she is very much a Negress. One-quarter, on her mother's side. I knew the family well." Sir Walter's chest seemed to expand with satisfaction.

The room fell silent. All except for the gasps and exclamations firing from the throng.

Morgan charged the man, grabbing his neckerchief and twisting it until Sir Walter's face reddened and his eyes grew wide. "Take that back, sir."

Gasping for air, Sir Walter clawed at Morgan's hands, trying to dislodge them, while Hadley and Emerald merely stood by, chuckling. Adalia must put a stop to this before Morgan killed him and she would never discover where the brute was keeping Joy. She grabbed Morgan's arm, tugging him back. "No, Morgan. Don't."

Still holding Sir Walter, he faced Adalia. "Did you hear what he called you? Why are you not outraged? Why do you not deny these baseless lies?"

"Let him go and I will tell you." Adalia glanced over her friends.

Emerald's expression reminded her of a child anticipating a treat. Drayton frowned, while a tiny grin formed on Hadley's lips.

Morgan released Sir Walter, shoving him backward. The fiend bent over, coughing and gulping in air. Turning toward Adalia, Morgan straightened his coat. "Give me one reason why I should not call this cretin out to a duel?"

Adalia swallowed. "Because he speaks the truth."

Exclamations from the crowd shot through the air like a quiver of arrows, some she dare not repeat. She glanced at the horrified faces of Charleston society—met each gaze with intensity. She wanted them to know she no longer feared their opinions. She was proud of who she was. Still, she searched for a sympathetic gesture, a smile, a kind expression among the sea of ashen faces gaping at her. People who had only recently greeted her as one of their own. She found none. In fact, several backed away from her as if she would infect them with her Negro blood. One lady fainted.

Adalia faced her friends.

"Oh my!" Emerald feigned shock, but the giggle that followed gave her away. Drayton shook his head and excused himself. Hadley barreled over in laughter. "My brother engaged to a slave! It is too much!"

Morgan released her hand. It dropped to her side, abandoned and cold. He gazed at her as if she had suddenly grown two heads.

Sir Walter recovered and adjusted his neckerchief, eyeing Morgan with contempt. "So, you see why I have come to bring the rebellious Negro home."

Placing a hand on Morgan's arm, Adalia tried to explain. "I would have told you, Morgan, but I feared you would be angry, that you would never see me again."

Shoving past Morgan, Sir Walter wrenched her away from him. Yet Morgan only stared at her. His jaw bunched. Pain and confusion knotted his forehead. Yet his silence gave her hope. A hope that was soon trampled beneath the loathing that emerged in his eyes. With mouth open, he backed away and darted from the room.

⁂

Forcing his way past the crush of people, Morgan blasted out a side door, stumbled to the hedge, and disgorged the contents of his stomach into the bushes. He leaned over, hands on his knees, and wiped his mouth. Breath heaved from his throat as his world spun around him.

A Negress? A slave! She'd deceived him, lied to him. He'd trusted her. Believed in her. Fallen in love with her. Kissed her. Scads, he'd nearly married her! How could he have been so fooled?

The door opened. Scoffs and jests—all at his expense—tumbled out on streams of candlelight before it shut. No doubt, he had been deemed the town idiot—a mockery of society.

The swish of satin sounded. Emerald touched his arm.

"I'm so sorry, Morgan. She fooled us all." Though she tried, she could not keep the elation from her voice. Morgan knew her too well.

He tore from her grasp and backed away. "Don't." He pointed a finger at her. "Don't you dare." He shook his head. "You forced me to come tonight. You knew about this, didn't you?"

She attempted a pout. "I did it for you, Morgan. To save you."

"Pishaw! It's always been about you, Emerald," he spat in disgust.

She took a step toward him, her eyes swimming.

"Leave me be!" he shouted. Then spinning around, he marched through the gardens and out onto the street, ignoring her calls.

Anger, confusion, shame, and heartache brewed a wicked tempest within him. He wanted to punch something, call someone out to a duel, drink himself into a stupor.

Would he be shunned from society forever? Gadzooks, what would his father say? No doubt Franklin's new-found confidence in his son would disintegrate, and the belittling would start all over again. Yet, as Morgan stormed down the street, his heart crumbling to dust with each step, none of those things mattered as one dreadful realization struck him. . . .

He would never see Adalia again. He *could* never see her again.

෨ଡ଼

Sir Walter shoved Adalia into the hackney. Pain shot through her palms as they slammed against the floor of the cab. A gasp brought her gaze upward to a figure sitting on one of the seats. The woman angled her face slightly, allowing the lantern perched outside to flood her with light.

"Joy!" Adalia rose and engulfed the young girl in her arms. She began to sob, latching on to Adalia as if she were a lifeline in a turbulent sea.

"It's going to be all right now, Joy." Adalia rubbed her back. "Shhh now. You are safe."

The carriage pitched, and Sir Walter climbed in, plopping onto the leather seat across from them. "Oh, how quaint." He snickered then pounded the top of the coach for the driver to take off.

Ignoring him, Adalia gripped Joy's shoulders and forced her back. She wiped moist hair from her face as the coach trundled down the street.

Joy's eyes skittered to Sir Walter. The fear and repulsion sparking in them resurged Adalia's memories of her years beneath the man's rule.

"Where are we going?" Joy managed to squeak out.

Adalia glared at Sir Walter. "We are going to Doctor Willaby's to drop you off. Aren't we, Sir Walter?"

He cocked his head and studied her. Curtains of light and dark from passing streetlamps swept across his face in a demonic dance. "My, you have changed, my pet."

Adalia ground her teeth at the repulsive moniker. She never realized how much she hated it until this moment. "You didn't answer me."

"Of course." He heaved a sigh of boredom. "Of course. I will keep to my bargain." His eyes glinted steel. "If you will keep to yours."

A burst of night air filled the coach, bringing the smells of Charleston: honeysuckle and the salty scent of the bay. Adalia swallowed. She would miss this city. "I will give you no trouble if you release Joy unscathed." She faced the girl again.

A tear slid down Joy's cheek. She gazed at Adalia in disbelief. "You gave up your life for me. Why?"

"I couldn't bear for you to end up like me."

Sir Walter gave a maniacal chuckle. "Ah, come now. You make me out to be a monster!"

Joy shook her head. "But you'll be a slave again."

"In body only." Adalia took her hands and squeezed them. "Not my heart or my soul." She tapped Joy's chest. "For true freedom exists within us"—she shot Sir Walter a scathing glance—"and no one can take it away."

He snorted and continued looking out the window.

Adalia brushed a tear from Joy's face. "Greater love hath no man than this that a man lay down his life for his friends. Do you know who said that?"

Joy looked down. "No."

"Jesus. He sacrificed everything to set us free. Free from death and sin. The only two things that can enslave you forever."

Joy met Adalia's gaze, and she squeezed her hand. "You have made me believe that, miss."

"Finally." Sir Walter groaned as they halted before Doc Willaby's home. "Enough of this nonsense!"

Light spilled from the drawing room window, where the doctor, no doubt, was reading his Bible. The thought brought a smile to Adalia's face. She glanced over the iron fence, the roses and jessamine dotting the garden, the gables, and balustrades. The familiar scene sliced her heart. Home, comfort, protection. At least it had been for a short while.

The footman leapt to the ground and opened the door.

"Off with you, slave." Sir Walter waved Joy away.

"Take care of M, will you?" Adalia asked.

"Of course, miss."

"And please tell the doctor I said good-bye." Adalia didn't blame him for his part in this. He had only done what he thought best.

Joy nodded.

Sir Walter groaned and squeezed the bridge of his nose. "By the saints, if I have to endure any more of this sentimental poppycock, I'll stuff rags in your mouths and take you *both* to Barbados!"

Joy shrank back at his outburst, her eyes flickering between him and Adalia. But at Adalia's urging, she rose and climbed from the coach. The door slammed, the carriage jostled, and Adalia hung her head out the window and extended her hand.

Joy grabbed it.

"Go and be free, Joy. For now, only on the inside. But someday I know you'll be free on the outside."

"Balderdash!" Sir Walter laughed. The whip sounded. The carriage lurched and started down the road. Joy ran alongside, clinging to Adalia, until their hands finally ripped apart and the young girl halted, tears streaming down her cheeks.

Unable to bear the sight, Adalia sat back on the seat and avoided gazing at the smug look on Sir Walter's face.

Thankfully, he didn't speak to her the rest of the trip. Not when they arrived at the wharves and he paid the driver. Not when his men rowed them out to a ship. Not until he shoved her into a tiny cabin. Only then did he look her up and down with an odd combination of disgust and desire. "Humph. You can dress a slave up like a princess. But she's still nothing but a slave."

With that, he walked out and slammed the door.

Chapter Thirty-One

"Do you know what you've done, boy?" Franklin paced the drawing room like an angry bull, his snort only confirming the analogy. "You've disgraced this family. Made a mockery of the Rutledge name!"

Wishing the man would lower his voice, Morgan faced the window and closed his eyes against the incessant pounding in his head.

"Come now, dear," Morgan's mother said, her tone one of pleading and pity. "How was Morgan to know who she was?"

"Humph." Franklin growled. Morgan heard him march to the sideboard and pour himself another glass of brandy. "I can smell a Negro a mile away."

Morgan turned to face him. "Then why didn't you warn me, Father?"

Franklin's eyes narrowed. "I *did* warn you. I was against this courtship from the beginning. But no." His face scrunched like a coiled rope. "You had to have her. Couldn't control your base impulses. Why, you're worse than Hadley." He thrust his glass at Morgan, the amber liquid sloshing against the sides.

Morgan licked his lips. What he wouldn't give for a drink right now. But that would make his efforts to sober up a complete waste of time. After that fateful night at the Brewton ball, Morgan had spent days hiding among the seediest taverns in town trying to drown his sorrow. But no matter how hard he tried, no matter how much he drank, he could not get Adalia out of his mind.

Or his heart.

Everywhere he turned, he saw her face in the crowd, heard her voice in the wind. Even smelled her rosemary scent on the breeze.

"What a shame." His mother gripped the back of the settee, a look of genuine sorrow tugging the lines of her face. "Such a sweet girl. And smart too."

"She still is, Mother," Morgan said.

"Blast you for a fool!" Franklin's face bloated. "Surely, you can't still have affections for this lying slave!"

Even Morgan's mother looked mortified. "It isn't right, son."

Martha, one of the house slaves, peeked in the room, but upon seeing Franklin's face, she skittered away. Morgan sighed and picked up a porcelain figurine from atop a table. He ran his fingers over the smooth glass formed in the shape of a young lady donned in finery. A young lady of class and position and white as the new snow. Memories assailed Morgan of Adalia's hatred of slavery. How she insisted he set the slaves free after they were married. Her hesitation in accepting his proposal. Now it all made sense. "Mother, you tend to the slaves. You care for them. They are people just like us."

His mother moved toward him, clasping her hands in front of her. "They are people, son, but they are not like us."

Franklin snapped his drink to the back of his throat and poured another. "Thank God you didn't marry her. People will forget this reckless blunder before too long."

Morgan cringed. Reckless blunder? Was that all Adalia had been reduced to? Still he saw nothing in the situation he should be thankful for. To God or anyone else. *God.* How often had Adalia spoken of God like a friend, a father. A kind father. Not like the one towering over Morgan now.

Lizzie tumbled into the room, a bundle of lace and giggles. She halted when she saw her father. "Papa, are you angry?"

"Not at you, sweetheart." But his harsh tone sent the girl dashing to her mother, who quickly drew her close.

Morgan thought of the way Adalia had prayed over his sister and saved her life. She never took credit for it, but gave all the glory to God. But where was her God now? Why had He allowed this to happen?

Morgan set the figurine down and faced his parents. "What does it matter if she has Negro blood in her?" He voiced the question that had been grinding at him all week, grinding and clawing and poking at his mind, his conscience, and at everything he'd been taught to believe.

Franklin's face grew ruddy. His eyes fumed. He charged toward Morgan as if intending to strike him. Oddly, Morgan felt no fear. He felt no remorse, no concern that he'd once again disappointed his father. Instead, he felt nothing.

Franklin's gaze landed on Lizzie hiding in the folds of her mother's skirt, and he halted. Instead, he pointed a finger at Morgan. "If you think to go after that slave"—he gritted his teeth and wiped spit from his lips—"if you dare even consider marrying her!"

"That option has been taken from me, Father. She is gone."

A flash of surprise at Morgan's commanding tone crossed his father's face, but Morgan's heart ached too much to relish in the victory. Adalia *was* gone. He swallowed down a burst of agony at the thought of what she had endured—what she *was* enduring at the hand of that bedeviled swine, Sir Walter.

Franklin turned away. "That you would even consider it disgusts me."

Morgan glanced at his mother, but even his sweet-tempered, kind mother was not on his side.

No wonder Adalia had lied to him. Look at the reaction from his parents. He hung his head. Look how *he* had reacted.

Everything he ever believed in, everything he had been taught—the fortress of ideas, values, and beliefs that had formed his world—was crumbling around him.

"If you chase after that Negro whore," Franklin spat. "If you marry her, I will disown you. I will toss you on the street without a coin in your pocket. Mark my words!"

෧෯

Halting just outside the drawing room, Adalia closed her eyes and lifted up a silent prayer for strength and protection. Though her heart still pounded in her chest, she felt God's presence surround her, cloak her with love. It was late, near midnight, and Sir Walter had summoned her to keep him company. As he had done nearly every night for over a week. She knew he was besotted before she entered the room. But now as she took a step toward him, she also knew from his eyes and the way he slouched on the sofa that he was angry and libidinous.

A horrifying threesome.

"You called for me?" She tried to keep her voice steady but knew she had failed when his lecherous grin widened.

"Come sit, my pet." He patted the cushion beside him, but Adalia lowered herself onto the high-backed chair across from him instead.

He frowned and lifted his drink to his lips, studying her.

Adalia spread her skirts around her feet, ensuring every inch of her

289

was covered. Though the maid had awakened her from a deep sleep, Adalia had donned her most modest gown. Not that it took more than her presence to elicit that lewd sparkle in his eyes. Still, it had been over two weeks, and he'd not touched her. Though why, she could not say. She sensed something different about him—a hesitation, a curiosity, perhaps even a doubt that seemed to keep him at bay. Instead, he had ordered her about as if she were a field hand, working her from dawn till dusk until she all but fell into bed each night. She clasped her hands in her lap, feeling the blisters on her palms even now.

"It doesn't have to be this way," he said.

Adalia pursed her lips. A breeze fluttered the gauze curtains, drawing her gaze to the window. Thick black coated the landscape much like the darkness that coated her heart.

He sighed. "You are different somehow."

Adalia met his cloudy gaze. Yes, she supposed she was. She'd learned so much in the past six months. She'd wandered away from God. But in returning, she'd grown so much closer to Him. And she'd discovered who she was—who she truly was. Who God made her to be.

"You don't have to work so hard," Sir Walter continued, his words slurring.

"I am your slave, sir. It is my job to work hard."

"And yet there is a better way."

Adalia swallowed. "What way is that? To live a life of ease and yet be a slave to your desires. Is that what you consider better? I'd rather work in the kitchen or the fields."

Face purpling, Sir Walter rose and tottered to the window. "That can be arranged! I can work you day and night until you fall over dead from exhaustion."

"If that is God's will, so be it." Adalia tightened her jaw. In fact, she had begged for death every day since she'd arrived at the Miles Plantation. Begged for an end to the ache in her heart—an end to the memories of Morgan Rutledge. An end to the dreams of his love that invaded her sleep at night. And the vision of disgust on his face that haunted her thoughts during the day. She loved him still. She would always love him. And that made his rejection hurt all the more.

"God, bah! What has He to do with anything?" Sir Walter held out his empty glass. "Get me another drink."

Making her way to him, Adalia took the crystal goblet and refilled it from the carafe sitting atop the buffet. "What difference does it make whether you work me to death or keep me in the house? You always take what you want." She handed him his drink.

The smell of brandy and bergamot cologne stung her nose. With one hand, he took the glass, with the other he clutched her arm. Pain throbbed into her shoulder. He thrust his face into hers.

"I want you to come to me willingly." A momentary flicker of longing—no, vulnerability—appeared in his glassy eyes.

She tore from his grasp and rubbed her arm. "That will never happen."

He sipped his drink then set the glass down on the table. . . methodically, slowly, like a predator trying not to frighten its prey. Then he struck her across the face. Adalia stumbled to the side, the sting radiating down her jaw and neck.

"You impertinent wench!" He raised his hand to slap her again and would have if he hadn't staggered and been forced to grip the back of a chair to keep from falling. He ground his teeth together. "You will obey me."

Adalia rubbed her cheek and leveled her shoulders. "I will."

He blinked, his gaze wandering over her. "What did you say?"

"I said I will obey you. You see, Sir Walter, I have made good use of the long hours you put me to work. I have been praying and talking with God. And He has told me three things. Do you wish to know what they are?" Strength surged through Adalia, encouraging her to continue. To no longer fear this pathetic, little man.

He snorted but did not answer.

"The first," she said, "is that to enslave another person against their will is a grievous sin. Secondly, that as long as I am your slave, I am to obey you and serve you with all my heart until such a time as God delivers me from your hand."

Sir Walter gave a malignant grin and grabbed his drink again. "Bah! No one is going to deliver you, my pet. But the obeying part, I find quite to my liking." He slid a finger down her jaw and twirled it through a lock of her hair.

Adalia stepped back, out of his reach. "And three. I am not to tolerate your lecherous advances. You may work me to the bone, order me to do whatever you wish, and I will obey you. But I will not allow you to touch me inappropriately again."

His wicked chuckle filled the room. "Indeed? Is that what your God told you?"

"It is." And so much more that she wouldn't mention. That God loved her, that He was with her. And that He would never leave her. No matter what happened.

Sir Walter contained his laughter then tossed the rest of his drink to the back of his throat. After setting down his glass, he grabbed the lapels of his coat. "And how is this God going to stop me from having my way with you?"

"He may not. Or He may. I am merely telling you that I will fight with everything I have within me."

A flicker of sorrow crossed Sir Walter's eyes, quickly doused by fury. "It's that foppish toady, Morgan Rutledge, isn't it?" He swayed on his feet.

The sound of his name sliced through her heart. She lowered her gaze. "This has nothing to do with him."

"You love him." Sir Walter snorted. "But he loathes you. Rejected you." He gripped her arm again and shoved her against him. "Yet I adore you. Love you, even." His breath sent a shiver of disgust down her neck. She turned her face away.

"This is not love, Sir Walter."

He tightened his grip, grabbed her other arm, and splattered kisses down her cheek and neck.

A bitter taste coated her mouth. She jerked from him and backed away. "I beg you, Sir Walter, ask God to help you, to forgive you. You can still be a good man, an honorable man."

Lip curling, he started toward her. But then he froze as if some invisible barrier forbade him go any farther. He grabbed his glass and brought it to his lips. Upon finding it empty, he tossed it against the stone wall. It shattered on the floor in a dozen glittering shards. "Get out of my sight!"

Adalia dashed from the room before he changed his mind. Yet as she mounted the stairs to her chamber, she knew it was only a matter of time before Sir Walter's anger and lust overcame his need for her compliance.

And then no one could rescue her but God.

❧

Morgan went to the one place where things made sense. He went to sea. Thankfully, Captain Bristo had made a full recovery and enlisted Morgan's help on a run to Jamaica with a load of rice, finely crafted furniture, and various musical instruments. Yet even after they'd anchored at Kingston, offloaded their cargo, and were heading back to Charleston, Morgan found no solace in the waves or wind. In fact, the ache in his heart had grown worse and began to spread throughout his body until he'd contemplated jumping overboard to end it all.

The evening breeze blasted over him, tossing his loose hair and filling his lungs with the smell of brine and tar. Unable to sleep, unable to shake loose the memories of Adalia, he'd come above deck to clear his head and seek answers. Yet now as he gazed over the onyx sea, he only felt more confused. Leaning over the railing, he watched the wake bubble like liquid crystal in the moonlight—frothing and churning and blistering just like the chaotic thoughts battling in his mind since Adalia left.

He loved her. He didn't want to live without her. But the truth that she was a Negro slave made him question his own sanity. How could he have fallen so deeply in love with a Negress? A Negress who was smart, kind, generous, fun, innocent—wonderful in every way. He'd never met a woman like her and probably never would again. But how could he reconcile everything good within her with *who* she really was? Weren't Negroes ignorant beasts—kind, yet incapable of taking care of themselves? Wasn't that why they were suited so well for slavery?

Morgan rubbed his head. None of it made sense anymore.

Then there was Adalia's God. Morgan felt Him everywhere. In the sea, the creak of the ship, the thunder of the sails. In the sunshine and the rain. Morgan saw His face in the clouds drifting overhead. Even now he heard Him in the whisper of the night as if God were calling to Morgan, as if He had an important message to give him.

Yet Morgan wasn't ready to hear it.

Footsteps told him he wasn't alone. Captain Bristo slipped beside him. "It's nearly dawn. Have you been up all night?"

"Couldn't sleep." Morgan shifted his shoulders.

"Something troubling you?"

Morgan gripped the railing, his jaw clenching. "Yes" was all he could manage.

"Miss Winston?"

Morgan nodded.

Leaning back on the railing, Captain Bristo crossed his arms over his chest. "Want to tell me?"

Before Morgan even stopped shaking his head no, he'd already begun to spill the gruesome events of the past weeks.

Captain Bristo listened intently, offering the occasional nod and grunt and the expected start of surprise at the news of Adalia's heritage. Surprise but not abhorrence.

When Morgan finished, he shoved off from the railing and took up a pace across the quarterdeck. "She lied to me." He tried to conjure up the anger he initially felt, but it had long since abandoned him. "Made a fool out of me."

Morgan braced himself as the ship bucked over a wave.

"Yes." Captain Bristo's gaze followed him. "She didn't disclose the truth. But do you blame her? You offered her luxury, wealth, and delicacies beyond her imagination? Not to mention, love."

"Still, she should have denied my suit. She knew who she was. Who I was." Morgan shook the sea spray from his face. Yet, now that he thought of it, she did try to discourage his advances. Quite vehemently in the beginning.

"Perhaps." Bristo shrugged. "But perhaps she fell in love?" He cocked one brow.

Morgan stopped. If Adalia's feelings for Morgan were anywhere near what his were for her, ending their relationship would have been as impossible as stopping a wave crashing upon the shore. He stared at his friend, envying the peace that always seemed to surround him. "You aren't shocked at who she is? Disgusted?"

"Shocked? Quite." Bristo smiled. "She doesn't look like a Negress, I'll give her that. Disgusted? No. She is one of God's glorious creations, as we all are."

Morgan ran a hand through his hair. He gazed at the myriad stars sprinkled across the black sky, longing for their light to penetrate the darkness churning in his soul.

"Only one question remains," Captain Bristo said.

Morgan huffed. The man had a way of simplifying life that always put Morgan at ease. "And that is?"

"Do you still love her?"

Morgan released a sigh. "With all my heart."

"Then why are you allowing Sir Walter Miles to have her?"

Morgan shook his head. A sail snapped above him. "I cannot marry her." He fisted his hands and took up a pace again.

"Why not?"

"My father would disown me."

"And. . ."

"I would lose the Rutledge name."

"A tragedy. The men who bear it are so honorable."

"I would lose my place in society," Morgan continued, ignoring the man's sarcasm.

"Another tragedy since that position has made you so happy."

Morgan eyed him. How could the man disarm him so quickly? "I would be penniless. Have to work to earn my way."

Bristo chuckled. "Egad, unheard of!" He clapped him on the back. "However, I do know a certain merchantman with an opening for a first mate. And from the looks of things"—his face grew serious as he scanned the sea—"I may need a good privateer should war break out with Britain."

Morgan smiled. The thought of sailing for a living was exciting enough, but privateering? That sent his heart soaring into a dream world he never thought possible.

"I intend to purchase another brig, and I'll need someone to captain her. Privateering can be quite lucrative, you know. With the added bonus of serving one's country."

"And you would entrust me with your ship?"

"You've more than proven your skill."

Morgan rubbed the back of his neck. "What if I fail?"

"Trust God."

God again. "I do not know this God of yours."

"You can."

Seek Me. The gentle words floated past Morgan's ears. He drew a deep breath of salty air and snapped the hair from his face. "I've had my fill of fathers."

"This one is different. He cares for you. He has a plan for your life. Just turn to Him, Morgan. Seek Him. Ask Him what to do." The sincerity in his friend's eyes tugged on a longing deep within Morgan.

Gripping the railing again, Morgan stared out to sea. Hadn't God answered his prayer when Morgan had faced the British privateer? "I have felt Him. . . Someone. I don't know."

Bristo gripped his arm. "Then answer Him." Releasing Morgan, he headed across the deck.

Morgan closed his eyes and lowered his head. *God, if You're there, what would You have me do? About Adalia? About sailing? Do You even care?*

The brisk wind changed direction and began swirling around him.

Around and around, fingering his hair and caressing his skin. A tingle alighted upon his head and sped through his body as though the finger of God had touched him. *God?*

My son.

Son. Morgan fought back a burning behind his eyes. Instead of the expected disappointment, the chastisement from a demanding father, an overwhelming feeling of acceptance and love washed over him. A feeling of value and worth that made Morgan's desire for wealth and status seem like refuse by comparison. *I'm so sorry, Father. For everything. For not believing in You. For making such a muck out of my life.*

Still the sense of love remained, stirring his soul with hope, with meaning, with purpose. A breeze feathered his hair and flapped his shirt like a gentle caress.

God, what would You have me do?

Follow what I have put on your heart.

Morgan opened his eyes. A ribbon of gold tinted the horizon, pushing back the night. God was real! He was real and knowable and powerful and loving just as Adalia had said. His heart surging with hope, Morgan shook the moisture from his eyes and spun around. He marched to the quarterdeck railing and scanned the deck. Captain Bristo stood talking with another sailor by the foredeck ladder.

"Captain!" Morgan shouted. "May I borrow your ship?"

Captain Bristo's knowing smile lit up the deck. "For what purpose?"

"I have a lady to rescue!"

Chapter Thirty-Two

Adalia knew her period of grace had come to an end. She knew because she could hear Sir Walter thumping up the steps, bellowing a ribald ditty. He was drunk. Striking flint to steel, she gathered a flame in a tinderbox and lit a candle, then glanced at the clock. Four in the morning. He was usually passed out long before now—long before she normally rose at four thirty to help in the kitchen. But something had awoken her over an hour ago. A gentle nudge. . .a bright light. . .the man in white. She couldn't be sure. It seemed like a dream now. Yet, unable to fall back asleep, she'd lain in bed praying.

"With women and wine I defy every care
For life without these is a bubble of air."

Sir Walter's slurred voice caused her stomach to convulse. The singing grew louder. And more garbled.

Another footfall pounded on the tread.

Perhaps he was simply heading up to his chamber to retire. But Adalia knew better. His behavior had changed over the past week. He had become bolder, more insulting, more demanding. And the more obedient she was—the more she returned his furious outbursts with kindness—the angrier he became.

Adalia darted to her wardrobe, thankful Sir Walter hadn't shackled her ankles since she'd returned. Instead, he'd posted more guards around the house at night and ordered one to follow her everywhere during the day. She was never alone. Quickly donning her stockings and stays, tying them up as best she could from behind, she flung on her petticoats and tossed a gown over her head. With trembling fingers, she did her best to button up the front. Better to be dressed as modestly as possible when he burst into her chamber.

Another footstep echoed in the hall.

"For life without these
For life without these
For life without these is a bubble of air."

Still fumbling with her buttons, Adalia moved to look out the window. She gripped the bars and shook them, desperate to escape. But the moist iron bit into her skin, stinging her fingers and spearing her heart. A heart that now crashed against her ribs as she fell to her knees and peered into the darkness, searching for an answer to her prayers—a light, a hope, a rescuer coming to take her away. But all she saw were clumps of dark trees and shrubs dotting a bleak, moonless landscape. "God, please help me."

"Each helping the other in pleasure I roll
And a new flow of spirits enlivens my soul
Each helping the other in pleasure I roll
And a new flow of spirits enlivens my soul."

He stopped singing. She could hear his shredded breath though the door. The key jangled. Clasping her hands together, Adalia bowed her head and whispered prayers. The keys fell to the floor. Sir Walter groaned as he no doubt bent to pick them up. The lock clicked, and the door burst open, drawing a breeze from the window that swept away Adalia's prayers.

Rising to her feet, she wiped a tear from her cheek and stood to face the monster.

He staggered toward her, a besotted grin on his lips. "Ah, how unfortunate you have wasted your efforts in getting dressed."

Only then did Adalia notice the whip in his hand.

"I have work to do, Sir Walter. If you'll excuse me." She attempted a wide angle around him, but he leapt and grabbed her arm.

"Not so fast, my pet."

Pain shot into her shoulder. She winced. "Please, let me go." Though tears burned behind her eyes, she kept her voice steady and her gaze straight ahead. "You have no right."

"I've had enough of your impertinence." He shoved her. Adalia stumbled backward. Her legs slammed against the edge of the table.

"I give you all of this." He waved his hands over her chamber. "A room of your own, a soft bed, plenty of gowns, food. And what do I get in return?" Angry eyes shot her way.

"If I have offended you, sir, I'd gladly sleep with the rest of the slaves."

"If you have offended me! Bah! You offend me every day you reject me."

"As I have said—"

"Enough talk!" he roared, startling Adalia. Then drawing a deep breath, he pasted on a smile. "Come now, my pet, I give you your choice. Submit to me, or suffer the whip."

A quiver ran across Adalia's back, awakening agonizing memories. Pain like she'd never known before. But there was a different kind of pain—a pain that injured her soul—that was far worse. She swallowed. "I choose the whip."

The muscles in Sir Walter's face bunched into knots. His eyes became menacing steel. She didn't have time to react before he charged her, spun her around, and shoved her facedown onto the bed.

Adalia's breath came heavy and hard against her sheets, enveloping her in a cloud of terror. Cringing, she awaited the first strike. She heard him loosen the whip. Heard it snap in the air. He grabbed her collar and ripped her gown down the back. She closed her eyes.

Twack! Pain seared across her skin, releasing her tears. He chuckled and raised the whip again.

But no burning spasm struck her, no leather sliced her skin. Instead, she heard boot steps drumming over the floor. Sir Walter cursed. Shuffling sounded. The crack of a bone, a loud moan, another crack, a thud, boots scraping. Adalia peered through the tangle of her hair to see a large man tear the whip from Sir Walter's hand and toss it into the corner. Sir Walter swung at the intruder, but the man slugged him across the jaw, sending Sir Walter tumbling backward. His head struck the corner of Adalia's dressing bureau before he slumped to the ground.

Her mind spun. Who was this man who dared defy Sir Walter? Was he friend or foe? With his back to her, she could not see his face. But she could hear his heavy breaths. She must leave before he turned his attentions her way.

She struggled to rise when strong hands lifted her from the bed and drew her close. No, not again! Raising her fists, she pounded the intruder's chest. His scent filled her nostrils.

Morgan.

"Are you all right?" His voice confirmed the hope rising within her. She opened her eyes to find him gazing down at her.

"Morgan?"

"Yes, sweetheart, it's me." He wiped the hair from her face and pressed her against him. The muscles in his chest twitched beneath her fingers. She listened for his heartbeat. There it was, strong and sure. Tears spilled down her cheeks.

"You can't be here. I'm being whipped, and the pain has made me delirious."

But the press of his lips on her cheek and his warm breath on her neck told her he was anything but a dream.

"You're safe now," he whispered, wiping her tears. He peered over her shoulder at her back. "You're hurt."

"No, I'm fine." She gazed up at him, still not believing her eyes. "But why. . . ? How. . . ?"

"That beast whipped you." Morgan hissed, glancing at the unconscious man lying in a heap on the floor.

Sorrow broke through Adalia's joy as she remembered the look of repulsion on Morgan's face at the Brewton ball. "It's not the first time. I'm a slave, after all." She pushed away from him, hearing the bitterness in her own voice. Candlelight wove gold through his hair, angled over his strong jaw, and reflected such love and affection in his eyes. "I don't understand, Morgan. Why have you come?"

"Shhh, now. I'll explain later." He reached out for her. "We must go!"

A moan sounded.

Adalia tensed and glanced over in time to see Sir Walter rising from the floor, rubbing his head. He started for them, his face blistering with rage.

Morgan pushed her aside, drew his sword, and leveled it at Sir Walter's chest. Adalia's throat went dry.

"How dare you invade my home!" Sir Walter raged. "Rodale! Kemp!" He shouted out the door. "My men will be upon you in a second."

"I doubt that. *My* men had no trouble dispatching your pathetic guards." Morgan pressed the sword. Sir Walter retreated.

The pompous gleam left Sir Walter's eyes, replaced by a fear Adalia had never seen before in the man.

"Allow me to inform you how this is to be played." Morgan unclipped a pouch from his belt and tossed it to Sir Walter.

His bumbling attempt to catch it failed, and it landed with a clank at his shoes. He bent over and picked it up, testing the weight.

"One thousand dollars. More than the price of a good slave. I'm purchasing Miss Winston. You will agree to the price, and we will leave unhindered."

⁣

With Adalia safely behind him and his blade pointed at Sir Walter, Morgan's heart began to settle. When he'd first dashed into the room and seen the man slash Adalia's back, it took every ounce of Morgan's control not to kill him on the spot. Even now as the buffoon fingered the bag of coins and grinned as if he had won the game, Morgan's fingers twitched in an effort not to end his miserable life. Instead he plucked a receipt of sale from his pocket and laid it on the table.

Adalia was alive! And she was with him. That thought alone kept his temper at bay.

Sir Walter's narrow eyes flitted between Morgan and Adalia. The malevolent sparkle within them brightened with each passing second as if were planning their demise.

Morgan sighed, tired of the man's theatrics. "Do we have an agreement, sir? I haven't all day."

"Do I have a choice?"

"No. But you can make it easy on yourself by yielding."

Sir Walter thrust out his chin. "Very well, but I have no pen."

Morgan produced pen and ink from a pouch clipped to his belt and forced them into Sir Walter's hand.

After scribbling his signature on the document, the swine handed it to Morgan. "I dare say you won't be at all pleased with your winnings." He looked Adalia up and down as if he were gazing at a spoilt piece of meat. "She's nothing but a Negro whore."

Blood surged into Morgan's fists. Folding the receipt, he stuffed it in his pocket, sheaved his sword, and barreled toward the miscreant. Grabbing him by the lapels, he slammed his fist across Sir Walter's face. The man jerked to the side and tumbled to the ground. Diving for him, Morgan picked him up by the neckerchief and fisted him again. And again. Sir Walter groaned and cringed, holding up his hands.

But Morgan didn't care. He would have struck him yet again, if Adalia's touch on his arm and her gentle pleading for him to stop had not stayed his hand. "Leave him be, Morgan. He's not worth it."

Breathing hard, he turned toward her. Ebony hair circled her flushed face. "Let's go." She caressed his cheek with the back of her hand.

He released Sir Walter. The beast dropped to the floor with a thud and a moan. Morgan didn't give him another thought—wouldn't waste another thought on the mongrel. Cupping Adalia's face, he showered her with kisses, finally absorbing her lips with his.

Ah, the sweet taste of her! He'd missed it. But now wasn't the time. He forced himself to withdraw.

"I can't believe you came for me." Her eyes shimmered with tears.

"I'm so sorry, Adalia. I was wrong. So very wrong. About you. About so many things."

He kissed her forehead and swept an arm around her. She winced, reminding him of her wounds and causing his anger to resurge. Shrugging out of his coat, he swung it gently over her shoulders and helped push her arms through the sleeves. To protect the open gashes on her back as well as her modesty. But now, they must hurry. There wasn't much time.

He led her out the door, felt her tremble as they descended the dark stairway. His whispered words of love and encouragement seemed of no effect as she cast a wary glance over the dark house. Even as they emerged onto the veranda, she jerked as if expecting a guard to force her back inside. He rubbed her arm and drew her near, wanting to reassure her—hating what Sir Walter had done to her. How could Morgan have ever let that man take her away? How could he have left her in this hellish place for even a moment? He ground his teeth together, fighting back a burst of self-loathing as he led her down the front drive.

A moonless night offered them no view save murky shifting shadows. A breeze shivered the palm fronds above them as gravel crunched beneath their feet. Adalia tensed. Morgan caressed the hair tumbling down her back in an effort to soothe her. Lifting fingers to his mouth, he whistled, and a dozen shadows, armed with cutlasses and pistols—Captain Bristo's men—emerged from the shrubbery lining the drive. Men who had knocked all the night guards unconscious when they'd first approached the house. Adalia seemed to relax at the sight of them.

The journey through the jungle to the coast was made in silence. Nothing but the snap of twigs, crunch of leaves, and buzz of katydids filled the air. Morgan kept one arm draped around Adalia and the other hand on the butt of the pistol stuffed in his trousers. Though he couldn't imagine Sir Walter following them, Morgan wasn't taking any chances. Not with the most precious cargo in the world at his side. Though her body still felt as taut as a sail under full wind, Adalia finally leaned her head on his shoulder with a sigh. A sweet sigh that told him that with each step they took, she believed more and more that this was no dream.

Batting aside a leafy branch, he caressed her arm, relishing in the feel of her by his side. He thanked God for the easy rescue. No one had been killed, though Sir Walter's guards would have a headache come morning. And with all of them out cold, surely Sir Walter wouldn't attempt to confront twenty armed men on his own. In fact, once they emerged onto the beach, they had only a mile's trek down the coast to where Captain Bristo's ship was anchored offshore. Morgan took a deep breath, smelling the salty sea already. Nothing could possibly go wrong now.

CHAPTER THIRTY-THREE

Adalia had a sick feeling in her gut. Something wasn't right. It was why she refused to allow herself to relax, refused to give in to the joy that longed to burst from her heart. She trusted God, but she had grown enough spiritually to know that His plans didn't always match her hopes, nor her dreams. Nevertheless, she would enjoy every precious moment with Morgan. Just the fact that he had come for her, just seeing the love pouring from his eyes once again, was all she needed to die a happy woman. For now, it was enough to feel his arm circling her like an impenetrable fortress. It was enough to feel his muscles move beneath her cheek as she laid her head on his shoulder and breathed in that masculine scent that was purely Morgan. Yes, she would cherish every second.

After some time, the mud transformed to sand, and the sound of waves crashing ashore muffled the hum of the jungle. By the time they emerged from the wall of foliage onto a wide beach, a strip of gold lit the horizon, inching fingers of light over sea and sand.

Morgan gave her a squeeze as they trudged toward the firmer ground near the water, his men following behind him. Adalia clutched her skirts. Sand scratched her feet through stockings that were now hopelessly torn from tromping over twigs and stones. She lifted her face and took a deep breath of salty air, tainted with morning dew.

Mr. Griggs came alongside her, hair still like scraggly twine and musket in hand. "It be good to see ye again, miss."

"And you, Mr. Griggs. Thank you for rescuing me."

He seemed to blush. Or was it dawn's glow? "It was Morgan's idea," he said. "He planned it all. We just came along fer the fun."

She chuckled and glanced up at Morgan. The wind tossed his

loose hair over his shirt. His jaw was tight, determined. Something was different about him. Even in the way he walked. More assured, confident, serious. As if to defy her last thought, he gave her that wickedly delicious grin of his, topped it off with a seductive wink. And she thought she might become one of those foolish coquettish ladies who swooned in men's arms.

"That's far enough, you pampered fop!" The loud declaration was immediately followed by the click of several pistols.

Sir Walter's voice sliced through Adalia's heart.

Every muscle in Morgan's body turned to stone. He swung to stand in front of her.

Breath in her throat, Adalia peered around him. Several dark figures emerged from the jungle like demons escaping hell. The arc of the sun peered over the horizon, spreading a fan of light over sea and sand, revealing the ghosts for what they were—merely men. Sir Walter and his paid henchmen, in fact. Though from the looks of them, they were mostly slaves.

Captain Bristo's men swerved about, pistols cocked and at the ready.

"What is it you want?" Morgan's tone was more one of annoyance than fear as he marched toward the front of his men.

"Need you ask?" Sir Walter gestured toward Adalia with his pistol. "I want what is mine."

"And yet there is nothing here that is yours. I paid for the lady fair and square."

"You forced an agreement at the tip of a sword," Sir Walter said. "I hardly think that is valid."

Mr. Griggs eased beside Morgan and whispered, "Want me to shoot him betwixt the eyes?"

Morgan's lips curved. "No, my friend." He cast a worried glance at Adalia. "Watch over Miss Winston, if you please."

Adalia's insides turned to mush. She didn't want to be watched over. She wanted Morgan's arm around her again. She wanted to leave this horrid place.

Morgan edged his fingers toward the pistol stuffed in his breeches. "There is no need for innocent blood to stain these sands," he said.

"I beg to differ, sir. These sands are all but pleading for the blood of a daft aristocrat such as yourself."

Adalia scanned Sir Walter's men. She recognized Mr. Pope, Sir Walter's valet, and Mr. Kerr, the groom, and the overseer, Mr. Milson.

They looked none too happy to have been awakened in the middle of the night for one of Sir Walter's mad schemes. The rest were field slaves wearing their usual masks of apathy.

"This is between Sir Walter and myself," Morgan addressed them. "Do you wish to die on this beach? For what? For this lady?" He waved toward Adalia.

Sir Walter studied his fingernails. "They are my slaves. They will do what I say."

Yes, the slaves would, but the disgust registering on the servant's faces gave Adalia a measure of hope. Especially Mr. Milson's.

"Seems we are at a standstill," Morgan said. "Surely, there is a better solution than all of us shooting each other."

"Yes, give me the girl."

"Never." Morgan replied. "You will die on this beach before you lay a hand on her."

Mr. Milson rubbed his chin. "How about a duel?"

Sir Walter shot him a seething glance.

"Aye," Mr. Pope chimed in, avoiding his master's gaze. "Seems a fair way to settle things."

Frowning, Sir Walter faced forward. His glance took in Morgan as if sizing him up. He rubbed his sore jaw before a grin seized his lips. "Perhaps they are right."

Glancing back at Adalia, then over at his men, Morgan released a sigh. She knew what he was thinking. He didn't want to risk any more lives than he had to. "Very well."

"No, Morgan," Adalia cried out.

Sir Walter chuckled. "No, Morgan," he repeated in a mocking tone that made his men laugh. "Seems your lady has no confidence in you, Mr. Rutledge."

"Her confidence is not what should concern you."

Sir Walter snorted. "The winner takes the lady. What say you?"

Tugging from Mr. Grigg's grasp, Adalia dashed toward Morgan and gripped his arm. "No. He's skilled with a sword."

Morgan raised one cocky brow. "So am I, milady. Besides, he's drunk." He gestured for Mr. Griggs to take her away, following her with his eyes as the man obeyed. "Don't worry."

But she *was* worried. Sir Walter prided himself on his swordsmanship, even engaged in contests with the neighboring landowners. And he didn't appear drunk anymore. No doubt the trek through the jungle had done much to sober him. Dragging her feet, she allowed Griggs to lead her to the side.

"Well?" Sir Walter asked.

Adalia knew Morgan had no choice. It was either a duel or a blood-bath. "Agreed," he finally said.

Sir Walter leaned in to whisper something to his overseer, and then he smiled at Morgan. "Very well. Whoever survives gets the woman."

Adalia's head spun. Waves thundered. Foam churned onto the shore. Though the dawn was muggy, a chill gripped her. Sir Walter was up to something. She knew it. But how could she stop this madness? "Oh, God, please help us."

Plucking out his pistol, Morgan tossed it to the sand and pulled out his blade. Sir Walter shrugged out of his coat and handed it to one of his men. Drawing his sword, he held it out before him, one hand in the air behind his head. The rising sun reflected off the metal, nearly blinding Adalia.

Sucking in a breath, she leaned on Mr. Griggs for support. He patted her hand, though his eyes reflected fear.

The ring of blades echoed across the sand. Sir Walter, in his classic impudent pose, short-stepped toward Morgan, his sword slashing before him.

Morgan dipped and dodged each swipe, pretending an incompetence that seemed to embolden Sir Walter. He charged at Morgan full force. *Clank!* Their blades met. The edges ground together in a metallic chime. Adalia shivered.

Morgan forced Sir Walter back. In a surprise move, Sir Walter swooped to the left and dove at Morgan's right. Morgan twisted and met the attack first with a defensive block and then swung his blade up to slash his opponent's side.

Sir Walter leapt back, barely avoiding the tip, then backed away to catch his breath. "Well, well, well, the dandy has played with a sword before." His imperious tone hid a strain of unease that only Adalia would have detected. It gave her hope.

"Though I doubt you have acquired my level of experience," he continued.

Stabbing his sword into the sand, Morgan leaned on the hilt. The wind flapped his shirt. Sweat glistened on his powerful chest. "It takes more than experience to win. It takes courage and honor. Neither of which you possess."

The sun rose higher over the horizon as if anxious to watch the altercation. Sir Walter's men did not share its enthusiasm. Aside from a slight grin from Mr. Milson over the last comment, boredom stole all expression from their faces. Captain Bristo's men, however, cast anxious glances at one another and seemed to be having difficulty restraining themselves from jumping to Morgan's aid.

Sir Walter's nostrils flared. A vein pulsed in his forehead. Lifting his blade, he barreled toward Morgan.

Ching! Ching! Ching! The deathly chime tolled over the crash of waves. Both men were now fully engaged. The lines on Morgan's face grew taut and deep with determination. The aloof confidence had faded from Sir Walter's eyes, replaced by pure hatred.

Back and forth they parried, dipping, swooping, spinning with extraordinary skill. The only difference being that Morgan remained calm, focused, barely winded, while Sir Walter spewed curses into the wind between gasps for air.

Growling, and with sword pointed before him, Sir Walter rushed blindly at Morgan.

Morgan stepped aside with ease and struck Sir Walter's back with the hilt of his sword. Sir Walter stumbled, arms flailing. A wave struck his shoes, spraying water onto his trousers. Catching his balance, he swerved around. His eyes took on a maniacal gleam. He circled Morgan, taunting him just out of sword's reach. Methodically, calmly, Morgan followed him. Sir Walter spun and dove in to Morgan's right. Sunlight flashed on metal. Blades clanked. Morgan thrust the tip of his sword into Sir Walter's shoulder.

The villain yelped and dropped his blade. Maroon blossomed on his shirt. Pressing a hand on his wound, he tumbled backward, shock and rage screaming from his face. He plucked the pistol from his breeches and pointed it at Morgan.

Adalia screamed.

The pistol fired. A red flame jetted from the weapon. Black smoke coated his face. Adalia struggled against Griggs's meaty grasp, terror choking her, but he wouldn't let her go. Yet no blood appeared on Morgan's shirt. He shook his head in disgust and sheathed his blade, then wiped the sweat from his brow.

"Why, that cheating toad tried to shoot you!" Mr. Griggs spit to the side.

Mr. Granger shouted, "A fair fight, to be sure! Morgan has won."

"Aye's" sounded from the men on both sides.

Sir Walter dropped to his knees and nodded toward Mr. Milson.

The overseer leveled his pistol at Morgan's chest.

Captain Bristo's men began plucking their pistols out of braces and trousers, but the foreman held up his other hand. "Put them away, or I'll shoot Mr. Rutledge where he stands." Yet a slight tremor, a hesitation, broke into his authoritative tone.

Plucking a bag of gunpowder from his pocket, Sir Walter scrambled to reload his pistol. "Shoot him! I order you to shoot him at once!"

Adalia's chest felt as if a thousand horses stampeded over it. Sweat trickled down her back. Morgan snapped the hair from his face and folded his arms over his chest as if he hadn't a care in the world.

The overseer's eyes bounced between Sir Walter and Morgan. Adalia knew he wouldn't hesitate to kill an innocent man. She'd seen him whip a boy to near death without so much as a flinch.

"I said shoot him, you fool!" Sir Walter finished reloading and pointed his pistol at Morgan.

Without warning, Mr. Milson swung his pistol toward his boss and fired. The shot echoed across the blue sky. Shock widened Sir Walter's eyes. His mouth opened, and he glanced at his overseer before a vacant expression claimed his face. His body went limp, and he fell backward with a thud.

Adalia's knees gave out. She sank to the moist sand, hand on her mouth. For seconds that seemed like hours, the two bands of men stared each other down. Sun glared off the hilts of their swords and the silver on their pistols as their eyes twitched beneath drops of sweat. But then one by one, Sir Walter's men turned to leave. Mr. Milson gave Morgan a nod of approval before he followed the others, disappearing into the web of green. Leaving Sir Walter's body to bake in the sun. A wave bubbled over him, depositing foam on his shirt.

Oddly, the sight saddened Adalia. Though it was a fitting end for the vile man, she sickened at the thought of where his spirit might have gone.

Struggling to rise, she clutched her skirts and rushed into Morgan's arms. His warmth and strength surrounded her.

It was over. It was truly all over. She peeked at Sir Walter one last time then turned away. She would never be his again. Morgan held her for several minutes, rubbing her back. He settled his chin atop her head, and the muscles in his chest loosened. Twice now he had dueled for her.

Could she ask for a more dashing, chivalrous prince?

At her insistence, the men buried Sir Walter in a shallow grave at the tree line before heading down the beach in a much more jovial mood than before. As soon as they spotted the ship anchored off shore, the men went ahead to ready the cockboats.

Morgan tugged on Adalia, stopping her. "I need to ask you something." He brushed a curl from her face. "Actually, I've already asked you, but after everything. . . I need to ask you again." He took her hands in his, caressing her fingers, his green eyes shifting between hers. Then he got down on one knee. "Will you marry me?"

Adalia drew in a breath of surprise. "I haven't changed my mind." She ran her fingers over his stubbled jaw. "I'll always love you, Morgan."

"But after what I did. . ." He dropped his gaze.

Though Adalia tried to prevent it, the memory of Morgan's look of disgust flashed in her mind, renewing her pain. "You don't mind marrying a woman with Negro blood?"

He shook his head, stood, and cupped her face with both hands. "I care not whether you are Negro, French, Arabian, yellow, purple, or green. I love you." Lowering his lips to hers, he caressed her mouth, deepening the kiss until Adalia's toes tingled with delight, and whistles assailed them from the men down shore.

With a chuckle, Morgan drew her into his arms.

She laid her head on his chest. "I can't believe your father agreed to the marriage after he discovered who I was."

"Well, I didn't say that."

Adalia tensed and backed away. "He didn't agree?"

Morgan chuckled. "If I recall, my father's words were something more like"—he mimicked his father's harsh tone—"'If you marry her, I will toss you on the street without a coin in your pocket.'"

Adalia bit her lip, finding no humor in the impression. "But your status, your wealth, they are so important to you."

"Not anymore. Honestly I can't fathom why I ever valued them so highly." Salty wind blasted over them, drawing his gaze out to sea. His eyes held a sparkle she'd not seen before.

"I've given my life to God," he said. "I've had much time to think—and pray—on the voyage over here. A veil has been lifted. I see everything so clearly now." Excitement sped across his face.

Adalia flinched. "Did I hear you say God?"

"Yes, shocking, isn't it?" He grinned. "It took the possibility of losing you forever to bring me to my knees. But once I did, God was right there like you said He'd be."

Adalia's breath escaped her, and she flung her arms around his neck. "I'm so happy, Morgan!" She had no idea how to process so much good news at once! "I, too, wandered away from God. I hid behind a veil—ashamed of who I was, of who God made me to be."

Wind flapped the hem of her moist gown across her legs.

"I don't fault you for it. There was a huge price to pay for your honesty." Morgan eased a lock behind her ear. "And what I thought was a huge price to pay for mine."

"It *is* a huge price, Morgan." Her vision blurred with tears. She loved him too much to see him lose everything that was dear to him. "I thank you for rescuing me, but I release you from your promise to mar—"

"Do you think I care about such things anymore?" He pulled her arms from his neck and squeezed her hands. "Without you they are meaningless."

Adalia searched his eyes for any hesitation, any untruth. She found none. She wanted to sing, dance, frolic in the waves! Instead, she wiped a tear away before it had a chance to spill down her cheek. God had worked a miracle in both of their lives. He had removed their shackles and set them both free. Truly free!

"What will you do?" she asked.

His gaze shifted to Captain Bristo's brig floating off shore as the wind fingered his light hair. Purpose and confidence tightened his expression. He wasn't the same spoiled, aimless man she'd met six months ago. He had grown up. Like her, with God's help, he had faced his deepest fears and found them naught but cowering dwarfs. He turned toward her, brows lifted. "How would you like to be married to a merchantman or perhaps a privateer?"

Adalia squeezed his hands, elated. "It's what you were meant to do, Morgan. I know it."

"But I'll be away from home a lot."

"Good thing I won't be there to miss you." She gave him a coy smile.

His brows crossed. "And just where will you be?"

"Why, with you, of course. You'll need someone to cook and tend to the sick on board the ship, won't you?"

He frowned. "No. I won't stand for it. It's far too dangerous."

"I'm not letting you out of my sight, Morgan Rutledge." Adalia speared his chest with a finger. "Not after all we've been through. You are my prince. And a prince never leaves his princess."

"Hmm. Then I suppose I don't have a choice." He gave her that disarming grin of his. "Besides, having my wife on board will have its advantages." He lifted his eyebrows.

Adalia smiled. "Of what advantages do you speak?"

"Why, getting started on a family, of course. I did tell you I want lots of children."

Heat swirled in Adalia's belly and flushed her face. "Well, then, I shall be happy to comply."

Offering her his arm, he gave her a delicious wink. "Our ship awaits, milady. Let us not delay."

Author's Afterword

By the time Morgan and Adalia arrived in Charleston, war had indeed broken out between the United States and Britain—the War of 1812. It may please the reader to know that Morgan accepted Captain Bristo's offer and became the captain of his own privateer, the *Liberty*, but not before he and Adalia were married in a small ceremony at St. Mary's, performed by Father Mulligan. Also present at the joyous event were Caroline Johnson, Doctor Willaby, Hadley Rutledge, and Joy.

Doctor Willaby repented of his prejudice and, soon after, freed Joy and his other slaves. She continued to work as a maid in his house, and he came to care for her deeply. Though it took much help from God, the doctor finally released the bitterness in his heart over his family's death and forgave Hadley for his part in the tragedy. Afterward, he became the most joyful doctor in all of Charleston!

Hadley and Emerald were also married in an extravagant ceremony at the Rutledge estate that was the talk of Charleston society for the entire season. Adalia and Morgan were not invited.

Soon after, Hadley moved his new wife into the big house and took over the running of the plantation. It didn't take long, however, for him to realize that what he'd so desperately longed for in Miss Emerald Middleton was but a mirage of beauty cloaking a shrewish woman who was never satisfied with anything. Consequences can be hard to live with.

When Adalia wasn't at sea with Morgan, she continued her work with the doctor, as well as helping tend the orphans at St. Mary's. In her spare time, she instructed Joy in the art of herbal healing and found that the young girl had a quick mind for learning.

Disowned by his father and shunned by society for marrying Adalia, Morgan tossed their opinions aside like so much chaff and began his new adventures at sea, his wife by his side. With Morgan as her captain, *Liberty* became one of the most successful privateers sailing from Charleston, capturing over fifteen British merchant brigs, five sloops, and two schooners.

Adalia overcame her seasickness and became an invaluable part of the crew, assisting with the cooking, mending of sails, and ministering to ill seamen. Though Morgan feared for her safety, he was glad to have her aboard and thanked God for her every day. By the time the war was over, he'd made a fortune in prize money, enough to purchase a beautiful and spacious home in Charleston close to Doc Willaby's. Soon after, Morgan joined forces with Captain Bristo and became a successful merchantman, while Adalia became equally successful at bearing children.

In the years to come, when the citizens of Charleston happened to be strolling down Calhoun Street in Charleston, they would hear nothing but words of love, laughter, song, and gaiety pouring from the Rutledge home, and inevitably, they would scratch their heads in wonder at how a simple, common family could be so happy.

Discussion Questions for *Veil of Pearls*

1. Slavery is one of the themes throughout the book. At the beginning of the story, Adalia is a physical slave, but after she gains her freedom, she becomes a new kind of slave. What did she become a slave to?

2. How did that affect the way she behaved? How did it affect her values, her relationship with God?

3. Morgan Rutledge was one of the wealthiest men in Charleston. He had money, charm, wit, status, and the eye of every lady in town. Yet he was a slave too. What was he enslaved by? How did that affect him and his life?

4. Almost everyone in the story was enslaved by something. Can you name what the following characters were slaves to? Emerald, Caroline, Drayton, Hadley, and Doctor Willaby? What about Sir Walter?

5. The Bible says that whatever we put above God is an idol. And whatever we worship, we become a slave to. In each of the characters in question 4, how did their slavery affect their lives? How did it keep them from what God had planned for them?

6. The fear of man is an unhealthy, consuming concern with what other people think of us. It has its roots in pride, which is a sin that can destroy your life. Don't believe me? Read about the kings of Judah and Israel in the Old Testament! But, let's face it, it is human and natural to want to be liked. Amazing how the devil can take something that is an innocent desire and pervert it into an atrocity that can ruin our lives. Have you ever felt an overwhelming need to fit in? To be popular? If so, what are some things you did to make people like you? Have you ever compromised who you are, your values and beliefs, just to be liked? I have.

7. If you answered yes to the question above and you named some things you did, what was the result? Did it work out as you planned, or did it backfire on you? Where are those people now whose good opinion you sought? Are they still your friends? Funny thing, I haven't kept in touch with anyone in that popular crowd in school that I so desperately wanted to belong to (and never did, by the way). I wonder if they had accepted me into their group, whether we'd still be friends.

8. As an author, I deal with the opinions of others quite often. Some are good. Some are not so good! It's been a difficult journey for me to learn to shrug off both the good and the bad. The good can puff me up. The bad can depress me and lead to stress. You may not be an author, but I'm sure you are bombarded daily with opinions about your performance. What did you learn from this story about the opinions of man? What did the characters say about Charleston society's favor?

9. The Bible says the fear of man is a snare. In other words, it traps you and keeps you from going forward. It literally keeps you from the abundant life God has for you. What happened in the story to both Morgan and Adalia to make them realize their bondage? How did they get set free?

10. The first step to breaking free of the fear of man is realizing how valued and precious you are to God. Once you accept that and begin to know how much He loves you, you are on the road to freedom! In the end, His opinion is all that matters. On Judgment Day, do you think God will ask you how many Facebook friends you have? Do you think he'll ask to see all your awards and accolades, your promotions, your status, your wealth? Aside from whether you believe in Jesus, what is the one thing you think God cares about the most?

About the Author

MaryLu Tyndall

MaryLu Tyndall dreamed of pirates and seafaring adventures during her childhood days on Florida's coast. She holds a degree in math and worked as a software engineer for fifteen years before testing the waters as a writer. Her love of history and passion for storytelling drew her to create the Legacy of the King's Pirates series. MaryLu now writes full-time and makes her home with her husband, six children, and four cats on California's coast, where her imagination still surges with the sea. Her passion is to write page-turning, romantic adventures that not only entertain but also expose Christians to their full potential in Christ. For more information on MaryLu and her upcoming releases, please visit her website at www.mltyndall.com or her blog at crossandcutlass.blogspot.com.

Other books by MaryLu Tyndall

SURRENDER TO DESTINY SERIES

Surrender the Heart
Surrender the Night
Surrender the Dawn

CHARLES TOWNE BELLES

The Red Siren
The Blue Enchantress
The Raven Saint

THE LEGACY OF THE KING'S PIRATES

The Redemption
The Reliance
The Restitution

The Falcon and the Sparrow